Snow Eagle Down

BY NANCY VELDMAN

ISBN: 1506161081
ISBN 13: 9781506161082
Library of Congress 2015900567
CreateSpace Independent Publishing Platform
North Charleston, South Carolina

We learn many things in life

that we store away,

hidden in some

compartment in our brain . . .

never dreaming

we just might need

that one bit of information

that was oh so boring

to us

when it was spoken.

And at the right critical moment

we would give

almost anything

to remember it.

Preface

My great grandfather on my father's side was a full-blooded Sioux Indian. His Indian name was Snow Eagle. I never met him, but I saw plenty of photos of him. He was big and had dark hair pulled back into a ponytail. But it was his face that stayed in my mind. It was wrinkled so deeply that it was like rivers had been cut into his face with tributaries that shot off in all directions. So many wrinkles that I couldn't find the skin; only lines that told about where he'd been. What he'd suffered. But his black eyes shown through like an eagle's. People swore that he could see anything for miles. And when he was hunting, he could become invisible in his environment.

My father sat for hours when I was a child, telling me story after story that his father passed down to him. And the generations behind that. He always told me that if he didn't share them with me, then they would simply stop. And he couldn't bear to know that how his grandfather lived would fade away into the air just because he decided the stories weren't important anymore. I had a temperament like my father and I loved to sit and watch him work with his hands. He could do absolutely anything. But while he was working he spoke of things from the past. The ways of his grandfather were embedded deeply into his soul. And as I sat and listened, they became a part of mine.

There were many things he shared with me that I couldn't understand. Because the world I lived in was so different from the pictures he drew of his grandfather's life. In all the stories that he shared, one in particular stuck with me through my whole life. Even though I was a girl, I was fascinated by it. He explained very clearly to me through this story that the survival of an Indian depended upon how he could live in the wilderness on his own. With nothing but what he found, what he ate, and how he handled the changes in weather. All Indians were hunters and warriors. But survival was critical to their villages. To their people.

My mother was a city girl who loved the arts and exposed me to dance, music, and movies. I read constantly and even now as an adult, my library covers three walls of my living room. I was taught in my youth to take in words and let them become who I was. I was told they would teach me things and stay with me for the rest of my life. My father told me that what I read could never be taken away from me. And even if I forgot the title of a book or the author, the words I read were inside me and they would find their way out at the right time.

I didn't know that I would ever need the words from any book I read or any story my father told me. But one time in my life, when an event happened that I wasn't expecting, I was forced to pull from every single thing I'd ever read or been told just to survive it. I learned what it meant to become one with my surroundings. To be as quiet as snow. And as observant as an eagle. It all came rushing back.

Chapter 1

Morning came like an unwanted guest. And the deceiving warmth from the sun's rays lying across the blankets on Elizabeth's bed caused her to stir and waken before the alarm clock rang. She hurriedly slapped the top of the clock before it had a chance to wake the dead. The curtains were open and she could see the backyard with all of its barren trees. It was early winter in Knoxville, but for the moment the sun felt like a summer sun and she was going to enjoy it for another five minutes.

Her bedroom was luxuriously decorated—long drapes that puddled on the floor, a thick silk duvet cover that hung precariously on the edge of the bed, and a magnificent chandelier over the bed that was covered in crystal that sparkled in the morning light. Her long brown hair was strewn out across the pillow and the darkness of it made her skin look like porcelain. Her eyes were dark brown, mistaken for black too often. And her lips were full and pink, dry from the winter wind that was always blowing when she went to and from her car to work.

She slowly sat up, stretching, and slid off the side of the bed, stepping into her slippers and grabbing her fluffy white robe that was hanging across the arm of a white leather chair near the bed. Now out from under the warm covers, she felt chilled as she brushed her teeth, combed her long hair, and pulled it back in a ponytail to get it off her face. The carpet felt thick as she shuffled across the floor, and when she reached for the doorknob and opened the French doors to the hallway, a burst of cold air hit her in the face. She'd forgotten to turn up the heat downstairs and it almost felt like a window had been left open. When she walked down the stairs to the kitchen she hurriedly made some strong coffee, wrapped a warm fur throw around herself, and walked down the driveway to get the paper. Half running back inside, she slammed the front door, locked it, and sat down at the kitchen table to scan the paper. She didn't expect to see anything drastic, but some of the Fortune 500 companies she consulted were struggling in the present economy. She had to keep her eye on the numbers. The phone rang and jarred her head. Who would be calling so early? It had to be Leigh.

"Good morning, dear. Did you sleep well?" Leigh's voice was loud and too cheerful. Something had to be wrong.

"I just woke up. What are you doing sounding so chipper at 6:30 in the morning?"

A sneeze. "Oh, I'm a morning person. You already know that from college days. You free tonight for dinner?"

"I have no idea. What day is it? Wednesday?"

"Come on, 'Lizbeth. Yes, it's Wednesday."

"I think I'm free. Let me get to my office and check my calendar. What did you have in mind?"

"I am having a small dinner party with close friends and wanted you to come. I think you need to be there."

"You aren't matchmaking again, are you? Because we both know how the last time turned out, don't we?"

"Uh, and whose fault was that? You didn't give the guy a chance. Besides, you haven't been too good at getting yourself a date, now have you?"

Elizabeth smiled. Forever playing Cupid. "Okay, okay. I'll come. What time and what do I wear?"

"Six o'clock sharp and dress down. Nothing fancy. I want him to see who you really are. Not wearing some stupid Jimmy Choo shoes that are impossible to walk in."

"I'll be there in my jeans, then. What do you need me to bring?"

"A bottle of your favorite wine. Nothing else. We're having filets on the grill so don't blow it by eating too much at lunch. God only knows how small your stomach is. You eat like a bird. And don't pull your hair back. You look like a schoolmarm, for heaven's sake."

"I'm forgiving you early for all the little things you are going to say about me. And I'll see you at six. Thanks for the wake-up call."

"My pleasure. Have a nice day, girl. And come with a smile. When you frown your wrinkles deepen between your eyebrows. So think happy."

"Got it. Bye, Leigh. Got to get ready for work. Not all of us are so lucky to be able to stay home and do nothing but plan dinners."

"I have plenty to do!"

"Just kidding. See you later."

Elizabeth ate a quick breakfast of warm oatmeal, cleaned up the dishes, and hurried to the shower. She wasn't looking forward to this next job. Walmart had hired her to check out all the stores in the Southeast. It was overwhelming because of the number of stores, but critical to the company as a whole to keep tabs on how each store was run. How they treated and communicated with employees. She was tired but pasted a smile on as she walked into her office to get her Mac notebook and files. Her secretary was a little overweight, young, and didn't know how to dress. But she was a quick study.

"Misty, we've got a ton of work to do today. I hope you are not in one of your lazy moods?"

Misty frowned and brushed back her long straight hair. "Nothing wrong with my mood, Liz. We got Walmart today. And for the next century. So what's your plan?"

"I'm headed out to the three Walmarts here. Then I'll be on the road for a few days. So keep your phone on and be checking your emails. I'll be sending you information all day about their books, employees, and all that. You know the ropes. This is big. Real big. I don't want any mess-ups. So stay focused even though you are in the office alone all day. No boyfriends, okay?"

"Got it, Liz. I learned my lesson the last time I brought someone in here. You failed to let me in on the small fact that the president of Exxon Oil was going to be dropping by some files. He got his eyes full that day. Pretty funny, actually. But not."

"'Not' is the word. I was embarrassed and how do you think that affects us getting the other accounts? We look like idiots. And I'll not tolerate it. Anyway, we've been through all of this and you have promised not to do that again. No drinking, smoking, or drugs. Okay? Just do your job."

"Okay, so let's drop it. Today's a big day and I am all ears. And by the way, your shoes don't match. Better pick up a pair on the way to Walmart. They're not like dealing with Goldman-Sachs but you still want your shoes to match." Elizabeth looked down in horror, grabbed her computer and files, and rushed out the door.

As soon as Misty heard the elevator ding, she pulled out her cigarette and lit it, blowing out the smoke slowly, watching it curl all the way up to the ceiling and across like a giant long finger. It was going to be a long day and the tension in the air was as thick as pea soup. She pulled the Walmart file up on the computer and minimized it, opened her drawer, and pulled out the folder marked "Walmart I." The she pulled her personal notebook out and connected to the Internet. She spent the next couple hours sending out emails to friends and going on Facebook. She forgot to check her emails on the work computer until nearly 10:00. When she finally did check, the phone rang and it was Liz. *I'll be lucky if I don't get fired today*, she admitted to herself.

Elizabeth worked into the afternoon and was frustrated because she was having trouble communicating with Misty all day. Her first thought was that it was an Internet issue, but her gut told her that Misty might be pulling something again. She hurried back to the office and found an empty chair. Misty was gone for the day and had left a note about her mother being sick. Liz sat down in a chair by Misty's desk and blew out a sigh. Without hesitating too long, she dialed Misty's number, leaving a message on her answering machine that had an unmistakable sharp edge to it. "*Misty, you're fired.*"

She was frustrated, tired, and knew she had to fake a smile for dinner later. Why did she allow Leigh to talk her into this? This deal with Walmart was huge and she needed to be able to concentrate on it one hundred percent. There was no room for error. She picked up the phone, opened her Rolodex, and dialed Stephanie Carnes' number. This girl was a whiz on computers and maybe, just maybe, she was looking for a job. If the money was right, she just might jump ship if she was already employed.

"Stephanie? Elizabeth Stone here. How are you?"

"I'm fine, Miss Stone. You caught me at work, though."

Liz frowned. "Oh, I'm sorry. I thought I dialed your home number. Will you call me tonight when you get off work? Any time will do, actually. I have a proposition to make and I think you might be interested."

Stephanie paused and Elizabeth sensed a change in the tone of her voice. "Of course, I'll call you back. Probably be around 8:00. Is that okay with you?"

"Perfect. Have a wonderful day. Your life is about to change."

Liz hung up and walked into her office. She had tried several times to hire Stephanie, but this time she was going to make it work. Money talked. And she had the money to give her. She was going to have to stay and enter the information she'd sent to Misty, or she would get too far behind. And as good as Stephanie was, she didn't want her to have to pull in two days' work on her first day.

She was feeling the pressure as she drove home. It was cold and the temperature was dropping fast. Winter had always been one of her favorite times as a child because of the snow. The crisp air. The million stars in the sky that she stared at outside her bedroom window. But now, as an adult, it was annoying. She opened the door to her house and slammed it shut, jarring the framed photos along the wall near the door.

She ran a hot bath and dropped out of her clothes, not even bothering to hang up anything. A good suit on the floor. Her mother would die if she saw it. She poured a little wine in a glass and stepped into the foamy white bubbles, feeling the stress drain out of her as she lowered herself into the tub. The phone rang and she cursed as she dashed to pick it up, leaving small puddles of soapy water on the floor. It was Leigh.

"I hope you aren't coming down with a mysterious illness so you can't come tonight?" Leigh asked.

Liz stood there dripping wet, water going all over the carpet in her bedroom. "Well, I might catch cold if you don't let me get back into my hot bath! Did you call for a reason, or just to make me get out of my bath?"

Leigh laughed loudly. "Sorry, Liz. Just making sure you don't duck out of my dinner invitation. I really want you to meet Jim Wilson. He's already here and such a nice guy."

"Yeah, yeah. They're all nice guys. I'll be there in about forty-five minutes. Wearing my jeans."

"See you then. Sorry about the bath thing."

Liz walked carefully back to the tub and climbed in. She picked up her wine glass and sipped it, feeling the warmth go down her throat. *Jim Wilson.* She picked up the soap and lathered up the sponge. She was out in ten minutes, pulling on her jeans and a ruffled top and jacket. Drying her hair would take thirty minutes but she couldn't go out with a wet head in such cold weather. She put some makeup on, red lipstick, and a dash of her favorite perfume. Wouldn't hurt to smell nice. Even if she didn't like Jim Wilson.

Chapter 2

Leigh Miller was five feet eight inches tall with legs that lasted forever, a full mouth, auburn hair, and a smile that would stop a freight train. She was married to one of the best airline pilots in the Mid-South. Joe had flown for Delta for years and had his own plane. Handsome with a great personality. Everyone loved him. He'd given Elizabeth flying lessons and she'd finally gotten her pilot's license. The three had been inseparable for years and while Elizabeth dated from time to time, her job kept her travelling just enough to where it was impossible to keep a relationship going. Most men were intimidated by her beauty. Others were just not able to take her being gone so much.

Leigh, on the other hand, had become comfortable just being Joe's wife. She was talented and had been a prominent artist, showing her work in fine art galleries around Knoxville. She'd been written up in many art magazines. But her desire to paint was waning as she aged. Joe and Leigh travelled all over the world, visiting remote places, giving to charities. She was on a lot of boards but hated every one of them.

Tonight she'd planned a small dinner with Joe, including Elizabeth and Jim Wilson, a new friend of theirs. He was from Montana and had been in Knoxville for a seminar. He was a cardiologist and people from all over the United States came to him for surgery. He was handsome but quiet. Odd combination for someone who dealt with people all day long. His bedside manner was the talk of the hospital. In spite of his subdued personality he was quite successful and had acquired some wealth that he'd invested wisely. Leigh wanted Elizabeth to meet him because he was so unlike all the other men she'd seen with Liz. He'd been married before but his wife had died from some strange illness. No children. It was a perfect situation if Liz didn't blow it.

Just as Leigh finished setting the table, Liz walked through the door looking like she'd stepped out of *Vogue* magazine. "Elizabeth! So glad you could come! Please come in. I want you to meet Jim!"

"Good to see you too, Leigh. Thanks for the invite." She turned to meet Jim. He was standing away from her with a slight smile.

"Hello, Jim. How are you? Nice to meet you."

He stepped up and took her hand. "Nice to meet you, too, Elizabeth. I've heard so much about you."

Liz looked at Leigh and rolled her eyes. "I'm sure you have. You'll have to forgive her for exaggerating."

Jim laughed and walked Liz to the table. "Please sit down so we can talk. I don't think she's exaggerated at all. You look beautiful."

"It's a cold night out, Jim. And windy. But I guess we expect that in the winter in Knoxville. Snow will be coming soon. I don't look forward to that at all. Makes getting around so hard. And I travel so much with my job."

"I understand you are a consultant for some of the Fortune 500 companies. Sounds interesting."

"I hear you're a cardiologist. Now that's interesting! How long are you here?"

"Leaving this next Monday. Heading back to Montana. Now you talk about cold; it's below freezing in Montana during the winter. And the snow is so deep—lasts a long time up there."

"I don't know how you stand that, Jim. I can hardly make it through our winters. I guess you adjust no matter where you live."

Leigh came through the door with a huge platter of steaks and Joe came in behind her with fresh green salad and rolls. She also brought out fruit and sautéed mushrooms. Too much food. But she loved cooking and she loved to see people enjoying their meal.

"Okay, guys. Serve up. Let's eat and then we can have our dessert. It's a surprise!"

Wine was poured and the conversation went on for three hours. Dessert was crème brûlée, which was the perfect light dessert after a meal of filet mignon.

"Elizabeth, I hear you have your pilot's license. I'm impressed."

Liz blushed and took a small bite of the crème brûlée. "Yes! I love flying but haven't been able to do much lately. Walmart has hired me as a consultant so I will be flying quite a bit until I have seen most of their stores that are not making a good profit. I was going to talk to Joe about using his plane on weekends for some short flights."

"Have you ever been to Montana? That would be quite an adventure." Jim was staring at her with a questioning look.

Liz shook her head. "No, never been there. It would be cold there this time of year. And snowy."

Leigh looked at Joe and nodded. He raised an eyebrow and looked at Elizabeth.

"You're headed home on Monday, aren't you, Jim?" Leigh asked, glancing over at Liz.

"Yeah, I have to leave out on Monday."

"Liz, why don't you fly Jim home? You need a break, anyway. All you do is work." Leigh said in her high-pitched pushy tone.

"You want to do that, Elizabeth?" Joe remarked before Liz could even answer. "It's fine with me. But if you're going to fly to Montana, you would need to do it sooner rather than later. The snow gets so deep and the winds pick up. Wouldn't be conducive to flying, if you ask my opinion."

Liz was caught off guard. "I'll have to check my schedule, of course, Joe. But it would be a nice flight. I haven't seen Montana in the winter. I bet it's lovely from the air."

"More than lovely. See if you can arrange it. If not, I'll book my flight Monday and head home." Jim reached over and touched her arm gently.

"I'll see what I can do. This is an important account for me, so I can't make any promises."

"Wouldn't want to ruin that for you. Just let me know."

"Anyone want any coffee?" Leigh asked, winking at Liz.

"I'm fine." Jim remarked, taking his last bite of dessert.

"I'm really going to have to head home. Been a long day and tomorrow is another one just like it." Liz wiped her mouth and scooted her chair back.

Jim jumped up and pulled her chair out a little more and waited for her to get up.

"I'll get your coat for you, Liz." He moved quickly and found the coat tree in the hallway. He brought it to her, helped her put it on, and then turned her around.

"I've enjoyed meeting you. Let's go out for dinner Friday night. I'd love to hear about your job and also your flying. You're quite the Renaissance woman."

Liz took two steps back so she could see his face better. "That would be nice, Jim. I'll give you my card and you can call me to make plans."

Leigh got up and walked her to the door, smiling glibly. "You have a nice time?"

"Yes, it was nice. But don't go getting your hopes up. It's just a dinner date, okay? Not an engagement."

"You don't like him?"

"I didn't say that. But you'll have me married by next week if I don't watch it."

"I just wanted you to like him. If I got that accomplished I'll be happy."

"I don't even know him. Give me time. Is that asking too much?"

She shook her auburn head no. "I guess not. But don't do anything stupid. Give yourself time to see if you enjoy being around him. He seems like such a nice man and very intelligent. Isn't that what you like? Intelligence?"

"Yes. But it wouldn't hurt if there was some sort of chemical attraction going on. So give me space. It will either work out or not. And I don't know what to think about flying him home. I thought that was a little bold of you to ask."

"I thought it was a chance for you two to get to know each other. But see how different we are?"

"No shock there. I'll see. What did Joe think about you asking me to fly him home? I'd be using his plane, for heaven's sake."

"He said he didn't care at all. As long as he isn't planning to use the plane; he trusts you totally. You know that. He taught you everything you know. But the snow might be an issue as you head that direction."

"I've flown in snow before. But yes, it is risky. Ice on the wings is deadly."

"You go home and rest. We'll talk about this over the weekend. I'll get Joe to check the weather for the weekend and Monday."

"Good. I'll talk to you soon."

"You bet you will. I'm going to want to know how Friday goes."

"Quit grinning. It's going to be our first date. We don't know each other at all."

"Bye, Liz. Talk to you soon."

Elizabeth pulled out of the driveway and headed home. It was pretty cold outside and she was looking forward to snuggling under her thick downy covers and watching a little television before she fell asleep. It just occurred to her that she hadn't heard from Stephanie. She checked her phone when she pulled up to her house and found out that the ringer had been turned down. Stephanie had phoned her and left a message. She walked into the kitchen and set her purse down and took off her coat, hitting redial on her phone and crossing her fingers.

"Stephanie? I missed your call. My ringer was off. Go figure."

"So did you want to talk to me about a job, Miss Liz?"

"Call me Elizabeth, please. And yes, I need someone like yesterday."

"You know I already have a job."

"I do. But I am willing to make it worth your while to change jobs."

"And what does that mean? Ten dollars an hour? 'Cause that won't do it."

"No way! How does twenty dollars an hour sound? And insurance. And vacation pay the first year?"

"Hmmm. Sounds tempting. Can I get gas allowance since your office is a good distance from my home?"

"No problem. We start at 8:00 sharp. Is that going to be a problem?"

"Never has been."

"Can you work until 5:00? And sometimes we have work to do on weekends, but it's rare and you might could take a day off during the week if you needed to."

"I'm all about the money right now, Elizabeth. My parents aren't footing the bill anymore. So when do I start?"

"You could start in the morning, but what do you need to do to leave this job?"

"I don't owe them anything. I just started a week and a half ago. I'll call and tell them I'm quitting. "

"Don't worry. I just need someone who will hang with me and get this job done. I need a 'right arm' person."

"I'm your girl."

"Great. See you in the morning. You know where my office is?"

"Sure do. Suite number?"

"Suite 600. See you tomorrow, Stephanie. And hey, thanks so much. You're a lifesaver."

"I hope this is a long-term thing, Elizabeth. I hate jumping jobs."

"I'd like it to be for a long time, too, Steph. We'll talk about that in the morning."

Elizabeth put the cell phone down and sighed with relief. *Thank heavens she's willing to make the jump. I was going to be in the biggest pickle tomorrow if she wasn't going to be there.* She took off her clothes and grabbed her flannel pajamas, brushed her teeth, and made some hot cocoa. Then she climbed into bed, shaking because the sheets were cold. It took her a while to warm them up, but she sipped on her hot chocolate and watched the news, still smiling about Stephanie. She'd almost forgotten about Jim Wilson.

Chapter 3

The alarm went off at 6:00. Elizabeth was out cold. She'd fallen asleep with the television on, so the early morning news was on. She rolled over sleepily and turned off the alarm. It was cold in the room, which was great for sleeping but not for getting out of bed. She yawned and rubbed her eyes. That was a quick seven hours of sleep, she thought, as she brushed her hair out of her eyes. She sat up, grabbed her thick robe lying at the foot of her bed, and peered down at the floor to see if her slippers were around. Swinging her legs over the side of the bed, she stuffed her warm feet into the cold slippers.

Chills ran up her spine as she headed to the bathroom. The pale blue walls made the room feel colder than it was and she hurriedly washed her face and walked downstairs to the kitchen. The hot coffee and oatmeal warmed her up and got her blood moving. She decided to break down and turn the thermostat up; it wasn't worth walking around shivering to save a few dollars.

She pulled out a pair of wool pants, tall boots, and a warm red sweater from her closet. She was going to be working inside some of the day, but when she had to get out, she was determined to stay warm. What she didn't need was to come down with the flu that was going around.

As she walked into her office she saw Stephanie coming off the elevator. She waited for her and they walked in together. "Hey, Stephanie! So glad to see you this morning. Thanks for coming in on such short notice. I really appreciate it. I'm going to take my coat off and put my things in my office and then I'll show you the ropes on the computer. It'll be a cinch for you."

"I can't wait to get into this program. I'll put my things in a drawer here and be ready when you come out."

Liz hurriedly put her purse down and came back out to the receptionist desk. She pulled up an extra chair and sat down, allowing Stephanie to sit at the computer. She'd already turned it on and was checking out the program before Liz could say a thing.

"This is going to be easy for me. I see what you're doing, posting the financials on their page and the employees and their responsibilities."

"Correct. I'll send you information during the day and you can go ahead and post to their page. I will run some numbers when I get back to work to see where the company is failing. Where the weak spots are. It all comes down to numbers. But also, how the employees are doing their job. Often it is the boss who is making all the mistakes. And let me tell you, that's not a pleasant conversation to have."

Stephanie laughed. "Yeah, it could cost you your job!"

"Exactly. But it's what they hired me to do."

"So you'll contact me today and I'll enter information into their file. No problem. Is there anything else I can do while you are gone?"

"Please look through the other files and get familiar with the other companies. There are quite a few. Get a feel for what I'm doing and what I'm looking for. You'll be a great help to me once you see how I come up with the numbers."

"I'm a numbers person; guess that's why you hired me."

"Yes. And I know how quickly you learn things. I've kind of kept up with you through your mother, so I know you've got what it takes to do this job. Doesn't take a rocket scientist. But the more you understand what I do, the quicker we can move through these companies and the more money we will make."

"I like the sound of that, Liz. I need to pay off school loans and get myself an apartment. It's time I move out of the house. Mom has remarried and needs some alone time with her new man. As long as I'm coming in and out of that house, they'll never feel like they're alone."

"Do you feel pushed out?"

"No. Not really. It was time for Mom to remarry. I like the guy, really. But they need their space. And frankly, so do I."

"I'm out of here. I need to get to Walmart in the next twenty minutes. I don't like to be late. You'll learn that about me. I'll be texting you and please check your emails regularly. If I need anything, I'll call you on the land line here at the office."

Stephanie spent the next three hours studying the program, surfing through the current files and studying the information that Liz had wanted posted. She entered what she could from yesterday, wrote down some questions to ask Liz when she called, and grabbed a bit of lunch. She checked her emails and printed them out so she would have hard copies to look at and to back up what she posted on the computer.

So far, she was comfortable with the computer. But to learn what Liz was doing would take a little more time. She just wanted to get everything entered so that when new figures were added, the program would calculate them automatically. She wanted to please Elizabeth and stay in this position long enough to pay her loan off.

Stephanie was a tall, slim girl of twenty-five who wore glasses and pulled her hair back in a ponytail. She had gone to college early and aced all her classes. She had a no nonsense attitude about everything except men. And in that area she was petrified. She'd had a few dates but hadn't found anyone who could match her brains. She intimidated them. So she gave up for a while and finished college and now she was working in a high-powered job. If there was a man who could use his brain, she hadn't found him yet. But there was hope. She was young. And her mother had it on her agenda that her daughter would marry before she was thirty years old.

Taking a break every few hours, she walked around the office and even went into Liz's office. She stayed out of her desk but looked at photos and familiarized herself with the file cabinet. Down the hall from their office was a Coke machine and vending machine. She'd brought her own sandwich but it was nice to find out that snacks were available. By the end of the day she felt very at home in the office. It really hadn't had that "first day at work" feel. The desk had been rearranged and she'd rounded up some pens and pencils so that she had plenty in her desk. Liz had a great supply of computer paper, file folders, and other small items needed for her job. There was a small refrigerator in Liz's office and they had a break room with cans of soup, crackers and a microwave. In the lounge area there was a sofa where Stephanie sat for a while, killing time. She turned on the television for the local news, waiting for Liz to return.

At 5:00, Liz walked through the door and plopped down on the sofa. She was worn out but smiling. "You have no idea how tired I am. But it felt so good to come back to the office knowing you would be here."

Stephanie smiled. "It's been a long day, but I've learned so much while you were gone. You'll be pleased to know I've posted all the things you emailed me, and have sort of learned the program. A little rough around the edges, but not bad for my first day."

"I'm not surprised at all. But I am glad you feel comfortable. Did you eat? Did you find everything you needed?"

"Yes, I did. How was your day? Anything I need to do before I head home?"

"I'll get all the files ready for you and they will be on your desk in the morning when you get here. Tomorrow's Friday so you will get a paycheck to cover what you missed on your other job. Did they keep your pay?"

"Yes. They weren't too happy. But they sort of understood when I shared the pay raise you offered. I think it actually made them feel bad."

"I imagine it would. Okay, you go home. You've done a great job for today. We'll talk in the morning before I head out. I think I've got this store figured out. Not too many issues. Have a good night and thanks so much for coming on board. It means a lot to me, Stephanie."

"My mom is thrilled. I'll tell her you said 'hello.' See you tomorrow. I really look forward to this, Liz. I think I'm going to like it here."

"That's what I want to hear. You are going to be bored for some periods of the day, and then you will have other times when you are slammed with deadlines to meet. You'll adjust to it. And so will I. We'll make a good team, and that's what I need here."

"Terrific. See you tomorrow. Get some rest. Sounds like you're going to need it."

Liz sat in the office smiling. The day had gone very well. The manager at Walmart was warm and helpful. The other employees were easy to work with. Her job there was almost done and the weekend would be relaxing. For a moment she allowed herself to think about Jim Wilson and the possible flight to Montana. It could be exciting if the weather held out. She could use a short break. Even two days. And this one store's project had moved so quickly that she wasn't too worried about the missed time.

Jim seemed nice but she needed to know more about him. That bothered her some but she tried not to size him up too fast. Just as she was putting the files on Stephanie's desk, the phone rang in her office. Her private line. She answered and sat down in her chair and leaned back.

"Hello, Liz? Jim Wilson. Checking to see if you've had a nice day." Leigh must have given him my *work number*, she thought.

"It's been busy. How are you, Jim?" She grinned at the sound of his deep voice. But he couldn't see her so she was safe.

"Been sitting in a meeting all day. Boring. But I have to do it. Sort of updates me on new techniques. And we all need that from time to time."

"Did you decide about Friday night?"

"I have chosen a restaurant and will pick you up, if that is okay with you. Or would you rather meet at the restaurant?"

Liz hesitated. She just wasn't sure about him yet. "I think I'll meet you there. What time is our reservation? And where?"

"The Oasis at 6:30. Is that too early for you, after working all day?"

"No, it will be fine. Tomorrow will be an easier day for me. I'll be more than ready to have a nice meal. So I look forward to it, Jim. See you there at 6:30."

"Great. Have a good restful night. We'll have a great time getting to know each other."

She hung up the phone and laid her head back on the sofa, closed her eyes, and fell asleep for about an hour, waking up with a little chill. She'd had a bad dream but she couldn't remember what it was about.

She picked up her things, put her coat on, and turned out the lights. Tomorrow was going to come quickly and she wanted to pick out something to wear on the date. She wasn't going to call Leigh until Saturday. She wanted some time to think about Jim after the date was over, without Leigh jabbering her head off about how many chances did she think she would have. Sometimes married friends were a pain in the neck. Because all they wanted to do was get you married. It never occurred to them that one might like to remain single. She was actually content with her work and friends. And the occasional chance to fly. She decided to phone her parents on the way home to check in and see how they were doing. Her father had flown when he was younger so she just might ask him about the Montana trip. Wouldn't hurt to have his opinion about the weather. You couldn't be too careful when it came to the wings of an airplane where ice was concerned.

Chapter 4

Jesse Stone was an ex-pilot and former president of Bank One. He was a stiff sort of guy, tall, thin and wiry, a bookworm who sat in a corner at parties and jogged five miles every day of his life. He didn't smoke or drink and had little tolerance for those who did. When he ran Bank One, he was like an army sergeant in one way, but he had a soft spot for the older ladies who came into open accounts or talk about a loan.

His relationship with his wife Martha was peculiar to most. But she loved him and understood his temperament, so it worked for them. He hadn't really wanted children, but when Elizabeth was born, that baby girl broke down part of a wall he'd built around himself in his younger years. He fell head over heels in love with her. And then Zach was born. Tall, dark, and handsome after his father. He grew into a strong man with huge muscles and was very athletic. His eyes and hair were dark like Elizabeth's. Martha's hair was blond. So both children looked like Jesse, leaving Martha the odd one out. It sort of fit with her personality and she adjusted to it very quickly.

Jesse was an excellent pilot and that perfectionism carried into all areas of his life. There was no room for error in flight, and he couldn't stress that enough to Elizabeth. When Zach was killed in a car accident at eighteen, his death tore the family apart. But Martha hurt the most. She was the closest to Zach and she never really got over it. Jesse and Zach had argued since the boy was old enough to talk and they never saw eye to eye on anything. This continual conflict only added to the distance that had grown between Jesse and Martha. But as time went on, they pretended things were fine and soon it got easier to believe.

Martha was not as tall as Elizabeth. She had short blonde hair, a perfect figure, and an easy smile. She dressed tastefully and had a thing for shoes and purses. She also loved wearing pretty jewelry and had a drawer full of it; not the real thing, but casual jewelry. Elizabeth had turned out a little plainer than Martha had hoped for in the way she dressed. She wore little jewelry and didn't like much frou-frou. The issue of ruffles or no ruffles had been a point of contention when she was raising her daughter.

Martha was strong and independent, which kept her from losing it with Jesse's apparent indifference to matters of the home and their intimate life. But she was very loving to her children and made their lives as pleasant as possible. Inside she wanted to leave sometimes, but she had found a love for Jesse that somehow lasted through the years, giving her comfort in times of stress or disappointment. Now in his retirement, Jesse and Martha had found some common ground in the game of golf and they travelled often in the States visiting friends and family scattered across the West. But the hole that Zach's death left in the family was like the elephant in the room. It remained unspoken but everyone knew it was there.

When the phone rang, Jesse was sitting in his worn leather chair in the den watching the local news. He picked it up, chewing a mouthful of peanuts.

"Elizabeth? How nice of you to call. Things going okay at the office? Haven't heard from you in a couple weeks."

"Not like me, huh, Dad? I'm on my way home now; it's been a tough day. You knew I got the Walmart account, right?"

"Yep. You told me that. How's that going?"

"Great. Nice people to work with. I've enjoyed it and I've only done two stores. Got a few more to go. But that's not why I called."

"What's going on? You got a problem with your car?"

"No. Nothing like that. I met a gentleman the other night at a dinner party at Leigh's. You remember her? She's my best friend. I knew her at college."

"Oh yes. I remember her. The one with auburn hair and a temper like a redhead."

"That's her. Well, she introduced me to a man named Jim Wilson. He's a cardiologist here for a seminar. He is from Montana. Found out I was a pilot and that Leigh's husband Joe had a plane. He asked if I would consider flying him home, and I was wondering about the weather this time of year. A lot of snow I hear."

Jesse was quiet for a moment, thinking. "I'll have to check, Lizzy. Not sure that is a good idea. Can I get back to you? It won't take me long to find out how things are going to be for the next week. When were you going to try to do this?"

"He wants to leave on Monday."

"Not much time. Okay. I'll get on it right away. But I can tell you right off if they're having a bad winter, then the air will be full of water. You know how that affects you when you're taking off or landing. That's the time you need to worry about it."

"I know all that. But just wondered how you felt about my doing it this time of year. How big is the risk?"

"I'll give it some thought and call you back later tonight. You be careful driving home and we'll talk shortly."

Elizabeth was in deep thought when she got home. She'd acquired a slight headache driving home and walked into the house looking for some medicine to take. She realized that she was hungry so she fixed some leftover lasagna and French bread and tossed a small salad. She was pouring her tea when her father called. It had begun to rain outside and she could hear it hitting the windows.

"Lizzy, it's Dad. I've been studying the weather maps for Montana and the surrounding area for the next four days. It looks like there is snow on the ground and in the mountain areas, but no new snow forecasted for the next week. However, the temperatures are low so there could still be some issues as you land and take off. I don't feel too bad about you going but I say that with caution."

She could hear the hesitancy in his voice. It worried her some, but the forecast was pretty stable. She knew she would have to give Jim an answer at some point so that he could make other arrangements if she said no.

"I'll take my chances, I guess, unless something changes between now and Monday. I need to check the plane out, even though I know without a doubt that Joe will do that this weekend. He wouldn't dare send me up without checking his plane. But I always feel better giving it a once-over myself since I'm the one whose life is at risk."

"I taught you well, dear. I'm a little nervous. Wish I could go with you. It'd be fun to fly together again."

"Wish there was room. I'd take you in a New York minute."

"Well, we'll have our time to fly, sweet one. Just watch for any changes in the weather. I'll do the same. Even if you have to cancel at the last minute, it's worth it to save your life. And his. Although I don't know this coot. What's he like?"

Liz laughed. "Dad, I told you he seemed like a nice guy. Intelligent. Just a little forward about asking me to fly him home. Well, actually Leigh started it. I'm sure he means well. And I don't have to say yes."

"True. You seeing him tomorrow night?"

"Yes. And I'll decide how I feel about it after we get to know each other a little more. Hard to do that when Leigh is sitting there glaring at me."

Jesse laughed at his daughter's sarcasm. "She just wants you happy and so do I. But that doesn't always have to include a man. Right?"

"Exactly. I'll keep you posted, Dad. Thanks for the flight information; I really appreciate it."

Her gut feeling was no. But she was going to decide after their visit tomorrow night. In a way, it would be exciting. She'd missed flying. But this Walmart gig was so big that she sort of wanted to remain on the job. She was type A in her career. She learned early that to get anywhere she had to work like a man. Driven. And it fit her personality to a T.

She'd blocked off her heart pretty well. Insulated it. After being hurt years ago, she had decided not to fall in love again. She had loved Tom more than anything in the world and one day his heart had turned towards someone else and it had nearly killed her. She'd never seen it coming. He'd given no hint that he was unhappy. There were whispers of marriage, but nothing definite. When he left her, there were tears in his eyes. She wasn't sure why he left, but he hadn't contacted her since. It was going to be a question that haunted her for the rest of her life.

She decided to take a shower instead of a bath and stood in the hot spray for a long time, allowing her mind to let go of the pain that had returned from remembering Tom. She also set a new plan for her career goals. She wanted every Fortune 500 company as an account. That was a huge target but she knew she could do it with someone like Stephanie alongside. The girl was driven—a little too much like her, but that was why it would work so well. She wanted the money and had a desire for bettering herself. It took that kind of drive for a woman to succeed.

And it also took a will of iron not to allow your friends to marry you off to the first man they could get their claws into. She laughed as she dried herself off. Jim was Leigh's catch. She was so proud of herself. It almost made her not want to like him. Not to even give him a chance. He was nothing to her now. She could care less if she saw him again or not. If love were allowed to creep in it would ruin her plan. She had to keep her guard up until she knew he could be trusted. And not many passed that requirement. In fact, none. Zero.

She climbed into her soft bed and snuggled into the covers again. Her long hair was stark against the white pillowcase, and when she closed her eyes, her lashes were long and thick, and her skin pale. Men stared at her constantly, but were afraid to approach her. She was almost untouchable. Almost.

Chapter 5

Jim Wilson sat in the last hours of a seminar, listening halfway to a presentation about a new technique that had not been introduced yet in the States concerning heart valve replacement. His mind kept wandering to Elizabeth. She was an enigma to him. Pulled back. Hard to read. He was usually good at reading people but she was an exception and it was driving him nuts. He didn't really get to talk to her that much because of Leigh and her loud mouth. She was a doll but she talked too much. It was way too obvious she was trying to hook them up. He despised that and it almost made him not want to come to the dinner. But after meeting Elizabeth, he was glad he did. Leigh meant well but she was one hair short of pushy. Meddling. And if he remembered correctly, that wasn't a trait you wanted in a woman.

His cell phone kept going off and he ignored it until the break. When he checked it, he had ten texts from Sheila Gordon. She sounded furious. She wanted to know why he wasn't responding to her texts. He grinned. She was a hot little thing who'd been after him for the last year. Sure, he had flirted with her and even had lunch with her once. Actually, they'd slept together. But it was a bad idea that had turned into a nightmare. He couldn't get rid of her. He texted her back saying he was in a seminar and had been for a few days. That he'd get back to her when he got home. She texted that she had relatives in Knoxville and wanted to come over to see him. He discouraged it, saying he was going to be tied up the whole time.

When the seminar was over he walked out and his phone was ringing.

"Hello? Sheila? What's up with all the texts?"

"What's up? I've been trying to get in touch with you for the last two days. I'm in Knoxville. I'm at my brother's house and wanted to have dinner with you tonight. Why are you ignoring my texts?"

"I'm not ignoring them, but I already have dinner plans. I had no idea you were coming here."

"That's because you didn't read your text messages. Now don't tell me you can't cancel your plans. I'm sure you don't have a hot date in Knoxville. You don't even know anyone there."

"I have a business meeting with a pilot who is going to possibly fly me back on Monday."

"Why couldn't I come along?"

"That wouldn't be possible. I hardly know this pilot and it just wouldn't be appropriate."

"You know what, Jim? You've led me around like your little prize thing and I'm pretty sick of it. You were all over me and then you just cut me off. What kind of woman do you think I am?"

"I thought I was just having fun with you. I didn't promise marriage. Now you need to cool it, Sheila. This is childish. We had a good time; that's all it was. A good time."

"You let me fall in love with you, Jim. You knew full well that I was falling hard for you. And you did nothing to stop it as long as you got to sleep with me. Now that you did, it's over? No way. You're not going to treat me like that. I've flown here to see you and I expect you to see me. You can't treat me like that."

Jim rubbed his face and shook his head. She was crazy. He didn't invite her to come; she just came on her own. She was stalking him. He had to get rid of her somehow. "I'm not going to change my plans just because you decided to show up, Sheila. I'll talk to you tomorrow. I have plans tonight and they aren't going to change."

"Okay, okay. Sorry I was so pushy. But at least tell me who it is you're having dinner with. At least give me that."

He was quiet for a moment. He didn't want to give Elizabeth's name. He decided to tell her about Leigh's husband. That way she wouldn't be jealous. "I'm meeting Joseph Jordan for dinner. He has his own plane. I'll call you tomorrow and we'll talk. Now I've got to run, Sheila. Have a nice evening."

He cut his phone off and walked to the car. He was uneasy about her being there but hoped he'd satisfied her curiosity for a while. He didn't want anything to ruin his dinner with Elizabeth. He should have listened to his colleagues about dating a patient. It wasn't a smart idea.

He drove back to the hotel and took a hot shower. Sheila had really gotten under his skin. He'd thought she was a nice lady, nice to look at. But now he was feeling like she was mentally unbalanced. It could get out of hand really fast. He decided to contact Fred, his best friend from medical school, to see what the best way to handle her would be. This could turn into a nightmare, and maybe, just maybe, there was something he could do to knock her down a notch or two. Or five. The fact that she had flown to Knoxville raised all kinds of red flags.

The Oasis was crowded and Jim was thankful he'd made dinner reservations. He got there before Elizabeth and the host seated him in a quiet corner on the right side of the restaurant. There were green fake palms everywhere and all the waiters were from China. It was family owned and each one of them was friendly. He felt good about inviting Liz there and this would give them time to really talk.

The walls were gold and covered in Chinese art. The lighting was subtle and each table had a candle and an orchid flower in a small clear vase. The décor was a little cheap looking but the aroma coming from the kitchen smelled wonderful. He was looking over the menu when he spotted Elizabeth walking through the door. He jumped up and strolled over to her, smiling big.

"Hey, lady. So good to see you again! Please come and sit down. They've been so kind as to give us a corner table."

Elizabeth looked ravishing. She was dressed in a long skirt and sweater with boots. Her hair was pulled back and she had silver hoop earrings on. He ushered her into her seat and sat down across from her, holding her hand.

"It's good to see you too, Jim. How was your day?"

"You wouldn't believe how boring it was. I sat through another day of that seminar, although I might add I have learned a few things I didn't know."

"Well, then, it wasn't a waste of your time. You're in a pretty important position and I would say learning something new would be critical to the patient."

"It is. And I don't really mind these long weekend seminars. But they can be boring. The companies that represent new techniques or medical instruments tend to like to hear the sound of their own voice. So half of the time no one is listening. We really just want to know how to use the piece of equipment or understand the new procedure."

"Is the last one today?"

"Unfortunately, I have another one tomorrow, but Sunday is free. What about your day?"

"Well, my day has gone well. I finished up at Walmart early and was able to come home and relax before I got dressed to meet you. The weather held out and that made it even better!"

They ordered their meals and the waiter poured glasses of Chardonnay. Elizabeth's cell went off and she looked to see who it was. Stephanie. She apologized and checked the text: "Going into office on Sat. Will go over computer program again. Don't wanna waste time next week learning it."

She's going to be amazing when she really understands the protocol, Liz acknowledged to herself.

Jim was staring at her the whole time, watching her hands. Watching her eyes. "So tell me about your flying experience. What made you want to fly?"

"Long story. But the short of it is, I love the outdoors. I am part Indian. Not much but a little. And when Leigh married a pilot, well, I sort of took advantage of it and talked him into teaching me how to fly. My father is a pilot, also, but was always gone. Too busy to teach me. And maybe it was better having someone I wasn't related to, to teach me. I was able to concentrate and not feel like I had to do it perfectly to please my father. It's what I love the most. And for some reason it came easy for me."

"I'm impressed. Never have met a woman pilot before. How do you feel about us flying to Montana on Monday? Have you made up your mind yet?"

Their food arrived and Elizabeth took her first bite, blowing on the sweet and sour chicken to cool it down before she put it into her mouth. "I've been checking the weather patterns and it appears to be okay for us to make that trip. But I'll be checking it up through Sunday to make sure there are no sudden changes. It's critical that we not fly through moisture that could freeze. Mostly during takeoff and landing. It's very dangerous if ice forms on the wings."

Out of the corner of his eye Jim saw a woman come into the restaurant and she caught his attention. He thought she looked familiar but he was captivated by what Liz was saying. He looked once more as she was being seated and recognized Sheila. His heart began to race. *What in the world is she doing here?* He tried to listen as Liz continued talking, but he was afraid Sheila was going to come over to the table.

"I know it's risky and I wouldn't dare want you to risk your life or mine just to fly me home. So I trust you to check out the weather and make your decision on what you find. I have no idea how dangerous it is to fly in the winter over Montana. I just thought it was a great idea and would be fun for us."

"It would be. I'll be checking on things and will keep in touch with you, Jim."

He took a bite of his rice, beef and peppers, and just as he was taking a sip of tea, Sheila walked up.

"So this is the male pilot that you were talking to me about today. Is your name Joe?" Her voice was shrill and Jim could tell she was over-the-top angry.

"Sheila, this is Elizabeth. She is a consultant for the Fortune 500 companies. And yes, she is also a pilot."

Elizabeth offered her hand and smiled. "Hello, Sheila. Nice to meet you."

Sheila ignored Elizabeth. "Jim, are you telling me you stood me up for a date with her?"

"Now, Sheila, you and I had no date. You need to back off. Excuse me, Elizabeth. I'm going to walk Sheila out of the restaurant."

The two left, with Sheila talking loudly as Elizabeth watched in shock. She couldn't imagine how Jim knew this woman, not to mention how she'd found out they were eating at the Oasis. Five minutes later Jim walked back in and headed towards the table. He was red-faced and perspiring even though it was freezing outside.

"Please forgive me, Elizabeth. That was one of my patients and I'm afraid she's become a stalker. I had no idea she had a brother here in Knoxville. She followed me here without my knowledge and texted me all through the seminar today. I finally had to tell her I had plans for tonight so she would leave me alone. I guess she got on the phone and called all the restaurants in the area to see where I had reservations. Obviously, she was successful in finding me."

"She did seem quite upset. Do you need to go, Jim? I can finish my meal and head home. After all, I did bring my own car."

"There's nothing I would rather do more than to finish this meal with you. Even if you don't fly me home to Montana. I wanted so much to get to know you better. I apologize for her outburst. Hopefully, I took care of it."

"So you dated one of your patients? Isn't that unethical?"

"Yes, it is. And I made a very stupid decision at a weak moment. I was lonely and she was nice to me and we went out for a glass of wine. One thing led to another and we were intimate. But I really wasn't planning on a relationship with her. That was not my future at all. However, she put her claws into me and she doesn't want to let go. I'm not sure how to handle it. If I get rid of her as a patient she could lambast me on Facebook or Twitter. It could go viral. Not sure how or what to do."

"I'm so sorry, Jim. I know it's hard on doctors when patients get attracted to them. It seems restricting but it's probably best in the long run not to go down that path."

"I so wish I hadn't. Now we were talking about you before she interrupted us. How long have you been flying?"

"It's been about ten years. But this contract I have now has taken up so much of my time that I haven't had a chance to fly. I really would love to take you home, but it will depend on that weather forecast on Sunday. I'm a career woman, Jim. I always have been. And I really love what I do. I feel privileged to be able to find ways for a company to improve its profit margin."

"Makes everybody happy, doesn't it?"

"Sure does. So usually, it ends well. On some occasions, people get their feathers ruffled, but they hired me to do the job and they have to prepare themselves for what I will find. It's an interesting situation."

"I bet. Is it common to find that it is employee theft or issues that cause a company to be struggling?

"You won't believe it, but often it's the top guy that's causing most of the problems. So they really are shocked when I walk into their office with that news. They are fully prepared to have to fire someone or talk to a group of employees who are not pulling their weight. When I identify the bosses themselves as the problem, they freeze. They are embarrassed. They fight it a little but I give them all of the numbers and if it points to them, they really don't have a leg to stand on. Hard to argue with the facts."

Dinner was over and they decided to forgo dessert. Jim walked her out to her car and gave her a hug.

"I sure hope we get to see each other again. I am so sorry about Sheila showing up. That was very uncomfortable for us both."

"I just hope you get it settled. Could turn into a nightmare for you professionally."

"Yes, it could. But I'm going to do whatever I have to to avoid that situation."

"I'll talk to you tomorrow or Sunday. We will know more by then about any weather changes."

"I was hoping to maybe take you to lunch Sunday. Is that a possibility?"

Liz wanted to dodge that question but he was standing right in front of her. "I guess it's feasible. Call me Saturday night and we'll make plans. Thank you so much for dinner. It was good to finally get to talk to you."

"A little late perhaps, but you look lovely tonight. I'm the one who should thank you for such a pleasant night. I'll call you Saturday night. Have a good rest, Elizabeth. You are a joy to be around."

She blushed as she turned and got into her car. It felt good to just sit there and think about the night. The confrontation Sheila had brought to the table. His reaction. And all the things they had talked about. She still was not sure about him and she wasn't dead sure about the flight, either. She started the car and pulled out, noticing he was sitting in his car watching her, smiling. She waved and smiled as she pulled away, anxious to get home to her bed. It had become a sanctuary to her in the evenings since it was so cold outside.

When she walked into her kitchen she saw the light blinking on her phone. She pressed the play button to hear the message. And her eyebrows went up as she heard the voice on the other end. "Lizzy? It's Leigh. Just wondered how your dinner date went! Not trying to rush you or anything, but give me a call when you get home. That is, if it's not too late. I want to hear all about your date with Jim! Now, don't ruffle your feathers. I'm not pushing you two together. I just want you to be happy; you know that. Call me. I'm up. No matter how late you get in. Love you, girl. "

Chapter 6

"Leigh, you've got to stop doing this. I'm not dating this guy just to please you."

"Don't I know it! I'm not trying to force you into anything. What makes you think that?"

Liz sighed. There was no hope. "I know you want me happy but what you don't realize is that I am happy. I don't have to be married to be happy."

"I know you say that, but you want someone to share your life with. I know you do. All women do. It's how we're made."

"Then I may be made differently. I really am content at home alone. Now that doesn't mean I don't want friends to go out with. I love a good dinner and movie. Or a man to take me dancing. But I don't have to get married and I'm not going to unless I am in love with the guy and he is right for me."

"Only God knows where that man is. I sure don't. We've gone through at least ten men and none of them suited you. Can you at least admit you are picky?"

Liz laughed and bit into a hangnail. "Ouch! No, I'm not picky. It just hasn't clicked. Jim and I had a good night. There was a little distraction from some woman who is a patient of his, though. She flew here and is staying at her brother's and is stalking Jim. It was kinda creepy, to tell you the truth. I almost decided to get up and leave."

Elizabeth could hear the shock in Leigh's voice. "What? A stalker? How did he handle it?"

"He took her arm and walked her out of the restaurant. I have no idea what he told her but she didn't show her face again. We ended up having a decent conversation but it was a little strained because of what happened. He told me he did take her for drinks once and they ended up in bed. But he was done and she thought it was the beginning. You know how that is."

"Yeah, and you know I've been there myself a time or two. Well, what is the plan? You flying him home or not?"

"I have to check with Dad and Joe on Sunday. They both are watching the weather for me. I don't mind doing it if it's safe. I just don't want to do something stupid and regret it."

"I agree. I totally agree. Well I know you're tired; I'll let you go. I'll see what Joe thinks about the flight. He wasn't too keen on it at first but when he saw the weather forecast he lightened up about it. So guess we'll see how it goes then."

"Thanks for the call, Leigh. Love you and you guys have a good night."

Liz hung up and walked back to her bedroom to change into her pajamas. She made some hot chocolate again and slipped under the covers. It felt so good to be home. She was really glad that Jim hadn't tried to kiss her. That would have been too awkward. Too soon. She thought he was handsome but there was something about him that just didn't sit well. It wasn't his dress or how he treated her. She couldn't put her finger on it. They hadn't talked about whether or not he'd been married. Or why she hadn't. She was pretty sure he was about forty years old. He had to have been married at some point. She'd been in and out of relationships through the years but for some reason none of them had lasted. She was afraid of commitment, that was clear. And she wasn't even sure why. But she was curious about his past. They'd wasted too much time talking about her flying ability when they should have been talking about who they were. What they wanted in life. She was angry at herself for allowing that to happen.

She was about to get up and brush her teeth when her cell rang. It was Jim.

"Hey, lady. Just checking on you to see if you got home all right."

That's nice of him, she thought, smiling. "Yes, I'm good. Almost under the covers."

"I'm headed in that direction myself. It's pretty cold outside."

"Yes it is. Typical winter for us in Knoxville. We usually get snow around this time. I'm sure it's coming."

"You tired, Liz?"

"Not too bad. I have the television on and had just finished a cup of hot chocolate. Leigh called to check on our date, so I filled her in."

"I guess you had to tell her about my stalker!"

"I did add that in to the conversation. Hard to leave it out, really."

"I'm just sorry it happened, Liz. Won't happen again, I assure you."

"So, Jim, we let the whole night pass without really asking each other anything personal. Can I ask you if you've been married before?"

"You sure can. I was married to a lovely woman for ten years. Her name was Susan Bentley. She passed away from a strange illness that caused a massive heart attack. You can imagine how I felt being a cardiologist and I couldn't save her. It was a nightmare."

Liz was quiet for a moment. He'd really been through something tough "I'm so sorry, Jim. I had no idea. Does Leigh know that?"

"Yes, she and Joe both met my wife on a trip they made to Montana quite a few years ago."

"Oh, okay. Well to answer your unasked question, I've never been married. I know that seems strange, but I've worked so hard that I really didn't have time for a long-term relationship. I dated several wonderful men but they were intimidated by my aggressiveness in the work field and I guess I wasn't ready to settle down and get married. Have children. "

"Hard for you to commit?"

"I'd say so. I'm not sure why."

"That's okay. We're all hiding something. Or coping with life."

"So has it been difficult for you to have another relationship since she passed away?"

"It took me a long while before I even wanted to date. I still don't like dating. That may be why I succumbed to Sheila. I was really not looking for anyone right then. I guess I was going through a weak time. It hits me from time to time and I really miss Susan. But life goes on and I know I have to make a new life for myself. I really enjoyed seeing you, Liz. Let's get together tomorrow even though I'm supposed to go to the seminar. I hope you don't think I'm being pushy, but either way, I am going home on Monday. So you won't ever have to see me again."

"I have a few errands tomorrow. But after lunch I am free. Why don't you come here to my place and I'll fix us dinner? That way we'll have more time to talk without interruption. And hopefully Shelia won't follow you to my house!"

They both laughed and said good night. Liz rinsed out her cup, brushed her teeth, and climbed back in bed. It had been a long day and she was tired. But she was glad Jim had called. It showed he was considerate and they at least hit on some important points by talking about his marriage. He'd suffered the death of a spouse; that was tough to go through. So he wasn't just a shallow cardiologist who was trying to impress women. That made her feel a little better. But she wasn't going to just jump into anything with him. He lived far enough away that she would probably never see him again. A couple meals together and maybe the flight to Montana. But that was it. She had a full schedule through the winter and into the spring and her career was very important to her. She wasn't going to do anything to mess that up. There wasn't a man alive who could tempt her into stepping out of her career now.

Morning light crept into her bedroom through the curtains that were slightly parted. She hadn't moved all night. When her eyes opened, the sun was streaming across the room and it felt like it was noon. She squinted to see the clock and barely could make out the time. It was 8:00. She stretched like a cat after a long nap and snuggled under the covers. It felt so good not to have to rush around. But she knew the morning would get away from her and she needed to run some errands. Jim had said he wanted to see her, but it would be after lunch. She decided to phone Lynda, a friend from her childhood whom she hadn't seen in ages. She reached for her cell and dialed the number. Hard to talk to someone before coffee. Her throat was a little dry as she waited for her friend to pick up.

"Lynda? It's Elizabeth. How are you?"

"It's too early to tell. What in the world are you calling so early for, on a Saturday morning?"

Liz laughed and pulled the covers up over her shoulders. "I'm lying in bed being lazy, enjoying my morning in. Just thought we might catch lunch today. Any chance?"

"Well, let's see. Janie needs to be taken to a friend's house to spend the night. Spencer is playing football at 11:00. So I guess I could eat with you if we time it right."

"That's terrific! Let's meet at the Brighton Cafe and eat a healthy lunch. Sound good? I love their soups."

"I do, too. Great idea. See you at noon."

"Perfect. Look forward to it."

Liz smiled and lay back on the pillow. She'd need to pick up groceries for the meal she was going to fix for Jim tonight. She had to drop clothes off at the dry cleaners, pick up light bulbs at the hardware store, and wash a load of whites. She threw the covers back and grabbed her robe. Her day was rolling and it wouldn't stop until she went to sleep that night. She was determined to nail down her feelings about flying Jim to Montana. And maybe her friend Lynda could tell her why she was so darned afraid of anyone getting close to her. But that was like asking for the moon—which any woman would want but no one would ever have. *Even if I could lasso the moon myself, who would it impress if no one else was watching?*

Chapter 7

The Brighton Café was on Main Street and at 11:30 it was buzzing like a beehive. People were everywhere; shopping, eating out, and enjoying the sunny day. The café was noted for its posters of the rich and famous and the red leather seating that went in a horseshoe around the edges of the room. It was small but the food was fabulous; thus the popularity. The crowds of people who lined up to eat there proved it was worth the wait. Fortunately, Elizabeth got there a little early and grabbed a two-seat booth. She ordered a cup of hot coffee with heavy cream and watched the steam drift up into the air and curl around the foggy panes. Her thoughts drifted from her date with Jim to flying to Montana and her pulse quickened as she thought of the chance to fly again. It had been too long.

All the men in the place were staring at her dark hair and beautiful face. What made her so beautiful was the fact that she was oblivious to it.

She looked up and her friend was coming through the door, dressed to the nines, with her hair blowing in the cold wind. She pulled off her leather jacket and smiled, walking toward Elizabeth with an easy gait. They hugged and sat down to catch up with each other. The room was filling up quickly.

"So tell me how your job's going! You still involved in the big 500 companies?"

Liz swallowed a bite of her fish sandwich and grinned. "I sure am. Landed Walmart recently. It's a big job but I'm not finding that much that needs changing. Just a few stores that are weak in their numbers. Some managerial issues."

"That's going to take you a while. At least you can set your own hours. That's true, right? They don't own you when you are investigating their company, do they?"

"No one owns me. But they do expect it done in a timely manner. I'm not working on weekends or anything. But I do feel the pressure to get the job done. How about you? How's your business?"

"I'm really digging the photography. I'm broadening my areas of work and word is getting around. The phone is ringing so much now that I've hired a secretary. So all in all, I'm happy. Jerry is pleased with what the business is doing, so that makes it easier at home for me. He wasn't at all into me doing photography for a living. Didn't believe I could pull it off. So it's a nice feeling to be doing well so early."

Elizabeth grabbed Lynda's hand and squeezed it. "I'm proud of you, girl. I knew you could do it."

"You always did encourage me. Now, tell me what's new in your world. Any man in the picture yet?"

Elizabeth frowned and shook her head. "No. I guess you can give up on me ever finding someone to marry. I guess I'm too picky. I did meet someone recently at a dinner who was intriguing, but he doesn't live close so the odds of us connecting seriously are very slim. He does want me to fly him to Montana on Monday, so we will be spending time together in the air if I do it."

"Are you serious? Fly him to Montana? Is that home for him?"

"Yes, he's a cardiologist. He found out I was a pilot and just asked if I would consider flying him home. I thought it was rather bold of him, but he seems like a nice man and Leigh is crazy about him. You know how Leigh is, always trying to find me a man."

Lynda laughed and rolled her eyes. "Oh yes, I know Leigh. I bet she called you right after your date, didn't she?"

"She sure did! But I told her to stop trying to get me married off. It's not going to happen. I would love to find that right man, but it doesn't seem to be in the cards for me."

"It'll happen when it is supposed to. Don't worry about it. And besides, you seem perfectly happy with your life as it is now."

"I am. Work is keeping me very busy. I hired a young girl recently to be my assistant and we're going to make a great team. So things are looking good for me right now. The short trip to Montana will just be a nice break. But I'll have to get back to work quickly; I don't want to mess up the contract with Walmart. I'm also working on a few of the other Fortune 500s. They seem very interested, which only means I will have more work than I can handle in the future. I like that. It keeps me pushing harder than I would normally push."

"Somehow I find that difficult to believe. Any dessert? Let's split something."

"I would love to. A great day to indulge ourselves."

"Your parents good? They both in good health?"

"Oh, yes. Dad's fine. In fact, he's researching the weather for me for that flight out on Monday morning. I'm not attempting it if Dad says the weather is too risky. It's not worth that this time of year."

"I wouldn't want anything to happen, Elizabeth. So please be careful. And I want to meet this guy if he ever comes back here! We'll have dinner together!"

They laughed and ordered a warmed brownie with ice cream and ate until they were stuffed. The café had filled up to its capacity and people were lining up outside. The waiter took Elizabeth's card and after she had paid, they left the café arm in arm.

"Let's not wait so long to do this again, Lynda. It was so good to see you."

"You are as beautiful as ever. Take care of yourself and I want to hear how it goes if you choose to fly him home. I'm available for lunch any time."

They kissed each other good-bye and Elizabeth headed to the grocery store and cleaners. As she got out of her car with a few grocery bags in her arms, her cell rang. It was Jim.

"Hey, lady. How's your day been?"

"Great! Just had lunch with an old friend. We had a great time catching up with each other."

"Super. Well, I'm out of the seminar early, so what time would you like me to come over?"

Elizabeth looked at her watch. It was 2:30. "I was thinking around 4:00. Is that okay for you?"

"Sure. That's fine. I'll be at your house at 4:00 sharp. Can't wait to see what we're having for dinner!"

"Don't get too worked up over a home cooked meal! I'm not the best cook in the world, but it'll be good. I'll do my best."

"Don't worry. My wife used to tell me I would eat dog food if a pretty woman served it to me."

"That's good to hear. I'll remember that if I decide to make meatloaf!"

He smiled. "See you soon."

The afternoon flew by as Elizabeth readied the house, made the salad, and got the steak and potatoes ready to cook when Jim arrived. She made fresh peach cobbler and had purchased her favorite vanilla ice cream. Then she hurried to her bedroom to change clothes. It was 3:30 and she didn't want to be in the middle of dressing when he came.

For some reason she was nervous. She wasn't sure if it was because she already liked him, or if she was fighting allowing him in at all. Either way, she couldn't decide what to wear. She finally picked her gray sweater and black jeans with some brown boots. She pulled her hair back and tied a scarf around the ponytail. After checking her makeup and touching up her lipstick, she was ready at last. Just in time, because the doorbell rang when she was coming down the stairs.

She opened the door and Jim was standing there in a black leather jacket and black boots. He had on jeans and a light blue shirt. Pretty striking, even if she was holding back.

"Hey! So glad to see you. Come on in, Jim. Let me take your coat. I've got a nice fire going in the living room."

"Hey, girl! Good to see you, too. I could use that fire. The temperature is dropping out there and it's only 4:00. Wonder what we'll end up with by midnight?"

"I think the forecast is saying it'll go down to the 30s tonight. Not unusual for us here. I'll get you come coffee if you like, or a glass of wine."

"Coffee sounds good. I'll save the wine for dinner, if you don't mind."

"Please have a seat and I'll get it for you. So how was the seminar?"

Jim followed her into the kitchen and sat down on a bar stool, watching her pour the coffee. She felt his eyes following her.

"The seminar? Oh, it was boring as usual. However, I did pick up some new techniques, as I mentioned before. So it wasn't a total waste of time. Not as many people came to this one, and I bet on Sunday it will be empty."

"You aren't required to go to these things?"

"We are, but this one was optional and I just wanted to get away for the long weekend. Now that I'm with you this afternoon, I'm so glad I did."

She smiled warmly and handed him his coffee. "Let's go sit on the sofa. It's more comfortable than these barstools."

He followed her into the living room and sat down not too far away from her. "So any news on the weather for Monday?"

"I haven't heard from Dad today. I'll call him before you leave tonight and ask him what he thinks. We may have to wait until early Sunday to make up our minds. I hope that's okay for you, since you may have to make reservations to get home on Monday."

"I'm counting on this working out. Thinking positive."

"Did you have any children in your marriage to Susan? I don't remember you telling me if you did or not."

Jim paused and sipped his coffee. "Yes, I do have one son. His name is Peyton. Nice kid. But he has drifted off a little since his mother died."

"Might have been difficult for him to deal with, Jim."

"I'm sure it was. It was hard for both of us. But he's out of college now and running his own computer store. He repairs computers and sells new ones. Very high-tech guy. He stayed in Montana, so it's not like we couldn't see each other. But he chooses to stay away and I'm sure it's because when he sees me he thinks of her. I haven't dated that much, so I don't think there is any resentment towards me there."

"It's been long enough to where I would think he would expect you to date."

"Children aren't as accepting of that as you would think. They like to hold on to the family unit as long as possible. His dissipated into thin air. And it was hard on him, being an only child."

"I see. Would you ever want another child?"

He looked at her seriously, searching her eyes. "I think I would like to have another one, if that was what my wife wanted. It's not like I'd be against having more children. But it's not on my mind, if that's what you mean. I haven't gotten close to a woman since Susan died, so it hasn't been an issue."

He paused and touched her hand lightly. "What about you, Liz? Do you want children?"

She moved away from him slightly. "I'm not sure. I think I would like to have at least one child, but it doesn't seem to be in my future. I just haven't had the best luck finding someone that I would want to share my life with. I guess you'd say I am picky."

"Picky is good. At our age, it's a waste of time to go out with someone you wouldn't want to marry. So I've sat home a good bit in the last few years."

Liz found herself relaxing a bit. She was trying so hard to get to know Jim, and his last statement gave her a little peace inside. She just needed to know he wasn't a womanizer. A big flirt.

Two hours had passed since he'd arrived and Liz decided to start dinner. She stood up and took his coffee mug and smiled as she pointed towards the kitchen.

"You want any more? I'm going to finish cooking our dinner. It won't take long. Just steaks."

"Can I help?"

"You can turn on the stereo and find us some good music. And I'll start the potatoes and steaks. Normally I would grill outside but tonight's just too cold."

He smiled and sauntered over to the stereo and shuffled through her CDs. He pulled out a James Taylor/Carole King CD and turned it up a little. He glanced into the kitchen and she did a thumbs-up and smiled. Once she got the steaks browned she turned the heat down and waited for the potatoes to cook in the microwave. She pulled the salads out of the fridge and handed them to Jim. The dinner was ready in about thirty minutes and they both sat down at the table. She pulled some wine out of the refrigerator and uncorked it, pouring two glasses. She handed him one. He proposed a toast, looking directly into her eyes. "Here's to a wonderful friendship and perhaps a flight to Montana in the winter. One we will never forget."

She smiled, hoping that they would get to make that flight. When dinner was over a sadness came over her when she realized that he had to leave. He'd been great company and made her laugh. They'd danced a time or two to some of the music, and it felt nice to have a man's arms around her. When she walked him to the door he hesitated before he opened it.

"I'd like to thank you for a lovely evening. I know I've been pushy with you a little, but knowing how far apart we're going to be after I return home, I thought I'd best grab hold of the time we have and make the most of it."

"I've enjoyed our night, too, Jim. You're a great dancer."

He lifted her face gently and kissed her lightly. "Good night, Elizabeth. Sleep well. And I'll see you tomorrow at lunch. Perhaps you will have some good news for me by then."

When the door closed she leaned against it and smiled. *A nice evening. A nice man.* Her eyes wandered around the living room and she locked into a single photo on one of the bookshelves behind the sofa. It was a picture of her great grandfather, Snow Eagle. As she drifted off to sleep later in the night, she thought about her father's words to her when she was a child. "Never go anywhere unprepared for the worst. That way you'll never be caught unaware." She brushed it aside and allowed Jim's face to come into her vision. She wondered for a moment before sleep took her over if he was just a friend or the love of her life. And would she be willing to go there, if he was the one…

Chapter 8

Elizabeth slept in on Sunday. Without opening her eyes she could tell it was cold outside. She could hear the wind blowing the bushes next to the house and they were scraping against the windows in her bedroom. She was expecting a call from her father at some point during the day, but for now, she hunkered down under the covers, wanting to stay warm. The week ahead of her was going to be a busy one. A trip to Montana and a short visit with Jim. Then back home and back to work at another Walmart. She wanted to overtrain Stephanie so that she could handle anything that came up while she was out of the office. It was critical that she not miss any calls from the other Fortune 500 companies. This was her time to get in the loop with all of them. And she was willing to do anything to get them.

She finally talked herself into getting out of bed and made her way down the stairs to the kitchen for some hot coffee, turning up the heat on her way into the kitchen. She fixed some hot oatmeal and added some blueberries, a little sugar and milk. The paper was outside and she wanted to read it, but just couldn't face that cold air just yet. It was 9:30 and she knew her father was up. It was getting down to the wire on the trip to Montana. She had to decide which way she was going so she could check the airplane. She decided to call Joe and see which way he was leaning on the flight.

"Hey, Lizzy. How's it going?"

"I'm surprised that Leigh allowed you to answer the phone." She laughed at the joke. Only it was so true. Leigh never let anyone answer the phone. She was afraid she'd miss something.

"She's in the shower. You and I both know that's the only reason she didn't pick it up!"

"How's the weather looking up north? You feeling good about the flight or not?"

"There's no direct forecast for snow on Monday. But it is cold. Very cold," he said. "I guess I'm leaning towards giving you the go-ahead. But with some small reservations."

"We both know it's always a risk in the winter. Especially when mountains are involved. And cold damp air."

"Yep. I just don't want anything to happen to you. I've already checked out the plane. It's in great shape and full of fuel. It's all set for the flight. I know you'll want to check it yourself and I'd feel better if you did. Since you're the pilot."

"I could come over after lunch and check it out. You want to meet me there? If I'm going, then I want to pack it for emergencies. You know how I am about that."

"Yeah, I know you got Indian feathers in your blood. Besides, it never hurts to be prepared."

"I'm going to dress like an Eskimo. And I'm going to insist that Jim does, too. We're going to have food and emergency supplies, medical supplies, and flashlights. Plenty of batteries. The works."

"That's what I would expect of you, Liz. I'll see you later then. Have a good morning."

"Tell Leigh I'll talk to her later. I'm meeting Jim for lunch and I'm sure she's dying to know how things are progressing."

Joe laughed. "That woman can drive the most patient human being nuts with her nosey ways. I'd tell her to back off but it does no good. Once she is on to something, she won't drop it. But you know her better than I do!"

"She means well, Joe. I need to go, but thanks for everything. I'll see you this afternoon. I'll text you before I head over."

"Sounds good. See ya."

Elizabeth shook her head. *So the trip was on.* Now that she knew she was going, it made her day easier. She could pack and get things ready for the flight. Her nerves were on edge because of the risks involved but she also didn't want to overreact. The odds were about 60/40 that nothing would happen that she couldn't handle. But that was true only if it didn't snow or moisture didn't collect on the wings or tail. She grabbed a manual she had tucked into her bookshelf and threw it into a backpack. She had insulated underwear, snow jacket and pants, extra heavy socks, boots and a knife, flashlight and batteries. She packed matches and first aid equipment, looking around her bathroom and kitchen for anything else she might need if they crashed. Of course, she was supposing they would survive a crash. The alternative wasn't an option.

Her phone rang. Jim sounded anxious to see her again. "Hey, girl. You okay with eating at the deli on North Street? I can't think of the name of it but I passed it the other day going to the convention."

"Nooks Café? Yeah, I love that place. You picking me up or you want to meet there?"

"I'll pick you up. At noon. So be ready!"

"I will. And good news… the trip is on."

Jim sighed. "What luck! Sounds wonderful. I was really afraid we wouldn't be able to do it."

"I'm going to check out the plane after lunch and make sure everything is solid. I'm also packing extra things in case anything should come up unexpected. We'll talk about it when I see you."

"You sure your father said it was okay to make this trip? I sure don't want to take any big risks, Liz."

"Not to worry. If he had big doubts he would nix the trip. We'll check the weather again in the morning. It's going to be cold so we will both have to pack warm clothes. Always be prepared for the worst. That's what my father used to say."

"Okay. I'll pick you up in a couple hours. Looking forward to it, Liz."

It was cold outside and Elizabeth pulled her coat up around her neck. The wind was blowing and it felt like it was going to be a bad winter. Jim held her arm as they walked to his car; he was talking nervously and she could tell he was excited.

"I'm so glad you agreed to this lunch. Now that I know we are going to make the trip together, it's not as important. But I originally thought this would be the last time I would see you."

"That sounds a bit dramatic, Jim. You just met me the other night!"

"It doesn't take long when you find someone you really like. Connect with."

Liz's instinct was to pull back, but she knew it was a destructive habit she'd had for years. "That's sweet, Jim. I am looking forward to the flight. We'll probably take off early, so that we have plenty of daylight. I wouldn't want to make this trip in the dark."

He helped her get into the passenger seat and closed the door, breathing out a sigh of relief. After he got into the car he started up the conversation again. It was obvious that he was so thrilled to have this time with her again.

"So, are you planning on staying a couple of days; I sure would like to show you around a little bit."

"No. I'm sorry, Jim. I really need to get back to work. But maybe I'll make it your way another time and you can take me on a tour."

"I'd love that, Elizabeth. Here's the café. Let's grab a seat. Looks like there are a lot of cars out front. Didn't think it would be so busy."

"It's a favorite around here. I love this spot."

They walked into the café and a hostess seated them right away. It was cozy inside and music was playing overhead. Being a small café, the aroma from the kitchen was enough to woo any hesitant customer inside. Elizabeth decided on a bowl of chili and a salad. Jim ordered seafood gumbo in a bread bowl and some iced tea. They both leaned back and took in the crowd that was pouring in the door.

"It's funny how the locals love this place. Well, usually the small deli restaurants and cafes are the places locals go. The food is good and it's a great atmosphere for not a lot of money."

"Probably common in most towns. We have places up home that tourists don't know about that have the best food in the world."

"So let's talk about your work. Do you love it or are you hardened like most doctors I've met?"

"That's a bit harsh, isn't it, Liz? Sounds like two extremes to choose from!"

Liz smiled and nodded. "You got me there. I didn't mean to be so hard on you. It just seems like doctors often get hardened if they stay in the business long enough. So that they really don't care about the patient anymore and treat each one of them with textbook-like medicine."

"Who in the world have you been seeing? My gosh, that sounds like a freaking nightmare!"

She laughed and took a bite of the steaming chili. "I guess I've met the wrong doctors, huh?"

"None of my colleagues are like that at all. They love their work and do their best to treat each person with dignity and respect. Especially in heart surgery, it's a pretty serious operation. The doctor needs to reassure the patient that he will come through it. I couldn't possibly just operate the same way on each patient. The outcome would be disastrous."

"That's true in your field, perhaps. But I have met many doctors, internal med doctors, who really are in it for the money. Or they've gotten burned out by seeing too many patients."

"That can happen easily. Some young doctors go at it like a bull in a china shop. They book too many patients and are worn out at the end of every day. Unfortunately, you can't hold up long doing that. Something suffers, and often it's the doctor's health."

"I couldn't handle that kind of pressure. How do you do it?"

"I couldn't at first. But I learned that all I am required to do is the best that I can. I study and read up on any new techniques that are brought to the forefront, and I also try my best to understand the patient. How they live, what they eat, how they've treated their body. All that plays into the success of the surgery. I'm not a miracle worker, you know. And some doctors feel they are supposed to be."

"That's an awful lot of pressure to put on one's self. Medicine is at best guesswork in some form or fashion, it seems to me. A diagnosis is made and a procedure is done, but each body is going to react a little differently. You do have people's lives in your hands, literally. My job seems quite trite in comparison."

"It's not a common attitude that you've shared, but that is my job. Just like you have a job. Mine just happens to be working on people's hearts. It is critical and there is a massive amount of pressure involved. But your work causes stress on you. I've seen it in just the short time I've known you. We do our jobs well, and that's the best we can do."

Elizabeth thought for a moment and smiled. "You're right. But I couldn't do what you do. It's much too serious. Critical, in fact. Life and death situations every single day could wear on a person. How do you keep your sense of humor?"

"I didn't for a long time. But I have learned to have a life outside that hospital. What I do in there is important but it cannot be my whole life. A person is complex, made up of so many parts. My work is only a part of who I am. Just like you."

"Well, I haven't developed myself very well. I've pretty much worked all my adult life and haven't taken the time to have hobbies or test the waters for any talents that might be hidden in there."

"That's not totally true. You're a pilot. And I thank God you are. We're going to have so much fun on this trip home."

"That reminds me. You need to pack some extra warm clothing—even if you have to buy it. I want us to be prepared for the best and the worst that could happen."

"The best is that we really fall for each other up in the air. The worst is a bit morbid, I might add."

She laughed but was serious when she answered him. “It’s critical to be prepared, Jim. In a plane, anything could happen. It has always gone smoothly in the past but that’s not to say it couldn’t change on this trip. The weather is a huge factor. And I’m a tad worried about the cold weather and the snow. Things change quickly over a mountain range. Believe me, we could get into trouble very fast if the weather takes a turn for the worse.”

He put his hand over hers. “I’m counting on things going well so that you’ll come back soon and visit.”

Neither had paid much attention to the food in front of them. They finished their meal and walked out of the small café, noticing again the line of people waiting to get in.

“Let’s go for a short drive before I take you home.”

“Sure. But I do have some paperwork to do before Monday, so I can’t be out too long. I also need to stop by the airport to see Joe and check the airplane.”

“Did he check it?”

“Always does. But I’m prepared to do a preflight check. After all, I’m the pilot on this trip, not Joe.”

Jim drove around midtown looking at the architecture and shops around a circle that included the courthouse.

“This is a nice place. Plenty big and high traffic. But I’ve enjoyed being here. Quite different from Montana. You’d be bored up there unless you enjoy riding.”

“It’s been a while since I’ve sat on a horse, but it is fun. Challenging. Do you ride?”

“I have my own horses. Didn’t mention that to you. Not that I have that much time to ride. Someone else keeps them and also teaches riding lessons to the underprivileged children in the area. Pretty amazing woman, actually. Her name is Dana. I’ve known her for years and let me tell you, she’s a horsewoman to the bone. Tough as nails. But you would love her. The children adore her and she has done wonders with them.”

Liz was seeing another side of Jim the longer they talked. It made her wonder about her judgment of him at Leigh's house. He was deeper than she surmised after her first visit with him. "I'm impressed. There's a lot more to you than meets the eye. Not that being a cardiologist and heart surgeon isn't enough."

He grinned and grabbed her hand. "I'm having a wonderful time with you. I guess I need to let you get back to your work. And we both have to pack."

He pulled into her driveway and she raised her hand up. "I'll walk myself to the door or we'll never let this day end. I've enjoyed our lunch and chat very much. I'll call you tonight to let you know where to meet me. Get a good night's sleep. You're going to need it!"

He leaned over and kissed her lightly. She didn't pull away outwardly, but inside she could feel herself wanting to run. But she didn't. She fought that desire and just leaned into him for a moment. It was kind of nice to smell his cologne and feel his beard against her face. She climbed out of the car smiling, and turned to wave. He waited for her to get inside and pulled away, looking back at her house in the rear view mirror.

She leaned against the door and let her mind relax. He was a lot of man to get to know. How many more secrets did he have in that six-foot-three-inch frame?

Chapter 9

It was a beautiful Sunday early afternoon. Elizabeth noticed the drop in temperature and shook her head as she walked up to the Skylane Cessna T182 RG. It was not a new plane but in great shape and it handled like a dream. Joe had taken excellent care of it; it was in pristine condition. She walked around it, checking the flaps, the wheels; her hand ran across every inch of the plane as she sought to notice even the slightest defect.

Joe had been standing by his car waiting for her to show up. When he saw her he walked towards her with a huge smile. "Hey, lady. You getting excited about the flight?"

"A little concerned about the weather change here. You worried at all about it?"

"I'm not tickled about your heading to Montana with my friend, but I think you'll be able to handle anything that comes up. Both with the plane and with Jim. He's a good guy, Liz."

She shrugged, finishing her checkpoints. "I am sure he is. I'm not anticipating anything happening with someone who lives so far away. I have enough trouble keeping a relationship going with a local man, much less someone who lives over two thousand miles from here."

"He lives in Helena so I would gas up in Ottumwa, Iowa. That's exactly halfway between airports. I'd feel better you keeping some reserve in your tank just in case."

"That phrase 'just in case' pops up in my head at every turn when I am preparing for this flight. I don't want to overreact but I do want to be as prepared as possible."

"I taught you well. Any questions about the controls? You've flown this plane a hundred times."

"No. It's been a while since I flew, but I feel comfortable with it. I just want the weather to hold when we get near Montana. What I don't want is a whiteout. You know?"

"We won't even talk about it. You have a GPS system that you can count on; I just replaced it last year. And I know you're bringing flashlights, batteries, and other emergency gear."

"I'm ready. It really boils down to the weather holding out."

"Nothing we can do about that from here. Your dad and I will be available on your radio at all times in case you run into something difficult. Between the two of us we can talk you through almost anything."

Liz smiled. "I know you can. You've been terrific with me and I really appreciate your allowing me to fly Jim home. Of course, he's your friend, not mine. At least not yet. We have enjoyed a few meals together so at least he's not a total stranger."

"You'll like the guy if you give him half a chance. If I were you, I would go home and rest up. Get a good dinner and make it an early night. You're going to feel the strain when you get close to the mountains. That's when you will need full concentration and I want you to keep your eyes on the altitude and any changes in the weather. You know all of this. I just don't want anything to happen."

"I appreciate your caution. I will be careful, Joe. I want this to be an enjoyable flight and Jim is really looking forward to it. We've had some talks about his past and mine, so we are slowly getting to know each other. I was hesitant to meet him for lunch and dinner, but now I'm glad I did. It will make the flight even more enjoyable."

Joe grinned, caught off guard by the news of their dining together. "I think that's terrific. Just relax and have a good time with him. Nothing serious has to happen. I was surprised, frankly, that Leigh mentioned you flying him home. He'd just met you. But we men tend to move fast when we are attracted to a woman. So keep that in mind. He probably is very attracted to you!"

"Did he say anything to you?"

"No, but we men pick up on each other's body language. And he was smitten, I can tell you that. But I'll let you make up your own mind about him. He's just a good friend of ours, and well, you know how Leigh is. She's always thinking of you when we have a single man around."

Liz laughed and gave Joe a hug. "Thanks for your help and the chat. I'll be here in the morning early, before Jim gets here. I want to get the plane loaded and be ready to take off by the time he arrives."

"See you then. Hope you can get some sleep."

She grabbed her phone in the car and dialed her father. Jesse answered when he saw her number come up on the phone.

"You ready to go on this trip, Lizzy? You made up your mind?"

"I just spent time doing preflight, Dad. I guess I've settled on going. How do you feel about it?"

"I been talking with Joe and we both agree it's edgy. But you can handle it. I know you can. Just keep your eyes open. Don't take any chances you don't have to take. And stay in touch with the National Weather Service so you know what's going on. You already know these things; just reminding you, girl."

"I know, Dad. You nervous at all about me going?"

He sighed and shook his head. "Yeah, I'm nervous. You're my little girl. But you're tough and a darn good pilot. You can make it and I want you to have fun."

"Okay, Dad. Thanks for the pep talk. Get some sleep. I'm going to do the same. I'll catch you before I leave in the morning."

"'Night, honey. You'll be fine."

By the time she got home, it was 5:00 and dark. She wrapped her coat around her as she walked in the door off the garage. The light on

the telephone was flashing; she had two messages. She played the first one and it was from Jim. He was just checking on her and said he was excited about the trip in the morning. She pushed the button again and walked over to hang up her coat in the closet off the living room. She could barely hear the second message and had to replay it after she got back into the kitchen. She nearly froze in her tracks when she heard the voice.

"Elizabeth, I was so hoping you would be home because I didn't want to leave a message. We haven't seen each other in so long and I don't feel it appropriate for me to just leave you a short message on here. Even though you may already recognize my voice, this is Tom Thornton. A voice from your past. I'm in town and would love to see you. If that's possible, call me on my cell. I really want to see you again. Please call me back."

Liz stood still, her heart racing in her chest. *Tom Thornton? What in the world is he doing in Knoxville?* She was shaking as she picked up the phone. She couldn't decide whether or not to return his call. It could open up all kinds of emotions that she really wasn't ready to feel. He was her first love. And he walked out of her life with no explanation.

She put the phone back on the receiver and sat down on the sofa. She couldn't think straight. Her hands were shaking and her heart hadn't settled down yet. She couldn't believe she was reacting to a voice message from someone she'd not seen in years. She had to admit to herself that she really had loved Tom. He was her first love. But what was he doing in town? And why in the world would he call her? She fixed some coffee and grabbed the phone, blowing out a huge breath in an attempt to calm herself down.

The phone rang several times before his deep voice answered. Her stomach was up in her throat and her knees were weak. "Elizabeth! I'm so glad you called me back. You don't know how good it is to hear your voice after all these years. How are you?"

She tried hard not to sound shaky. "I'm fine, Tom. What a surprise to hear your voice. What are you doing in Knoxville?"

"Well, I've been through a pretty tough divorce in the last year and have had some time to really think about my life. You came into my mind and I decided to look you up. I have so much to talk to you about and I really want a chance to see you. Can I come over? I'm staying at the Holiday Inn not too far from your house."

So he'd taken time to look up her address and pick a hotel close to her. That was impressive. "I'd love to see you, but I'm leaving in the morning for Montana. A short flight. I won't be gone long. Can we do it when I get back?"

"I really want to see you before you leave. Couldn't we have dinner at your house? I'll bring something in so that you don't have to cook. Please let me see you."

"You sound so urgent about it. Is anything wrong?"

"Yes, something big is wrong. And I want to make it right. I'll be there at 6:30 with food. You just pour us a glass of wine, and I'll bring the rest. I cannot wait to see you again."

She hung up and shook her head. What in the world was she thinking? She needed to go to bed early so she would be alert for the flight. But for some reason she couldn't tell him no. She grabbed some clothes she left draped over a chair and straightened the pillows on the sofa. Then she went into the kitchen to get the wine out and two glasses. Heading towards the bedroom, she checked her hair and makeup, changed her blouse, and put a pair of flats on. There was no reason to dress up, but she didn't want to look like a hag, either. She had no idea what she would say to him and was wondering what he had to talk to her about. Her feelings for him had been shoved so far back that it was difficult for her to really know how she felt about him. He'd left her hanging many years ago. She had cried and fought back emotions for a couple of years. Now that he was coming to her house, all those old emotions came rushing back.

Thirty minutes later the doorbell rang and she ran to open the door. He was standing there holding some bags of something that smelled delicious and looking as beautiful as ever. When he saw her, he sat the food down and wrapped his arms around her and picked her up, swinging her around. "Elizabeth! I've missed you so much. You look wonderful! I'm so glad you let me come over."

Catching her breath, she came up with a smile. "It's so good to see you, too, Tom. Come on in. I've got the wine open and our glasses ready. Let me take your coat."

She could feel him watching her every move as she walked over to the sofa and sat down. He grabbed the food and set it on the counter and followed her to the sofa. She was shaking inside; she'd never dreamed she would ever see him again. *Of all times for him to show up.*

Tom leaned near her and took her hand. She wanted so much to pull it away, but there was no energy left in her to fight it. He felt her release and squeezed her hand. "Lizzy, please. Don't pull away. You have every reason to hate me. I pulled out of your life so fast it made your head spin, and I didn't give you any reason. Any excuse. I disappeared and never contacted you. I knew it threw your world upside down, and I kept on going, anyway."

"That about sums it up, all right. It nearly killed me when you left. It haunted me for years as to why you would do it. Why you would leave when we loved each other so much."

He was quiet for a moment and then looked up at her. His eyes were sad and he was dead serious in his answer. "It was the stupidest thing I've ever done in my life; giving you up. I was scared and stupid. Young. I was afraid of commitment and you were so serious you scared me to death. So I ran. I knew you would hate me and I didn't know what else to do. We were at a place where the choices seemed slim and I felt pressured to take us to the next step. I wasn't ready and I didn't see an alternative. You would not have understood if I had told you that I was afraid of commitment. It wouldn't have been an acceptable excuse to you. I was going to hurt you no matter what. So I ran like a scared rabbit."

She had tears in her eyes listening to him talk about it. All of the emotion she felt then was coming back and it was almost too much. She took a sip of wine and sat back. "Tom, it was so long ago. We've both moved on. I heard you got married; is that true?"

"Yes. I married a girl I met in Texas. Sara Bane. We lasted about five years and then she said she wanted a divorce. That she didn't love me anymore. I've been single ever since, and wanting to contact you for so long. I was afraid you wouldn't talk to me, and for good reason. I had some business here in Knoxville and decided that now was my chance. My one chance. I just couldn't let this opportunity to see you slip through my hands."

Liz wiped her eyes and shook her head. "So you're telling me that you left me because you were afraid of commitment back then? And you married Sara and it only lasted five years. Did you love her?"

"If I'm honest, no, I don't think I did. I couldn't ever put you out of my mind completely. And maybe she felt that. I tried but it wasn't real. It had no depth."

"I'm sorry, Tom. I'm really sorry that marriage didn't work out."

He got up and brought the Chinese take-out to the table and they ate slowly and talked. Liz had mixed emotions and also knew she needed to go to bed early.

"Tom, I have to make that trip tomorrow to Montana. I'm flying a doctor I recently met home to Helena. I will be back in two days. Will you be here when I return?"

"Yes, I will. I'll be here for a week. Come here, Lizzy." He reached over and pulled her to him, wrapping his arms around her. It felt so good to be in his arms that she really didn't want to move. But she pulled away and looked into his blue eyes.

"Tom, this has been quite a shock to me, seeing you again. Do you think it's possible to regain our relationship after all this time?"

"I want that more than anything, Lizzy. I have missed you so much. We have so much to catch up on; I want to hear about what you're doing, and hear how your parents are doing. So much to talk about."

"I wish now that I wasn't leaving. I've wanted to talk to you for years. I still can't believe I'm sitting here looking at you. You really haven't changed much at all."

"My hair is getting a little gray in it. Never thought I'd gray early, but it's happening and there's nothing I can do to stop it. I guess it's better than going bald."

She laughed and touched his face. "I kind of like it, if you want to know the truth. It's very becoming on you. Shows off your eyes more."

He grabbed her face and kissed her quickly. "You are gorgeous. Always were. I miss you so, Lizzy. Can I kiss you again?"

She felt helpless in his arms. She kissed him long and hard and pulled away. "I've really got to get to bed. I hate it. I would love to sit up all night talking to you. But maybe when I get back we'll have a few days before you have to head back to Texas. Is that where you are living now?"

"Houston."

She stood up and walked him to the door, holding his hand. "I've been so angry and hurt. You have to give me time to adjust to seeing you again. I understand about commitment. I've not had a close relationship since you for the very same reason. So it's really hard to stay mad at you. I've run off several men because I wouldn't let them in. I think subconsciously I was thinking if I couldn't have you, then I wouldn't get close to anyone. Didn't want to be hurt again. Not like that."

He hugged her and kissed her again. "I'm so sorry I hurt you like that. I want to make it up to you. I'm so thankful you saw me tonight, Lizzy. I never stopped loving you. Never. I just wish I'd called sooner. Didn't have the nerve. You sleep and let me hear from you soon. I wrote my numbers down on your pad by the phone in the kitchen. I'll miss you while you're gone. Be safe, angel. Come back to me so we can see if there's a chance for us."

"'*A chance for us.*' That sounds so good to me. I'll call you as soon as I land the plane. It won't be long. Thanks again for calling me and for such an honest talk. Wish we could have had this sooner."

"Timing is everything. And I think this was the perfect time. I still love you, Lizzy. You're still my girl."

She smiled and yawned. “Sorry, Tom. I’m tired and I have a long journey ahead of me. But I will call you soon.” She kissed him lightly and shut the door, leaning against it for a moment in disbelief. He was the last person she ever thought would call her. But now, after talking to him, she felt so much better. That commitment thing was a demon. Somehow, she had a feeling that it might not be an issue anymore if they could work things out. She was hesitant only because it had been so long. But he seemed like the same man, only better. *He called me his girl.* She turned out the lights, brushed her teeth and fell into bed without washing her face. And her dreams were of Tom and the kiss that just might have turned her world upside down.

Suddenly remembering Jim, she snapped awake and dialed his number. “I forgot to tell you to meet me at 7:00 at the airport on Northside Road.”

“Good thing you called. You okay? You sound upset.”

“I had a visitor tonight. Tom, a guy I dated in the past. Haven’t seen him in years but we were very close. I am tired and you hear that in my voice. And that visit with Tom brought back a world of emotions that I didn’t need on my mind right before this flight. I’m sorry if I seem distracted to you. Tomorrow I will have my focus completely on getting us to Montana.”

“I knew you sounded different. Maybe even strained. You sure you want to make this trip? It’s not too late to cancel it.”

“No way. I’m committed to it now. Just feel like I’ve seen a ghost from the past. Someone I really loved at one time. I know you can understand that.”

“Not what I expected to hear tonight, but I do understand. You get the rest you need, Liz. We can talk more about it tomorrow if you like. I’m looking forward to spending some focused time with you. We’ll have fun.”

“Thanks, Jim, for understanding. Sorry I called so late. See you tomorrow. Sleep well.”

Chapter 10

A ghost out of the past, Tom Thornton counted himself a very lucky man. He had to pinch himself just to see if it was real. She'd let him back in, at least to a point. It was hard to believe after so many years apart. At six-foot-two inches, he was a striking figure in a crowd. He had an incredible mind and sense of humor and was very quick-witted. No comment could catch him off guard.

But this one thing, this seeing Elizabeth again, had really knocked him for a loop. As a corporate attorney, he represented huge auto manufacturers and was used to surprises. But in matters of the heart, he was helpless. He knew that like many men, he had few coping skills when it came to a broken heart. Or decisions about relationships. There weren't enough books written for men on how to understand women, because no matter how many he'd thumbed through, most of the suggestions fell flat in real life. And his cluelessness left him looking like a fool.

He sat in his car outside her house for about thirty minutes, thinking about all that they'd talked about. He would have given anything if they'd been able to talk all night. This trip she had committed herself to really threw a wrench into the mix. But he would wait for her if it took a week. He could reschedule his appointments if he had to. She promised she would be back in a couple days and he could certainly handle that.

She was so beautiful. Just like he'd remembered. His heart jumped in his chest when he saw her. She was a little different in that she'd matured since he'd seen her and had developed her own business. She knew where she was going. But the girl he loved was still in there. It would take some doing to pull her out. He felt the wall she'd erected and he didn't blame her for that. She'd been hurt when he left her suddenly without cause. Looking back, he realized they had been so young. So unready for a serious relationship. But women mature earlier, he admitted, and she had really loved him. He just hoped there was some of that love still hanging around deep inside of her. He would do all he could to bring it out.

He started his car and pulled away, looking one more time at the window to see if he could catch a glimpse of her. He did see the bedroom light go out, so he knew she was going to sleep. What he would have given to have tucked her in. To see her brown hair spread out on the pillow. Her eyes were darker than he'd remembered and he got lost in them within five seconds after she opened the door. She was hypnotizing without even trying. She had no clue how lovely she was. But there was a coldness in her eyes that wasn't there before. And he knew he'd helped to build that icy wall.

The motel wasn't too far away and he pulled in and walked inside, heading for the elevator. Once in his room he opened his computer and checked his emails. He'd left her his email on the pad in her kitchen, but didn't expect to hear from her just yet. But just as he was about to close his computer, an email came through from her. His heart started racing and he feared she was regretting their visit. But it was a short note that was touched with the grace he'd always loved.

"Tom, I never dreamed I'd ever see you again. What a wonderful surprise when you knocked on my door. I really thought I'd be angry at you if I ever saw you. But your usual charm and openness pushed the anger away. I'd nursed that wound for so long it had become a friend. I so look forward to our talking again when I return. Thanks for waiting. It will be a short flight and then we'll have our time to catch up. Say a prayer that we have a safe trip. Good night. Elizabeth."

He stared at the email and wondered if he should reply. He watched the cursor flashing. He'd waited so long to call her, and the miracle was that she actually allowed him to come in. To sit down and talk. He'd expected a lot of resistance. He had so much to talk to her about but emailing wasn't how he wanted to do it. It had to be face to face. It was getting late and he had an appointment in the morning early. He watched the white screen for a few minutes and put his fingers on the keys. Slowly he typed out a message to her.

"Lizzy, I am the one who is grateful for the visit. As usual, you blew my mind away with your grace and beauty. I really don't deserve your forgiveness. On another note, I'm very impressed with how far you've come. I just hope we'll find our way back to each other, and that the years we've lived without each other would only be stepping stones that bring us back. I hope there is an 'us.' And I'll pray you make it home safely. I'm not letting you go this time. Good night, Elizabeth. You take my breath away."

He hit send and watched it leave the in box, and leaned back against the headboard, waiting to see if she responded. The screen stayed quiet so he closed the computer and got up and brushed his teeth and went to bed. Sleep was long in coming because his mind was running rampant on what might have been and what could be.

Finally, he fell into a deep sleep and didn't wake up until the next morning at 6:30. The first thing he did was open his computer to see if he had an email but the box was empty except for some random notes from his secretary. He jumped into the shower and let the hot water drench his back and face. Outside it was cold so he dressed for the day and grabbed breakfast at the Waffle House next door to the motel. His day had begun, and he was certain Liz had started hers. He said a silent prayer she would have a safe flight. And he asked a God he rarely spoke to, to bring her home.

Elizabeth woke up with a start and looked at the clock by her bed. It was 6:00 and she wanted to get to the airport before Jim did, so she hurriedly made her bed and jumped into a hot shower. She dressed warmly with long underwear, jeans, boots, thermal undershirt, sweater, and scarf. In the kitchen she made a thermos of coffee for her and for Jim and wolfed down some oatmeal. She packed some extra snacks, grabbed some water bottles out of the refrigerator and slung the backpack over her arm with her purse. Her suitcase was already in the trunk. She headed out the door, looking back one more time to make sure she hadn't forgotten anything.

It was going to be a long day and she took a deep breath as she pulled out of the driveway and drove along the side roads to the airport. She had texted Stephanie to let her know she would be out of the office for two days. She was hesitant to do the flight with Jim, but decided to go with it because she didn't know when she would take another day off. Now that Tom was waiting for her, she was really looking forward to getting back. *Odd timing of things.* She pushed Tom out of her thoughts as she climbed out of her car, hauling as much as she could carry to the plane. Joe was waiting for her, smiling. It was hard to beat that guy. He was always early.

"Hey, Liz. You ready for this flight?"

"As ready as I can be. It's a pretty day here. Clear skies. Feels good to be flying again."

"I left you a map inside the cockpit and rechecked everything. Should be an uneventful flight for you guys. I guess Jim's on his way. I tried his cell and he didn't answer."

"I haven't spoken with him this morning, but we agreed to meet here by 7:00. So I'm sure he'll show up any minute. I just wanted to be early so that I could load the plane. I'm going to get the rest of my stuff out of the car."

Joe walked with her and took her suitcase out of the trunk. "You've packed for a week. Thought you were coming back tomorrow."

She laughed and slapped his arm. "You know I'm going to over pack. Like all women do. Besides, with this cold weather it's hard to know what to wear."

"Well, I'm going to make a few calls in my truck and let you get settled in. When Jim drives up I'll walk over to talk to him."

Liz made herself at home in the plane, putting things where she wanted them. Jim drove up at exactly 7:00, smiling big and ready to go.

"I am so excited about this flight! How did you sleep?"

"Pretty well, under the circumstances. How about you?"

"Not that well, but it was because I was so excited about today. I ate a good breakfast and brought some things with me to snack on. Really looking forward to some time with you."

She smiled but didn't comment. Her mind was on Tom. But she shoved her thoughts aside and put her mind on the flight schedule and on making sure things were tight. She loaded Jim's suitcase and computer and got him strapped in. Joe was already at the door of the plane watching her like a hawk.

"You guys ready to go? Get in your seat, Elizabeth, and let's crank her up. It's about time for you guys to take off."

She shut the door and climbed into her seat, buckled up, and put her headset on. When she started the plane, it sounded smooth so she waved at Joe and rolled down the runway. Her stomach was in a knot but she had to admit to herself she was looking forward to flying again. She contacted the tower and a controller gave her clearance to depart. The plane rolled down the runway picking up speed, and as they rose, her flying skills kicked in and she leaned back in her seat and took in the view. She stayed in communication with Air Traffic Control for the altitude and direction of her flight. As the plane climbed and leveled out at around eighty-five hundred feet she talked to Jim to get him to relax. She'd noticed his white knuckles.

"You can relax, Jim. We're flying now. We'll be fine and I want you to just enjoy the view. Isn't it fantastic up here?"

He laughed and tried to relax his grip on the arms of the seat. "I guess I'm a little nervous because there's quite a difference in this plane and a commercial airliner. Didn't think about it until we took off. But I can see a lot better and it is a beautiful sight. I just feel like I'm in a taxi."

She laughed and rolled her eyes. "We'll head straight to Ottumwa, Iowa, and land there for refueling. This will be the easiest part of our flight and will take a little over three hours."

"I can't get over the difference between this plane and the ones I'm used to being in. This plane feels so lightweight."

"It weighs in at about two thousand six hundred pounds, so yes, it is lightweight. But that makes the plane fly easier. We will remain at about eighty-five hundred feet, where a commercial plane flies between thirty- and forty-thousand feet. Quite a difference. We'll top out at around twelve thousand five hundred feet when we reach the mountains. I'll let you know because we'll use oxygen then."

"You know what you're doing. I'm really impressed, Elizabeth. I'd say this is one of the best dates I've ever had!"

"Well, I just want you to sit back and enjoy the ride. Relax. I'd hate for you to make the whole trip gripping the seat."

The light dusting of clouds made the flight seem like a dream to Elizabeth. She was hardly listening to Jim as they headed towards Ottumwa. Her mind was on Tom. And as Jim rambled on about his work and the new techniques he'd heard about, she wondered if there really was a chance that she and Tom might reconnect in a big way. Even better than before. The plane was handling like a dream. But dreams could turn into nightmares.

Chapter 11

Three hours and twelve minutes later, Ottumwa was visible. The flight had been inconsequential and very enjoyable. They had laughed about their teenage years, talked about restaurants they liked, and she'd lightened up about her daydreams about Tom long enough to get to know Jim a little better. She at least acknowledged that he was a nice guy. He'd been a perfect gentleman so far on the flight. So as Elizabeth landed at the small Ottumwa airport, she found herself admitting that she did like him a little. They could be friends even though she was pretty darn sure Jim already wanted more than that from her.

They climbed out of the plane and walked to the FBO where the restrooms were. It felt good to move around a little and get the blood circulating. They both grabbed some coffee before walking back to the plane.

As they buckled up, the atmosphere started heating up on Jim's side of the plane. "I really am enjoying this ride with you, Elizabeth. I was nervous at first, as you noticed, but it's really not all that bad riding in a smaller plane. A lot more private." He reached over and took her hand.

She slowly pulled it away and adjusted some of the controls, checking with the tower about takeoff.

"I've had a good time, too. It feels so good to be flying again." She smiled at him but noticed the look in his eyes. It told her that he liked her way too much.

"This could become a habit, you know. Flying back and forth. Just wait until I show you around. You're going to love it in Montana, lady."

"I'm sure I would. But remember, I won't have time on this trip for much. I need to get back to work."

She glanced over at him as she was going down the runway. "You do remember that, don't you?"

"Yeah, I do recall you saying something about your needing to get back to work. But I took that as an excuse because you weren't too sure if you liked me or not."

She laughed but shook her head. "Nope. It's real. I have to earn a living like you do. And this account is really important to me, as I've said too many times since we met."

"One day won't hurt, Lizzy. One single day…"

"Not even that. I've already risked disappointing them by leaving today. I did call, but they want this taken care of in a timely manner. My going on a trip to Montana isn't a good excuse."

"I know. I'm sorry for pushing this. I just know if we could spend some time together we'd really hit it off."

"What do you think we are doing now up here in the air, alone?"

He nodded and grinned. "I have a lot to show you in Montana. And not from thousands of miles in the air."

"Some other time, Jim. We'll get to it. But just not this trip."

"How long we got before we hit Helena?"

"About six more hours approximately, give or take. But the weather could worsen as we near the mountains."

"Let's count on that not happening."

In a little over two hours cruising at the same altitude of eight thousand five hundred feet, there was increasing cloud coverage as they approached Rapid City, South Dakota for another refueling. They got out of the plane and walked to the FBO for more coffee and a restroom break. Jim tried to hold her hand but she pulled away and brushed her hair out of her face. The wind was blowing and the fresh air felt good.

"Not that I'm picking on you, but every time I try to get close to you, you seem to find a way to pull away. Am I imagining that or?"

Elizabeth was embarrassed. He'd picked up on her seeming disinterest. "I move slow, Jim. Don't be offended by that. It's just the way I am."

Jim half grinned but she could tell he was discouraged. They parted at the restroom doors and then met back up at the free coffee near the door. Jim grabbed a candy bar in the vending machine and tore it open, taking a huge bite. He offered it to her and she took a bite and smiled.

"Not good for us, but it sure tastes wonderful. I try not to eat too much sugar on a flight, but I'll make an exception this time. We have plenty of food in the plane that we can eat anytime, Jim. In another hour or so we should be at our destination."

"For some weird reason I get hungry when I fly and usually we get nothing but peanuts. My mouth is so dry I can hardly swallow them!"

"I know. Commercial flights aren't what they used to be. We used to get a full course meal."

"What is Flight Service saying about the weather ahead of us?" Jim asked. They were back at the plane and climbed into their seats.

"We are facing some strong headwinds that could cause a problem. I'm going to be in touch with them the whole time as we approach the mountains. We'll see what's ahead."

She announced their takeoff and climbed again to eight thousand five hundred feet. Then she made another climb to twelve thousand five hundred feet, telling Jim to grab the oxygen. They were quiet for a while, as talking with the oxygen wasn't easy. She could tell that Jim was less comfortable with the mask and more uneasy as they went through some tough winds.

As they approached the Beartooth Mountains the terrain would not allow them to fly lower to get better winds, which was a disadvantage, causing them to head straight into a storm. She was in constant communication by that point but the plane was being blown off course and the signal for navigation and communication was getting weaker and weaker. She noticed the outside air temperature was at 32 degrees and an alarm went off in her head. Ice was forming on the wings and the plane was losing altitude fast. For some reason the electric deicer wasn't working and she kept flipping the switch to see if it would cut on. She felt panic rise in her chest as she fought to hold the plane steady.

The Denver Center reported they were losing her on radar and her transmissions were breaking up. Soon she had no signal at all. As she tried to push the nose up, the plane began to buffet. She tried to pull the nose up but it wasn't responding. She kept trying to get the radio to work but to no avail.

She looked at Jim and their eyes locked. They both knew they were about to crash. She kept her hands on the controls, leveling out, and looked around frantically for a place to try to land the plane. There were a lot of craggy peaks but she suddenly spotted a lake that looked like it was frozen solid. It was their only hope. The downside was that it was surrounded by forest, which she knew would do massive damage to the plane. In her mind she had calculated that if she could possibly land on the lake near the edge, the plane would slow down as it hit the bank. It was a long shot, though, and there was no guarantee that the lake would be frozen solid.

"Prepare for a rough landing and a possible crash," she said. He squeezed her arm and nodded.

It happened fast. At the speed of light. She was able to keep the nose up, aiming at the bank, hoping it would slow them down and lessen damage to the fuselage. It was very cloudy and there was frozen precipitation on the wings mixed with snow. As the lake approached she tried hard to land it angled towards the right bank. They came in a little too fast and landed hard on the frozen ice.

The silence inside the plane was deafening. She was sure she was screaming but she couldn't hear herself. Instinct told her to slowly press down on the brakes so that they wouldn't lock up. It seemed like nothing would stop the momentum of the airplane on a solid block of ice at the speed of sixty knots. They hit the bank hard and jumped it, skidding into the trees that she was hoping to avoid. She blacked out and slipped into a dark void.

Jim lay motionless in his seat with part of the cockpit pressing on both legs. Blood was pooling on the cockpit floor in front of his seat and nothing was moving but the oxygen masks hanging from the ceiling. An eerie silence lay over the crash site. They were in the middle of nowhere and it was 28 degrees.

Chapter 12

Jesse Steele looked at his watch and shook his head. He had a bad feeling in his gut but didn't mention it to his wife. He thought he would've heard from Lizzie by now. She'd had plenty to time to land and even get Jim off. She had planned on staying the night and flying home tomorrow. It was 7:00 his time, which put it at 6:00 in Montana. Martha saw him staring out the living room window.

"You worried, Jess?"

"Yeah. Hate to admit it, but I am. Not like her not to call. She knows we're waiting."

He knew what Martha was thinking. That there was nothing she could say to him to ease the worry. She had had a severe headache all day and he knew it was probably from stress. Their daughter was brilliant, but this flight was a little over the edge. Risky. She'd had no say in it, as usual. But he knew she hadn't felt good about it all along.

"Have you tried to reach her? Did you try her cell?"

"I wasn't going to tell you, but I've tried several times and didn't get an answer. The only hope we have is that she got delayed in Rapid City and was late landing in Helena. I'm holding out for that. I think I'm going to call Joe."

Martha sat down in the kitchen and sipped her hot tea. She was shaking inside, but she didn't want to add to his burden. He loved his daughter more than anything in the world. More than her. It was something she'd accepted long ago. She watched quietly while he dialed the number and sat down in his leather chair by the window.

After one ring, he answered. His voice said everything Jesse was thinking.

"You heard from her yet, Jess?"

"Hey, Joe. No, I haven't. Was hoping you had. What do you think?"

"I think we're like two mother hens worrying over their chick. She's good. She knows what she's doing. But like you, I've been pacing for the last hour."

"I tried her cell. No answer."

"I called Rapid City and they said she left at 3:00 heading northwest to Helena. No problems were detected with the aircraft."

"So we know she left Rapid City within a reasonable amount of time. If something went wrong, it happened over the mountains. I pray to God it didn't."

"Jess, let's not go that far yet. She could've gotten tied up with Jim and just forgot to call us. Kids do that, you know. We're not the only thing on their mind."

Tom sat on his bed in the hotel room and checked his emails. He had spent a long day with a client and it felt good to be back in his room. His mind was on Elizabeth. In fact, he could think of nothing else. He'd had no hope of ever getting back with her. He'd made some stupid decisions in his life and walking away from her was one of them. He was amazed that she even considered talking to him, but he was grateful she did. Their relationship was nearly perfect when they were close; about the time he walked away they should have gotten married. Quite a few years ago. Now he was as deep into his career as she was. That could be the thing that kept them apart this time. She'd really become very independent; he could hear it in her voice. Her body language. In some ways she was a different Elizabeth now. But he still saw that girl in her that he had fallen in love with. She'd just hardened a bit.

He glanced at the clock. It was 7:30. He wanted so much to dial her cell phone number. But she was taking a cardiologist back to Montana and he didn't want to butt in. Well, actually he did. But he would respect her enough to wait until she was home. Even though they'd been apart, he felt a twinge of jealousy sitting there waiting for the hours to pass. He wished he was the one in that airplane. When he saw her it was like they'd never been apart, even though he'd spent years running from that commitment. When he married Susan he hadn't felt the same love he'd had for Elizabeth. And in his gut he knew one day they might have a chance to get back together. He just didn't know when. Or how. His parents had thought they would get married and were angry when he left her. It was one of those decisions that you would look back on for the rest of your life, knowing you'd changed the course of your destiny with that one choice. And it wasn't that your life would be bad; it just wouldn't be as good.

He called room service and ate in the room. He watched television until he couldn't stay up any longer. Soon his eyes closed and he dreamed a dream. But he woke in the middle of the night sweating and his heart was racing. Something was wrong, but he didn't know what. He picked up his cell and checked for messages. He looked at his email. Nothing. He got up and splashed water on his face and drank some watered down iced tea by the bed. He tried to shake off the feeling that something was wrong. Bad wrong. But the feeling hung with him all night long. He lay there trying to sleep but his mind wouldn't turn off. Finally, he gave it up and sat up, watching television the rest of the night. When he couldn't take it any longer he dialed her cell, but she didn't answer. Of course, she was probably asleep. He felt silly worrying so much and took a cold shower to wake himself up. He had another meeting and luncheon to attend. He had to be on top of his game. But one thought stayed with him all day long. She would be flying home and he'd hear from her by dinnertime.

Chapter 13

The plane was getting covered in snow and there was no movement in the cockpit. When Elizabeth came to, the first thing she saw was Jim slumped over, leaning against the broken window. There was blood spattered on the windshield and she could see blood on the floor. She feared he was dead. Her whole body was freezing and she was afraid to move in case there were broken bones. She checked her arms and fingers and moved her legs. She was so stiff she could hardly move and the cold was unbelievable.

After a few moments she realized she had come through the crash basically unscathed, with a few cuts on her arms and a slice on the side of her head. She had blood on her legs but wasn't sure where it came from. She unhooked her seat belts and tried to climb out of her seat. Standing up, legs shaking, she brushed the glass from her clothing, being careful not to cut her hands. She was so dry in her throat that she could hardly swallow. Underneath her seat was a half filled bottle of water that she grabbed, noticing that the water had started to freeze. She then leaned over to feel Jim's pulse in his neck and there was a slow heartbeat. So he was still alive.

Her brain wasn't working very well and her movements were slow. Some of that was because of the severe cold but she could tell she was in shock. She decided to see if she could ascertain Jim's injuries and decided it might be smart to try to wake him up. Looking at her watch she saw it was 5:30 and the sun was setting fast. She grabbed a few flashlights, blankets, and checked the battery on her cell phone. She had plenty of battery left but no service.

Quickly she put her arms around Jim and whispered in his ear, trying to awaken him. He moaned and she felt hope rising inside her chest as she slowly checked his arms and hands, legs, and face. The upper body had glass everywhere; in his clothes, hair and in his lap. His forehead was bruised and cut. There was a small cut over one eye. His legs were under part of the cockpit, which had been shoved inward when they hit the trees. Her heart was racing trying to figure out how they would dislodge his legs. They had to be crushed and she was worried about the condition of his ankles and feet.

He stirred a little and opened his eyes. She turned on the larger flashlight so he could see her face. He winced and turned his head towards her, looking straight into her eyes. In a raspy voice he spoke to her, and she had to lean forward to hear him. "Do you know how beautiful you are?"

She shook her head and spoke back softly. "Jim, we need to find out what injuries you have. I'm afraid about your legs. Can you feel them at all?"

He looked down slowly and moved the flashlight with one hand so that it shone on the crumpled instrument panel and realized the whole front of the plane had been shoved into the cockpit. His legs were trapped underneath all the twisted metal. He winced again. "I think I can feel my feet. Not too much pain but my upper legs feel numb. It's freezing in here. We need to get my legs out so I can tell what we need to do."

"That's what I was thinking, but I was afraid to try to move you without knowing about what your other injuries might be. Can you move your arms?"

Jim tried to move his arms and shoulders, and he didn't seem to have injuries in those areas. There was blood on his face and shirt from the smaller cuts. He had a deeper gash on his head and his shirt was torn on the window side. But basically, his legs were the problem.

And if they didn't get him free, he would freeze to death sitting in the cockpit.

"I think we need to put blankets over the broken windows. Don't you?"

"Jim, I'm going to take care of that right now, but I wanted to make sure you were alive first of all, and secondly, that your injuries weren't life threatening. Not that we could do much about it here, in the middle of nowhere."

"Are you okay, Elizabeth? No deep wounds? No broken bones?"

"Oddly, I seem fine. Just a few cuts and very sore. Tomorrow the soreness will be worse." She reached over and picked up the water bottle and gave him some big swallows before she grabbed the blankets.

"I have no idea how difficult this is going to be with the snow coming down and we don't know what shape the plane is on the outside. I'm assuming that we hit the trees and at least one of the wings is gone. It makes no difference in our survival but I need to assess the damage in the morning. I'm going to go outside and secure blankets across the broken windows here in the front. We need to stop this cold freezing air from coming in or we're going to die. And that's not an option, Jim. You hear me?"

He managed a slight smile and shook his head. "If we survive this, Elizabeth, it will be nothing short of a miracle." His voice was weak and raspy.

"Well, right now, I'm choosing to believe we'll make it. We have to work from that assumption or the alternative is to just sit here and die."

"You want me to keep the flashlight aimed at the windows? How can I help?"

"I'll take one of the flashlights with me. We're going to have to really preserve the batteries. I brought some extra ones with me but we don't know how long we're going to be here."

She climbed back into her seat and kicked the door open. It was jammed, but finally, after kicking as hard as she could with her boot, the door opened. She stepped out and immediately sank up to her ankles in snow. She pulled her coat around her and buttoned it. She had a hood that she pulled up and secured with a tie. It was too cold to stay outside very long. There was a wind whipping around the lake and it made the air feel even colder.

She shined the light on the front of the plane and it was just as she had feared. The whole front of the fuselage was shoved inward. They were lucky to be alive. She grabbed the front of some bent metal, trying hard not to slip, and pulled herself up where she could throw some blankets across the windshield. Then she climbed back down and tried to find some broken limbs that she could lay across the blankets to secure them. Her hands were in gloves but she could still feel the cold through them. She draped a smaller blanket over the right window near Jim and walked around the plane to her side. The cockpit was small. This was all they had to protect them from the cold.

She knew she had to get Jim's legs out. Because they didn't know the extent of his injuries, she feared he might lose his legs if there was enough blood loss. She sat down inside the plane and covered herself and Jim with a blanket. It was so cold that she really needed to build a fire outside the plane. She looked over at Jim and he was nodding off, and she knew he probably shouldn't sleep until they could get his legs out. The clock was ticking and the temperatures were going nowhere but down.

"Jim! You need to wake up! I need you to help me get your legs free before we both fall asleep from exhaustion."

Jim stirred and opened his eyes. "I'm sorry, Liz. Can I have a sip of water? My legs feel numb now. I cannot feel my legs at all."

"They could just be cold. Let's hope that's the issue. I don't know how much blood you've lost, but we need to see how bad it is."

"I'll tell you what to do if we can get them free from the wreckage." Jim winced at the thought of dealing with broken bones.

Liz went outside one more time to find a sturdy limb she could use for prying. She climbed back inside the cockpit and shut the door, pulling her hood up tighter around her face. Jim was shivering and she was certain he was still in shock. She aimed the flashlight downward and studied the situation carefully. She didn't want to do any more damage trying to get him loose.

"Jim, I'm going to place the limb between your legs and try to pry the metal off your legs. Even if I just get a little movement, it'll help us when I try to move your seat back. You may feel some pain when the pressure comes off your legs."

"I'm sure I will. But the cold is helping to keep them numb. That can be good and bad. Just do the best you can. My arms are fine and I can help you push upward. Just don't know how much good we'll do."

Elizabeth placed the limb between his legs, finding a place that she could lift upward. Her body was aching and she was so cold. But this had to be done, and adrenalin had kicked in the moment she understood their situation. They simply had to survive. Jim grabbed the limb with Liz and they pushed with all the strength they had. The metal creaked and groaned but didn't seem to want to budge. They repositioned themselves and Liz leaned into the limb. On the count of three they both pushed and finally something lifted. Jim cried out in pain and turned white as a sheet. Liz hurriedly climbed behind Jim and tried to slide his seat backwards. She jerked as hard as she could, knowing she was trying to pull a seat that held a six-foot-four-inches tall man who probably weighed two hundred and fifty pounds. Jim was helpless in trying to assist her in moving the seat back. His legs were lifeless and he was in great pain. But he finally put his hands on the busted control panel and shoved backwards. He pushed and she pulled and suddenly the seat gave way and moved back a few inches. Jim shouted and Liz climbed over the equipment into the front seat. His legs were almost free. She moved the flashlight closer to his legs so they could determine where the damage was.

"You got a knife, Lizzie? I need to cut this left pants leg to see if something is broken."

"I hate that you have to cut your jeans. It's so cold in here."

"It's the only way we'll be able to find out if my leg is broken and where the blood is coming from."

"I'll get my knife. I want you to drink this water." She handed him another water bottle and he drank the whole thing down. He was going to have to go to the bathroom pretty soon. That would be another thing they would have to work out.

The knife was in one of the bags she had brought along with the medical supplies. She took it out and wiped it with alcohol.

"Here, Jim. It's clean. Do you want me to do it?"

"I'll get it started, but you'll have to take over. I can only bend so far."

Liz cut through the jeans and they spread the pieces open so Jim could see his leg. Part of the shinbone was cracked. The good news was it was a simple fracture. But he'd have to splint it just the same. There was blood still dripping out of the other pants leg so they cut that one open, too.

"I think there's a cut on the right side of my leg. Looks like it's a clean cut; we need to rinse it out and bandage it up. Stop the bleeding. Can you get me another bottled water? And some alcohol?"

"That's going to burn like hell, Jim."

"I know. But we have no choice. It'll keep the infection down until someone comes to our rescue."

After rinsing the wound, Elizabeth bandaged it and covered Jim up with several blankets. They both were worn out, but at least his legs were freed from the metal that was cutting off circulation.

"Are you in much pain?"

"I think I'm still in shock. How are you? I know you're exhausted. You've been a trooper, Liz. You've got to be sore from the crash."

"I'm numb, too. But I am more worried about the cold right now since we have bandaged your leg and discovered what your injuries are. I'm scared to fall asleep."

"We need to get all the blankets we have left and huddle together. I really think we need to move to the seats behind us, shove my seat forward, and that way we're not sitting in glass and twisted metal."

"I agree."

Liz climbed into the back seat and cleared a place for them. Then she helped Jim pull himself to the back, stopping to get a better grip on his jacket. He was tall and heavy so it was difficult to move him around in such a tight space, and he was in great pain with every movement. But finally, they collapsed in the back seats, out of breath and tired. Fatigue was setting in and a realization that this was just the beginning of their survival. In the morning they would have to face other difficulties, but for now, sleep was pulling them away. They leaned in towards each other and fell asleep in spite of the fear of freezing to death. Outside, the snow was falling and the temperature dropping. As Liz fell asleep, she knew that her father and Joe would be frantically trying to locate them. There was nothing but silence as she drifted away.

Chapter 14

Jesse and Martha headed down to the Rocky Top Pub in hopes of having a good dinner and putting their worries aside for a while. The pub was cozy and the locals loved it because of the casual atmosphere and good food. The seats had duct tape on them and there were local photographs on the wall of people who had visited the pub. Thousands of dollar bills hung from the ceiling and the lights were low. Jesse was a big fan of the Pub's spicy garlic wings, and Monday was fifty cent night. Martha didn't like the wings, but she was addicted to the celery and homemade blue cheese dipping sauce that came with every dozen wings. They sat for a while and picked at their plates, neither enjoying the food. Jesse reached across the table and touched her hand, but noticed that she wouldn't look him in the eye.

"Martha, come on, we need to have some trust. Liz is a good pilot. She knows what she's doing. I have to believe they're alive somewhere, even if they had to make an emergency landing."

Martha kept her eyes down as she took another bite of food. "I know, Jess. Something in my gut tells me she's in trouble. That's our daughter out there. It's hard for me not to worry."

"I'm worried, too. But I'm choosing to think positive about it until we know different. The location where she may have gone down and the environment would make it difficult for them to have any communication ability. But I know she'll be trying to find some way to reach us."

"I didn't think it was a good idea for her to do this. You and Joe are the experts, Jesse. I should have spoken up, but I thought you knew best. Sometimes your gut feeling is right. And this time it was, for me. Flying to Montana in the dead of winter with the possibility of more snow was stupid. When you crash in those conditions, what are the odds of being found?"

"We're gonna find her, Martha. I promise you that. I'll call Joe when we get home so we can find out if he knows anything."

The pub was filling up and the noise was too distracting for them, so they finished their meal and left without speaking to the other Monday regulars. As soon as they walked in the door, Jesse was on the phone with Joe.

"Have you heard anything yet? We haven't heard a word."

"I don't have much to report, Jesse. I looked at the Rapid City chart and going west, they should've been talking to Denver Center. I think we should call them next."

"Do you want to make that call, or should I?"

"I'll do it and call you right back."

Finally, after what seemed like an eternity, the phone rang.

"Jesse, Denver Center said they'd been talking to Elizabeth, but the airplane started going off-course and Center warned her that they were losing contact. The radio broke up, and shortly after, the transponder went off the screen."

After a long silence, Joe said, "Are you okay, Jesse?"

"I'm okay, but I can't believe this is happening. We should've gone with our instincts about the weather this time of year. You and I both know that this kind of weather change can occur without any warning. Did you ask Center where they were when they went off radar?"

"Apparently the plane was over a huge wilderness area in the mountains where they must've gone down. Their ELT is signaling that the plane is somewhere near a place called Beartooth Mountain."

"We've got to get Search and Rescue in there right away."

"Well, it won't be tonight. That whole mountain range is socked in with high winds and blinding snow."

They agreed to speak first thing the next morning, knowing it would be a long, sleepless night.

"Sounds like it's not good news." Martha wiped her eyes. He could tell she was worn out with the worrying.

"No, not the news we wanted. But they'll get the right people on this, Martha. I know you feel like everyone is just standing still. But the weather is keeping them from searching. No one can go in there at this point. I am counting on Liz's knowledge of survival to kick in, and Jim is a doctor. The two of them should be able to survive for a while out there. I know Liz packed that plane with what she thought she would need if anything went wrong. I also know she packed her Weatherby. I taught her a lot about survival when she was younger. Now she has to pull from that knowledge or she may not make it. I'm betting she will."

"I know that's supposed to give me comfort, and I understand how close you are to her. But she's still a woman and I don't know how strong she can be in freezing weather, outside with no way to communicate. How long can anyone survive that, Jesse?"

He shook his head and stood up and walked over and hugged her. "We need to be strong for her, Martha. We've got to believe that she'll pull through this, no matter what she's facing out there. Now let's attempt to go to bed. We're both exhausted and we need to be rested for tomorrow. Each day that passes is chipping away at her chances of being found and whether they live through this or not. Her life is not in our hands right now. I just pray to God that they get to them in time. That's all we can hope for right now."

Martha lay down and turned towards the window. The night was clear and the moon was shining through the opening between the curtains. She knew somewhere out there her daughter was cold and tired, and maybe injured. She closed her eyes but sleep was not going to come. It was going to be a long night. As if sensing her distress, Jesse reached over and put his hand on hers. It was hours before either of them fell asleep.

In Montana, the snow was coming down, erasing traces of the wreckage. The beauty of the winter wonderland in the Beartooth Mountains became a death trap to the two people huddled inside the cockpit of their downed plane, grasping at a thread of hope that the snow would let up and they would be found. The night was long and cold, a frigid cold that got into their bones. And even in their intermittent sleep they felt only slight warmth from each other under thin blankets.

Chapter 15

Morning came quietly but with it came a new awareness of their situation. Elizabeth sat up and immediately felt the soreness in her entire body. Like she'd been hit by a truck. She was warm under the covers but as soon as she stuck her head out, she felt the bitter cold. Her back was so sore and stiff that she could hardly move. She'd slept bent over, seeking the warmth of another human body, and she was paying for it after eight hours in that one position.

Jim stirred, opened his eyes, and just looked at her. Sometimes words weren't needed. A tear formed in her eyes. She knew he was in pain. He cleared his throat and spoke. "Liz, I don't remember ever hurting like this. I've been awake off and on all night trying to forget how bad my leg hurts."

She reached out and touched his shoulder. "I know you are hurting. I do have Motrin if you think it would help."

"I'll take the whole bottle. This is serious pain."

"Hang on and I'll get it for you. I've got some water by our feet. As soon as we eat something, I'm going to build a fire outside the plane."

She dug through the medicines she'd packed and found the Motrin, poured out three pills and gave them to him. He drank some water and downed the pills, wiping his mouth on his sleeve.

"We do need to eat something. I'm feeling pretty weak. What you got back there?"

"I brought protein bars and fruit. And if I can build a fire, we might could heat some snow and make coffee. That is, if you drink it black."

"I'd drink it black even if I hated it, just to warm myself up. No telling what the temperature is out there. Because in here we could hang meat."

She managed a smile but it didn't last long. "I'm going to take some Motrin, too. I'm stiff and sore and feeling a little shaky this morning. And I'm tired of being inside this plane!"

After they ate the bars and a banana, Jim announced that he needed to use the bathroom.

"I've been waiting for that to come. I have a cup you can use for now. That's the best we can do until we get you a little more mobile."

"I was going to talk to you about that very thing. We need to make me a splint so I can wrap this leg. It's swollen so I can't wrap it too tightly. But it does need to be set and it's going to kill me to do it."

Liz looked at him and shook her head. "You use this cup for now and I'm going to go outside to take care of myself. While I'm out there, I'll collect a few dead branches and try to start us a fire. It would be nice to be able to get warm for five minutes and it wouldn't hurt in case someone is looking for us. I'm sure the transponder is sending out a signal. But in this weather, that may not do us a lot of good."

"I was going to ask you about that. Guess I have my answer."

Liz went out the door of the plane carrying a small hatchet, dreading the cold. It hit her in the face as she closed the door. Her feet also sunk down into a foot of snow. It was difficult to walk in it, and she was already getting too cold. She pulled her coat and hood tighter around her and walked a few feet into the woods to relieve her swollen bladder. Then she grabbed some fallen limbs and dragged them into a clearing near the plane.

The huge Aspen pine trees had sheltered a spot from the snow, and it was a perfect place for a fire. She got the fuel drainer from the back of the seat in the airplane and drained some fuel from the tank. She could use it to ignite a fire that might warm them and help save their lives. It might also become a signal to anyone who was brave enough to look for them. The branches were full of ice and snow but she cleared them off the best she could and stacked them in a pile, pouring the gasoline on them as thoroughly as she could. Her hands were cold and her feet were freezing, but she worked quickly, hoping to get the fire going so that she could hunt for food. Something to kill. Her survival instincts were kicking in and the words of her father were coming back to her. A new hope was growing, even though things looked grim for them.

Remembering that Jim needed to splint his leg, she looked for a limb that they could use. She found one and used the small hatchet to clean the small branches from it. As she opened the door of the plane and looked inside, she saw Jim staring back at her. His face was distorted in pain.

"I need to set this leg. Did you find something?"

"Yes, I did. Sorry it took so long. I need you to look at it to tell me if it'll work." She held up the limb and watched for approval.

"Perfect. I really could use two if you could find another one the same size."

"Give me five minutes and I'll be right back. Jim, I'm so sorry you're in pain. It's bad enough to be this cold. But to be hurting like you are is just too damn much."

"I'm pretty tough, lady. But this is more than I want to go through. Have you tried your phone again? Mine is dead."

"I have no signal. None."

"Okay, just thought I'd ask. Find me that other limb. I'll be waiting right here."

She smiled at his attempt at humor and shut the door. She was worried about the fact that he might not be able to get out of the plane at all, and he really needed to be near the fire to warm up. The plane merely blocked them from the wind. But it was almost as cold in the plane as it was outside.

The fire was going nicely and she warmed herself before hunting for the second limb. She walked a little ways into the woods and found another clearing and some fallen branches, grabbed one that looked like it might work and pulled it back to the plane She chopped off some branches, bracing her foot on the edge of the limb. They snapped off leaving little jagged pieces, but it was the best she could do. She walked back to the plane and opened the door, and Jim nodded.

"That will have to do. Let's get going on making the splint. Did you bring any tape by chance? I ask, because it seems you brought everything out of your house you thought we might need for survival!"

"I do have some duct tape or rope. Whichever one might work best for you, Jim."

"I'll take both. I'm not sure which one will hold those limbs next to my leg. This isn't going to be pleasant for either one of us, but it has to be done. My leg is in bad shape and it's getting pretty stiff."

"I'll do whatever you say, Jim. But I'm not going to enjoy hurting you."

"Well, if we move me at all, it's going to hurt. So just accept that. I'll tell you exactly what to do, and you have to do it no matter how much I yell. Is that clear?"

"Yes. I understand. " She cringed at the thought of hurting him like that.

"Come on, girl. Bring the branches here and tape them together. Then lay them underneath my shin. They aren't that big around so we'll use them like one branch. My pants are cut, so we shouldn't have any problems doing this."

He was shaking from the cold and the pain. But Elizabeth knew she was going to have to get this done so that they could cover him back up again. She'd already decided she would heat up a blanket and lay it over his legs when they were done. She taped the branches together and pulled them underneath his right shin. He groaned every time she touched his leg but he still yelled at her to get the branches in place. They took a short break so that he could breathe deeply and drink some cold water.

"I don't want to pass out from the pain. If I do, I won't be able to instruct you. I want you to tape my ankle to the branches. Then I want you to slowly come up the leg to my knee, taping it as snug as you can. It's swollen, so you aren't going to be able to do it as tightly as I want you to, but we'll adjust that as the days go by. Maybe we won't be here that long."

"We can hope. Now I'm going to tape your ankle. Just try to relax and separate yourself from the pain. I'll be as gentle as I can, Jim."

She taped his ankle and tried to ignore his writhing. As she moved up near the break on his shin he screamed out. But she wrapped tape around his leg and kept moving upward. When she got to the knee, she cut the tape and stepped back. He was white as a sheet but nodded, holding the leg with both hands.

"The reason I didn't want you to get a full length branch is that I will probably be spending most of my time sitting in this seat and it would be impossible to do if my right leg was totally straight. I need to prop my leg up as much as possible to keep the swelling down. I'll go outside some to put snow on it to help with the swelling. At least then the cold will be working for me."

She grinned and leaned over and kissed his forehead. "I know this is a nightmare for you, but you've been very brave."

"I'm a professional, a doctor. This should be a piece of cake for me. It's what I'm trained to do. But damn, it hurts."

They both laughed as a gust of wind came through the window of the plane. They were constantly being reminded that their survival was on the line. Jim sat for a few minutes and then looked out the window at the fire.

"I'd really like to go outside of this plane for a few minutes. I haven't moved much since we landed. Notice I said 'landed' and not 'crashed.'" He raised his eyebrow and looked at her.

"I was trying to ignore it. Do you think you can move around that much? I know you're stiff because I am. I was having trouble outside trying to gather firewood. But the more I moved the better I felt."

"Adrenalin kicks in. And we really do need to get some protein in us. I see in the back you have a bow and a rifle. What made you pack that?"

"I knew where we were headed. And I knew the risks. My father has always told me to be over prepared. It might have been an overkill but once in a while my obsessiveness works for me. I'd say this was one of those times."

"At this point I'm thankful for that imbalance. Let's get me up and out that door so I can feel the fire and fresh air. I'm sure I won't last long but it'll do me good to move around. Need to get that blood moving in my veins."

Elizabeth moved slowly, knowing it was going to be not only painful but nearly impossible to get him out of his seat and through the door. The plane was small and cramped for someone with a broken leg taped to a couple of branches. They maneuvered between the front seats and Jim had to sit down in her seat to catch his breath.

Jim was grateful he had both arms to assist because he was so much taller and heavier than Elizabeth. He was amazed at how strong she was and unafraid of the elements. He caught himself watching her and the feelings that had been new were growing rapidly. She was so feminine and graceful that this new survivor mode was throwing him off guard. He'd heard about her great grandfather being a full-blooded Indian, but he hadn't taken that too seriously. Evidently, there was something to that relationship and what her father had taught her when she was young.

Elizabeth's mind was on killing something to eat. She'd been taught how to use a bow and a gun and had gone hunting with her father numerous times. But that was when she was younger. She hadn't shot a gun in years. Now all the things she'd learned were being put to use, just like her great grandfather had said would happen. She was impressed with how tough Jim was. He'd been a real trooper handling the pain and trauma of a crash landing. She hadn't had time to sit around in shock. There environment was too critical for them to stay down long. And she had no idea when someone would be searching for them. The snow was still coming down pretty steadily and it didn't show any signs of letting up. Her mind reluctantly raced to her father and Joe. They would be frantic and her mother would be sick. Last of all she remembered Tom; she hadn't thought of him all morning. That seemed like a dream, so far away. Now it was she and Jim trying to live through a nightmare.

Chapter 16

The fire was blazing and smoke was billowing up to the already gray sky. The heat from the fire felt like a million dollars to Jim after being inside the cold airplane since the crash. He put snow in a cup and sat it on a stone near some hot coals. The water heated up pretty quickly and Liz handed him some coffee to stir in with a stick. He took a sip and smiled. It warmed him all the way down to his stomach. But he felt the cold in his feet and hands. It was so cold outside that their breath almost froze in the air. Liz drank her coffee and sat the cup down just inside the plane. It was time for Jim to return to the plane, even though she knew he was enjoying the fire.

"Jim, it's time I go hunt for some food for us. We can't live on those snacks in this cold. We need some protein and I'll have to admit that I'm a bit worried about hunting in the snow. I'm hoping for some rabbits. But who knows what I'll be able to find."

"I hunted when I was younger and loved it. I wish I could go with you. But this damn leg just isn't going to allow that. Will you be okay, Liz? The snow is picking up and I'm worried you might get lost out there."

"Don't think that hasn't crossed my mind. But I can follow the smoke back. I know the snow is disorienting and anyone could get lost in it. I just can't allow myself to think that right now. We have to find food and I have no choice but to go out there and kill something. Let's get you a branch you can use for a cane so that if you needed to come outside you'll be able to manage it."

"Good idea. I really want to stay here by the fire a little while. We have an afternoon of daylight and it shouldn't take you that long to find us something. You won't last that long out in the cold, anyway. You have to remember about hypothermia. It can sneak up on you, lady."

"I'll layer some more clothes so that I'm protected. It's mostly my feet and hands that will get cold."

She walked back to the plane and climbed in, digging around in her clothing to find a sweatshirt and thermal t-shirt. Then she found another pair of socks that were thicker. She could hardly put her boots on but managed, because the snow was only going to get deeper. She wouldn't allow herself to get nervous thinking about the cold. It was critical for her to keep her wits about her and think about the purpose of her hunt. They would starve to death or freeze if she didn't find some food.

She took a few snacks and another banana with her, slipping a water bottle into her coat pocket, along with plenty of bullets and the Weatherby rifle that was given to her by her father. He would die knowing she was about to use it to save herself.

Outside the plane, she stepped through the snow to where Jim was huddled next to the fire. Her heart went out to him but she knew what she needed to do. Nothing could stop her from going out now. There was no one else to do it.

"Jim, will you be all right? You know where the food and water are. Please drink plenty of water while I'm gone. And eat something else. You are going to need the food to withstand the cold."

"I remember that part, Liz. You keep forgetting I'm a doctor! I'm more worried about you getting lost in all the white. I thought about tearing up a shirt for you to put on a stick to use a marker. Why don't you do that?"

"Great idea! I'll get a shirt and you can help me rip it up. We need to make sure the sticks are thin and light weight so they won't be heavy for me to carry along with a rifle."

She hunted around and found some thin sticks that were tall enough to be seen sticking out of the snow. Then she went to the plane and grabbed a red shirt, and she and Jim ripped it into shreds of material that she could tie on the sticks. She tied them before she left in case her hands were too cold once she got out in the deep snow. Then she pulled her hood up tight around her face and told Jim to do the same."

"You can't allow yourself to get cold right now. So if I'm gone very long, go inside the plane and rest, and try to keep the fire going if you can. I'll be back soon. Before I go, I'm going to show you how to drain the gasoline to ignite the fire in case it goes out. It's going to be your lifeline right now and my way back home."

After showing him where the stopcock was, and the cylindrical cup that she used to hold the gasoline, she said good-bye and started out into the whiteness. Her heart was racing as she walked into the blinding snow, worried now that she might not find her way back.

She put her first stick in the ground, and watched the wind blowing the red tie. She was hoping it would hold long enough for her to return to the site. It wasn't long before she was far enough into the white blanket of snow that she could no longer see Jim or the plane. She took a deep breath and remembered her father telling her about Snow Eagle. *Be still and listen.* She wasn't sure what animals lived in the mountains, but figured there would be rabbit. A deer would be a prize at this point, and she sure didn't want to run up on a large animal. Bears would be hibernating so they didn't worry her. However, her father did tell her they could wake up easily.

She tried not to go too far away from the crash site, marking her path carefully. Finally, she reached a place where the woods came to an end and there was an open field of snow. The trees were laden down with snow and looked like tall old men leaning forward. She stayed hidden in them for a short while listening to any noises she could hear. The wind was blowing loudly as it whipped through the trees. She moved to the edge of the forest, and she crouched down and lowered her heart rate, just as her great grandfather had done, to stay warm.

The words of her father were coming back to her. *Invisible. You have to become invisible.* She took another slow deep breath and let her mind become still. Her main job at the moment was to listen. She began to hear some noises that sounded like birds. She saw a grouse sitting on a low tree limb but she decided not to shoot it yet because she was hoping for a larger kill. An hour passed and she still had not seen a rabbit or larger animal. The snow was falling and it was extremely quiet. She felt oddly peaceful out there alone, but she knew time was critical and she had to remember that Jim was back at the crash site alone, cold, and hungry. *This is just day one in our attempt to survive,* she realized, trying not to feel hopeless. Her mind wandered, worrying about how long they could realistically hope to survive.

Suddenly she saw something move in the woods. It was a larger animal. It almost looked like a bear. She kept low and didn't move. Her jacket was white so she blended in to the surroundings as long as she kept her dark hair tucked inside the hood. Her father had taught her as a child to become still, but now it was just as important that she blend in. She could try to shoot the bear, or let it pass her by. The decision time would be short. If she waited too long she could be killed. If she shot and missed it would be the same outcome.

She decided not to shoot and remained in her crouched position, waiting to see if the animal walked out of the woods. Minutes went by and she heard nothing. She glanced in the direction of the movement without turning her head. She could no longer see the animal. So she didn't know if it had moved away or was closer to her. Her rifle was by her side, her finger near the trigger. If worse came to worst, she would be able to pull the trigger. But the snow was steadily coming down and covering her up. She couldn't sit there too long without standing up and shaking the snow off.

She watched the bird sitting on the limb for any signs of nervousness. The grouse was looking around and fluttering her wings. But she didn't look like she was about to fly away. Liz took that as sign that the animal had moved away and stood up slowly. Her movement was so slow that the bird did not seem to even notice that she'd moved.

Suddenly she saw a small deer staring right at her on the edge of the woods. Its body was turned away from her, but its head was facing her direction. She looked him straight in the eyes without moving a muscle.

Slowly she raised the rifle up and aimed. She had one shot. One chance. She pulled the trigger and the animal fell silently to the ground. She must have hit him dead on. It was a miracle. The grouse had flown away at the sound of the gunshot.

She walked in the deep snow towards the deer and bent over to make sure it was dead and then grabbed hold of the dear's ear, dragging it behind her as she walked back in the direction of the plane. She could not see where she was going and suddenly realized she couldn't see the smoke from the fire. But she did find the first flag and that gave her hope of finding her way back. Her footprints were covered up by now and she smiled, realizing how brilliant Jim's idea of the sticks and red flags was. She was proud of herself for killing the deer, but, it was heavy, and she had to stop several times to rest. Her body was still sore from the crash, and she was using muscles she didn't know she had to pull that deer back to the plane.

One thing crossed her mind while she was dragging the deer in the snow. She was leaving a blood trail the whole way back. An animal could track her back to the crash site. That wasn't smart. She tried to zigzag her walking but it was just too cold and the snow was too deep. The snow was still coming down and covering up her tracks, but she knew the smell of blood would still be there. It was a risk she had to take, because they needed the meat to survive. She continued to walk and came upon on the second flag. Then the third. Soon she was back to the crash site, totally exhausted.

Jim was peeking out of the plane with a worried look. She almost laughed at his expression. "Hey! I've got us a good meal here. You feel like helping me prepare this deer? I'm not sure I can pull the skin off this animal. You ever done that?"

"I've done it, but it's been a while. I can tell you how to do it, though."

She rolled her eyes. "You mean I have to kill the animal and clean it? That just doesn't seem fair to me."

He laughed. "First thing we need to do is gut the deer. I want you to take this rope and tie it around both back legs and loop the rope around a lower limb to pull the animal up. Tie the rope off so that you can begin to cut the hide off. I know it sounds dreadful, but we have to do it. When you hang the deer, blood will be running off the deer as you pull off the hide."

Elizabeth shook her head as she tied off the back legs and dragged the deer over to a lower limb. After trying several times she succeeded in looping the end of the rope over a limb. She pulled the deer up, tied the rope off, and sat down on a fallen log to rest. She was out of breath and hungry.

It was nearly 4:00, and she wanted to get this part done before dark. The fire was still burning, but she decided to throw more wood on it to build it up. It was really putting out a lot of heat and the warmth felt good to her. She didn't remember feeling so tired. She warmed her freezing hands and went back to cutting the hide.

"Tell me what to do next, Jim. I sure wish you could help me do this."

Jim moved gingerly out of the plane and used his cane to hobble over next to the fire. "Now, cut the legs straight down towards the abdomen and then make a slice all the way to the throat. Remember to keep the cut shallow, because you don't want to cut into the meat."

She made the cut and stepped back. "Now what do I do? Blood is running down the deer onto the snow."

"Start pulling the hide down from the legs. Anything that gets in the way just cut it off."

She pulled hard on one leg and got it started, and then went to the other leg. It was harder than she thought it would be. But once she got the hang of it, the hide started coming off. She had to pull the hide away from the fat on the inside of the legs and abdomen all the way to the throat. Then she moved to the backside and began to pull the hide from the deer. It was coming off in one piece, but occasionally she had to use the knife to cut away the fat.

She was getting very tired and her arms felt like dead weights.

"Let me help if I can," Jim said. He hobbled over to the deer and leaned on his good leg against her. He reached up with both hands and pulled down with all his strength. He made some headway and was going to pull again when he suddenly got weak.

"Jim, you need to sit down and rest. Neither of us is as strong as we normally would be. This crash has taken its toll on our energy. And besides, we've not had anything to eat to speak of that would help us restore our energy. You got the hide started, so I'll try to do the rest. Just sit here and talk me through it and then we can cook this thing and eat some meat. I think it'll make a difference in how we feel and help us withstand the extreme cold."

"You're so right. I didn't realize how weak I was until I pulled on that hide. I feel like a jerk watching you do all the work."

"It doesn't matter now who does it. We just need something to eat and I want to get this done before dark. Now tell me what to do."

"Pull the hide the rest of the way down to the neck and just cut it off from there."

"Okay. I'm to the neck now. So I just cut the hide off now?"

"Yeah. We're not trying to save this hide or anything. We just want the meat."

Liz cut the hide off and threw it aside. Then she let the animal down slowly and it hit the snow with a thud. "Now what?"

"We're going to just cut as much meat off as we want and haul this carcass off into the woods, well away from this site. Some animal will track it down and have a meal or two. But we sure don't want them coming around our site."

Liz laughed and slapped her leg. "I like the 'we' part of your instructions! You mean *I'm* going to drag this carcass into the woods." She paused and wiped some sweat off her brow. "I'm not sure where to put the meat after I cut if off. I know it doesn't matter too much because it's so darn cold. I guess I can lay it on the snow. It's as pure as anything else around here that I could use."

It took her about thirty minutes to cut off enough meat. She had blood on her sleeves and face and was pretty sick of the deer by this time. She needed a hot shower and a change of clothes, none of which was at her disposal. She did have a clean sweater and jeans, but it was so cold she really didn't want to take her clothes off to change. They found another sweatshirt to put the meat on, wrapped it up, and laid it in the snow so that it would get good and cold. Liz kept a few pieces out and skewed them on a small stick and held them over the fire.

"Here, Jim. Cook us a little meal, will you? I'm going to try to clean up this mess and drag the carcass off into the woods. The longer I wait, the more risk of an animal showing up. And I don't feel like sharing my meal with a bear right now."

The roasting deer meat sent a wonderful aroma up into the cold air. The sun was getting close to setting and both of them were exhausted. Liz had taken snow and cleaned off her hands and jacket. She stood by the fire to dry her clothes and hands, warming herself and enjoying the smell of the cooked meat. They left the meat on the stick and carried it into the plane. She also grabbed the wrapped raw meat and put it in the back of the plane behind the seats.

Jim had become more adept at climbing in and out of the plane, so it didn't take near as long to make that transition. Inside the plane felt cold after being so close to the fire, but they were hungry and tired and wanted to eat the meat while it was still warm.

Elizabeth had eaten deer meat before but it had been disguised with herbs and a sauce. Now it was gamey and a little undercooked. But she didn't complain. Neither did Jim. They ate all they had cooked and wished for more. They added a piece of apple to their meal and called it quits.

Jim leaned back in his seat and closed his eyes. It wasn't ten minutes and he was asleep. Liz looked outside the window and saw the sun setting. The fire was still going, and she felt safe for now. She drifted off to a restless sleep, halfway worrying about what animal would intrude on their camp. But finally, deep sleep came and she slept through the night.

It was pitch black and deadly quiet except for the animals that moved in the darkness around the plane. The smell of deer was so strong that even with the fire burning, it did not keep them away.

Chapter 17

Stephanie sat at her desk on Wednesday morning, taking calls from Walmart. She had no idea where Liz was, but her job was to assure Walmart that everything was going as planned. She was getting worried that she hadn't heard from her boss even one time since she left, and had tried to no avail to reach her on her cell. She had decided that Liz and Jim had hit it off and that Liz had decided to remain in Montana for another day or two. That was just wonderful, but she had no idea what to tell the testy Walmart V.P. who kept ringing the phone. Her paperwork done, she spent the morning cleaning the office and rearranging the files in Liz's office. She redid the phone numbers and addresses in Liz's computer and worked on her own computer, studying the files of the other companies that Liz had consulted. Her admiration for her boss had grown the more she dug into the files. This woman knew what she was doing. None of which added up when she couldn't get in touch with Liz by email or cell.

By the afternoon Stephanie was getting worried and looked up Liz's parents' number. She hesitated a moment but then thought, *what do I have to lose?* She dialed the number and the phone rang a few times before someone answered.

"Hello? Mr. Stone? This is Stephanie Carnes. I work for Elizabeth and was wondering if everything was okay. I haven't heard from her at all since she left for Montana. I may sound nosy, but is she okay? Have you heard from her? I mean, it's just not like her to leave and not contact me at least twice a day. I haven't heard one word from her."

Jesse could hear the frustration in her voice. "It's perfectly fine that you called, Stephanie. In fact, I know you're worried about her. I have some bad news to share with you. Liz has probably had to make an emergency landing somewhere in the mountains of Montana. We believe it to be the Beartooth Mountains but we're not sure. Her cell phone won't work in that location, especially with the snowstorms they've been having in that part of Montana."

Stephanie panicked. "You mean to tell me that you haven't heard from her, either? Oh, my gosh! Do you think she's okay? Is anyone trying to find them? You've got to be out of your mind with worry, Mr. Stone."

"We are worried, but we're staying in contact with the right people, hoping that the weather will clear up so that they can send in Search and Rescue."

Stephanie was quiet on the other end of the phone. She was shaking and didn't know what to say.

"I know this has caught you by surprise, Stephanie. I'm so sorry to have had to tell you this on the phone. Elizabeth is fully prepared to survive an emergency landing, barring any severe injuries that might have occurred. She's a strong woman, as you probably know, and was flying with a doctor. So between the two of them, they have the ability to survive. But it's very cold there and we don't want too much time to pass before someone can locate and rescue them from that mountain."

"I'm sick about this. She's so brilliant and has been so kind to me. I've loved working for her, but frankly, Mr. Stone, I don't know what to tell the Walmart people. They are ringing my phone off the wall. I can only stall them for so long."

"I'm sure you'll think of something. And hopefully, you won't have to do it much longer. We are watching the weather forecast to see if there is going to be a break in the snow that has pummeled that area for a few days now. That is what has made it impossible to search for them. I'll keep in touch with you and let you know immediately if we hear anything."

"Please do! I want to know if you hear anything at all. I don't want her to lose this account, but her life is more important. She can get another account. I'll do my best to take care of things here. I'm so glad I called you. I was afraid you would think I was interfering."

"Not at all. Please call me back if you have any other questions. I'm not much help to you, but I will let you know if we hear from her or the rescue team."

"Thank you so much. Take care and I'll be thinking about you and your family. I sure hope she is found soon. I miss her."

"So do we, Stephanie, so do we."

Stephanie hung up the phone and sat at her desk with tears pouring down her face. *What would happen if they couldn't find her? What would her parents do?* The phone rang and she snatched it up, hoping it was Elizabeth. It was another client wanting Liz to consult their company. She took down the information, her hands shaking as she wrote, and hung up the phone. She decided to get up and clean just to keep sane. This could possibly be a long wait and there was no way she would make it sitting in a chair at her desk. She had to get busy doing something. Anything.

Tom left his appointment with Baum, Sheffield, and Holmes feeling pretty good. They were co-representing the same client and met with an investigator concerning faulty parts on a specific automobile. The lab work was being done in Knoxville. Interesting meeting and productive. But he had Elizabeth on his mind as he walked to his car. He was dying to hear from her and very disappointed that she hadn't made it back home yet. His worry was that she was falling for the doctor that she flew home to Montana. After all the years they'd been apart, he didn't want anything to interfere with his chances to revive their relationship. After seeing her and spending some wonderful time with her, he felt like there was more than a good chance for them to get back together. He loved her. He had never stopped. And when he saw her face as she opened her door to let him in, it felt like a time warp had occurred. Nothing had changed. Except she was more beautiful than ever.

He stopped and got lunch at a local diner, trying her cell phone again. No answer. He'd left a few messages already and didn't want to annoy her. It was difficult to hide the anxiety in his voice. He was starting to get worried that something could have happened to them. He was pretty confident that she would've responded if she'd gotten his messages. There was no reason to believe otherwise. But sitting alone in the diner eating meatloaf and mashed potatoes and gravy, he missed her. He really wanted to talk to her. To see her again. He was going to try to remain in Knoxville as long as he could. But at some point he would have to go home and take care of business. There were a couple more meetings during the week, but by the weekend he would be making plans to return to Texas. He didn't want to leave without seeing her again, so his stress level was rising. Not that there couldn't be other arrangements made to get together. But he was here now. In her town. And he was waiting eagerly for her to return so they could talk further about working on a new beginning.

He had already looked up her parents on the Internet and knew where they lived. He had their phone number programmed into his phone. But he didn't want to call them yet; he wasn't sure about how he would be received after the way he'd treated their daughter. Even though they were young at the time, she was committed to the relationship and he had run like a scared rabbit. Although it might be uncomfortable, he would relish the opportunity to talk to them and explain himself. But the real issues were between him and Liz. No one else.

He drove back to the hotel room feeling lonely and a little anxious. They'd had such a wonderful reunion that he was really looking forward to seeing her again. *Maybe she's flying home in the morning,* he thought. *It's not like I don't have enough to do while she's gone.*

Just as he was getting into the elevator his cell rang. His heart jumped but then he noticed the number. It was his secretary. "Yes, Morgan. What's up?"

"Nothing too critical. But when are you coming back?"

"May not be until next Monday. Is there something going on that I need to know about?"

"No. Just the usual phone calls and an urgent call from Levins and Miller. They hadn't heard from you and I told them you were out of town. Didn't sound too happy."

"I'll call them now. I spoke to them before I left and everything sounded good. These things change like the weather. I'm getting pretty sick of it. What's that number?"

"1-800-755-3333. Levin's secretary's name is Martha. And she's a piece of work. Just sayin'.

"I'm well aware of ole Martha. I've got her wrapped around my finger. Or I did last week. Like I said, everything is subject to change. Thanks for the call. I'll keep in touch with you, Morgan. Have a good day."

"Sure. You're away in Knoxville, and I'm here slaving over stacks of files."

"You not happy with your pay?"

"No, I'm just giving you a hard time. Take care of yourself. Eat right. And keep me posted on Levin and Miller. Talk to you soon, Tom."

He hung up the phone and smiled. He loved his work but the hassle of dealing with some of the law firms was getting to be a real headache. He made it to his room and lay back on his bed, his head resting against the headboard. He had a meeting in two hours. Plenty of time for a quick nap. He closed his eyes and all he could see, all he wanted to see, was Elizabeth. Dark thick hair that smelled of heaven. Dark eyes he couldn't see his way into. And a smile that erased all the years of kicking himself in the butt for letting her go. He snuggled down into the bed and dozed off for an hour and a half.

Chapter 18

Day three brought its own set of problems along with several more inches of snow. The sky was gray and heavy looking, even though there were areas of strong light from the sun. And there was a light snow falling that looked like it would be around the entire day. Liz woke up with a start and sat up, feeling sore and still fatigued in her muscles. There wasn't a place on her body that didn't hurt. She felt dirty and could still smell the odor of the deer's blood on her hands. Under her nails. She would have given anything for some hot water and soap. Her hair was in a permanent ponytail and her makeup gone from her face.

Without waking Jim, she reached behind her seat and shuffled through one of her bags that carried supplies to see if she'd missed a bar of soap. At the very bottom of the bag, wrapped in paper, was a bar of soap she had put there a year ago. The soap was cracked and dry but it would be like pure gold to use on this cold morning.

She looked outside and saw the fire had dwindled down, and she also knew their water was getting very low. She would have to melt some snow for them to drink and fill the empty bottles. The one good thing was that they wouldn't have to worry about running out of water. She tried not to think about being there much longer than a week. Surely, someone would discover them by that time. She had eaten more deer meat in the last day and a half than she'd eaten in her entire life, trying to stave off the hunger that kept returning. It would be nice if they had something else to eat besides deer.

Jim was stirring so she grabbed the soap and a granola bar, some coffee, their cups, and a spoon and headed out into the cold. She'd slept with her coat on and her hood up, so she was prepared for the bitter cold. For some reason there was always a slight breeze blowing, which made it seem so much colder.

Jim caught her before she made it out the door. He sounded rough. "Liz, where you headed? Bathroom?"

"Yes and no. I've got to stir the fire and add more wood. Then I'm going to make us some coffee, which I know you're dying for. And our water is low so I need to melt some snow and fill the bottles."

"I can help do that. What about us catching some fish in that lake? Is that a possibility?"

"I toyed around with the idea last night. I'm not that fond of deer meat, but it is keeping us alive. I'm concerned that the ice is too thick. What do you think?"

He rubbed his eyes and tried to stretch. His leg was still extremely sore. "We need to do something today. We can't just sit here waiting on someone to find us. Let's build a bigger fire so that the smoke will attract attention. And maybe we could find some rabbits today. I've heard they taste like chicken."

"Exactly what is this 'we' business?"

He laughed. First laugh of the day. "I can help. Just get me outside and I'll work on the fire."

"Jim, we have no idea if this transponder is sending out anything. We don't know how long we'll be here. And I'm not sure how long we can last in this freezing temperature."

He wrinkled his nose and frowned. "Do you have to be so morbid this early in the morning?"

It was her turn to laugh. "Sorry. I'm hurting and tired and I guess my sense of humor is wearing thin. Let me get our coffee made and take my bathroom break. Then I'll be much friendlier to talk to!"

She climbed out the door and braced herself for the wind and cold. It was amazing how warm they were under the blankets inside the plane. She shivered as she headed into the woods. When she came out, she was dragging limbs to throw on top of the hot coals. It took a few minutes to heat the wood but soon a roaring fire was going and the heat felt wonderful to her body. She put one of the metal cups on a stone that was sitting on top of some small hot coals. The water heated up pretty quick and she used a folded rag to pick up the cup and stir in some coffee. She poured the coffee into Jim's mug and walked back to the plane and handed it to him. He smiled but kept his mouth shut. Then she fixed her own coffee and went back into the plane.

"Can you stomach any more of that deer for breakfast? I think we have a couple more protein bars, one apple and one almost too ripe banana."

Jim rubbed his beard and shook his head. "I am getting pretty tired of eating deer meat too, but it's all we have at the moment. Let's skewer some and get it on the fire. For some reason I'm hungry this morning."

Liz pulled her ponytail holder out of her hair and ran her fingers through the tangled mess. She leaned her head back on the seat and turned to look at Jim. "This is what my father and Joe were hoping we would avoid. And here we are stranded, not knowing if the transponder is even working. What's worse is that until this front moves through and it quits snowing, no one will be looking for us."

He touched her arm and reached over and rubbed her neck. "Listen, Liz. You're doing a great job of saving us. We just need to take it one day at a time. This is only our third day here. We've done well to survive this long and really the main complaint besides the cold is that all we're eating is deer meat."

She looked down and blew out a long breath, which was white and rose up to the ceiling. "I'm tired of being in this cramped space. We cannot keep sleeping like this. My back is killing me and you're not propping your leg up enough. It's swelling; don't think I haven't noticed."

Jim looked down at his leg. "Yes. I need to keep it up. You would think the cold would help keep the swelling down. But I've been outside more than I've been in here. Somehow, when I'm sleeping I need to find a way to prop it up on the seat in front of me. We'll figure it out, Liz, but I don't want you to get discouraged. And don't think I don't realize how much you've done to save us. Liz, look at me."

She turned her head and looked into his eyes. "I had hopes of showing you Montana and the world I live in. But as it turned out, we're seeing Montana in a way I've never seen before. If I had to go through this nightmare, I'm glad it's with you. You've been amazing. And I'm falling in love with you, Liz."

She looked away, tears coming down her face. She was so tired and frustrated. Worried. Jim had been a real trooper dealing with the pain and fear of being stranded for only God knows how long. "Jim, we're on a learning curve here. We both are coping as best we can. Feelings arise in situations like this that may or may not be real. We hardly know each other and we've been thrown into a situation that is causing us to be more intimate than we normally would've been at this point. So we should be careful what we say to each other out here in the wild. The real world is there, Jim. And when and if we get back to it, all these words might come back to haunt us."

She reached over and kissed his forehead. "I care about you, too. And I want us to survive this nightmare. But while we're here, we need to use all the creativity we have, all the strength we can muster, to make us safe until we're found. I know my father will be doing everything he can to push the powers that be to search for us. But the weather is our enemy. The snow is keeping them away. I agree a bigger fire might help. But as long as it's snowing, no one is going to be looking."

Jim leaned his head against the side of the door and thought about what she had said. He knew she was right. His emotions were running wild. He wanted to make love to her. He wanted to hold her. But the feeling of closeness was more physical than emotional.

"I am so sorry for blurting that out. You are so right, Liz. And we'll survive this. I have a gut feeling about it. But you are beautiful to me. I can say that honestly. I've seen you at your worst, and you're still beautiful."

She laughed and climbed to the front of the plane. "We best be getting our breakfast on the fire. And I have an idea that I want to share. Can you get yourself out of your seat and come outside? Let's get by the fire and warm up, get some water in those bottles, and then I'll think of something. The fresh air and a bite to eat will help us both."

When she stepped outside, the breeze was still blowing and the snow had not let up. Another long day waiting. She looked up to the bleak winter sky and listened. There was no sound at all. It was so odd to hear absolutely nothing except her own breathing. Her own heartbeat. But someone was going to come. It was just a matter of time. If they could last long enough, they would be found.

Chapter 19

Snow was continually collecting on the plane and the ground, making it more and more difficult for Jim to get around. Elizabeth was watching him move about and was concerned that if it kept snowing she would have to keep a path cleared out from the plane to the fire. She looked upward and saw nothing but gray skies and snow coming down. No sight of it clearing up for a good while. She walked over to the plane and pulled out some deer meat and skewered it on two small branches.

"Here, Jim. Can you cook these while I gather a little more firewood? We have to really work at keeping this fire going. And I've used up most of the wood directly surrounding the crash site. I notice each time I gather wood that I'm having to go farther out."

Jim frowned and shook his head. "I'm no help at all, Liz. I feel like a jerk watching you do all the work. My leg is not quite as sore but I can't put any weight on it at all. I don't think my hobbling around in the woods would be a smart move at this point."

She shook her head and agreed. "No way. You're just now able to move around without making grunting noises. And I've noticed that you have cut back on the ibuprofen. Does that mean you aren't hurting as much, or that you're afraid we'll run out?"

"Both, I guess. Nothing worse than running out. I'm halving my pills now. It's just enough to take the edge off."

"Probably wise since you are lying around so much." She headed towards the woods and was gone about five minutes, returning with a load of wood in her arms. She dumped the load and returned to the woods for more. After three trips she sat down, winded.

"I want to talk to you about something I saw when we were forced to land. In the back of my mind, I recall seeing what looked like a cabin somewhere near the lake. I'm going to pull out the map in the back of the plane and look again at our location to see if I can guess what direction that cabin is in relation to where we are."

Jim looked at her. "So you think you saw a cabin out here? That would be a boon. We would both benefit from getting out of this cold. The fire is great but my whole backside stays cold while I'm warming the front. There's no way to really get the chill off my body. I know you feel the same way. We are sleeping in 28 degree weather, huddled together. I wake up sometimes shivering and I can feel you doing the same."

"So you noticed? I was hoping you wouldn't. But you're right. We could use a shelter that could possibly be heated. I guess I was bringing it up because I thought I might venture out pretty soon to see if I could locate that cabin or whatever building structure it was."

"It's a risk, Liz. I don't mind us taking one, but it needs to be a planned risk, don't you agree?"

"Hard to know how to plan for this one. I have the map and my memory. I'm pretty sure I saw something. A building of sorts. But just not dead sure which direction to go. The only thing I know to do is to head out and just not go too far. I'll mark my path so I can find my way back. The snowfall makes it difficult because if I go very far at all, my footprints are covered up by the time I return. I can't risk getting lost. That would be a disaster in this cold. But if I'm careful and take my compass, I think I'll be okay."

"Eat some of this meat and maybe add on a little more clothing. An extra pair of socks. How are your hands? Do you need another pair of gloves on?"

"My hands get cold but at least I can use my pockets in my jacket. I'd say my feet are at the highest risk of getting cold. I'll be fine. I don't want you to worry. Just need to keep that fire going. That's the main thing."

They both sat down on a log and ate silently, thinking about what was ahead. The thought of being stuck outside in the snow with minimal food and no communication with the outside world wasn't very enticing. Elizabeth's mind was racing, thinking about Stephanie and the complications that would arise with Walmart if she didn't show up pretty soon. Of course, this was a disaster and they would understand. But there was no way for her to communicate with her secretary to let them know. She was hoping that her parents had stayed in touch with her office so at least Stephanie would understand that something had happened.

Jim's mind was moving in a similar direction. He was worried about his office and the several patients who had been lined up for heart surgery. Things would fall into place but the initial mayhem wouldn't be pleasant for his staff. He looked at Elizabeth and he could tell she was also preoccupied. He wished he'd not been in such a hurry to sweep her off her feet. This was no way to start a romance, that was for sure. They were forced to be together in the worst situation two people could be in, and that wasn't necessarily a good platform to build a lasting relationship on. In fact, it could do quite the opposite. He vowed to keep his emotions in check and be a gentleman to her while they were stranded. The memories she would have of this accident would at least not be negative about the time she had to spend with him.

Elizabeth stood up and wiped her hands on her jeans. "I guess I'd better get going. It's not getting any warmer out here, and it might take me an hour or so, maybe longer, just to locate the cabin. Then I have to find my way back. But again, I'm making something out of nothing. I know I can take care of this with no problem."

"You're tired, Liz. You've worked so hard in the last couple days. Not to mention the shock of the crash. Don't push yourself so much. You don't have to go unless you feel up to it."

She turned and smiled. It was a weak smile but it was there, peeking out from behind the worry lines that had developed since the crash. She was looking pale and worn out. Dark circles were around her eyes and he could tell she was worried. Not so much about their survival, because so far they were doing fine. But about the rescue situation. And the damn snow.

"I probably should go while I have the energy. We don't know what tomorrow will bring. I'm going to pack my backpack with a couple of snacks, a piece of cooked meat that I'm going to ask you to put over the fire right now, and some water."

She handed him a small piece of deer meat and he skewered it onto the branch and held if over the fire. While it was sizzling, she packed her backpack, put on another pair of socks, and layered a couple of thinner shirts underneath her thick sweater. She put her compass in her pocket and an extra pair of gloves and then added the hatchet and the rifle, wishing there were two guns. She would've loved to be able to leave a gun with Jim. When she returned to the fire, the meat was done and she wrapped it in a towel and stuffed it into her pack. Jim was looking pale and weak. But he was smiling as always and she thanked him for that.

"I really appreciate your spirit, Jim. It does help. I know you feel frustrated because you're the man and you want to fix this. But you can do a great job keeping the fire going, and I'll be back soon. Don't give up on me if it takes longer than you think it should. I'm coming back. I wouldn't miss another deer meal with you for anything."

Jim smiled and gave her a hug. "Take care and go slow. I'll be praying. I'd be in a real fix here if you didn't come back."

She didn't answer and turned and walked away. But she knew what he meant. She walked slowly, marking her way by tying red material on the trees as she went through the woods. She was travelling N.E. and used her compass to set her course. The wind had picked up and that would work against her, but she pulled her hood up and zipped her jacket all the way to the neck. She was as warm and protected as she was going to get.

There was no path for her to follow, so she was walking in snow and pushing aside branches that kept slapping her in the face. Sometimes the brush was thick and other times it had thinned out to nothing. The woods were quiet except for the occasional bird or rabbit but she kept her eyes open for any sign of bears or larger animals. The deeper she went into the woods, the more she began to relax and pull from her knowledge of survival. Because she'd not been in such a serious situation before, she hadn't had to use any of what her father had taught her about Snow Eagle. But her breathing slowed and her feet were light as a feather. She hardly made a footprint in the snow. Her ears tuned in to every single movement or sound and she felt more alert than she'd ever felt in her life.

After about an hour of walking, she sat down on a log and pulled out her water. Her movements were subtle and she made no sound at all. When she put the bottle to her mouth to drink she looked to her left and there was a male elk standing not twenty feet from her. She could see his antlers between the trees. She had her gun by her side and was so tempted to shoot, but there was no way she could drag such a huge animal back to camp. He was beautiful and it appeared as though he hadn't spotted her yet. She kept still and closed her eyes, almost invisible in the snow. When she opened them, he had moved on, looking for food. She stood up and began the difficult task of making her way through the thick growth and trees, still not sure if she was going the right way to find the cabin. Another half hour passed and she was still in the woods but as she walked farther and farther in, she came up on a clearing where the snow had piled up. There were no footprints anywhere except for her own and no movement at all.

Suddenly she saw about ten rabbits coming out into the open. She was sure they'd seen her but they didn't run away. They were white rabbits and they almost blended into the snowy mounds. She was again tempted to shoot them but decided to try on her way back. Her father had told her on one of their hunting trips that rabbit was good to eat, but very high in protein. Rich. That you couldn't eat it every day. But she knew it would taste good for a change after eating so much deer meat.

After walking through the clearing and rechecking her compass to get her bearings, she saw a wood structure surrounded by trees. There were so many trees close to the cabin that she couldn't imagine how it could have ever been built. The roof was covered in a foot of snow and it was impossible to see much of the cabin itself.

She walked up slowly and called out. No one answered. She knocked on the wooden door but still no one responded. It looked empty. In fact, it looked like no one had been there for years. She tried the door but it was stuck so she walked around to the back and found another door. It had a latch on it but it was broken. She pushed it aside and lifted the metal latch, and the door slowly came open with loud creaks. As she walked inside, she noticed how dark it was because of all the trees that surrounded it. She walked around to see if she could find out if there was electricity but she didn't see any light switches. There was a fireplace that hadn't been used in a long time and a kitchen with all the appliances and a row of cabinets. She looked inside and the only thing she found was a can of sardines, some peaches, and beans. There was one bedroom with a bed fully made and a bathroom with no plumbing. That was still an improvement over going behind a tree.

It was a very small cabin, perfect for a hunter who only needed a roof over his head. But it would be a palace to Jim and her after sleeping in the plane. The only detriment was that it was so far away from the crash site. It would take her two hours to get Jim there, if not longer. She wasn't sure about whether it was worth moving their blankets and pillows to the cabin and a little water and food, or if it was best to remain at the plane in case someone should fly over and spot them.

She began to nose around and found a bookshelf with books stacked everywhere. Dusty and worn. She opened one of the books and a letter fell out. It was addressed to a Robert Benford. No return address. She opened the letter, feeling almost like she was snooping, and scanned the words. It was a love letter of sorts and she folded it back and placed it in the pages of the book, and placed the book back on the shelf. After looking around a little more, she opened the refrigerator and there was one single beer stuck in the door. She took it out and placed it in her backpack, thinking it might do wonders for Jim to drink a beer. She had no desire for it, but if he liked beer it would be a nice surprise.

Closing the door tight, she turned and made her way back to the clearing, hoping to see the rabbits again. As she approached she did spot two sitting near a tree. She lifted her gun and shot the largest rabbit and walked towards it. The other one had run off into the woods. She carried the rabbit by its ears and laid it on her shoulder as she walked into the thick brush.

It took her almost two hours to return to the camp, and she found Jim still sitting by the fire. He'd obviously added more branches, because the fire was roaring and a lot of dark smoke was billowing up towards the sky. Jim looked relieved to see her, and he got up with his crutches and limped towards her with a big smile.

"What have we here? Did you go hunting? I thought you were looking for a cabin?" He gave her a quick hug.

She managed a laugh and handed him the rabbit. "I shot this on my way back. Here, let's sit down. I have something to talk to you about."

"I tried not to worry but it's so cold. When I hugged you, I noticed your hands were still warm. How could that be possible?"

"I'm not sure, but I didn't get cold at all when I was walking through the woods. I didn't notice the cold once I got started. But I want to tell you that I did find an old cabin about two hours away. It's a one bedroom that obviously is perfect for a hunter. Someone built it in the middle of a heavy growth of trees. I don't even know how they fit it in there. But they did a great job. The back door latch was broken so I was able to go inside." She pulled the beer out of her pack and handed it to him nonchalantly.

"What in the world is this? How did you find this beer out in the middle of nowhere?"

"It was in the refrigerator. So I took it with me. I knew you would get a kick out of that."

"I love beer. But I'm so cold I would die for some more coffee. Can I make you a cup?"

"Sounds heavenly. But what do you think of the cabin? Should we try to make it there before dark or trek there tomorrow?"

After a few moments of thought, Jim turned to her and spoke. His voice was getting stronger and deeper. "I would like to get this fire roaring and pack some things and go to the cabin for the night. But I know you are worn out and maybe you're too tired to walk that far again. Two hours is a long time for a walk in the snow. You've already made that trip twice today."

"True. I think we should go tomorrow. It would give us something to look forward to, and we would have time to figure out how to carry some gas we would need to light the fire. We'd have to carry some of our deer meat or rabbit, either one. Our coffee and mugs. And something to snack on if we have it. How are our supplies going, anyway?"

"I'm not sure. I think we have a few bars left. Not much."

"We might should save them until another day. We can do with the rabbit meat for now."

Jim fixed them both some coffee and they sat by the fire and watched the darkness creep over the day. They ate more deer meat by the fire, skinned the rabbit, and Liz walked the carcass into the woods a ways and left it. She felt bone tired suddenly and told Jim she was heading back to the plane to rest.

Jim watched her go, staring at a body that was so worn out. She'd done a great job finding that cabin. She had killed a rabbit. And she'd even had the wherewithal to come up with a beer. When she'd shut the door of the plane, he turned around and loaded up more branches on the fire. It roared and the heat hit him in the face. It felt so good for a moment to be really warm. But when he turned to head into the plane the snowfall increased so he quickly pulled the door shut in the plane, shivering. Liz had already tucked the blankets in around her and he had to sneak in carefully without waking her. He watched her sleep for what seemed like the longest time, and then allowed sleep to overtake him, too.

Darkness swept over the crash site as the snow kept coming down. There was no moonlight coming through the broken windows of the plane. Only darkness and a snowfall that just wasn't going to stop.

In the quiet of the night Elizabeth awoke and felt Jim's hand on hers. Deciding not to resist the warmth, she closed her fingers around his and fell back asleep. She had always been so independent and loved being alone. But not this alone. There wasn't another soul on earth that knew exactly where they were. Not another soul. Only God knew, but he apparently wasn't sharing that information with anyone just yet.

Chapter 20

Jesse awoke Thursday morning with a smile on his face. He'd been dreaming of deer hunting in his youth in the Great Smoky Mountains, and the memories of those times always made him feel alive again. He turned over lazily but the stark realization of the situation they were in came rushing back when he saw that Martha's side of the bed was empty. When he put his hand on her pillow it felt cold so he knew she had probably been up for hours. He turned over and rubbed his eyes. The tension and stress were getting to both of them. And it was only going to get worse as the time went on. He put his feet on the floor and stepped into his worn out house shoes, slipped into a sweatshirt, and headed to the bathroom. When he wandered into the kitchen he found Martha holding an empty coffee cup, staring out the window. Tears welled up in her eyes and her voice was tight.

"Jesse, what are we going to do? This is the fourth day she's been gone, and we still don't know anything!"

"I know. Waiting is pure torture. We have to get something in motion. I'm going to call Denver Center again to see if they know if Search and Rescue has been out there yet."

"Why don't you call Joe first to see if he knows anything new?" Uncannily, the phone rang at that very moment. Jesse grabbed it up.

"Hey, Jess, Joe here. I hate to do this to you but I need to tell you something that you're not going to want to hear."

"What is it, Joe? Did you hear something about Elizabeth?" Jesse's heart had begun to race at Joe's words, and Martha rose up, her face ashen.

"No, no, nothing that extreme. Last night I just realized that the emergency locator transmitter was just the second generation of the 121.5/Mhz. I never had the latest one installed, because it was going to cost one thousand dollars even without installation. I should have just bitten the bullet and had it done."

"That doesn't seem like a life or death situation, Joe. At least there's still an ELT."

"You don't understand, Jesse. After January of 2009, the satellite-based monitoring system doesn't pick up that frequency anymore. The only way it would be picked up is if an aircraft overflew the area."

"Have you checked the weather forecast up there for today? Last night the Weather Channel said they thought the storm was starting to break up."

"Actually, I did. It didn't look too promising, so I called Center to see when the search could start. They said the clouds at 14,000 were overcast, but at 12,000 they were scattered and broken. The snow seems to have stopped, at least for now. They indicated that they might send an aircraft up at 12,000 feet to see if anything pops up. However, they stressed the point that if it started closing up, the flight would be over."

"If they go up, what are the chances they would pick up the signal?" Jesse could feel his blood pressure rising.

"The chances of finding them right away are slim. That mountain is large, and we only have information about a particular sector of the chart they were in when radio contact was lost. They could be anywhere in a fifty-square-mile area. But it's still possible that the first sweep over the area might find them. You never know."

When Jesse hung up, Martha's face was a mirror of his, full of despair, confusion, and loss of hope.

"It's worse than we thought, Martha, but I believe there's still a chance for our Liz. All we need is one of those Search and Rescue planes to fly over the crash site and they'll hone in on her ELT signal."

"Is the weather any better?"

Not wanting to completely dash her hopes, he tried to hide his true feelings. "They think they'll be able to get a plane up today to start the search. We may hear something even by this afternoon."

"What's an ELT?"

"You've forgotten, Martha. It's an emergency locator transmitter. Remember it sends a signal up from the ground if a plane is down. They will find our Lizzy with that." He sounded far more convinced than he felt.

At 3:00 Jesse's phone rang again. Racing to get it, Jesse and Martha almost collided.

"Hello?" It was Joe again."

"I just talked to Center again for an update. I know they're probably tired of hearing from me, but I couldn't wait any longer."

Jesse interrupted with a loud voice. "What did you find out?" As the day had crept by, he and Martha hadn't been able to concentrate on anything and caught themselves looking at the phone frequently to make sure they didn't have a missed call. His nerves were about shot.

"Well, I have mixed news. They did get a plane up for about an hour and a half, before the sky closed in. They started a pattern looking S.W. of the last signal. They covered a good amount of territory, but there's still plenty left. In parts of it they could even see trees on the ground. Of course, trees would obscure a visual sighting unless the airplane was hung up in one. Obviously, they didn't find anything yet or we would've heard. You and Martha need to try to relax and get some rest. I know you're both tired of waiting, but I'll call you if I hear anything at all."

"Thanks, Joe. You're a good friend."

As he filled Martha in on what he'd learned, he saw her anxious expression turn into despair again.

"Martha, we have to be strong for our daughter! Lizzy knows what she's doing and all that she's learned from my grandfather will keep her in good stead. I know she took ample supplies, so I'm sure she'll hunker down and wait out a rescue."

Jesse was convinced now that the plane was down, but he couldn't let himself think that Elizabeth wasn't okay. Needing to be alone for a little while, Jesse made up an excuse that he wanted to read and went into his study. There was an extra bedroom in the house that had been converted into a "man cave" that had two recliners, a flat screen TV, and some shelves with books that were Jesse's favorites. The subject matter ranged from books on flying, do-it-yourself projects, and historical reference books to detective and courtroom mysteries that he'd grown to love. Without picking up anything, he sat down in one of the recliners and shut his eyes. Sleep was not in the picture, but he wanted to think. Looking back to the time when he and Martha first met, feelings of guilt washed over him as he realized how far apart they seemed to have grown in the last few years. Back then, he'd been full of himself, thinking he was a real player. Certainly a fine catch for any of the single ladies in town. He was an outdoorsman who loved hunting and fishing and would even grow a mountain man beard in the winter. When he got his pilot's license, he felt he could do anything. He loved impressing his dates by taking them to some little restaurant half an hour away by plane. After a fun dinner and flight, he could have his way with almost every woman he took out. But then he met Martha. She was so different from the others. When he saw her for the first time at a pub, he couldn't take his eyes off her. He sauntered over to her table, so certain that she would be as easy as the rest. He talked her into giving him her phone number, but she held him off for two weeks. Feeling rather humbled when they first went out for a drink, he backed off from his usual brashness. He knew she was something special. So much more sophisticated.

Opening his eyes, he knew these memories were a waste of time at the moment. He needed to concentrate on Liz. She was his baby, his reason for living. When she was a small child she followed him everywhere, helping him with his projects. She loved listening to the stories about his grandfather. His life had been powerful. And he knew in his heart that the stories that were woven into her childhood were the driving force that formed her character. She'd inherited a lot of her great grandfather's stubbornness and this made Jesse smile. She would need to draw on that strength to make it through this catastrophe. If he ever got her back home, they were going to have a long talk. It was okay to take risks if you didn't put your life on the line. And she'd done that this time. He just hoped she lived through it.

He didn't see Martha standing in the doorway. He didn't see the tears streaming down her cheeks. And he had no idea she was yearning for the love they used to share. He'd always been her hero until he shut her out. This traumatic situation had thrown them together in a new way. But as she stared at him, trying to guess what he was thinking, she wondered if he would ever find his way back to her. He'd always been able to fix everything, to make things happen. But this one time he just might not be able to pull it off. This one time.

Chapter 21

The phenomenon of the passage of time was a mystery to everyone. But stranded in a snowy tundra for four days caused time to walk in quicksand. Because of the whiteness around them, days seemed to run in nanoseconds. In slow motion. Every single hour was broken down into minutes that were insignificant except for the fact that it simply meant they'd survived another minute, another hour, another day. Jim yawned and stretched slowly, not wanting to wake Liz up. But they were sleeping so close together it was impossible not to. It was too early to get up. His watch said 4:00 a.m. and he needed to use the bathroom. The curse of drinking anything after 10:00 p.m. He needed to climb over her, which was humanly impossible with his leg splinted. So he begrudgingly woke her up by kissing her forehead and asked her to let him by so he could go outside and relieve himself. Liz stretched and kept her eyes closed as she stood halfway up and moved to the side so he could pass through to the front and climb out the door. A rush of freezing cold air blew in and she shivered uncontrollably. There was no point in doing it differently. Some things were habit now.

He refrained from talking to her and slipped back into his seat. She sat back down and they pulled their bodies as close together as they could without sitting in the same seat. They drew the blankets around them and tried to retrieve the warmth they'd given up when he had to go outside. It was a silent dance that remained inside the plane. They never mentioned it to each other but when night came, a resignation to the close proximity in which they had to sleep was done without a word. The first night they were more timid about it. But as they came to understand the depth of the cold, they burrowed into each other more easily to keep warm.

Several hours passed and they both remained in a deep sleep. They awoke at the same time, opened their eyes, and looked at each other. It was brighter outside and the snow had backed off to slight feathers floating from the sky. They were hoping it was a good sign.

Liz whispered in a low voice. "I am thinking this might be our lucky day. I'm not seeing a curtain of snow pouring from the sky."

"I noticed. But I was afraid to even say it. Should we go stir the fire, put some logs on, and make our coffee?"

"I think that's a great idea. Who's going first?"

"Damn. Let's flip a coin. It's so darn cold out there. How do you feel?"

"Worn out and a little sore from walking so far. But glad that I found that cabin."

He smiled. "Me, too. Just wish it wasn't two hours away."

"If you're going to wish, let's wish your leg wasn't broken."

He laughed out loud, his voice stronger. "Oh, you! I wish it wasn't broken. Don't rub it in. I already feel like a dog for not being able to help you more. If we're going to walk to that cabin today, we better get up and move around. We need to melt snow again for water?"

"Don't know. But that's easy to check. I guess we'll both get up. You tend to the water issue and I'll get the fire going out there."

Liz got up and wrapped her jacket tight around her, pulling up her hood. She never got used to the feel of the cold when she opened the door. No matter how she prepared herself, when that blast of cold hit her face it was like diving into a freezing cold pool of water. It took her breath away. It went to her bones. She shivered again and headed towards the fire, which had died down considerably in the night. She walked over to the slowly disappearing pile of branches and grabbed several to throw on the fire. The sky was still gray and it was very cold. But for some reason, there was a break in the continual downpour of snow. She stirred the fire and soon the branches caught and there was a roaring flame in the middle near the coals. The heat felt so good to her that she didn't want to move. But coffee sounded so enticing that she made herself walk back to the plane to retrieve their cups and the coffee. She piled snow into their cups and melted it on the stone near hot coals. The water boiled soon and she picked up the cups and stirred in the coffee. She dreamed of the rich cream she normally used in her coffee. And a teaspoon of sugar. But the blackness of the coffee sort of snatched her awake. The coffee was strong and it did its job to run the sleepiness of the night away.

"I don't know about you, but I'm starving. How about rabbit this morning? Doesn't that have a nice ring to it?"

She smiled but she still hadn't warmed up enough. "I think that's a great idea. I really want eggs with it. Wouldn't that be nice?"

"Don't go there, Lizzy. I'll take you to the best restaurant in Helena when we get rescued. But right now, this is our only choice. I'll get the rabbit and skewer it for us. I'm anxious to see how it tastes."

She nodded her head and put her hands in her pockets. It was going to be a good day if the snowfall stayed light. Perhaps a plane would venture out and they'd be discovered. It was early yet. But she knew Joe would be checking constantly to see if the weather forecast had changed. Even a window of time would be enough for them to send a plane out. But she also knew they would not risk another crash just to find her. So again they would live out this day with no communication, no way of knowing if someone was looking for them or not. It made her feel so out of control. It made her have to trust. And that was the most difficult part.

The flames licking the rabbit meat caused a wonderful aroma to waft in the air. It stirred their hunger. When the meat was done, they allowed it to cool a little and then bit into it. Liz had cut up the last apple, which was very cold and crisp. Even though it seemed like an odd combination, it tasted wonderful with the rabbit meat.

"Not so bad, huh?" Jim smiled as he licked his fingers.

"Not bad at all. But I need to kill more rabbits. It's a nice change from the deer meat."

"We have to alternate now. We shouldn't eat rabbit every meal or every day. Remember that."

"I got it. But I'm really enjoying the taste right now. How was our water supply?"

"We could fill up the six empty bottles. We both need to drink more water. I'm forgetting because I'm so cold half the time. And we don't have tons of coffee so no more coffee during the day except this one cup for breakfast."

"I agree. It's hard not to drink one in the late afternoon. But rules are rules, and we have to watch our supplies like a hawk."

Jim sat down on a log near the fire and warmed his hands and feet. His leg was hurting and the heat felt good.

"Do you really think I can make it to the cabin? Should we stay here and see if someone flies over, since the snow has slowed a bit?"

Liz nodded while she sat by the fire, warming her hands and feet. "I'll admit it's a long walk. And we have a lot of 'ifs' in this decision. We don't know how hard it's going to be for you to walk on those makeshift crutches, and we aren't sure if the heavy snowfall will return. My guess is that it will. I just thought it might be nice to sleep inside one night with a fire in the fireplace. I bet it would heat that cabin right up."

"It should. I can't say how difficult it'll be for me, but we can always rest halfway. I know it's going to be cold but we'll be moving. As long as the wind doesn't pick up and the snowfall stays light we should be okay. But we need to take enough meat to eat. We can always melt snow there for water. Did you really search the cabinets for any food?"

"I didn't open every single one of them. I was in a hurry, frankly, to get back. It looked pretty empty, but hey, I did find that beer! So I guess we could look when we get there. But I wouldn't count on there being much of anything in those cabinets. The place was pretty dusty; it may have been months since anyone was there."

Jim nodded and stood up. "I'll go pack my backpack with things that I think I'll need. Won't be much. We're down to the basics now. Toothbrush, toothpaste, ibuprofen, water bottles, and any food we have. Let's start out early in case we do get more heavy snowfall."

Liz walked back to the plane and gathered some things to put in her backpack, including some deer meat and the last three protein bars, and one pack of peanut butter crackers at the bottom of the bag. She grabbed an extra sweater, clean socks, the small bar of soap, and a hairbrush. In fifteen minutes they were ready to leave.

"Think we ought to leave a note just in case Search and Rescue happens to show up?"

"Not a bad idea. I've got some paper in my purse and a pen. I'll leave a note on this seat by the door. We're going to leave a roaring fire that will last for most of the day. I hate that it's going to die down a good bit by nightfall. And we won't be here in the morning to build it back up again. I'm torn between staying and leaving."

"I feel the same way. But a night on a bed sounds too good to pass up. Even with my leg in a splint."

"If we stay, we know we can survive the night, but my throat is getting sore and I felt chilled this morning when I woke up. I sure don't need to be getting sick now. I guess we can restart the fire when we return here tomorrow afternoon or the next day. I am taking the rifle and my knife. You sure you have everything you need? Your wallet? We sure don't want to leave anything like that here."

"I've got everything I own in this backpack. Wasn't that much to bring. I only took another pair of jeans and a sweater because my luggage is full of clothes that I won't need here."

"Okay. So let's build the fire up and head out to the cabin. If we run into that group of rabbits again, I'm going to shoot one of them. And maybe a bird or two. Wouldn't hurt to have extra meat there. I am a bit uneasy leaving the crash site. All manuals tell you not to. But we sure could use a warm place to sleep. So we'll do this at least for one night. And we can decide tomorrow whether we're returning here or staying one more night."

"Sounds good to me. I'll help you with the fire."

They piled all of the remaining branches on top of the blazing fire and made sure the blankets were secure that covered the windows of the plane. At least five or six inches of snow sat on top of the plane so the blankets over the windshield were under snow and that meant they were going nowhere. Jim hobbled behind Elizabeth and they used the markers she had placed on the limbs yesterday to find their way to the cabin. The trudge seemed longer this time because Jim had to go slow, but it gave Elizabeth time to check for any signs of wildlife. They also were listening for any sound of an engine overhead. But as they trekked through the woods, there was no noise but the sound of their own breathing. It was cold and the wind had picked up a little, and after an hour and a half of walking, they noticed that the snowfall was beginning to increase. When they reached the clearing where Liz had seen the rabbits, she spotted three more and lifted her rifle. Jim noticed there was dried blood on her jacket from the last rabbit she'd shot. He had never seen her shoot and remained quiet as she aimed at the largest rabbit. The noise of the gun firing off echoed for miles around them. The rabbit fell silently in the snow and Liz walked over and picked it up by the ears and slung it over her back. This was a larger rabbit than before and they would have more meat to eat.

The thought occurred to Elizabeth as they were walking closer and closer to the cabin that it was their fourth day they'd been stuck in the Beartooth Mountains. Four days. She'd really hoped someone would have been there by now to rescue them. But the time just kept going by and no one came. The snowfall was picking up gradually and she could tell they were in for another blizzard.

"Jim, I know you're worn out and your leg is probably aching. We're almost there. Hang on. Just a few more minutes and we'll see the cabin."

"I'm good. I'm not going to be complaining, Liz. It's bad enough that I'm useless to you. You might as well shoot me for the amount of work I'm doing. It's more than frustrating. It's driving me mad."

"Don't focus on that, Jim. I need your brain to help me think of ways to survive. To keep us sane while we're waiting. My female tendency is to crawl up in a corner and cry. But I've been taught about survival and that's what you see now. But inside, I'm sick of this. I'm tired of the cold. And—"

"I see it! There's the cabin! You were right, Liz. It's crammed into those trees. Incredible."

She looked straight ahead and saw the log cabin standing in the growth of trees. As they approached it, Jim saw how small it was and laughed. "Not much more room than the cockpit of the plane."

"Well, now, it's not quite that small. And we'll have an indoor fireplace to keep us warm."

"Sounds good to me. Let's get inside."

They walked around to the back of the cabin and Liz opened the door. It was always good to check for animals who might have decided to come inside to get away from the cold. But it was empty, just like before.

"Jim, put your things down and have a seat on that old leather sofa. You need to put your leg up for a while and rest. I'll get you some water."

Jim sat down and almost cried out with pain. His leg was swelling a little and his whole body ached from having to walk with the limbs that were his crutches. Under his arms were blisters forming where the limb had rubbed the skin raw through his jacket. But he'd made it and that was his goal. Liz brought him some water and helped him prop up his leg on the edge of the sofa. Then she headed outside to skin the rabbit and find some firewood. It took her about thirty minutes to get enough wood to burn in the fireplace. She had blood on her hands when she came in and Jim winced.

"I hate that you have to do all of the work, Liz. I could have cleaned that rabbit. I need to try to do more. I can't just sit around and allow you to take care of me. It's insane."

She laughed and went to the sink to see if there was running water. No such luck. As she headed outside to wash her hands in the snow, she saw a bucket under the sink and carried it with her so that she could melt some snow and use the water to wash with. Her hands were freezing and her face was cold. By the time she returned with the wood and built a fire, she was getting numb.

Soon there was a roaring fire going and the room began to heat up. It was a small room, about three hundred square feet, with a doorway that led to the small kitchen. The bedroom was off the living room and wasn't much larger. There was just enough room for a full-size bed and a small chest of drawers. Very rustic furniture. Liz walked into the bedroom and checked the sheets and blankets that were on the bed. They seemed fairly clean so she just aired them out and folded them down so Jim could get into the bed easily. Then she went through all the cabinets and found a jar of instant coffee with no expiration date on it. She also found a can of beans and a small unopened jar of peaches. No telling how old it was but the seal was still good so she felt comfortable risking eating it. She found a can opener in the drawer and a few knives and silverware. She almost felt like she'd found civilization for the first time. She laughed and Jim heard her and called out.

"What's going on in there, Liz? You talking to yourself?"

"No! I found some instant coffee, a can of beans, and some peaches. Then I opened a drawer and found a can opener. I feel almost civilized again."

He laughed and laid his head back on the sofa and closed his eyes. The room was beginning to warm up and he was already tired from the long walk. He slowly dozed off while Liz cut the rabbit up and put it in some snow on a plate and set it inside the refrigerator. She walked into the living room and noticed he was asleep and lay down on the bed and took a short nap. It felt like heaven to sleep on a mattress even though it was lumpy and sagged.

Inside the cabin at last, they both relaxed and let the stress of the last few days float away. The cabin was quiet, with just the sound of the fire crackling and the wind blowing outside. There was no electricity so it was dark inside except for the flickering firelight.

Another six inches of snow fell quietly through the next few hours, erasing their footprints. Neither one moved for hours, lost in their own dreams of another world that was out there. Their lives had been halted by the falling of snow. Beautiful feathery snowflakes that if allowed to accumulate could stop life dead in its tracks. And they had a lovely way of erasing all evidence that anyone had even been around.

Chapter 22

Elizabeth opened her eyes and for a moment she was disoriented. She got out of bed, stumbling on her shoes, and tiptoed into the living room to see how Jim was. He was still asleep and the fire had died down a little. She walked over and put a few more logs on the fire and watched the flames licking the Aspen pine. Her stomach was growling so she went into the kitchen and pulled out the rabbit meat, skewered it onto two sticks, and propped them up near the flames. Then she sat down on the sofa and touched his arm. He slowly opened his eyes and smiled.

"Jim, we've both been asleep for several hours. It's dark outside. I think we need to eat some rabbit meat while it's still fresh, and then we can crash. I know you're worn out from the long walk. How is your leg?"

"Throbbing. But I can take a couple pills and it will take the edge off. It was pushing it a bit to walk so far, but now that we're here it was well worth the pain I'm feeling now. How was the mattress?"

"Heaven compared to that seat in the plane. If we build the fire up, we can sleep in there and still feel the warmth. It's good that this is a small cabin. The fire will heat the whole place."

"I really conked out! Man, it felt so good to sit on something comfortable and with the fire going it just put me to sleep."

"You needed it and so did I. I bet the meat is almost done. I'll get the water for us and we can eat right here by the fire. It's weird not having electricity, but I've got two flashlights that we can use when we have to go outside for any reason."

"The meat smells good cooking, and I'm starving. Wish we did have something besides rabbit to eat, though. Wouldn't a glass of wine taste good?"

"It would. But we're dreaming again and that's torture!"

She handed him some water and his skewer and he took a small bite, blowing on the meat so he wouldn't burn his mouth. They ate in silence and when they were finished she laid the skewers in the sink and brought some snow inside and melted it so they could wash up. When she soaped her hands and washed her face, it almost felt like home. There was a mirror in the living room so she walked up to it and looked at her face. She was a little anxious about looking at herself and it was quite a shock. She looked so tired and old. Her hair was a mess. Jim saw her staring at herself and laughed.

"Don't even go there, Elizabeth. I know I look like an old man, beat up and put away wet. We've been through a catastrophe and are just trying to survive. I guess this is what it would've been like in the old days when they were making a journey across the Wild West."

"I don't think I could have made it back then, riding all day in a covered wagon. Although walking two miles in this deep snow wasn't a picnic, either. Did that meat go down okay?"

"It was delicious. I'm still hungry but maybe we need to save the rest until tomorrow. How much is left?"

"We have plenty and I'll shoot more tomorrow. We also have plenty of deer meat back at the site. I can make a trip tomorrow if I need to, to relight the fire and get that meat."

"I think we can make it here for a day or two, especially with Annie Oakley around!"

She laughed and sat back down on the sofa. Jim put his arm around her shoulder and kissed her face.

"You're really pretty amazing, Liz. I'm impressed. You've taken care of us like a pro and I haven't heard a whimper out of you. You've been so brave. This hasn't been easy for either of us, and I've felt so helpless in my efforts to help. But you haven't once made me feel small. I really appreciate that. I'd give anything not to have this broken leg. To have to watch you do all the heavy work has driven me crazy. Do you know that? It's not what a man does well. Watching a woman take care of him—"

She laughed and raised an eyebrow. "Now that's a statement that could be debated until the next Ice Age. I know it hasn't been easy on you. But thank God I was taught survival and all of that teaching kicked in just when I needed it. I can't tell you how many hours I sat with my father listening to him talk about his grandfather. So much of what we learn we never get to use. This one time I was able to pull it up and use the information. "

He leaned in and kissed her mouth, catching her off guard. She instinctively pulled away and saw him wince. "I'm sorry, Jim. I don't know why I did that. You've been nothing but a gentleman to me and I know you were just trying to be sweet. I'm sorry. I've pulled away so long I'm not sure how to allow anyone in."

He stood up, wobbling a little, and grabbed his crutches. "Don't worry, Lizzy. I'll stay in my place. I wasn't trying to seduce you. I genuinely like you. A lot. I'm going outside to use the bathroom. Where did you say those flashlights were?"

Liz could sense his disappointment. Her words had hit him like an arrow. "I'll get them. They're in my backpack."

She walked over to the corner near the kitchen door and pulled out the larger flashlight. When she handed it to him she kissed his cheek. "Don't be long or I'll have to come out there and hunt you down."

He smiled weakly and closed the door behind him. The air was cold and there was a strong wind blowing. It chilled the room in seconds. She went over to stir the fire and add another log. The Aspen wood burned well but quickly, and she would need to bring in more wood first thing in the morning. She grabbed the bucket and stepped outside the door to get more snow to melt, and sat the bucket on top of the one of the outer logs that was over some hot coals. The snow melted quickly and she had to use a shirt to grab the handle and carry the bucket into the kitchen. She heard Jim coming in and walked into the living room with a smile, trying to lighten the gray mood in the room.

"I thought I would wash up a little. This is my first chance to take a bath of sorts. I'm going to close the door to the kitchen for some privacy, but I am going to leave it cracked open so I don't freeze to death. I'll heat up some water for you when I'm done."

He looked at her and it was more than obvious that he was thinking thoughts he had no business thinking. "I'll guard the door with my life."

She smiled and went back into the kitchen, leaving the door ajar. She had a flashlight to light up the room and she used part of a shirt to wash with. It was primitive but it felt like the Taj Mahal to her as she washed off nearly a week's worth of dirt. She would have liked to have dunked herself in a large tub of water, but the bucket would have to do. *It was amazing what you could adjust to when things were difficult.* And she was a girly girl who loved nice things. Hot baths. Nice clothes. And perfume. Now she looked like a tough outdoorswoman with boots and a dead rabbit over her shoulder. She laughed and dried off with the corner of a blanket she'd dragged in from the bedroom. She put some clean jeans on and her dirty shirts and sweater. If they were stranded much longer she was going to find a way to wash out some clothes with that one single bar of soap. But the soap had become like gold to her and she didn't see wasting it on the dirty clothes when they were going to get dirty again in five minutes. Her hands and face became the most important parts of her body to keep clean. It was all she had left of decency.

She walked out of the kitchen and found Jim sitting on the sofa staring at the fire. He looked sad and tired.

"You think you could drag your dirty broken body into the kitchen while I heat up some water for you? I know it will make you feel better. It has done wonders for my spirits."

He turned to look at her and she stopped in her tracks when she saw the look on his face. "Liz, I know we really don't know each other that well. We've been shoved into a situation that is all about survival and raw emotions. But I've not found someone in my whole life that I would dare attach myself to until now. I'm sorry if this makes you uneasy but I feel it needs to be said. Can you come over here by the fire so we can talk?"

Liz walked over to the sofa and sat at the end near the fireplace. She had a nervous feeling welling up in her stomach and her mouth was as dry as cotton. "Look, Jim, I know this is a very emotional moment for you and I don't want to say anything that will hurt your feelings. We probably do need to have this talk because we've been through so much in the last couple of days that it might be healthy to let it all out."

He smiled and moved closer to her. "I know this makes you very uncomfortable but I'm enjoying every single moment I spend with you. Except for the forced landing and headlong crash into the trees!"

"Well, actually that doesn't count, does it?"

"Liz, let's be real for a moment. This is an opportunity of a lifetime for us to get to know each other. Even though we are roughing it a bit—well, guess it's an extreme situation, it's just you and I. No one else is around. We have to be open with each other or this won't work. I am falling in love with you. I know it's strange and you hate it, but it's the truth. And you know I'm not just interested in the fact that you're a pilot! At the moment, that's not seen as a plus."

She couldn't help but laugh. "Oh, you! If I hadn't been able to set this plane down like I did, we both would be dead right now. So I'd say it's pretty important that I'm a good pilot!"

"Doesn't play a role at all in how I feel."

"Well, you need a bath if you're going to sleep next to me in that bed. So let me heat you some water and you can wash up. It feels wonderful, trust me."

"Okay. I'll clean up. Wish I could soak my leg but at least I've been able to keep it elevated for the afternoon."

Liz went out and scraped up a bucket full of snow and melted it over the fire. She brought it into the kitchen and helped him up off the sofa so he could scrub the dirt off his face, neck and hands. While he was cleaning up she sat on the sofa with a blanket and watched the fire. It had been a strange week; one that she would never forget. Her life at home in Knoxville seemed so far away. Odd how quickly she had let all that go so that she could think about the tasks at hand. Like survival. Their lives had been reduced to food, water, and a place to stay warm. That was pretty much it. No phone, television, books, or any communication with anyone but each other. Almost the "lost on an island" scenario. Only this was for real. She wondered what her mother and father were doing, and what, if anything, Joe and her father had been able to find out about her location. She allowed herself a moment to think about Tom and wished she had some way to contact him. She knew he would be sick with worry by now. Or thinking she'd changed her mind and stayed in Montana for a few days with Jim. Which was exactly what she was doing but not by choice.

Jim came out of the kitchen smiling from ear to ear. Her attention was pulled from her own thoughts of home back to the present. She could tell by the look on his face that he'd enjoyed the hot water and soap. Such a small thing to bring such contentment.

"Man, that felt good! You were so right, Liz. I can't believe how dirty I was, when you did all the work."

She nodded and laughed sarcastically. "Oh, so you noticed, did you?"

"Yes, and I've mentioned it several times to you. And I'm sure I'll never live it down after things get back to normal."

"Let's just hope they get back to normal. Right now that's still up in the air."

"You tired?"

"Yeah, I was leaning towards climbing back into that bed. We've been sleeping sitting up and leaning into each other. The thought of lying down on a mattress is rather attractive at the moment."

"Let's go for it. Will the fire be okay?"

"I'm willing to take that risk since it's so cold outside and we wouldn't make it in this leaky cabin without the fire burning. I'll get up in the night to check on it."

They walked into the bedroom and suddenly the bed looked very small. Liz got in on the right side nearest the wall and pulled the covers up to her chin. Jim sat down on the left side, lifted his leg onto the bed, and shoved the other leg under the covers. He lay back against the pillow and looked over at her. She looked beautiful to him even though he couldn't say it out loud. She turned on her side and propped up on her elbow so that she could see his eyes. He turned slightly so he could see her whole face, and their eyes locked. Then she did something he had never expected her to do. Not in a million years. She leaned over and planted a kiss on his mouth and he was afraid to move. To respond. She pulled back and laid her head down on her pillow and closed her eyes. He watched her fall asleep, wanting to kiss her lips again. To feel her next to him. He would wait until she stirred in the night, and then he would try to snuggle up against her. But for now, for this moment, he was enjoying the memory of her lips against his. He dozed off listening to nothing but the fire crackling in the other room and the breathing of the woman lying next to him. The warmth of the mattress enveloped him and he fell into a sound sleep, not knowing she'd moved closer to him in the night. The hours passed and the snow fell silently as the fire burned down to nothing but hot coals in the fireplace.

Across the states, miles away, Tom lay in his bed with his eyes open, wondering if he'd ever see Liz again. After holding her in his arms after all those years apart, he couldn't bear the thought of losing her again. But how long could he wait with no word from her? Was she telling him without words that she was done? Or was there something wrong?

Chapter 23

When Jim opened his eyes the first thing he felt was the stiffness in his leg. The swelling had gone down but his leg was so sore he winced as he turned to see if Elizabeth was awake. One thing he noticed was that it was freezing in their room. The fire must have burned down in the night. He lay there quietly watching her sleep, noticing her thick dark eyelashes lying on her creamy cheeks. She'd lost weight during their days out in the mountains and he had, too. He could see the stress in her face. But she was so beautiful it didn't matter. He never thought he'd be lying in a bed next to her so quickly. He smiled at the irony of that thought. She must have felt his stare because her black eyes opened and she quickly turned away from him.

"What in the world are you doing staring at me? Gosh! I look horrible."

Jim laughed and lay back on his pillow smiling. "Don't worry. I was just seeing if you were awake."

Liz sat straight up in the bed and wrapped her arms around her body. "Geez, it's cold in here! One of us needs to get up and get that fire going again." She looked straight at Jim.

"Well, you know I would've already done it if I could. I'll get up and help you, though. Come on, let's get this place warmed up again. Without that fire we'll never make it in this cabin. The place leaks like a sieve."

A smile found its way to her mouth and she jumped out of bed and grabbed her jacket and zipped it all the way up, pulling her hood up as she ran out of the bedroom. She didn't wait to see if Jim was following her. It was too cold for that. She hurriedly went outside and dragged more small limbs to the fireplace, cutting off the branches that stuck out too much with her hatchet. She put a small amount of gasoline on the wood and lit it, and soon the fire was roaring again. It took a little while for the heat to come out into the room, but she just sat there stoking the logs until it was burning hot. Jim was sitting on the sofa and reached for the hatchet, cutting off other small branches she could add to the fire. Hunger was moving up the ladder of priorities so Jim got up and hobbled to the kitchen to get the meat and two skewers. He put the meat on the sticks and handed them to Liz. She leaned over and held then over the fire, which sent an aroma out into the room that made them even hungrier. It was getting old eating meat every single meal and Elizabeth felt the depression coming on when she suddenly remembered the one can of peaches in the cabinet. She went to the kitchen and opened the can and sniffed it. It smelled pretty fresh so she took the can into the living room along with two plastic spoons she'd found in the back of a drawer. They ate like kings for a few moments, savoring the taste of the peaches. They saved some of them for another meal and fixed some coffee to drink. With the warmth back into the room, their moods lightened up and they began to discuss what the plan was for the day.

"You think I need to make a trip back to camp to get more clothing and check on things? I know that fire has to be out and it might be good to build up a huge fire today. The snow is barely coming down."

"I hate to think of you out there alone, but you're probably right. If there's any chance of a plane being above us, we do need to get that fire going so they can see the smoke. Otherwise, the fuselage would blend right in to the surroundings. So much snow has fallen that it's covered up a lot of plane."

"I know Dad is frantic, and Mother, too. I've been thinking about them. And Stephanie, my secretary. No telling what she's come up with for an excuse when Walmart's people have called asking where in the world I am. We can only go so long out here before our businesses start to suffer. I've worked so hard to build up my company and now who knows what's going to happen. Someone's got to find us pretty soon."

Jim pulled her up on the sofa and hugged her. "Now, Liz, I know it seems bleak. But you know they're waiting for the first opportunity to put a plane up and it's been snowing pretty much the whole time we've been here. We landed during one of the worst snowfalls this area probably has ever had. And the longest. Of course, it's the dead of winter. It snows almost every day, anyway."

She pushed her hair back and nodded. She knew he was right. "I sure hate to worry every one like this. But there's nothing we could do. At least we're both alive and in pretty good shape. If you hadn't broken your leg, we might have tried to hike somewhere. But Dad would have killed me if we'd left the scene of the crash. That's in every handbook."

"I'm sure it is. We did the right thing and I think you're correct in saying we need to rebuild that fire at the site. You get dressed as warmly as you can, and I'll keep this fire going while you're gone. It'll make for a long day for us both; I'd go with you but I would only slow you down. You might bring some of that deer meat with you, if it's still there. We can't rule out the fact that a large animal might have found our site and shuffled through everything on the plane looking for food."

"You're right. I'll be careful. Heck, if I see any animal I'm going to kill it for food. So I'm not worried too much about that. Will you be okay here? I mean it's going to be at least three hours sitting in the cabin with nothing to do. And you need to keep that leg raised up as much as you can. How is it feeling now?"

"Kind of achy all the time, especially when I try to walk. I can't put any pressure on that foot at all or pains shoot up my whole leg. I'm sure the bone is going to try to set, but it's still very sore. The orthopedic surgeon will love this one."

"Oh, won't he, though. We'll be in all the papers in Montana, and at home. Our proverbial fifteen minutes of fame, which probably won't affect anything in our lives. But it will be so good to be home, Jim. I don't know about you, but I'm tired of roughing it. I'm glad I have used some of my skills, but I'm ready to get back to work."

"I never thought I'd say that, but I am sorta ready for that, too. But it has been kinda nice getting to know you. After all, that was the purpose of this plane trip in the first place!"

She felt an urge to leave the room but looked at him and smiled. "Yes, spending time like this out in the wild sure creates instant intimacy."

"That's not what I meant, Liz. I—"

She interrupted him quickly. "I know what you meant, Jim. And I agree. I just don't know how I feel at this point. I kissed you last night and it was on an impulse. But I just want us to be careful because when we get back to our lives, all of this could go away. Real fast."

"You better get going. You don't need to be walking back here in the dark, and who knows what the weather is going to do. It's still pretty gray out there."

Liz packed her backpack and threw it over her shoulders. She grabbed the rifle, made sure she had enough ammunition, zipped up her jacket, and raised the hood. The wind was howling outside and very cold; she was going to have to really be careful about hypothermia. She started out the door and looked back. Jim waved her on, so she turned and closed the door. It felt weird leaving him behind. But it was the best way for now. She would never make it if she had to worry about his leg and she needed to get this trip done as quickly as possible.

There was no path as she worked her way through the woods. The snow had completely covered where she'd walked before. She kept her eyes open for deer because she knew there was a chance that the deer meat had been found. A camp left unwatched was open game for any animal. The woods were thick and there were patchy spots where the limbs of the trees had kept the snow from reaching the ground, and it made her way easier as she moved from one bare spot to another. But as she moved into a clearing the snow was up to her knees in some places, so trudging through it sapped her energy and left her panting.

She stopped halfway to the camp and checked her watch. She was making good time but her feet were beginning to feel the cold. That wasn't a good sign. She felt tired and a little weak. She drank some water and ate a bite of meat she had cooked for breakfast, wishing for those peaches. They'd tasted so good to her after eating just meat. After about ten minutes of rest she started out again, determined to make good time so her feet would not get too cold.

The snow remained deep for the next thirty minutes and she wasn't at the campsite yet. She was really feeling tired when she finally arrived. Her first concern after resting a minute was the fire, which was nothing but a few embers glowing. She sat her backpack down and checked out the inside of the plane. Nothing had been disturbed. Maybe the snowfall had been so strong that it protected them from invaders. She dug around for the deer meat and found it underneath Jim's bags. It was frozen solid so she put some in her backpack and climbed out of the plane.

Outside the plane, she began the grueling job of cutting branches and stacking them in a pile. It took her longer than she'd planned to build up a good fire. She poured gasoline from the plane onto the logs to make them more flammable, but not on the top logs. She wanted this fire to burn all afternoon. There was a little snowfall but not enough to keep a plane from flying overhead. She was hoping the search and rescue team had heard a good weather report and were up in the air trying to find them. After she was sure the fire was burning good she went inside the plane and grabbed her one red sweater and tied it to a branch she stuck inside the windshield, in between the blankets. There was a lot of snow piled on top of the front of the cockpit and on the remaining wing. The plane might be invisible from the air. She was hoping the red sweater might stand out in the all the white.

Liz sat down on a log near the fire and warmed her feet and hands. It felt so good to feel the heat of the fire. She put her head in her hands and closed her eyes. The walk had taken a lot out of her and she was dreading the walk back to the cabin. For a moment she wanted to stay at the site and spend the night. But she knew Jim needed her to return. He would be worried sick. And it would be so much colder in the plane than the cabin. This whole tragic event had taken its toll on her. She felt a little depressed but she still had hope that they would be found. Her father and Joe would not stop looking; she was confident of that. *But would they really believe that Jim and I are still alive?* Or would they finally be accepting that after a week out in this weather no one could survive long if they were injured? There were so many unknowns for them, because there had been no communication from her or the plane.

She sat there for almost thirty minutes just absorbing the heat from the hot fire. She piled a few more limbs across the top and put her pack on her back before heading back to the cabin. The trip home was slow but she had her footsteps to follow. She drank nearly a bottle of water and ate another piece of meat while she walked. After she got into the woods, she began to sing, and the sound of her voice echoing in the quiet helped her to not feel so alone.

It was quieter than she had imagined it would be on that mountain. No sound at all. Not even a bird. And to be walking in that quiet for miles and miles was unnerving. She'd been prepared as a young girl to survive anything. And she would survive this. But at times she felt pushed to her limit. Her great grandfather would have told her that this was the point at which you pulled from deep within you. That you reached down and brought forth the meat of what you were made of. Her father had taught her to become one with her surroundings and she allowed these words of his to keep her company while she walked. He had always told her that if she could lose the fear of her surroundings, or the weather, whatever was causing her the most stress, and just accept it, let it flow, then she would begin to blend in. To become one with what she had feared.

At this point she felt worn out and feared the cold. In her mind, the cold was trying to take over her body. So she had to allow herself to give in and accept the cold and become one with it. She needed to slow her heart rate and allow her body to be able to survive in the cold, no matter how cold it got. It wasn't long before she didn't feel the cold anymore. Her mind was on what she was doing, which was walking back to the cabin. She didn't concentrate on the snow or how cold it felt. She concentrated on how warm her body was and how fast she was moving through the snow. It became her path to the cabin. Nothing else. She breathed in and out slowly and kept a good pace. In the open field just before the cabin, she again saw the family of rabbits looking for food. She shot one of the larger rabbits and carried it back to the cabin. It took two hours to the minute and she was back.

When she opened the door, she was breathing hard and sweating under her jacket. Her throat felt sore but nothing serious. She handed Jim the rabbit and unloaded her pack and pulled down her hood. She felt hot suddenly and took off her jacket. Jim saw her flushed face and told her to go lie down. He took the rabbit outside, skinned it, and brought the meat inside and put it in the refrigerator in a pan full of snow. He hobbled back to the bedroom to check on her and noticed she'd fallen asleep, so he carefully took off her boots. He was amazed that she didn't wake up, which made him realize just how tired she was. He put a light cover over her and walked back into the living room.

He was hungry so he put some of the fresh rabbit meat on a skewer and hung it over the fire. He looked into her backpack and found the deer meat she'd brought back with her and put it in the refrigerator next to the rabbit meat. He knew she was worn out, but he was more concerned that she might be sick. He let her sleep for a couple of hours and then walked back into the bedroom. She was burning up with fever.

"Lizzie. Can you hear me? You need to wake up and drink some water. You've got a fever."

She stirred a little and opened her eyes. "My head is killing me."

She tried to sit up but he could tell she was weak. "What in the world is going on with me? I'm cold but burning up. Chilled. Have I got a fever?"

"That's exactly what's going on, Liz. You're burning up with fever. Not sure why, but you need to swallow some of the ibuprofen to get that fever down. We don't want you getting pneumonia out here in the middle of nowhere."

She sat up slowly and drank the water Jim handed her. "I am so weak and tired! I made it back in good time, though. It was amazing to travel like that and not feel the cold."

"Well, your mind may have accomplished that, but I don't think your body did. I should have gone with you. I don't know how that would've helped, but this was too much for you, Liz. You are burning up."

She slumped back on her pillow and frowned. "I can't get sick. Not now. Did you keep up the fire out there? I didn't even notice."

"Yes. And I got the deer meat out of your backpack. I need you to get well. Are you hungry at all?"

"I probably should eat a little meat. Would you fix me some deer meat this time? I'm getting tired of the rabbit."

"Sure. You sit up and relax and drink your water. I know you're worn out, and a good night's sleep will do you wonders."

Liz lay back and listened to Jim fixing the meat. She was amazed at how quickly they'd settled into the cabin. It almost felt like home. Except for the fact that there was no running water or a bathroom. No one would ever believe she had survived such limited living conditions.

Before Jim could get the meat to her, she'd fallen into a deep sleep. Jim sat down on the edge of the bed and watched her breathing slowly, worried about her fever and how tired she was. After a few minutes he got up and walked into the living room and ate the rabbit he'd cooked for himself and a little of the deer meat. He kept the fire going and built it up so that when he lay down beside her late in the night, the fire would burn until morning. There was no sound at all in the cabin but the crackling of the fire and outside the snow was falling, putting down another layer of white. Jim's last thought before falling asleep was the fear that they would never be found. That was, unless the owner of the cabin decided to show up.

Chapter 24

The night was long for Elizabeth. She awoke several times coughing and chilled from the fever. She got up once and took more ibuprofen to get the fever down and checked on the fire. She wrapped up in a blanket and sat near the flaming logs, her mind going ninety miles an hour. After sitting there a moment, she decided to fix a cup of hot coffee and sat in the dark letting the fire and the coffee warm her bones. She wondered how her parents were holding up. And she wondered if Tom had gone home. Her dreams about him were so vivid that it made her even more anxious to get back to her life. She thought about Jim lying in the other room asleep. He'd been nothing but a perfect gentleman to her since the crash. Although his leg was broken and it hindered him quite a bit, he never forced himself on her. Never acted inappropriately. If she was honest, she did like him, but she didn't know if there was a future with him. And Tom had jumped back into the picture the day before she was leaving for Montana. If he hadn't come back, she might be tempted now to get closer to Jim to see if there was something there to hold on to. But she just couldn't let her feelings go with Jim, knowing Tom was at home waiting to see her.

Finally warmed, she climbed back into bed without waking Jim and snuggled down into the cool sheets and blanket. It took her a few minutes but she finally fell asleep and didn't wake up again until morning. When Jim woke up, he found her up and dressed, although looking rather frail.

"What do you think you're fixing to do, young lady?" His face was frozen into a frown from worrying all night about her.

"I feel some better. I was going to bring in some more firewood. We're going through it pretty fast.

"Well, I'm going out there with you this time. You really don't need to be out in the cold with the fever you had last night."

"I'll be okay. I won't be out there long. Put your coat on and meet me outside. There are plenty of fallen branches on the ground with all the wind that's been whipping around for the last day or two."

"Liz, you need to give your body a rest. I want to check your throat to make sure you don't have something serious going on."

"You worry too much, Doctor. I'm fine. Just a little fever is all. I pushed hard and got too cold. Besides, if it stops snowing we might get a plane flying overhead. It's about time, wouldn't you say?"

"As much as I love being out here with you, I'd say it's a perfect day to be rescued. I'll be right out."

Liz went outside and began gathering branches to bring inside, cutting them into smaller pieces so that they fit into the fireplace. She glanced up to the sky and shook her head. It didn't seem like the snow was ever going to stop coming down. It had been difficult this time walking back to the campsite. She couldn't imagine doing it again if it kept on snowing. It would be up to her knees in some places.

Jim came out and helped her carry a few branches inside. He looked pretty pitiful with two crutches and a broken leg. But she could tell he was worried about her and felt guilty for not being able to help.

"Liz, do you think we've made a wise move by staying in this cabin? I mean, if anyone flew over, they would never spot this cabin. Well, I know you thought you saw it when we were about to land. But I would hate to depend on that happening to the rescuers with the weather like it is. And to keep that fire going over there you'll have to make that trip every other day. Are you up to that?"

Liz sat down on the sofa, wiping her hands on her already filthy jeans. "What you say is true. We wouldn't be spotted here by a plane most likely, even though the smoke from the fireplace would send up a signal. Let's face it; the fuselage is being slowly buried in the snow. The main thing they would see would be the fire. And it is a pain walking that hour and a half trek in the deepening snow. This last time I walked it, I got out of breath. But it was mainly because the snow slowed me down and caused me to work harder. If I take my time and pace myself, I'll be fine. But this weather pattern is just hanging over us. It never stops snowing except at night and then it's right back on us in the morning. That's not helping us at all."

"I bet your parents are going nuts. I've thought and thought and I cannot come up with any way to communicate with them or with anyone for that matter. Our cell phones are dead. No use at all. I bet when we get back to civilization we'll have a million messages coming in."

"You're right. I worry about Mom and Dad, too. But we're doing pretty well as far as surviving. They'll be proud of us. I guess I better rest today because tomorrow I'll need to make that trip again."

"I'm going to bind my leg this afternoon and see if it helps me be able to put any weight on that foot. I know it's a gamble, but it's worth a try. It's very sore and I know the leg is weak. I don't want to re-break it if it's trying to mend. I'm pretty sure it's a simple fracture, but if I'm wrong and try to stand on it, I'm going to be in real trouble."

"No, that would set us back for sure. And because we can't see the news, we have no idea what the weather forecast is for the next week. It could be clearing up and it that's the case, then we need to just sit tight and do what we're doing. They'll find us one way or the other. We have to keep up our energy and drink lots of water."

"You're right. Eating just protein is hard on the kidneys, so water is critical. And I want to check out your throat. How do you feel?"

"Mainly washed out from the fever. Let's build this fire up and stack the wood, and then I'll get us another rabbit. We aren't eating enough, Jim. After breakfast, we don't eat again until maybe 2:00. We're going to have to make ourselves eat again around noon. And then an afternoon small meal. Our appetites have disappeared because all we're eating is meat."

"After you get your rabbit, as your doctor, I'm recommending complete rest for the rest of the day. Is that clear?"

Liz grinned and nodded. "Yes, Doctor. But right now get your little butt down here and help me with the wood."

They laughed and finished stacking the branches, and then Liz went out to kill another rabbit. After she had picked up the rabbit and was walking towards the cabin she thought she heard an engine. She looked up in the sky but it was so gray and hazy that she couldn't see anything. She ran into the house calling for Jim.

"Jim! I heard an engine sound. I think there was an airplane overhead!"

"What? Are you sure? Did you see anything?"

"No! It's too hazy up there to see anything at all. But I'm sure it was a plane. I don't know how they could see anything with the sky like it is. I could have been wrong. But it's so quiet out there that any noise stands out."

"Well, if it was and they spotted anything they'll circle back. Maybe we should go out there and listen."

They both walked outside and stood near the cabin for the next twenty minutes. Nothing else was heard. Not a sound. Liz was obviously disappointed and walked back into the cabin fussing.

"Damn. I just knew that was a plane. And we're not even sure that fire at the crash site is still burning strong. This is so frustrating, Jim. I can't be in two places at one time. One of us needs to be at that site every day making sure the fire is burning strong enough."

"Do you think we could survive in that plane for more than a day or two? We barely made it before. I'm willing to try if you think we should. But this cabin really protects us from the cold. We're able to sleep in a real bed and the fireplace puts out enough heat to at least knock the chill out of the air in the bedroom."

"I know. We're much better off here. But I wonder if we're making a mistake as far as anyone being able to find us."

"Well, there's no way to really know that, is there? We're doing the best we can to survive."

"I'll make the trip back to the site tomorrow as long as I don't have fever. It's only critical when it's not snowing. And who the heck can tell when that's going to be? It's a guessing game for us. The whole thing. It makes me tired just thinking about it."

Jim walked over and hugged her and smiled. "Now, now, Lizzy. Calm down. We've gotten ourselves all worked up over nothing. We're not even sure it was a plane in the first place. We have to have confidence that your father and Joe know what the heck they're doing. And that Search and Rescue won't just give it one flyover to see if they can spot us. I'm sure they are working that map to death trying to figure out where we landed. So let's relax and get through today. Both of us need to rest and get stronger for tomorrow. I am really leaning towards going with you this time. We'll see how we feel when we wake up."

Liz nodded and sat down on the sofa. She felt weak and discouraged. "If we can make it one more day, just one more day, maybe someone will find us. I'm sorry for being so pitiful. It's the woman coming out in me. But do you know how sick I am of roughing it? And you dealing with a broken leg? When I get home I'm not going to eat another piece of meat for a frigging year."

Jim laughed and sat beside her, pulling her close to him. "Relax, lady. We have to be patient. They're going to find us one way or the other. Now rest your eyes. I'll watch the fire for you. I don't want you worried about one single thing."

He looked at her throat and saw some infection. But there was nothing he could give her to clear it up. Tomorrow it would either be better or far worse. And either way, there was nothing they could do about it. Liz leaned her head back on the sofa and dozed off listening to Jim talk about his surgeries. The drone of his voice and the warmth of the fire put her into a deep sleep.

Jim finally closed his eyes and slept most of the afternoon. When he woke he saw the snow had stopped and the fire had burned down inside the cabin. Theoretically, he knew there was no way anyone would spot the downed plane that was nearly completely covered in snow. Not today. Not any day. A strong fire burning was the only way to signal another plane flying overhead. And from the cabin, nearly two hours away by foot, it seemed impossible to keep it burning strong enough.

Chapter 25

When Elizabeth opened her eyes the thought occurred to her that it was Sunday. Nearly a week since they'd crashed. It took her mind several minutes, like walking in quicksand, to catch up with that realization. For each day ran into the next and they were all alike. She lay there quietly, listening to Jim breathe in and out. The fire had died down to embers and again, and it was cold in the cabin. Her one small area in the bed was warm because of her body heat. Her fever had not returned but she felt weakened by it. She hated to move but she knew she needed to get up and build the fire, go outside to gather wood and use the bathroom. Then she would make the coffee and cook some meat. Her chores were pretty much the same every day since the crash. Food, water, and fire. She looked over at the now very familiar face of Jim, who had become a good friend to her if nothing else. She knew he wanted more. And in another world, time or place, it just might have happened. It still might. Jim was sound asleep with his mouth open. Which would mean that he snored at night but she never heard it. It also meant that he would be very thirsty when he woke up. They had learned each other's needs out of necessity.

She got up slowly, trying hard not to shake the bed enough to wake him. He stirred but did not open his eyes. She put on her jacket and boots and braced for the cold. No matter how she prepared for it, the freezing temperatures were ruthless as she relieved herself in the woods first and then gathered branches to take inside. Near the door she cut off the smaller branches and took them inside for kindling and knelt down and built a strong fire and waited while it began to burn. The warmth went right through her and made everything more tolerable. She hurried to get coffee as she passed the bedroom and noticed that Jim was sitting up in bed. He smiled weakly and put on his coat. It was his time to face the cold.

Some mornings they were quiet with each other, and other times they couldn't stop talking. This was a quiet one. She handed him his coffee when he came in from outside. He nodded and sat at the end of the sofa nearest the fire. She could see him shivering so she walked into the bedroom and grabbed a blanket to lay over his lap.

"I know you're freezing. I'm never ready to face that wind out there."

He whispered in a raspy voice, "Damn the cold. This coffee feels so good going down."

"I'm grateful for it. I just hope it lasts until they find us. I'm using less each time so it's more like colored water. But it's still better than nothing."

She left him alone and went into the bedroom to straighten the bed covers and fluff the almost permanently flattened pillows. Then she melted some snow to wash her face and hands, putting on a little makeup from her purse. At least she looked more alive and it made her feel better. She also brushed her hair thoroughly and pulled it back again into a ponytail. It was beyond dirty. She only hoped it didn't break off. When she walked into the living room after checking herself in the mirror, she saw Jim glance up smiling. She ignored his smile and poked at the fire, then walked back into the kitchen for the meat and skewers.

"Do you want rabbit or deer? I was thinking of cooking both this morning. We need to eat that deer meat and we're already into the new rabbit I killed. But I am glad we are eating more meat than before. Neither of us needs to lose any more weight."

Jim sat back on the sofa sipping his coffee. "I have grown to love the smell of the meat cooking over the fire. I'm hungry this morning. Stiff. But determined to make that trip with you today. How do you feel?"

She yawned and stretched hard. "I feel okay. A little washed out from the fever. But the meat will help me have energy. Wish we had some carbs. I'm going to look in the upper cabinets after our breakfast to make sure there isn't anything worth eating stuck away in a hard to reach area. I doubt I'll find anything, but it is worth checking. I know you wish I'd luck up on another beer."

He smiled but shook his head. "No. I'm more interested in those peaches. They were a great change of pace from the meat."

She got the meat off the fire and let it cool before handing it to Jim. When he took his first bite, he grinned. It was crispy and very tasty, like chicken. The deer meat could taste gamey but they had both acquired a taste for it. After she had finished her meal, she climbed up on the kitchen counter and looked in the upper cabinets. In the back of the one over the stove was a can of pork and beans. It was a large can, which thrilled her. Then she found more coffee that looked old and a can of Vienna sausage. Both brought a smile to her face. The other cabinets were empty so she climbed down and dusted off her hands. When she told Jim about the food he was delighted. They would eat a good meal for supper. That was something to look forward to after the long hike back from the site.

They started out with a good wind blowing from the northwest. It was tough with no scarf around their necks to help and their faces feel the bite of the cold. They lowered their heads and walked a steady pace based solely on how fast Jim could walk with the crutches. He had wrapped his leg tight and was able to touch his foot down lightly with every other step so he wasn't hobbling along like he had been.

Elizabeth felt the slower pace and knew it would take them longer to reach the crash site. They kept quiet for a while to save their energy and to concentrate on breathing deep enough. The cold made them want to take short breaths, which wasn't good long-term.

Jim watched Liz for signs of fatigue. She really shouldn't have attempted this trip again today. But the fire at the camp was critical so they took the risk. About halfway there Jim asked if they could stop. Liz was more than ready. They found two logs fallen in the snow and sat down for a minute to catch their breath.

"This is tougher than I thought it would be, but I'm glad I can touch my foot down. I don't think I'm doing too much damage to the leg but I'll find that out when I get home. How are you feeling, Liz?"

"I'm good. Not as strong as I was the other day. And it is taking us longer to get there. But maybe it's a good thing I'm not pushing so hard myself. It would've drained my energy too quickly."

"I'm looking forward to seeing the plane again and I'm curious as to how long that fire burned. You said you had it built up pretty good. We need to use that to gauge how long it will last next time."

"I'll know as soon as I look at it. I piled the branches pretty high and some of them were pretty large. It took all the energy I had to lift them onto the pile. I was thinking that the fire would last longer. Burn slower."

"Liz, what do you think you'll do when you get back? Call Tom?"

"I'm surprised you thought about him."

"Are you kidding? He is all I think about. Wondering what he's like. Wondering how you'll feel after you see him again."

"Don't let that play with your head, Jim. I've known Tom for years and we were very close. But he did walk out on me because he was afraid of the intimacy level. And I was ready to marry. Obviously he wasn't. He's changed, of course, and grown older. But I don't know him like I did before. We have a lot of work to do to find out if we still have something with each other. It was fun seeing him and it felt good. But that really means nothing when it comes to spending a lifetime together."

Jim looked down, feeling the sadness darken his face. "I was hoping you and I would get to that point. I know it sounds childish but we've spent so much time together over this last week that I feel like we belong together."

"I feel close to you too, Jim. It's impossible not to, being out here together. All we have is each other. But I warned you when this thing started that it would be hard to govern our emotions. I just want the chance to see if Tom is still the one I love. That would not be fair to you and me if I didn't. You wouldn't want that haunting me the rest of my life."

"No, I wouldn't. If you come to me, it needs to be settled. Done with. I'm not playing second fiddle to a ghost."

"Are you hungry? Do you need some meat?"

"I'll chew on a bite, but then we need to get going."

They both took some meat and chewed on it for a while, walking as fast as they could without injuring Jim's leg. They saw a few deer in the woods and one time they saw an elk that was in the distance on the edge of a group of trees. He was strong and his antlers massive. He didn't run, but stood there watching them struggle in the snow. Elizabeth was feeling tired but paced herself so that she could make it back to the cabin. But her mind was on Tom and what Jim had said. He was really serious about her. And it warmed her heart. She didn't want to make the wrong decision and miss something wonderful. She hadn't really allowed herself to feel romantic with Jim. She was afraid to let go. In the back of her mind she was always thinking that Tom was who she was supposed to be with. But she didn't want to look back and discover that the right man was with her all along in this critical time of survival.

They arrived at the campsite about two hours after they had stopped to rest. She'd made the trek much quicker alone. When Jim saw the plane he gasped at the amount of snow that had fallen. "Look at the plane, Liz. It's nearly covered in snow. I see what you mean now.

No one would see the plane from the air because of all the snow. Can you open the door of the plane or is it frozen shut?"

"It opened the last time I was here. It stuck some but I got it open."

"I'd love to get more clothes. Do you have more sweaters or a pair of jeans to take back with you?"

"I'll look. First, I want to check the fire. You see how low it is? Only hot embers glowing. It won't take much to flame it up again. I'll add these pieces that are already stacked near the fire and then go get more in the woods. You rest some. Get your clothes. And drink plenty of water.

I'll take some water with me and I'll be drinking that while I work."

Jim walked towards the plane and jerked on the door. It opened after a few tries and he leaned his crutches against the plane and climbed in. He was reminded of the days they'd spent inside the small plane. It was amazing how small it really was. He sat down for a moment to catch his breath and then reached behind him to open his luggage. He had another pair of jeans, more socks, and a sweater. He tucked them inside his backpack and looked for some clothes for Liz. He found another pair of jeans and socks and a sweatshirt. He folded them smaller and laid them on the seat so she could get to them easily. Then he got out of the plane to see if he could help her build the fire. When he got there she was nowhere to be found. He stood there listening but all he heard was the wind in the trees.

He waited for five minutes and then called out. His voice echoed for miles. She heard him and called back. It wasn't too long before she came through the trees dragging branches behind her. He knew she was going to be tired before they even started the trip back to the cabin.

"Let me help you. You can't drag that many branches at one time, Liz. You'll use up all your energy. Be smart about this. I know you want to get it started, but you're going to kill your energy."

"You're right. I'll slow it down. I'm just eager to get this thing going so we can head back. It looks like snow again."

"Hell, it always looks like snow around here."

They both laughed and he helped her drag some branches and toss them onto the embers. Liz got more gasoline and poured it on the lower branches hoping to start the fire but keep it burning slowly. She went back into the woods for larger pieces and came out with two at a time until they had a roaring fire and then she sat down on a long near the fire and rested, drinking water. She pulled out some meat in her pocket, handed some to Jim, and put some in her mouth. She knew she needed to rest before starting back. It was getting harder and harder to do what she needed to do for them to survive. At least he was able to walk now and help carry a few things. It wasn't his fault but the load had totally been on her back the whole time. She knew that he saw how she was wearing down emotionally because of the physical strain.

Jim could almost read her mind. "You've done a great job. I want you to sit and rest, angel. We got plenty of time to get back. I found more jeans for you." He watched her face for a response. "I knew that would make you smile."

She grinned and brushed some stray hairs out of her face. Her lips were chapped and her throat dry. She drank more water and put her head in her hands, closing her eyes. Jim thought she'd fallen asleep but she was just resting. When she looked up, there were tears running down her face. He knew then that she'd reached the end of her rope. It was just too much. He walked over and sat down beside her, laying his crutches on the ground. He held her in his arms and they sat there for a while just rocking back and forth in the cold, with their faces to the fire.

It was at that point that Liz felt something stirring inside of her for Jim. She didn't say a word. She didn't want to give false hope. But with tears running down her face she turned her face upward and kissed his mouth, knowing it would mean something more to him than her. But she did it, anyway. Because he loved her. And she was beginning to love him back in some kind of way that she didn't even understand.

Chapter 26

The trip home was slow and arduous. Some snow was falling and the sky was thick with a foggy haze. Another reason why a plane would not fly over them today. Elizabeth tried not to allow the discouraging thoughts into her head because she needed to be strong for Jim. They were doing well. Surviving as well as any trained outdoorsmen. But it did play with one's mind being out in the whiteness all the time. The dead quiet that surrounded them. It was hunting season and she knew there was a chance, a good chance, that the owner of the cabin might return. She was going to mention it to Jim but thought better of it for now. If it happened, it would be great. *But why put false hope into someone's mind who was already dealing with an injury?* They plodded along watching for deer or rabbit, and talking very little. At the halfway mark they stopped again to sit and rest.

"Have you noticed how tall these aspens are? And how many there are in here? A person could get lost so fast with the snow so deep. You can't tell what direction you're going because everywhere you turn it looks the same. The sky is so hazy we can't see the sun. Don't you dare lose your compass. We'd be lost and no one would know where to look for us."

She smiled. *He's worrying about losing the direction and I'm worried about surviving the hour.* "I have it in my jacket pocket. Guarding it with my life. So how do you feel? How's your leg? Do you need more ibuprofen?"

"No. I'm good for now. It's aching but it's sort of muffled. My back and arms hurt from using these make-do crutches. I have sores under my armpits. But I'm not complaining, really. I'm thankful I came with you, even if it's a struggle. Wanted to see the crash site one more time. It really hasn't changed that much. Except it's becoming more invisible. I don't feel good about that."

"You did see my red sweater hanging on that stick by the door?"

"I did. But now I'm wondering if I put it back. I opened the door and it fell to the ground. Damn!"

"I'll be back over in a day or two. I'll put it back up. At least we have a large fire going and it should burn through tomorrow. I don't see any other choice that we have, Jim, of staying in the cabin versus trying to keep the site active. If we hear a plane, I'm sure we will try to get here as fast as we can. They won't just circle once if they think they've spotted us. We haven't had a decent day yet for them to search. I know all of our families are going mad with worry."

"I'm sure they are. No one would miss me except my office and patients. And I'm sure they're taken care of by now. But my secretary will be worried and it might cross my son's mind even though we don't see each other that much. I'm certain we've been on the news by now as missing. Not sure how that works, but at some point they'll put it out there."

"I've thought of that, too. And how that will affect my accounts. Especially Walmart. That life seems so far away from here. Like a lifetime ago. Do you feel that way?"

"It does seem like we've been here longer than a week. It will be a full week tomorrow. Hard to believe. The days go by slower—and they all are the same. Maybe that's it. Like we're stuck in a frigging time warp."

"We better get going. Chew on this meat so that you don't lose energy. And we both need to keep drinking water."

"I've been noticing how dark my urine is. How about you? That's the protein and we do need to dilute it. A lot more water than we're drinking now. A couple bottles a day isn't going to get it."

"I agree. We don't have too much longer to go. Let's pick up the pace if we can but you tell me when you have to slow it down. I don't want to push you any more than you feel you can go."

"You're the one who had fever. What's the hurry?"

"Just don't want to take the chance of it getting dark on us. That would make it near impossible to find our way back. We do have flashlights but at night it would feel like tunnel vision. And the compass would help us but I just don't want to risk it."

They walked another hour, slowing down for Jim. The conversation was sporadic as they were both lost in their own thoughts, trying to sort out their fears about work and the emotions that were building between them. The snowfall picked up and that made it more difficult to see where they were going. Elizabeth kept them going in the right direction with the compass but the wind had picked up and she knew they were in trouble. She grabbed Jim's arm and yelled out to him.

"Jim! This whiteout is making it nearly impossible for us to see where we're going. But if we stop we'll freeze to death out here. So we have to keep going. I'm watching the compass and I'll try to keep us on track. After we get into the trees it will be easier to see."

Jim nodded and leaned closer into her. The crutches were digging into his armpits even though he'd tied some material padding on top of each one. His leg was numb from the cold. His toes were cold. He was miserable but knew it would do no good to tell Liz. They walked for what seemed like forever, going at a painfully slow pace, but moving in the right direction according to the compass. Eventually they moved into a more wooded area and could see much better. They both were worn completely out but they had to keep going.

"Liz, I swear this might be the last time we go to the crash site. I really think I need to make a call on this one. You've done this one too many times and it's wearing you out. And I know this will be my last time for sure. We need to find another way to alert a plane that might be flying overhead. This isn't smart, Liz. It's hard enough finding food and staying warm, much less traipsing back and forth from the cabin to the crash site to keep that fire going."

"I hear you, Jim. I'm as tired as you are of making this trip. But I'm not sure what we'll do as far as signaling a plane. The transponder will work if they fly directly overhead. So we do have that to rely on. That is, if the transponder is still working."

"We don't have to make a decision right now. But when we get back to the cabin and are warm and full, I want to discuss it."

Fifteen minutes later they were at the door of the cabin, out of breath and out of energy. Liz opened the door and they both walked in and fell onto the couch, laughing uncontrollably. After a few minutes she got up and started building a fire in the fireplace. The cabin was cold and they needed the warmth. After the branches were blazing she got a bucket and melted some snow to wash their hands and faces. She wished she could sit in the bucket and warm her whole body. Especially her feet. She felt good inside about how well they were managing. But there was little room for error. Hypothermia could set in and then they would be in serious trouble. Both of them were worn completely out.

"We need to eat, Liz. I'll get the meat and skewers out of the kitchen. You sit here and get warm."

She watched him wince as he put the crutches under his arm one more time. He was hurting pretty badly and she got up to help him get the meat.

"Here, Jim. Let me do it. You need to rest your arms and get that leg elevated. Isn't that what you tell me all the time?"

"Yeah, I do. But I can't sit here and let you do everything when I know you're just as tired as I am."

"We're both dead on our feet. We'll eat and drink plenty of water and then go to bed. I know it's going to feel so good to get in bed tonight."

"I feel good that we got a good fire going at the crash site. But who knows how it will be in the morning. You put enough wood on there for it to burn another day, I'm sure."

"I think so. I just pray someone comes for us soon. My parents are going to lose their minds if we aren't found in the next day or two. And

I'm going to have to kill a deer tomorrow. We've eaten so much meat. I didn't get all the deer meat from the crash site because I couldn't carry it all. So we need some in this refrigerator in case we don't return to the site."

The deer meat began to sizzle and their mouths watered. They both were starving.

"Tastes pretty damn good, doesn't it?"

"Man, this stuff grows on you! Not too bad."

Liz leaned back on the sofa and pulled her boots off. She decided to wash her socks and let them dry near the fire. She put new ones on and rinsed out her other ones, feeling like a pioneer woman. She was wearing out. Her back was hurting from lifting so much and her feet were throbbing. Her throat felt a little sore but she didn't want to mention it to Jim. What could he do but worry? She closed her eyes and just tried to feel the warmth of the fire washing over her.

Jim was quiet and sat back on the sofa watching her for a moment. He yawned and fought off the desire to fall asleep. He wanted to talk to her. To hold her. But he wasn't sure if that would be a dangerous move or not. They sure didn't need to get into a fight after such a long, exhausting day.

He leaned back and put one arm on the back of the sofa. She opened one eye and scooted over and snuggled up next to him. He smiled. If that was all he got, he would be content. He smoothed her hair and kissed her forehead. He began to hum a song he'd heard on the radio driving to the airport to meet her. He'd forgotten the words but loved the melody. Liz closed her eyes and smiled. After hearing absolutely nothing but a fire crackling, his humming was hypnotic to her.

She fell asleep lying against his chest until the fire had nearly died down. Jim felt like he better wake her up so they could build it back up again, so he gently shook her arm and she opened her eyes.

"I must have dozed off. What was that you were humming? It put me to sleep?"

"Oh, nothing. A song I heard on the radio the day we left. The fire needs building up and I know we need to get into bed. You ready, Liz?"

"I would love some coffee, but we need to leave that for mornings. So I guess it's time to hit the bed."

She added several bigger branches to the fire and left it roaring and walked into the bedroom. She carried a blanket into the living room and placed it near the end of the sofa so it could get warm. Then she went into the bedroom, closed the door, and changed sweaters. When she was ready to climb into bed, Jim had already beat her there. She walked into the living room and got the warmed blanket and laid it on top of them and pulled the covers over the blanket. It helped to warm the cold sheets and felt so good next to their skin.

Sleep came quickly as Liz rolled over next to Jim to keep warm. The bed was small and they'd learned a dance unspoken of when to turn and when to remain still. Things married couples took years to learn, they had picked up quickly. Because they had to survive the cold. The hunger. And the fear.

Chapter 27

The house was quiet and Martha sat on the sofa in the living room thinking back on the early years of her marriage to Jesse. The pregnancy had been very difficult, and she'd been sick day after day. During the last three months she'd been diagnosed with preeclampsia. The doctor had ordered bed rest for her the whole last trimester to try to avoid eclampsia. Jesse had been good to her, even though he'd never wanted children. When they had married, it seemed the first year had been an ongoing honeymoon. They couldn't do enough for each other. Jesse would have been content for that way of life to continue indefinitely. But when she found out she was pregnant, Jesse's joy could barely be contained. He was so in love with her that his misgivings about having children disintegrated. He bragged to his friends that his beautiful wife, Martha, was pregnant, and he was compelled to constantly caress her ever-growing belly. At first, she thought it was sweet, but as time went on and she continued to be sick every day she began to snap at him in irritation. She got so big that she was very uncomfortable and didn't think the pregnancy would ever be over.

Early in the pregnancy, before she started having morning sickness, she wanted to fly to Louisville where her parents were from and let her mom enjoy shopping for the baby. That had fizzled out quickly after the first morning she began throwing up. It never stopped for five months. Then shortly after it ceased she was confined to bed rest. By the time Elizabeth was born, she was almost indifferent to her because all she could think of was that it was finally over. It wasn't that she didn't think Elizabeth was tiny and adorable. She just didn't want much to do with her. She refused to nurse Elizabeth and didn't ask for her to be brought into the room. She perfunctorily held the baby when the nurse brought her in, but was ready to give her up right away when feeding time was over.

She knew Jesse thought that she'd been cursed with a difficult pregnancy, but that it would all be great when the baby finally arrived. Since this was their first child, he seemed shocked by her reticence when Elizabeth was born. He was patient for a long while, but he began to think she didn't love Elizabeth. Soon she seemed to draw away from him, too. Even Martha began to wonder what had happened to those days of carefree bliss they'd enjoyed, the days when nothing was quite as important as the time they could share together. After she distanced herself from the baby and Jesse for several months, he started pulling back from her, as well, and closely bonded with Elizabeth, beginning a bond that would be lifelong. As he drew back from her, Jesse's whole personality seemed to change. His outgoing, free-spirited joy for life was restrained. He began to stiffen up in his dealings with people. It wasn't as if he wasn't friendly; he just didn't have his former ease. Martha had brought a lot into his life, but she had taken away more.

As the tears streamed down her face, Martha relived those moments after Elizabeth was born. *Jesse and I had been so close that first year,* Martha thought. *Suddenly, everything just fell apart. I'm not really sure what happened. I know I had a very difficult pregnancy, and I remember being irritated a lot. But I never stopped loving him. Dr. Gilreath told me that postpartum depression was why I wasn't that interested in Elizabeth. But it seemed like during that time, Jesse got further and further away from me and closer to her. If only I could have that time to live over, I know I could change some things.*

As she sat there, Jesse became aware of her presence. He turned in his chair and felt a wave of incredible emotion that he hadn't felt for years; tenderness. Looking at her sitting in the dimly lit room, Jesse was painfully reminded of what had drawn him to her those many years ago. This woman was strong but still needed a shoulder to lean on. She was sophisticated and very intelligent, but even after all these years she was still naïve about so many things. She was brave but extremely fearful that something had happened to her daughter. She wouldn't be able to live through another tragedy like Zach's. On impulse, Jesse stood up and wrapped her in his arms and held her until her sobs subsided. And tears found their way down his own face in spite of his outward show of strength. A beginning of trust. And hope.

The sound of the phone ringing jarred both of them in the quiet house. When Jesse picked up the phone, Martha saw a change in his mood. He slammed the phone down and all the tenderness he'd just shared with her was gone.

With a questioning look Martha said, "Who was that?"

"You'll never believe it! It was Tom Thornton! I thought I'd never hear his voice again after how he treated Lizzie."

"What did he say?"

"He wanted to know if we'd heard from her in the past two days. The nerve of him. When he said that, I just hung up on him."

"I don't blame you, Jesse. He broke her heart and it took her so long to recover. And now he thinks he can just stroll back into her life as if he just left yesterday. Anyway, I thought he'd moved away. I'm glad you hung up on him."

Jesse continued, "I didn't like Tom at first, but I think it was probably just that a father doesn't want anyone to take his baby girl away. Liz loved him so much that I was finally able to see the good in him and had a glimpse of the man I thought he'd become. But then what did he do? He dumped her at the last minute. He sure didn't live up to my expectations!"

Martha nodded and shook her head. "Odd that he would turn up now, with all this going on."

When Tom hung up he was upset. It wasn't the fact that Elizabeth's parents hadn't wanted to talk to him. He certainly understood how they must feel. He was upset with himself for walking away from the one person who'd made him happier than he'd ever been. *What a fool he had been!* But what could he do now? If Liz's parents didn't want him around, Liz would never take him back. She'd probably had a weak moment the other night when she agreed to see him before she left. He knew she'd seen that doctor she was flying to Montana, anyway. Maybe he should just give up because in his heart he knew didn't deserve her. He decided to turn in; it was getting late, and there was nothing he could do at that late hour. But he would have given anything to know that she was okay.

The next morning when Tom awoke, he had a gnawing feeling he couldn't seem to shake, even through his morning meetings. He knew he couldn't return to Houston without finding out if Elizabeth was safe. If she was seeing that doctor, then he would let things be. But if something had happened and she wasn't okay, then he was going to pull some strings, do anything it took, to find her and try to win her heart back. At the lunch break, he jumped in the Nissan Altima he'd rented and headed downtown, turning left to follow the old familiar streets that led him to Liz's house. He knocked on the door, holding his breath and hoping they would let him in. The door opened and he could tell by the look on Jesse's face that this might not go very well.

"I thought I made it clear on the phone that we don't want anything to do with you! What are you doing here?" said Jesse harshly.

"Please let me come in to talk to you for a few minutes. After we finish, I'll leave you alone. You won't ever have to see me again."

Martha had followed Jesse to the door, and when she saw Tom standing there looking distraught, her heart softened, and she said, "Let him in, Jesse. Let's hear him out."

Jesse looked hard at his wife, but after a few seconds he stepped back to let Tom inside.

"Okay, then, what do you have to say for yourself?" Jesse still sounded angry.

"Mr. and Mrs. Stone, I have no words that could come close to explaining how sorry I am and what a fool I was to walk away from Elizabeth. I was young and immature and so afraid of commitment. I never meant to hurt her; Lord knows I loved her more than life itself. I just wasn't ready yet, and it scared me to go to the next step. So I ran. I've spent years regretting that foolish decision, and I know I don't deserve her. If she's dating that doctor that she flew to Montana, I'll step back out of her life and leave her alone. But if she isn't, I would like the chance to get to know her again. To see if we have anything to salvage. I'm in a profession I really enjoy, my life is stable, and I know I can make her happy." Tom paused with a pleading look in his eyes.

"But right now I'm terribly worried about her. We saw each other for a few minutes Sunday night before she flew out on Monday. She promised she would call me when she landed, and I haven't heard a word. Even if she didn't want to give me another chance, I know she would've called to tell me. Have you heard from her?"

Jesse and Martha found themselves being pulled towards the young man who had just poured his heart out to them. They decided to at least let him know what they knew, which wasn't much.

"We are as worried as you are, Tom," Jesse replied. "We know she was headed towards Helena and never reached her destination. The plane has gone down somewhere near the Beartooth Mountains. But there has been a record snowfall in that area for the whole week and Search and Rescue has been unable to fly. No plane would go out in that kind of weather. It's frustrating because we know she's out there, but we have no idea if either of them is alive or injured, or what. It was on the news last night. Didn't you see it?"

Tom stood there with his heart racing. Surely there was something they could do. "Are you serious? I missed it. Haven't been watching too much television lately. I sure wished I'd seen that. How do you take the waiting? I had no idea she'd gone down. What can we do?"

Jesse put his arm on Tom's shoulder and looked him in the eyes. "Son, we can pray. That's about the only thing we can do. I'm staying in touch with NTSB and with Search and Rescue. They're on it 24/7, watching for a window to put a plane up. I want you to know she's trained in survival. It doesn't help you much to know that, but her training will help her survive until someone gets to them. I have faith that she is strong enough to endure this. It's all we have to hope for, Tom. All we have. And Tom, I shouldn't have cut you off like that. But I'm very protective of my daughter. I guess that's quite I'm sorry for how I treated you on the phone. obvious."

Tom said good-bye and walked away with emptiness in the pit of his stomach. Elizabeth was out there with Jim, either injured, dead, or surviving one of the worst snowstorms in years. It didn't make him feel much better to know she was trained in survival. He knew he needed to fly home but he wrestled with that decision, even though he knew his practice would suffer if he remained in Knoxville much longer. He drove back to his hotel and packed his bags, booking the last flight home to Houston. He would have to trust the connection he'd felt when he'd seen her the night before she left. There was something still there between them, and he was going to hold on to that if it killed him. He texted her a note saying how much he loved her. And that he had waited a week before flying home. But even though the message was sent, he knew the words were out there hanging in the wind. She wouldn't get them until she was found. And he prayed to God she would be.

Chapter 28

Joe was standing at the window in the dining room looking at the front yard. The neighbor's kids were playing in the street, laughing and throwing a ball. It was cold and there was a threat of snow for Knoxville and the surrounding areas. He lit a cigarette and blew the smoke up in the air. He had never felt so sick in his life as he did now, knowing Elizabeth was down. He clenched his fist in frustration and helplessness. He felt partially to blame. What was he thinking allowing her to fly in conditions that were fluctuating? She had trusted him to make a wise decision and he'd failed her. If she didn't make it through this, her blood would be on his hands. He had noticed Leigh walking through the last few days with a dazed look in her eyes. A faraway look. Elizabeth was her best friend. And to think of her out there in the wilderness freezing to death was just about enough to put her over the edge.

Leigh walked into the room and he turned to look at her. They'd avoided each other for as long as they could because neither one of them wanted to talk about any possibilities. But it loomed in the air like a thick layer of smoke and he knew they needed to work through it. And now was the time.

"Honey, let's sit down in the kitchen and talk about this. We've been dancing around each other for days and nothing's getting said. I know you're hurting and I can't keep this up."

She walked into the kitchen and plopped down in a chair, lighting up a cigarette and picking up the ashtray on the counter. They usually didn't smoke in the house, but in this situation, the rules went out the window.

"I've had it, Joe. I don't even know what to say to you. So many emotions running around in my head."

"I realize that. I know you're angry at me. I can feel it. You could cut the air with a knife around here."

"I'm not really angry at you. It's just that this could have been avoided so easily. One word from you or Jesse and she would not have taken this trip. But both of you told her she could make it. And now look what's happened."

"Weather changes, Leigh. There are no guarantees any time you make a flight."

"You know what I mean, Joe. The room for error on this flight was pretty much in our faces. It wasn't a good decision to put her up in the air."

"Well, it's too late now. Believe me, if I could take those words back I would. I've beaten myself up for the whole week, worried sick about Liz and Jim. I don't know what else we can do right now. The NTSB is doing all they can to find out where she might be. But the damn snowstorm just won't let up. It's setting records right and left. I'm almost to the point of going there by jeep and finding a way to travel the roads up there."

Leigh rubbed her face and poured a glass of wine. She offered Joe one, but he refused. He was fit to be tied.

"I want you to know I regret this with all my heart. I know you love her, Leigh. We all do. She's a special person and one of a kind. I fear Jesse is going mad with worry. And Martha probably is on his back every day, asking him why he would put her up in a plane that was going to fly right in the middle of a possible storm. We just didn't see this happening. There was a clear window but it closed up on us."

"All this talk doesn't bring her back. It doesn't do one single thing, Joe. I feel like I'm going crazy inside worrying about her. And Jim. He's such a wonderful man and great doctor. They are too young to have their lives snatched out from under them. What chance do they have to survive that crash? Do you really think she's still alive?"

Joe paused and blew out some smoke. It bought him time to think. He didn't want to sound too certain, but he also couldn't tell her that there was no way they could still be alive after all this time out there in freezing conditions.

"Leigh, I believe that Liz could survive the crash. But in weather conditions like that, anyone would have trouble surviving for a long time. We are assuming neither of them is injured. If they are, then you have to add that into the equation. It gets pretty complicated. Now having said that, Liz is a brilliant woman and was trained by her father in survival. I'm sure she didn't think she'd ever have to use any of that information, but now that she's faced with a life or death situation, I imagine all of that knowledge is surfacing."

"I hope to God she is alive. What in the world would they exist on? Can they melt the snow for water?"

"In the mountains where there is little population, the snow would be fine to eat or drink. Here in the city, I would say no. And she took a rifle with her, a hatchet, and bow. A lot of emergency supplies and some food. Plenty of warm clothing, blankets, and flashlights. I knew she was preparing for the worst, but I never dreamed it would happen."

"A woman out there. I can't imagine that. She's not your average woman, Joe. I can't take thinking about her out there when we cannot do anything from here."

Joe leaned over and hugged her. It was good they were talking about it.

"Honey, I'm on that phone every hour trying to find out what's going on. They put a plane up once but the storm changed directions again and they had to return to base. I'm sure they'll send another plane up soon. Today doesn't look too bad. I was hoping to get a call from them saying that they'd put a plane up to look for them. The more time goes by, the less chance of finding them alive. However, if both of them are alive, they could be very ingenious and come up with some extraordinary ways to survive out there. You do what you have to do."

"I don't even want to go there. I just want her home, Joe. I want her home safe with us."

"So do I, Leigh. You don't know how much I want that."

Stephanie was sitting at her desk reading a book. The phones had quieted down since the short newscast about Elizabeth and Jim. She was surprised the family had approved it, but at least it helped Walmart settle down. People were praying for them all over the United States. If they were found alive, they would practically be celebrities. Their story would go viral on Facebook and Twitter. She had set up a blog about Elizabeth and people were reading it every day. She was worried sick that Liz might not be alive. She couldn't imagine being out in the wilderness in such cold weather for any amount of time. Not to mention having to scavenge for food.

She'd been through the whole office cleaning, organizing, and sorting through all the mail. Letters were coming in by the hundreds from people who were praying for them. She'd set up a file in the file cabinets to hold them but it was getting to be a problem. So she just got huge garbage bags and filled them up with the letters. Her blog was the best way for people to find out any information. She kept in touch with Liz's parents and then blogged that information out so others could read about it. It gave her something to do and kept her hopes up. But the dread was there, hanging over her like a ton of bricks, that Elizabeth might not ever be found. It was the worst thing in the world that could happen, so she pushed it way back in her mind. What she wanted to do was learn all about the ways Elizabeth did business with her clients so when she did arrive home safe and sound, she would be ready to work hard to rebuild the business.

Even though she never got any answers from her texts that she sent to Elizabeth, she kept on sending them. Hoping that one of them might actually go through and Elizabeth would answer. At the very least when her phone was in range again, Liz would see all the texts and know she was loved. It had only been one week, but it felt like much longer. The worry weighed on Stephanie all the time. But Walmart had been wonderful about the whole situation, which took the pressure off her until her boss came home.

She sent flowers to Liz's parents once, just hoping to give them a lift. But there was really nothing she could do but wait. And hope. And she did that with a vengeance. The minutes went by so slowly. It felt like the longest week of her entire life. But she was determined that she was going to be sitting at her desk when Elizabeth walked through that door.

So she came every day with the mindset of getting something done. And more than anything, she prayed that Liz was coming home. She was alone most of the day and at some point she would cry because of the silence that never stopped. No one on the end of that cell phone. No text. No call. Nothing. It was the lack of communication that sent Stephanie over the edge. She would have given anything to have a text come through that said she was alive. Just one word. One single damn word.

Chapter 29

Elizabeth opened her eyes and looked at the ceiling. She could hardly bear to think about the fact that it was Monday morning. A week had gone by since the crash. A whole frigging week. She glanced at her watch; it was 8:00 and freezing cold in the bedroom. The fire must've gone out. She was getting tired of always having to get more firewood and angry at the fact that no matter how large a fire they built at night, it was gone by morning. So there was no way to really keep warm all night. The blankets on the bed were thin and if weren't for Jim's body heat she wouldn't be able to sleep at all. The two of them together created just enough body heat to keep from shivering all night long.

She looked over at Jim and he was snoring. She smiled and climbed out of her side of the bed without waking him up. The floor was freezing as she fought to get her feet into her boots. Her clothes had become a part of her body, stiff and filthy. But for some reason, maybe because of the extreme cold, she didn't feel that dirty. A hot shower would have been heaven and she certainly wouldn't turn it down. But her hair was the worst thing that she had to deal with. Keeping her face clean and her teeth were what she counted as a bath. She washed her feet every day and also brushed through her hair. The one bar of soap they had was slowly melting. But they guarded it with their lives and used it as little as possible so that it would last. She didn't know what she would do if it melted completely to nothing. She vowed to take several bars with her on her next flight, no matter where she was going.

With her coat tight around her and her hood up, she walked outside to gather some wood. She had to go farther into the woods each time to find limbs that had fallen, and the trip back was more difficult. But she managed to haul them to the front door of the cabin and chop them up enough to build a decent fire. Jim was beginning to stir when she finally lit the fire. When she was sure it was going good, she went into the kitchen to get the skewers and meat for breakfast.

"Hey, you. I hear you up and moving around. Is breakfast ready yet?"

She laughed. "You need to get your lazy self up. It's cold in here. I can see my breath."

"I know. I bet that fire feels good. I'm hungry as a bear this morning. Is it rabbit or deer for breakfast?"

"Rabbit. I just can't stomach deer this early. In fact, we're just about out of deer. I'm going to have to hunt after lunch maybe at around 3:00, depending on what the weather is doing."

"It's snowing right now. Not too heavy. Sure wish this thing would clear up so they could put a plane in the air. I don't know about you but I'm ready to be discovered."

"No kidding."

"I know you're sick of taking care of me. It's a wonder that you'll even talk to me, I'm so worthless. I wish you knew how bad that makes me feel that you have to do so much of the work around here."

"I'm kind of liking being in charge, if you want to know the truth. Makes me feel like I'm at home."

"And what is that supposed to mean, Miss Stone?"

"It means that at home I have to do it all myself, anyway. So what's the difference here, except maybe having to go hunt for my food?"

"Oh, come on, Liz. I know you're independent, but I think it's stretching it a bit to say this makes you feel like you're at home. Besides, it isn't all bad having me around. You wouldn't have anyone to come home to if you were alone. And I warm the bed up pretty good, too."

Another laugh. "You are full of yourself this morning. How's your leg?"

"Sore, stiff, and aching. But I'm going to bind it again today so that I can hobble around a little better without worrying about injuring it more."

"Breakfast is ready, Jim. Come and eat before it gets cold."

Jim walked into the living room and sat down on the end seat, stretching his arms out to the fire. The room was pretty plain, with nothing on the wall but the one mirror that Liz loved to use. One single rug on the floor in front of the fireplace. You could tell a hunter owned the place and that it was rarely used.

He took a bite of rabbit and licked his fingers. "How'd you sleep, Lizzy?"

"Pretty well. Kept dreaming about Walmart, though. I'm sure they've heard that I'm lost. I know Stephanie has had her hands full with answering phone calls. No telling what she's having to deal with."

"My office, too. We're causing a lot of problems for people, being lost in the wilderness like this."

"I know. I hate it. I wish we had some way of communication. That's the worst thing about this, besides no indoor bathroom!"

"I knew that was coming. If we just hang on, someone will come, Liz. They have to."

"I sure hope so. I'm tired of eating meat, and I sure don't want to live out here in a cabin for the rest of my life. I like you, but I had a better life pictured for myself."

This time it was his turn to laugh. "Thanks for being so blunt. I like you, too. I think we're both sick of roughing it, but we've learned a lot about survival. And getting along with someone you barely know."

"Wonder what the owner of this cabin is going to think when he comes back to hunt here and someone's been sleeping in his bed? We'll have to leave him a note. He'll get a kick out of it."

"What would be funnier is if this cabin was on the news and he recognized it."

Elizabeth took the two skewers and walked back into the kitchen. She went outside to use the bathroom and brought in two buckets of snow to melt. It was time to wash her face and she knew Jim would love the hot water. Everything took longer, but it gave them something to do. She shut the bedroom door and took the layers of clothing off and tried to wash the upper part of her body. She dug some lotion out of her purse and rubbed it on her arms and chest. Her skin was drier than a cork. The bitter wind and cold were drying her skin out. And her hair. But being clean was worth a million dollars. She got dressed again and threw out the water. It was Jim's turn to wash.

At 3:00, Liz knew it was time to hunt. She had packed her backpack with extra bullets, a flashlight, and a little meat. She also took her hatchet, knife, and the rifle fully loaded. Jim was getting uneasy about her going, but there was no choice. They were about out of meat and they couldn't count on the weather to improve. The snowfall apparently was a permanent fixture in the Beartooth Mountains for the month of November. She went over her gun to make sure it was clean and ready to shoot. She layered her socks and another shirt so that she wouldn't get cold and took two pair of gloves and her white jacket. She wore white jeans and covered her boots with white socks so that she blended into the snow unless her hood was down, showing her long dark hair.

Jim watched her from the other room getting ready. His heart was beating fast and he felt the urge to hold her close. To kiss her. Even as messed up as she was, she was beautiful. Striking. Standing in the other room packing her backpack, she took his breath away. But he didn't say a word. She wouldn't want to hear it.

"You got everything, Liz?"

"Yeah. Just checking it over. Don't want to get out there and find out I left something back here."

"Wish I could go with you."

She looked across the room at him through the doorway of the bedroom. She caught the look in his eye and it made her stomach go into a knot. He loved her. She could feel it. And she couldn't respond like he wanted her to, because she'd had just seen Tom again. He was the first love of her life and seeing him dug up so many emotions she thought were dead. *How could she get involved with Jim if she was still trying to figure it all out with Tom?*

"I know you do. I know it's hard to sit here while I'm out hunting something down. But if I don't go, we don't eat. And I would rather you go with me than go out alone. It's not fun out there alone in all that white. I could get lost so quickly and also the cold is unbearable. After just thirty minutes I'm ready to come back to the cabin. I'm going to have to really watch the cold."

"I worry the whole time you're out. And I feel so friggin' helpless."

"It's okay, Jim. Just relax about it. I know your leg is killing you and half the time you don't admit to the pain. You've been very brave. We both have. I know my father would be proud of me for standing up to this nightmare. I feel like now that I could survive anything and I guess that's what he wanted me to come to. I just didn't want to do it this way. Maybe we don't get to choose how we learn things. They just happen."

"I'm beginning to think that myself. I wanted a date with you and now I've had a whole week out in the middle of nowhere in a cabin. Didn't do much for our romance, did it?"

She smiled but it was a sad smile. Because she could see the sadness in his face. He was a good man. He would be a good husband. But she was stuck.

She walked up to him and hugged him and smiled. "Be patient with me. I know you care about me and are wondering why I don't show more affection towards you. I'm holding back and I know you feel it. It's not because I don't like you, Jim. Because I do. We've already had this conversation. No point in going into that again."

He grabbed her arm and pulled her closer to him. He looked her straight in the eyes. "Liz. Listen to me. Sometimes things happen and we are put in a position to make a choice. I think we were meant to be together. I feel so comfortable around you. And I think you do me, too. We have become very close because of this horrendous situation."

He pulled her up next to him and kissed her long and hard. She didn't resist like he thought she would.

"I'm sorry, but I had to do that. I've been wanting to do it for the whole time we've been out here. I think you're the most beautiful woman I've ever seen in my life. And to think I'm stuck out here with you and cannot show you how much I feel—it's driving me nuts. Do you get that?"

"I do get it. And I feel something for you. I'm just not sure what. I'm afraid, I guess, to say it's love. Because I need to know if there is something there for me with Tom. That must seem very childish to you, Jim."

"I don't think it's childish. But I think you might be missing a very special moment in your life because you might be holding on to the past. You don't know Tom anymore. You haven't seen him for years. And you have to admit we've gotten along extremely well out here. With nothing to do but talk to each other, we've made huge strides in getting to know each other."

"I didn't know you knew so much about relationships, Jim. Most men don't. I'm impressed. But how do I put my feelings for Tom aside? How do I just say that it's over when I don't know if we would have anything now or not?"

"You will have to make that choice. But listen to what you're heart is telling you. Did you feel anything when I kissed you?"

She blushed. "Yes, I did. You are wonderful to me. I do feel very close to you, if I'm honest. But I feel myself holding back because of Tom. Or the wondering about Tom."

"You need to get going. It's getting later and I don't want you out there in the dark. Liz, be careful out there. If you don't find something pretty quick then come on back. Don't push it this late in the day. Mark your trees so that you can find your way back in case the darkness sneaks up on you. I wouldn't be able to find you if something happened. You're pretty much on your own once you leave this cabin."

"I'm aware of the dangers and I feel like I'm as prepared as I can get. I'll shoot the gun twice in a row if I'm in trouble. Our voices will carry like the wind out here. So you can call my name. I probably will hear you pretty well. But don't leave this cabin no matter what, unless I am calling for you, okay? You have to stay here and stay warm. We both can't be out here in this cold."

Jim didn't like what she was saying but he knew she was right. He hated sending her out there alone, but this was the deal and he had to accept it. He watched her walk out into the white snow, and it wasn't long before he couldn't see her. She blended into the snow like an eagle. A snow eagle. He shut the door and stirred the fire. It was going to be the longest two hours of his life waiting for her to come back.

Chapter 30

After nearly a week of snowfall, the fuselage of the downed plane was blending into the whiteness of the landscape that stretched out for miles and miles. Surrounded by mountains and trees burdened by the snow that constantly pulled their limbs downward, any traces of the crash were being hidden expertly by what seemed like an unending fall of white feathery snow. The whiteness was only surpassed by the constant silence of the mountainous region. No hunters had appeared and no overhead traffic. The skies were too gray and too foggy to get any visibility, and the amount of moisture in the air deterred any plane from searching for the crash site. However, on Monday afternoon a helicopter flew over the Beartooth Mountains for a brief time when the snow had ceased and there seemed to be a window of clearing skies. The sound of the chopper echoed around the mountains, seeming louder than it might have otherwise because of the lack of any other sounds.

The search for Elizabeth and Jim had been delayed for the entire week and while this window of time was significant, it wasn't going to last. The Search and Rescue team went as low as it could go but the weather was changing at every turn. They circled the mountains below for a few hours, not seeing anything that would give a clue to the whereabouts of the downed plane. The two officers were quiet, listening for the sound of the transponder sending a signal. They were in constant contact with their command post pertaining to the weather and their location.

After two hours in the air they got orders to return to base. Another front had moved in and more snow was expected immediately. The chopper circled one more time and then headed back to post. Frustrated, the officers climbed out of the chopper shaking their heads. It appeared that the mountains were like a white tomb that had swallowed the crash victims up.

The forecast for the next two days was snow. All they could do was wait, but the pressure from the families and the media was getting out of control. Everyone was wondering how anyone could survive the conditions on the ground in those mountains.

Everyone except Jesse, who was counting on the training his daughter had received when she was younger. And he was counting on another thing—for the weather to change—something to lift so that his only daughter could be found.

Jim entered the cabin and sat on the sofa. He thought he'd heard what sounded like a helicopter out there. It was loud but he couldn't see above the haziness. He built up the fire in case the chopper returned, hoping they would see the smoke coming out of the chimney, dark against the white of the snow that lay on everything.

He was frightened about Elizabeth's trip for some reason. Uneasy. She'd been farther than this before, and nothing happened. But for some reason he was worried and he couldn't shake the feeling. He straightened up the cabin and went outside to try to gather more wood.

He had bound his leg pretty tight but it still was fragile. He couldn't put much weight on it and that made it nearly impossible to go very far in the snow. He managed to gather a little more wood and take each piece one at a time into the cabin. It gave him something to do and he was desperate to feel productive. This whole time he'd felt totally useless. Watching her do everything had ripped his guts out. She was so brave. But he knew there was a limit to what she would be able to do, and he only hoped he could step in when that time came. He did some exercises on the floor to keep his other muscles from atrophying. He'd been doing that all along and it really helped to keep his strength up. But it was his mind that felt useless. No computer, no phone, no newspapers to read. He couldn't even pace the floor very well with the crutches. So he finally gave up and sat on the sofa with his injured leg propped up, hoping to keep the swelling down and help with circulation.

The passage of time played tricks with his mind. It seemed like it had been weeks that they'd been stranded on the mountain. But it had only been one week. How could that be? He went over every single day starting with last Monday when he came to and discovered just how bad the crash landing was. It was a miracle the cockpit had held together like it did. He was impressed with how much punishment such a lightweight plane had taken. He also thought about his son Peyton and how estranged they'd become over the years. He swore to try to develop that relationship if he made it home.

If. He didn't want to think about any other option at the moment, especially with Elizabeth out in the cold and snow about to fall again. The whiteness was delusional. It caused him to lose all sense of direction and time. And the silence was deafening. He decided to go outside and yell out her name to see if she could hear him. It was worth a try.

He hobbled out the door and moved out into the open and yelled as loud as he could. "Elizabeth!" He waited, listening to his voice echoing in the quiet. He was about to give up when he heard his name coming back to him. So it had worked! That gave him a false sense of peace and he hurried back into the cabin, rubbing his arms to keep warm. He sat back down and dozed off, enjoying the warmth of the fire. He had no idea how long he'd slept. But it was longer than he thought. Much longer...

Elizabeth was making her way into the woods. It was cold and she noticed that the snow was beginning to fall. She, too, had heard the chopper overhead and had almost run back to the cabin in the excitement of the moment. But the sound didn't last long and she could tell when it returned several times that it wasn't that low. She knew the snow had nearly covered the plane and the fire would have gone out by now. She was going to have to make another trip back to the campsite in spite of the objections Jim would have. There was no other way to handle it. And she could rest for a day before she returned. If he stayed at the cabin with a good fire burning, then she could travel faster and there would be two smoke signals going up into the white sky. Hopefully at some point the smoke would be seen and the transponder would come through that thick fog to the rescue team. She had to keep the hope going.

As she made her way into the woods she tied a piece of cloth on a few trees to mark her way back. But in the darkness it would do no good. She had to time this hunt and get back before it turned dark. Dragging a dead deer through the woods in the dark would be a death trap for her. She couldn't take that risk. Even if she and Jim were starving. The snow kept falling as she moved farther and farther away from the cabin. After hearing Jim's voice, she smiled and moved on. It made her not feel so far away from him and the safety of the cabin.

Chapter 31

The adrenalin kicked in as soon as Elizabeth spotted some deer down the hill from her. She had settled just short of a small ravine that separated her from the deer. She forgot how cold her feet were and how far away she was from Jim. It was just a beautiful sight to see the deer gathered underneath some trees whose limbs were bowed down with the weight of the snow.

There wasn't a lot of light in the woods but there was enough for her to be able to aim well and hit her target. She had to wait to choose a smaller deer because the larger ones would be too heavy to drag through the woods. She squatted down and waited until they moved away from all the trees. Scrubby undergrowth blocked her from having a clear view, making patience imperative or she would lose the shot altogether.

Her heart was beating fast and she feared that it could be heard. She slowed her breathing down and tried hard to relax and blend in. It wouldn't do for them to see her. Although she knew they'd already heard her she remained dead still so that they would adjust to her being around.

In the position she was in, she could see 180 degrees around her. The snow was coming down through the trees and slowly her footprints were being covered. Her gun was in front of her, balanced on her lap, and her hand was beside the trigger. She had her hood up and her jacket was zipped up to her neck, making her appear all white except for her face. Her eyes were on the deer and at the same time she watched for any movement outside the perimeter of her vision.

The deer were looking for food and staying close together. The smaller trees were in the way of her aim so she stayed calm and waited. She wondered what Jim was doing and how her parents were holding up. Her mind was moving from one thing to the other and she reminded herself to still her thoughts. Her father had told her that the deer sense fear, danger, and movement. She wanted to emit as little energy as possible, almost as if she were a stone statue.

Twenty minutes passed and she still didn't have a shot. If she moved around to get a better angle, they would see her and run. She really didn't want to go any deeper into the woods because if it got dark she would have a harder time finding her way back. She slowly leaned back on her heels to rest the muscles in her legs. It took a lot of discipline to sit totally still. When her father was training her in survival, he used to have her sit in an open field with wildlife around and not let any one of them notice her. It was an art that most people would never achieve. As she sat waiting for the right angle, she finally understood about blending in. Becoming a part of the surroundings.

She waited another twenty minutes as the deer moved slowly around the forest floor searching for food. She saw movement on the right side of the deer, maybe a hundred yards away. Just some dark shapes mixed in with the trees. At first she thought it was a pack of dogs but then she remembered that wolves were on the mountain. She was a little uneasy about knowing they were out there and kept her eyes on the deer to see if they were nervous. She knew they would sense the wolves quickly and their reaction would warn her of any imminent danger.

For a few minutes nothing moved at all. She had an opportunity to shoot but waited until the smaller deer moved out into the open. Finally, after watching carefully, she moved very slowly and raised her rifle up to aim at the deer. Her movement was detected quickly and all the deer stopped and raised their heads. She knew this was the only time she would have to shoot the deer. They were about to run. She aimed carefully and took her shot and a deer fell. The sound of the gun going off in the woods was so loud that all of the deer—she counted eight—ran off into the woods, leaving the dying deer out in the open.

Elizabeth saw the wolves moving closer, but she could tell they were being cautious because they weren't sure about her. The gun had caused them to slow their pace, but they smelled the blood and that was almost overpowering their fear. Elizabeth stood still and waited but realized the longer she waited to get to the deer, the more risk of the wolves moving in to take the kill.

She suddenly darted down the hill and tripped over a hidden log, falling into the ravine and dropping the rifle at the edge. In the fall, she hit her head and was knocked unconscious for several minutes. When she came to, she shook her head and tried to get her sense of direction. She looked up and realized it would take some doing to climb out of the ravine. Although not too deep, there was no way she could just walk up the side. The banks were most likely were full of rocks and limbs underneath the deep snow. She didn't want to injure herself while trying to climb out.

Slowly, without making too much noise, she moved from one limb or rock to the other and pulled her way up the ravine. But just as she got to the top she saw the pack of wolves on the deer carcass. They were tearing into the flesh of the deer and growling at each other as they fought over the kill. The noise was deafening and she was scared they would turn on her if she made a move to climb out of the ravine. She turned back and saw her gun on the back ledge of the ravine. She slowly climbed back down, her strength waning, and climbed up the backside to get to her rifle. The pack remained by the carcass fighting each other and digging into the fresh meat. Blood was dripping from their mouths. She reached for her rifle and it was then she saw another wolf staring right at her from behind a tree.

Just as she made the reach he growled at her with all his teeth bared. Her heart was racing but she stared the wolf down. She didn't want to show any fear although her pulse was racing. She knew he could sense the fear and she kept her eyes steady on him. She made a small lunge, grabbing the rifle, and shot at the wolf. He was lunging in mid air when she made the shot and he hit the ground near the edge of the ravine, still growling at her, saliva mixed with blood dripping out of his mouth.

She froze, shaking like a leaf, her heart beating in her throat. The fear made her lose her grip and she fell backwards into the ravine again. Her body was sore and beaten up from landing on the rocks and small limbs that were underneath the snow. She lay there for a few moments trying to decide if she had enough energy to climb the bank again.

Her thoughts then rushed to the fact that there was a pack of wolves eating on the carcass before she hit the wolf behind her. She was certain that the firing of her rifle made them run again. But how quickly would they return? She stood up, her legs shaking, picked up her rifle, and stumbled over to the other side of the ditch so that she could attempt to climb out of the ravine. She had to be mentally prepared if the wolves were back. She was sure they wouldn't wait for her to fire her rifle again before they attacked her. They had tasted the blood and the kill was theirs. She would be a threat.

She inched up the side and held on, her arms shaking. Her muscles were worn out. She looked closely and saw that the wolves were gone for the moment. Probably just inside the woods, far enough away where they could watch her but not be seen. She pulled herself out and stood up, ready to shoot at any moment should they reappear. The coast was clear so she walked over to the bloody deer and reached down and grabbed the ears. Luckily they had not eaten too much of the meat, spending more time biting each other and doing a dance around the deer, fighting each other off.

She began to drag the deer towards the ravine and stopped in her tracks. There had to be a way around the ravine. She knew she couldn't take that deer down and back up the other side. She decided to walk the length of the ravine away from where the wolves were. Surely, at some point she would reach a place where she could cross.

She figured she must have walked for fifteen minutes before the ravine stopped and there was flat ground. She dragged the deer past the opening of the ravine and turned back left so she could head back to the cabin. The snow was coming down pretty steadily and her energy was going fast. The deer felt like it weighed a ton, but she tried hard not to think of how far she had to go. Daylight was disappearing in the woods and she knew it wouldn't be long before it would be completely dark.

She knew the wolves wouldn't forget about the deer meat. Unfortunately, she'd left a trail of blood behind her so they'd have no problem finding out where she was. This was on her mind the whole time she was dragging the deer across the snow.

Jim was beside himself with worry. It was near dark and she wasn't back yet. He'd heard some shots and thought maybe she'd killed a deer. But he'd seen nothing the handful of times he'd walked outside to look. He decided to walk out again, this time with his jacket on, to yell out to her. He called her name three times and heard it echo across the wooded area. He could barely see anything at all. He listened closely to see if he could hear her calling back to him. He yelled one more time and then stood there watching.

Elizabeth thought she heard Jim calling out to her, but it was faint sound. Which only meant that she had a short way to go before she would be in yelling distance of him. She called back to him but was pretty sure he wouldn't hear her. She continued to the left until she felt like she could walk up the hill to the cabin. Dragging the deer slowed her down tremendously, especially going uphill. Even if Jim had heard her, there was no way with crutches that he could help her at all with the deer. It was totally up to her to get that deer back to the cabin before the wolves came after it. She tried to stay calm and stopped once or twice to look behind her with her flashlight. Darkness was setting in fast and she wanted more than anything to get back to the cabin safely with the meat they needed so badly. She smiled, knowing her father would have been proud of her. The odds were against her that she would make it back to the cabin without the wolves coming near. But she just kept on walking, stopping occasionally to let go of the deer and rest her hand. Surely it wasn't much longer and she would see the smoke from the cabin.

Chapter 32

Jim was pacing, dragging his crutches around on the wooden floor. He'd kept the fire burning so that she could see the smoke. The temperature was dropping fast and more snow was falling. He walked outside with the flashlight and called out her name. It echoed on all sides of him. He heard a faint noise in the far distance and wondered if she was calling back to him. If she was, she was pretty far into the woods. He wished he could go find her. *What if she needed help? What if she was injured?*

It was just driving him nuts hobbling around, unable to help her at all. He was almost at the point of going out to find her when he heard her call his name. He yelled her name back several times and then stayed quiet. He didn't hear anything again so he went back inside to warm up. He didn't know how she was taking the cold. It was bitter and he was so sick of the snow.

He warmed himself and went back outside, trying to keep his head covered from the wind that had picked up. He kept his flashlight on in case she could see the light in the distance. He looked for any sign of a light coming from the woods but saw none. He stayed out as long as he could stand it and went back inside to warm up again. He grabbed some meat and skewered it and ate a few bites, wondering if she was going to make it back. And what would he do if she didn't? His mind was running rampant with thoughts about what could be happening to her. There were wolves out there. What if she'd been attacked by a pack of wolves? Or bear? Or wolverines? There would be no surviving that. She did have the rifle but how could a woman fight off a pack of wolves?

He went out one more time and heard a voice calling in the distance. He decided to grab his jacket and zipped it up all the way, pulling the hood up over his head. Then he took his flashlight and headed out. He got to the edge of the woods and called her name.

Nothing. It was so frustrating to think he heard something and then when he called out, nothing would happen. Only more silence. The wind was blowing through the trees and that was the only noise. He stood at the edge of the woods waiting, with his light shining into the trees. He called out occasionally, hoping to hear back from her.

Elizabeth was about at the end of her rope. Her energy was gone. She was so tired she could hardly put one foot in front of the other. At one point she thought about just dropping the deer and walking out of the woods without the meat they so badly needed. But she'd come so far now that she hated to quit. She knew the wolves were back there. She could hear them in the background howling. She was shivering but determined to make it back to the cabin. It was just a slow process that couldn't be hurried.

She called out to Jim off and on, hoping he would hear and know she was okay. Once she thought she heard her name, but it was faint. She tried again and heard nothing, but she did see a light in the far distance. It had to be Jim.

Suddenly she heard the wolves coming closer and turned to shine her light behind her. The light hit their eyes and they were upon her. She fired the rifle once and they moved back away from her, hiding in the undergrowth under the trees. But she knew she'd only bought some time. She yelled out again and kept on moving forward, keeping an eye on things behind her by shining her light into the trees and moving it around to see if she could see their eyes again.

They are not going to give up the deer. She knew she should drop it and run but she hated letting them win. She stopped and reloaded her rifle, put her backpack on her shoulder, and picked up the carcass. She called out to Jim about five times and finally she heard him say her name. It echoed into the woods. She was getting closer to him.

Jim heard her voice and hobbled back to the cabin to get the bow. He wanted to have something to defend her if animals were coming behind her after the deer meat. He called to her, trying to get a bearing of where she was. The echo was throwing both of them off in pinpointing where the other one was.

She saw the rags tied on the tree limbs so she knew she was close. *The wolves are still following me. It's crazy how they won't give it up.* Without any warning, one of them lunged forward and tried to grab the deer out of her hand. In a split second the other wolves were on the deer, pulling against her. She fell to her knees and let go of it, calling out to Jim. He was moving as fast as he could when he saw the light of her flashlight. He shined the light on the wolves, stopped and pulled the bow out and set the arrow. He aimed at one of the wolves, hitting it square in the side. Elizabeth had grabbed her rifle by then and fired a shot in the air. The wolves fled deep into the woods but Elizabeth knew they had only bought time again. She stood up and took the ears of the deer and dragged it to the edge of the woods, allowing Jim to help her as best he could. He was so glad to see her that he almost cried. He saw tears coming down her face.

"Come on, Lizzie. We're almost back to the cabin. I want you inside and safe from these ravenous wolves. They want the meat. They're starving. But so are we. We need that meat and I'll be damned if we're going to give it to them after you've fought so hard to bring it home."

She smiled through her tears of exhaustion and nodded. "I wasn't going to drop that deer for anything. But I knew there was a limit as to what I could do. Those animals were ruthless. It was almost a losing battle and I was getting tired. I think they sensed my weakness."

They walked up to the cabin and Jim opened the door so she could get inside.

He took the hatchet and knelt down and dressed the deer and then dragged the carcass to the edge of the woods. He knew the wolves were there, watching. They seemed fearless, even with the last gunshot. He took the meat inside and got a bucket of snow and placed it on a tray in the refrigerator. This amount of fresh meat would last them a while. And he knew Elizabeth had to be starving. He skewered some meat and put it on the fire for both of them. Then he walked over to where she was sitting on the sofa and sat down beside her, wrapping his arms around her. She leaned into him and closed her eyes. She couldn't believe she was at the cabin at last.

"I really wondered if I was going to make it, Jim."

"I wondered myself. But I had faith in you, Liz. You've done some pretty amazing things since the crash. I think you reached your limit today, though. No more hunting at dusk. I'm putting my foot down."

She smiled. "That's about all you have, Jim, is a foot."

He laughed. "Let's take your boots off and warm your feet by the fire. I want to heat some snow and let you wash your face and hands. You've got to be absolutely exhausted, Liz. But you did bring the meat home. And for that I am thankful."

"Thank God I made it, Jim. They were right on top of me at the end. I'm glad you got one of them. I wasn't completely overtaken with fear until I was almost home. I knew they were behind me, which was a great disadvantage for me. Especially in the dark."

"No kidding. Now I want you to relax and sip some of this watered down coffee I fixed for you. And eat some of this meat. It's good and it's fresh."

"I never thought I'd be out there that long. And it seemed to take forever to get back. I haven't mentioned the ravine I fell into right after I shot the deer. That's what started this fiasco in the first place."

"A ravine? Oh, my gosh! I'm glad I didn't know that was happening. I'd have lost my mind. I worried the whole time you were out there."

"Stupid move on my part. But the snow was so deep I couldn't really see how steep the ravine was. And when I fell, I dropped my rifle on the edge of the ravine. When I climbed up to get it, I was looking square into the face of another wolf. The pack was already on the deer I shot. This one lone wolf was staring me down."

"How did you keep your cool?"

"I have no idea. My father told me to stare them down. Not look away. It worked until I reached for my gun. It was odd; almost seemed like he knew what that rifle was. He lunged as I reached and I got off a shot. It made the pack run away and bought me some time."

"I know all about bought time. So glad you are here, angel."

He hugged her again and kissed her forehead. She pulled off her jacket and boots and watched as he brought in the bucket of hot water. She walked into the kitchen and washed her face and hands and then went back to the sofa and soaked her feet. It felt so good to be warm and safe. Jim came over and pulled her up next to him and they stayed there for an hour or so, just watching the fire and talking in low voices. When it was time to go to bed, she climbed in and was pulling the covers up when he got in bed. He smiled and lay down beside her, holding her close. She fell asleep in his arms, dead to the world.

Jim remained awake feeling her breathe, loving the feeling of closeness. He wished more than anything that she would let him love her. He wanted to take her home with him and take care of her. Not just for the night, but for the rest of her life. If she could only let her guard down and trust instead of waiting for a dream to come true with an old boyfriend who was now a grown man she didn't really know anymore. He felt so close to her. So complete with her.

In the night he finally slipped into a deep sleep and she awoke feeling his arms around her. For once she didn't pull away and allowed herself to enjoy his covering. But when she closed her eyes the face she saw was Tom. He was smiling at her. She was weary of the pull and knew she would find out what it all was about when they made it back to their lives. Jim had been very good to her during this catastrophe. He asked nothing of her and she gave very little. But this love of his was finding its way into her heart. One snowy footstep at a time.

Chapter 33

The weaving of two hearts can happen so subtly that the two people involved aren't wholly aware of it. The slipping of the guard, the tearing down of walls, can be done in silence. Without strain. Elizabeth woke up on Tuesday morning with her legs entangled in Jim's. At first she felt nervous and then she relaxed. Every bone in her body ached. She felt like she'd been beaten. And the fear she'd felt when the wolves were at her back dissipated as soon as she'd seen Jim walking on his crutches towards her. In spite of her feelings for Tom, the kindness Jim had shown her throughout this whole fiasco had changed her attitude about him. Even though in some ways they were strangers, they knew more about each other than if they'd dated for months. They'd been forced into an intimacy that might have put an unforgiveable strain on their newly formed friendship. However, in this case, this one situation, it had worked just the opposite. She didn't move because she wasn't ready to get up and face the cold. The fire had obviously gone out and the room was freezing. But underneath the covers they had created enough warmth to sleep through the night without shivering. It was a miracle, nothing short of a miracle, that the both of them had not fallen sick with pneumonia. Or worse.

As she lay there beside Jim she went over the entire day yesterday. The hunt for a deer that had turned into a nightmare. She'd been so shocked to see the pack of wolves so close to her. The whole week she'd been hunting and walking back and forth from the cabin to the crash site, she'd never seen any wolves. Then all of a sudden there's a whole pack of them, and the one lone wolf staring right at her.

Her heart started beating faster remembering how it felt to stare that wolf down. She'd done well. She knew her father would agree. But it was a stupid move to come down that hill so quickly. She was too eager to get the deer back to the cabin. However, by that time she'd spotted the wolves and it was too late to alter her course. The fall into the ravine was a terrible mishap, but dropping her rifle was worse. When she had to face that wolf it aged her five years but also gave her an unbelievable feeling of strength. There was no time for fear. It was clear what she had to do, and if she didn't do it she would most likely die.

It was cloudy outside. She'd forgotten what the sun felt like. Especially in the morning. There were no curtains on the bedroom window but the sun had not awakened them once since they'd discovered the cabin. She yearned for the brightness and warmth of the sun. And the sound of a plane or helicopter that was going to take them out of there. She was more than ready to go home. And she knew Jim was eager to get back to his practice. When she thought of all the hours of waiting that moved like a sloth, and the hours of watching it snow...waiting for night so they could fall asleep...she felt like she just couldn't take it anymore. But the restlessness had to go. Because as long as she resisted the fact that they were not in control of their lives at the moment, the more difficult it would be to remain in that cabin. They were snowbound in the worst sense of the word. The lack of communication was the most difficult thing to deal with, especially in the techno age they were living in. At home she had numerous ways to contact someone. Here there was a smoke signal and that was about it. She didn't even know for sure if the transponder was sending out any signal at all. In fact, the way things had been going since the crash, she would almost bet that it was dead.

She slipped out of Jim's grip and rolled on her side, watching him sleep. Was this a man she could spend her life with? Have his children?

Grow old with? How would she know the answer to that question until she'd given Tom a chance? Was she stupid to keep on pushing that issue, when Jim was right here, right now, wanting to love her? Those questions plagued her every single day. And she knew that she'd probably hurt Jim more than once when he reached out to her. She was not giving him any signals except for the two times she'd kissed him, that there was any hope at all for their relationship to grow. If it hadn't worked out like it did, if she hadn't just seen Tom right before leaving for this trip, then she wouldn't be in this dilemma.

She almost reached out to touch his hand, but it would wake him up and she knew he probably needed the sleep. Even though she was sick of having to get up first, she rolled out of bed and tiptoed into the living room to see what shape the fire was in.

As usual, the coals were hot but the flame was gone. She added more wood and stirred the coals and it started to smoke and finally burn. She sat there warming her body until the flames were high and licking the raw wood. It felt so good to be warm.

"Hey, woman. You hogging all the heat around here?"

She turned and smiled. "Didn't want to wake you up; you were sleeping so soundly."

"Yeah, I was. But when you left the bed, I suddenly felt cold. You took the warmth with you, I think."

"Never thought of it that way. But it does take two of us to warm up that bed. I was freezing when I stepped out from under the covers. So tired of feeling cold."

"I'm tired of these dirty clothes. I'm going to burn them one day."

"Oh, gosh! You don't know how I hate my clothes right now. I don't even think about them anymore, though, because they have grown to my body. I'm not even sure I could get them off."

"Gross. That's a sick thought."

"Wouldn't you give anything to know the forecast for the next week? Is it ever going to stop snowing?"

"Nothing lasts forever, dear one. We haven't been gone but just a week. It feels like much longer because of the struggle we've had."

" A little over. It is so hard to believe. And I imagine my parents and Joe and Leigh are frantic. I keep thinking, maybe tomorrow. Just one more day here. And they just keep going by one at a time. At least we have more deer meat to eat. That was quite an adventure out there."

"Ha! An adventure? It was nuts. Absolutely crazy. You came so close to being mauled by those wolves. It's not going to happen twice, if I'm alive. No more going out alone at dusk."

"Okay, okay. I've learned my lesson. It was a fluke thing. Think of all the times I've been out hunting before and never saw one wolf. It surprised me to see such a large pack. They were hungry. That was obvious."

"Speaking of hungry, how about some deer meat this morning?"

"Sounds good. I've got to cut some small branches and make new skewers; those in the kitchen are burnt to a crisp."

Jim laughed and watched her go outside. The cold air came rushing in and he grabbed his jacket and zipped it up, moving closer to the warm fire. He was so grateful that they weren't still at the crash site. The cabin had turned into a nice haven for them, and the fireplace was doing a great job at heating the small rooms. He thought about the time when they did get rescued, wondering how he was going to feel when she had to return to Knoxville. All of his thoughts would be about how to get her back to Montana again. Or when he could make a trip to Knoxville. They'd spent so much time together that it would feel weird not having her around. Real weird.

And then there was the question of Tom. The thing that haunted her would become his worst nightmare. He knew she was going to contact him and he was so afraid that being away from him, she would forget the closeness they'd developed and seek to rekindle the flame that burned between her and Tom.

He didn't know if he could handle being away from her. He wanted to marry her and take her home with him. But that was out of the question. There was no way in hell she'd agree to that. But he was sure of her. He knew he loved her. She was on the fence and caught up in the emotions of a past relationship. What he feared was that she was so far into the hope of renewing her love for Tom that she was missing the rare connection they had found with each other.

Sometimes happiness is in front of our nose and we just can't see it because we are looking for it somewhere else. He decided to find a way to make his case to her before they were rescued. There was no point in waiting much longer because as soon as they were found, she would be going home. He might not ever see her again if Tom got hold of her. And he was going to do everything he could do make sure that didn't happen.

The decision to stay inside was made early in the day. The weather had remained the same; cold and snowy. So Jim and Liz made the call that it might be smart if they just hunkered down and made the best of the day inside. Liz did go out to cut more firewood and bring it inside. But they both spent the rest of the day taking naps, eating more meat, and they sat in front of the fire telling stories of their past.

Liz seemed more relaxed than he'd seen her since the crash. She laughed easier and didn't pull away if he reached out to her. He thought it might be a good time to revisit their relationship and his desires. This was one time when there was nowhere for her to run. He didn't want to corner her, but at the same time, if she was going to contact Tom as soon as she got home, he knew he'd better say all he had to say now while she was face to face with him.

He waited for her to get up from her nap. She came out of the bedroom and sat on the floor next to the fire, stirring the logs and warming her face. He sat on the end of the sofa near her and rubbed her neck for a moment.

"Liz, could you come up here beside me for a moment. I wish I could get on the floor, but my leg is a problem with this splint."

She moved up to the sofa and sat back, looking at him with questioning look.

"What's on your mind, Jim? You've been quiet this afternoon and I can tell something is on your mind."

He smiled but it was a weak one. "I do have a lot of thoughts running through my head. Ninety percent of them are about you. The other ten are about my work."

"I'm sure you're exaggerating about me. You care to share what you're thinking about?"

"Liz, I know you're tired of me telling you that I have fallen for you. You're going to say that it's too fast, and normally it would be. But we haven't had a normal relationship. Not one square inch of it has been normal. You have to admit I'm right about that."

"I do agree. So where is this leading?"

"I'm smart enough to know that when you get home the first thing you're going to do is contact Tom."

Liz winced and turned her head towards the fire.

"You don't have to say anything. I'm not asking you to defend yourself. But I want you to think about how well we've gotten along this whole week. Look what we've shared. What we've lived through. It's been absolutely amazing and I feel I've learned so much about you. I know you have to feel that way about me. Tell me you do."

"Of course I know you better. We've been roommates out here in the frigging middle of nowhere for a week and had to depend on each other to survive. I love how we get along and you have been a perfect gentleman. I never dreamed this would happen, even though I packed for the worst possible scenario. You've been very brave, Jim, and I've come to know what kind of man you really are."

"But how do you feel towards me, Liz? Can you tell me that?"

She sat and stared at the fire, running her fingers through her ponytail. "I really don't know how I feel, Jim. To be honest, I have strong feelings towards you, but I'm trying not to focus on them because this little nightmare we've lived in is going to end at some point and we will go back to our lives, or what is left of them. You live a good distance away from me. It won't be convenient to see each other. It has crossed my mind many times that it would be a struggle to keep up the intensity of a relationship when we live so far apart."

Jim nodded and stood up, moving towards the fire to warm his leg. "I agree totally. And I realize some of what I feel isn't reality. This way we have been forced to live here in this cabin alone in the woods isn't reality. When we get back to our lives, we will be hit with that. And it will snatch us away from each other, or try to. I'm not sure I want that to happen. I really am falling in love with you, and I just don't say that lightly. I love who you are."

Liz blushed and looked down. "You are making it very difficult for me to remain neutral. And I know how much you hate my passiveness. But is it wise for us to just give in to our feelings while cooped up in this small cabin, when we know things might be very different once we get back to our routines?"

"Usually it's the woman that's falling too soon. The woman who has all the emotion. But this time it's me. And I'm a doctor, for God's sake. I know all about life and death and the ins and outs of reality. For some reason you've gotten under my skin and I don't want to let you go. The thought of you calling Tom and meeting him somewhere really bothers me. I've become very protective of you. I falsely feel like you are mine. I'm just being honest here, Liz. I'm trying to let you know my feelings; where I'm coming from."

She turned and looked at him. He was a handsome man with blue eyes that were clear and true. He stood straight and had a great stride even with the bad leg. She felt pretty safe with him and admired his tenacity. They had made the transition smoothly to the pattern of her taking the lead in so many areas. He never fought her about the decision she made concerning hunting for food or her going alone to the crash site. They had begun to really trust each other's judgment. But she felt hesitant to let herself go with him. And he was feeling it strongly.

She stood and walked over to where he was standing near the fire. She raised up on her tiptoes and kissed his cheek. "I appreciate all that you are telling me. I know it's tough to open up like that. Especially for a man. And I know why you are doing it. I don't blame you one bit for wanting to protect me. I might not like another woman moving in on you right now, either. But I'm smart enough to know that when you go back home, things may not feel the same as they do right now. That could happen to either or both of us. I think we need to see how things are when we get back to our lives. Making any decisions now would be setting us up to fail."

He took her face in his hands and leaned over and kissed her slowly. She didn't move away, and he was so glad. He kissed her again, this time deeply. He felt her stirring and pulled his head back to look into her dark eyes. "I just love you. Is that so bad a thing to say to you?"

She smiled slightly and leaned her head on his shoulder. "No, it isn't bad, Jim. It's very sweet." She looked up at him and stared closely into his eyes.

Just for a moment their eyes locked and he thought he saw a tear forming in her eyes. "Don't be so afraid to let me in, Liz. We don't have to commit to each other. But let me in a little bit. I'm not going to bite. I'm not going to force you to do anything at all. Just let me in."

For a second something hit her and she got angry. All the emotions that she'd felt for so long came rushing into her mind and she suddenly felt like Jim was trying to take advantage of the situation to get his way.

"How can you do this, Jim? How can you push me to feel what you feel in a week's time? Give me a break here. I've been through hell the last seven days and have taken care of both of us beyond what I thought I was capable of doing. I'm worn out and scared and sick of being here. You've caught me at my most vulnerable time. I—"

He grabbed her and kissed her hard. "Stop it, Liz. Slow down. I'm not taking advantage of this situation at all, and you know it. I need you to be honest with yourself, is all. I want you to allow your feelings to surface because I see them in your eyes. You've kissed me on your own. You've given me signs here and there. But I know you are holding back for Tom. I just ask you to let me in. Give me a chance. And stop waiting for some fine day that may never happen with Tom, when you are sitting here in this tiny cabin during the worst snowstorms in the history of Montana with a man who is in love with you. I know you feel it. I know you feel something strong. I'm only asking you to let it come out if it's in there. Don't keep holding back until it's too late. There's no guarantee that you and Tom will get back together. We've been given this time with each other and I want to make sure we don't miss a chance to have a relationship of a lifetime. Do you get that?"

She nodded and hugged him, not wanting the moment to go any farther. The fire felt so good and the room was filled with warmth and peace. The only thing better would have been to hear the sound of a chopper dropping out of the sky to find them. But she knew in hoping that, that everything would change as soon as they were found. It would set in motion a series of events that would pull them apart and that separation was going to be painful for both of them.

They stood there for a while allowing each other their own separate thoughts. He held her hand and stayed by the fire with her, rocking back and forth, listening to the wood crackle under the flame. And inside each of them was a similar flame that needed more time. More freedom. And a belief that it was supposed to remain and not be snuffed out with all the reasons they could come up with that would make it impossible to last. They were in their own little cocoon and the world passed them by for one more night.

Chapter 34

"Jesse, this is Mark Gallagher with NTSB. We know how concerned you are about your daughter being down in the Beartooth Mountain area. We've been waiting on a much needed break from this tremendous front that has hung over that area this whole last week. I think we are going to get a small window of time today to search for the wreckage. Hopefully, we will have some news for you before nightfall. I just hope this time the weather holds out. We sent up a chopper not too long ago and they had to return pretty quickly. The weather changes so fast there that we can't count on anything for very long."

Jesse felt his heart rate increase as he listened to the good news. "I've been waiting on your call. You don't know how worried we are that we've lost our daughter and her friend to the elements, if not the crash."

"I've seen this many times, unfortunately. And I do know your worry. But we will do what we can once we get airborne. These men are trained and will find the downed plane, but we just cannot make any promises about loss of life. That all remains to be seen. I understand your daughter is a seasoned pilot."

"She is good. And trained well. But the conditions are so treacherous on those mountains that I should not have allowed her to make the trip. We just weren't sure about how long the conditions would hold. Now we know."

"Don't beat yourself up, Jesse. We'll find your daughter. Just pray to God that she is still alive. Both of them. I'll keep in touch with you and let you know the minute we find anything."

"I'll be sitting here by the phone, Mark. No matter what news you have, I need to hear from you."

"Got it. Stand by, Jesse. Talk to you soon."

Jesse put the phone down and blew out a deep breath. Martha could read his face like a book.

"They going to send up a chopper?"

Jesse nodded. He didn't want to talk too much about it. "Yep. We'll hear one way or the other from them today, unless the weather closes in on them again. We got to pray, Martha, that they are still alive. I'll be so glad when this is over, I don't know what to do."

"Me too, Jess. It's been long enough now. We need to know one way or the other. And if they are still alive, they need to get off that mountain before they die."

Jim woke as soon as the light hit his eyelids. The room was so bright it hurt his eyes to open them. It suddenly occurred to him that the sun was shining. It wasn't a clear blue sky, but the sun had found a small hole to shine through and it was blinding at first. Then a smile came across his face. The thought ran through his mind like the speed of light that this might be the day they were rescued. He stretched slowly and turned over to see Elizabeth lying there with her eyes closed. He reached over to touch her and she spoke quietly, never opening her eyes.

"Either you have a flashlight shining right on my face or the sun has decided to shine this morning."

"You sure know how to kill a surprise."

"How could I miss it? We haven't seen the sun for well over a week and it's so lit up in this room that it hurts my eyes."

Jim laughed. "Can you believe it? This means a chopper will be out today looking for us. We might be rescued at some point! Aren't you excited?"

She turned slowly and cracked her eyes open. "I have the worst headache known to man and I am awakened with nothing short of a laser light shining in my eyes, and Mr. Happy next to me in bed. Can you give me a sec?"

He laughed and got out of bed. "Oh, come on. We've been waiting for this day for what seems like forever. I know you are excited."

Liz sat up and rubbed her eyes. "My first question is, where did you put the ibuprofen?"

"I think we have one left. I'll find it for you."

"That would be so kind." She fell back on her pillows and a smile formed on her lips. "Rescued." Had a nice ring to it.

Jim brought her the pain pill that would smother the grouchiness in her and gave her a sip of water.

"I sure hope this works, 'cause this is a mother of all headaches. Can you start up the fire and get us some breakfast? I will get up and help. Just need to let this pill work a minute."

"You go right ahead. If the chopper shows up, I'll tell them you're not ready to go today. We need one more day to get rid of your headache."

That brought a chuckle out of her mouth, but she muffled it in the pillows. Her heart was beating fast and the excitement was building. *Could this possibly be the day when they would be found?* It seemed like they'd been in the cabin for weeks on end. She'd lost all track of time. Her real life seemed so far away, and she knew Jim felt the same way. Odd how a tragic event could erase anything that had taken place in your life that seemed so important. Suddenly only one thing was critical. That was staying alive.

The aroma of deer meat sizzling wafted into the bedroom and got her out from under the covers. The warmth she'd slept in was gone and the coldness of the room swallowed up any remaining warmth on her skin. It was freezing in the cabin. She could see her breath. She wrapped her jacket around her and hurried into the living room to stand in front of the fire. Never again would she complain about her electric bill. Or her water bill. She would've killed for a hot shower.

"Here's your breakfast, and I managed to scrape the last bit of coffee out of the jar for both of us. It's pretty watered down, but it's hot."

"So kind of you," she said sarcastically, but there was a slight smile lingering on her lips. "Thanks, Jim. Not sure why my head is hurting so badly."

"It's so cold that it's no surprise to me. Your body has been beat up pretty good lately. I'm very proud of you."

She grimaced and shook her head. "That was a pretty tough call out there with the wolves. Stupid on my part. I knew better. But the hill threw me. Running downhill and dropping my gun was the worst thing that could happen, but it did. I'm so glad I was able to kill that one wolf that was behind me. I never saw him. I wasn't paying attention like my father taught me. The whole thing went by so fast."

"You did fine. Stop beating yourself up. Um, you're not a type A personality or anything, are you? As if I didn't know. I mean, does everything have to go perfectly all the time for you?"

"Heck, no. But when it's a matter of life and death, you pretty much better be right."

"I can so relate to that. I'm just glad it's over. You're safe. I was worried sick, Liz."

"I know you were and I was very glad to see you coming. I was going to be a meal for them if you hadn't shown up. A very close call."

"Let's not rehash it. We need to be looking for a rescue chopper today. It really should happen with the weather clearing up a little bit."

Elizabeth walked over to the door and opened it, letting in a cold rush of air. She looked outside, squinting in the bright sunlight, and took in a deep breath. She noticed some blue sky between layers of gray clouds, and her hopes shot sky high. She closed the door and leaned against it smiling.

"You could be right, Jim. We just might be rescued today. That's going to feel so weird. I mean we've been in this cabin for what seems like ages. And the whole crash thing seems so far away. Does it to you?"

"It does. But my leg is a reminder of the whole situation. And we have no more ibuprofen. So I have had to bear the pain of it without any help from drugs. I'll be glad to get this taken care of."

"You've handled it very well. I'm sick of eating deer meat and rabbit. I cannot wait for some real food. But it did keep us alive. I'm not taking anything away from that."

"Liz, we could walk to the crash site. I mean, is that a possibility or do I need to shelve that idea?"

She thought for a few moments and rubbed her face. She leaned over and picked up a small piece of deer meat that was sitting on the sofa and popped it into her mouth. He laughed at her and sat down, waiting for her answer.

"I think it might be a good idea. But we may get there and the chopper doesn't show up. Then we have to walk through a lot of snow back to this cabin. It has snowed so much in the last couple days since the last time we made that trip. Remember how long it was and how cold?"

Jim shrugged and nodded. "How could I forget? My leg nearly killed me. But we did make it. It just took longer because I couldn't walk fast."

"We can build up this fire so that perhaps they would see the smoke from the air. I'm pretty sure they could. And there will be no fire at the crash site. The plane is nearly covered up in snow. That worries me a little because they will be looking for the fuselage. I guess we could pack some meat and take our backpacks and extra clothes and walk back to the site with the knowledge that they might not show up. We can build a big fire so that they will have no trouble spotting us from a low altitude. These men are good. They do this for a living and they know these mountains. I really think they'll find us pretty quick if we have a fire."

"Sounds like a good plan. Let's get dressed. I need to get some snow and melt it to wash up a little. We can pack our bags and if you'll get the deer meat, then we will be just about ready to go. What time is it, anyway? My watch is on the nightstand."

Liz glanced at her watch. "It's 9:00. We need to get going so we will have plenty of time to build a huge fire. It's kind of exciting, Jim."

He looked at her as he opened the front door to gather some snow. Even though her hair was a mess and she looked worn out and dirty, she was beautiful to him. She saw him looking at her and a smile ran across her face before she could pull it back. He almost spoke but didn't. She stared at him for a nanosecond, thinking what a perfect gentleman he'd been the whole time. Always saying the right thing. And even though they'd had to share the same bed, he never made a wrong move. Never pushed her. She did love his eyes. His laughter. His mind. So why was she holding back? What was she waiting for? Maybe he was right; maybe her time with Tom would never come. And then she would have missed a chance to have something wonderful with Jim.

He walked outside and came back with some snow, melting it over the fire just until it was lukewarm. He poured some in a bowl for her and then washed his face and hands. The soap was so small but it still gave him some lather. He packed his backpack and put it on his back, and walked back into the living room where she was packing her bag. He came near to her and she turned around. Their faces were inches apart. He was afraid to move, but he sensed that she was ready. He thought he saw her lean in slowly. He reached out and touched her arm and she didn't move away. He whispered to her softly.

"Lizzie, let me hold you. I want to feel you close to me."

She moved a little closer and he wrapped his arms around her. She laid her head on his shoulder, and there were tears that he could barely see running down her cheeks.

"You've been through so much, Lizzie. Let me take some of the weight of this off your back. I love you, Liz. I know it's fast, but we've been through a lifetime of emotions out here on our own. I—"

She pulled back, almost making him feel like he'd said the wrong thing. But she spoke in a whisper to him and he leaned forward to hear it.

"I've been thinking, Jim. Maybe you are right. I haven't given you much of a chance and you've been wonderful to me. I do care for you. I like you a lot. I don't know about the word 'love.' Haven't used it in years. But I need that in my life. I am ready for it."

She stood there with tears streaming down her face, and he couldn't take it anymore. He pulled her to him and kissed her hard on the mouth. He held her close to him and kissed her over and over. She finally wrapped her arms around his neck and they embraced, and it was then she cried like she had wanted to since the crash. All the emotions she'd been feeling came to a head and she just let them out while he held her. It nearly broke his heart, but he stood there like a rock until the crying stopped. He wouldn't dare move for fear she would take that as a bad sign. He would have stood there for an eternity if it meant he would have a chance to love her.

"You are so good to me, Jim. I'm sorry I've been so hard to read. I don't even know how to read myself. Much less let you in on my feelings. I guess I've shut out men for too long and dove into my work. Out here we've had to survive so I had that to think about. And yes, Tom. But like you said, there are no promises with him. I don't know him anymore. And he doesn't know me. It would be like starting over."

"That's all I'm asking you to do, Liz. Think about it from a distance and just allow your feelings for me to come out enough so that you can decide if you really like being around me or not. This situation we are in is extraordinary. Nothing normal about it. We both may feel totally different when we get back to our real lives. But I just know how I feel right now. I don't want to put either one of us on the spot or force something to happen between us. I think it's already there, frankly. Anyway, holding you feels good and I am grateful that you have opened up a little bit. I need to hear what you are thinking and feeling. It matters to me."

Liz nodded and wiped her face. "I guess we need to get going. It felt good to have this talk and I appreciate how sweet you are to me, Jim." She leaned over and kissed his cheek and turned around to leave.

Jim pulled her to him one more time and kissed her mouth. "Just one for the road. It's going to be cold out there and I know we are going to get tired. I love you, lady. Remember that, will you?"

"I will, Jim. Now let's get going. If we keep on, we'll never leave this cabin."

That wasn't such a bad thought to Jim as they headed out the door. The cold air hit them both in the face, a constant reminder of just how cold it was on the mountain. Their breath froze in the air and they had to adjust again to the wind blowing in their faces. The cold air went straight to their bones. But they both knew they were possibly heading towards a rescue and that kept them warm inside. The hope of being rescued off the side of the mountain was enough to give them the energy to keep on going. Their boots made footprints in the snow that had fallen during the night. In places it was very deep. But they plodded on, Jim with his crutches and Liz with a heavy backpack full of water and deer meat. Hopefully this would be their last trek to the crash site.

The silence outside caused them to remain quiet as they walked away from the cabin. They were both lost in their own thoughts, as had happened many times as they sought refuge from the frigid weather outside. It was going to be a long hike but this time they had real hope. And their ears were listening for the sound of a chopper off in the distance. At the moment there was nothing but the call of a bird they could not see echoing around the mountains.

Chapter 35

"Base to three."

"Three, go ahead."

"Where is your location?"

"We're finishing four and moving to grid five."

"Okay. Base out."

The helicopter lowered its altitude and the two men studied the area within the fifth grid. The sun was so bright that the reflection off the snow was blinding. But they were determined to find the crash site. There were two other choppers in the air and each had a set of grids to cover while the window of opportunity was there. A forecast for snow in the evening was always in the back of their mind. The weather changed quickly on the mountain this time of year, so they wanted to make the most of their time. The two people in the crash had been on the ground for over a week. If they were alive, they needed to be rescued off the mountain or their chances of survival would be very slim.

After four hours of searching, the clouds covered the sun and fog moved in over the mountain. The choppers were signaled to fly back to base. The sound of the helicopters echoed across Beartooth Mountain as they gained altitude and speed. The search was cut short but they could hope for a better day of searching tomorrow. Pressure was coming from the family of Elizabeth Stone to locate the plane and rescue the two people. No one was talking about the reality that they might not find them alive.

Liz was walking slowly so that Jim didn't push too hard. The snow was deep and wet. Harder to walk through. Their feet were freezing and their hands were getting cold. As soon as they hit the crash site they started building a fire so they could warm their bodies. They were beginning to wonder if they'd made a bad mistake. The sun was still out when they arrived at the site, but they could see that the clouds were building again. Jim saw disappointment creeping up on Liz's face and he was worried she would get depressed.

"I know you're watching the weather. It doesn't look good, Lizzie. I really thought they would find us, but we just may not make that goal today."

"I know. It's very disheartening. I thought I heard a chopper while we were walking, but I didn't say anything because I wasn't dead sure. Let's get this fire going because if there's a chance in a million that they're looking for us, I want them to have a signal of smoke to look at. We're going to make it easy for them."

Jim knew it was probably futile, but he helped place limbs on the already burning fire. It took so much out of him to walk so far in the deep snow, and now they were going to have to head back to the campsite or spend a cold night inside the plane. And there was no promise of what the weather would be like tomorrow.

"I know what you're thinking. They aren't going to find us today. That's great. We walked all the way over here for nothing, except to wear ourselves out, freeze to death, and build a frigging fire."

"Now, Liz. Don't get upset. I'm just as tired as you are. It's so dang cold out here that both of us are risking hypothermia, but we thought there was a good chance a chopper would be out. We've missed them, Liz. They've come and gone. The window of time was short and they had to return to base."

Liz looked at him and shrugged. "Now what do we do? Walk back to the cabin? Or do we stay here for the night?"

Jim looked around. It was no longer a place where he wanted to be. The cabin had become a safe haven and it was too cold to sleep outside anymore. "All our food is in the cabin except for the deer meat you brought with you. And we can sleep warmer in the cabin. I hate it that we have to hike back; I don't want to do it again. But we have no choice, do we?"

"No. I just wanted to hear it, I guess."

"Nothing's changed, Liz. We are making it fine. We have food and water and a way to stay warm. A bed to sleep on. And we can keep each other sane until they find us. And they will find us, I promise you that."

Liz sat down on a log near the fire and warmed her feet. Jim followed suit and sat beside her, letting his legs stretch out near the flames. They sat in silence for the longest time, just enjoying the heat from the fire. It was a huge bonfire and after about twenty minutes Liz stood up and got a long stick, put some meat on it, and held it over the flames. The smell of venison rose in the air and with it came a hunger for food. It didn't take long before the meat was done and they were sitting on the log eating it. They melted snow and drank lots of water before deciding to head back to the cabin. They couldn't wait too long because it would get dark, and they knew all too well about the wolves that were in the area. Neither of them wanted a confrontation with the wolves again. For this time they just might lose the battle.

On the long way back to the cabin, Liz spotted some rabbits and pulled out her small pistol and shot one of them. It meant she had to haul it home draped over her shoulder, but having something besides deer meat made the burden lighter. She was cognizant of the trail of blood she was leaving as she walked through the white snow. But they kept on walking, determined to make it back before it got dark or more snow fell. The woods were quiet and both of them chose to be silent for most of the first hour. It was a good time to just get lost in their own thoughts, but finally Jim broke the silence.

"I sure thought today would be the day."

"Don't even say it out loud. My mind was going in the same direction."

"First real day of sun and it just felt right, if you know what I mean."

"Hard to figure. But I know the window of time that it was safe to be out there in a chopper must have closed up and when that happens, they have to get out. It's just too risky."

Jim shook his head. His arms were so tired of walking with the branch crutches that sores were developing in his arm pits. He winced at every step.

"I get that part and I know your family is worried to death and my secretary is wondering if I'm dead or alive. It's not all about us. But in a way it is, Liz. They have no way of knowing if we're dead or alive, so we're the ones living out this nightmare alone on this frigging mountain. I would've been happy if the owner of the cabin would have showed up. He'd have a heck of a story to tell, wouldn't he?"

That brought a smile to her lips. "No kidding! No one would believe him, though. What are the odds of two survivors of a small plane crash ending up in his cabin trying to survive one of the worst winters this mountain has seen in years?"

"Pretty slim. But I think you have a habit of beating the odds. Look at you acquiring Walmart as a client! That's pretty amazing in and of itself. And you're a pilot. Not too good a one, I might add."

She threw him a dirty look and sneered. "I got you down safely, now didn't I?"

He laughed and it echoed across the mountains around them. "Well, yeah. But we could have been killed, the both of us. Do you remember what actually happened?"

"It hit us pretty fast. A wind came up and the weather had turned. I had to make instantaneous decisions that were going to determine whether we lived or died. I somehow remembered seeing the cabin in the woods or thought it was a building of sorts. Glad I recalled that part. It has been a blessing to have a bed to sleep in. Can you imagine what shape we would be in if we'd had to spend the nearly two weeks in the fuselage of that plane?"

Jim laughed. "I know one thing. You would be one grouchy woman by now."

They both laughed as they came nearer to the cabin. It was slowly getting dark and they both were tired and hungry. The snow crunched under their boots and although they'd grown accustomed to the cold, their feet were nearly numb from the frigid temperatures. The sky was gray and it almost felt like it could snow again. Jim hurried into the cabin to get a good knife for Liz. She gutted the rabbit and skinned it, preparing the meat so that they could eat some of it immediately. Jim remained in the house and built a good fire so that they could cook the meat. He was starving and the warmth from the fire felt good to his frozen body.

Liz came through the door and slammed it shut, handing the meat to Jim. She took her jacket and boots off and sat down in front of the fire, letting the hot flames that lapped the logs warm her. At that point nothing would've felt better to the two of them than the hot fire's warmth against their faces. The meat sizzled on the flames and dripped juices that caused the flames to flicker and shoot up inside the chimney. The smell was intoxicating and their mouths watered, waiting to get that first bite of rabbit meat.

Jim handed her the skewer and she pulled off some of the meat and placed it on a plate from the kitchen. She blew on it to cool it quicker and took her first bite. He watched her with a smile on his face as she bit into the hot meat and chewed it slowly, with her eyes closed. As messed up as she was, he couldn't keep his eyes off of her. Her jeans were so dirty that they were crispy. Her jacket had blood and dirt smeared on it. Her hair was a total wreck, and both of them were so overdue for a hot soapy shower that it was a joke. He resisted the urge to take her in his arms. He didn't want to ruin her private little moment of eating that rabbit meat. But it was tough on him to watch her and not be able to kiss her and hold her close. He couldn't ever remember loving someone like he loved Liz. And he'd dated his share of women. For some reason he hadn't been able to figure out, she had captured his heart and he couldn't shake it off. Even her attempts at being cold and unresponsive only drew him nearer. She was strong but there was a lovely feminine fragility about her that drove him up the wall.

Liz felt his staring even through the strong flavor of the rabbit that floated on her tongue. She didn't want to open her eyes. She wanted to eat and eat until she was so full she couldn't move. But she longed for vegetables and fruit. Something to drink besides melted snow. A good glass of wine. Anything but water. She cracked her eyes open and saw Jim digging into the meat on his plate. He was beaten up and filthy, his hair was going in ten different directions, and there was no telling what was underneath his fingernails. But she felt a tugging in her heart when she looked at him. It bothered her so much that she got up and went outside to get some snow to melt for hot water. She wanted to clean up and get enough water to wash the plates and the knife she'd used to cut up the rabbit.

She washed her hands and face and rinsed out her mouth, grabbed her toothbrush and used a small amount of toothpaste to clean her teeth. That was the one thing she could clean and she worked at it for a few minutes. When she had rinsed her mouth out she stood up and turned around and Jim was standing a foot from her, smiling.

"You scared me! What are you doing?"

He pulled her up next to him and grinned. "It's quite obvious what I'm doing, don't you think?"

She smiled but turned her face away from him. "You're being silly. Look how filthy your face is! Have you looked in the mirror lately?"

"No, I haven't. What's the point? And besides, you look the same way now, so hush. I want to be close to you."

She leaned in and hugged him, resting her head on his shoulder. It felt good for a moment to just hug.

"Let me get cleaned up and we can enjoy the rest of the evening sitting by the fire. I have some stories to tell you."

She walked away, leaving him to the hot water and what was left of the bar of soap. The fire needed stirring and she stood there moving the logs with a stick, letting her face get warm again. Her legs were tired so she sat down on the sofa and lay back against the cushions, closing her eyes. It wouldn't have taken much for her to have fallen asleep, but Jim was humming in the background and she kept one eye open to watch what he was doing. He had a way of sneaking up on her and she knew his motives weren't altogether innocent. In a few minutes he was right next to her with his bad leg stretched out. He leaned back against the cushions and closed his eyes. But he reached out and touched her hand, grabbing her fingers in his. The two of them dozed off for about an hour, and when they awoke they both were stiff and sore.

"I have a great idea, Liz."

"And what would that be?"

"I'm going to give your feet a massage. Would that feel good?"

"Might be a bad idea. I could be totally worthless if you do that."

"I'll take that risk. Lay the other way and put your feet in my lap."

She didn't argue the point and moved to the arm of the sofa and put her feet up on his legs. He pulled her socks off and started rubbing her feet with his rough fingers, pushing in just the right areas to make her groan.

"You've done this before, I take it?"

"A few times. But mainly I have had it done to me. After working on my feet all day in surgery, I have treated myself to a foot massage. It really was a life saver for me."

She yawned and closed her eyes. "I can certainly see why."

He smiled as he worked on the other foot. "Now don't go to sleep on me. You have to rub my feet, too."

"I didn't sign up for that, did I?"

"I think you did. This isn't a one way street, you know. I walked the same miles you did."

"That you did. And I will gladly rub your feet. But I better do it now, because I'm not going to last much longer."

Liz pulled his one good leg up on the sofa and pulled of his sock. He winced as she dug her fingers into his foot. After working on that foot for a few minutes she got on the floor and pulled off his other sock and worked a little longer on that foot. She wanted to rub his leg a little but he shook his head,

"I can't let you work on my shin right now. It's still too sore and I don't want to do anything to upset it. We have no ibuprofen, you know."

"You're right. I just thought it might feel good for me to rub it. Let's go to bed, I'm really exhausted, Jim."

He agreed and they walked to the bedroom, leaving the dirty socks on the floor by the sofa. Liz peeled off her jacket and jumped into bed, feeling the coolness of the sheets on her bare feet. Jim climbed in behind her and snuggled up against her, putting his feet over hers. They were asleep in five minutes, and neither moved all night. The trip to the crash site was getting harder and harder for them. It was just too cold.

Outside the wind had picked up and a light snowfall covered up their footsteps. Even the blood from the dead rabbit was nearly gone. The only thing that remained was a whitish-gray trail of smoke that found its way up into the dark gray sky from the fire inside the cabin. And one lone wolf who had followed the blood of the rabbit to their door. He sat for a while hoping to catch a scent of the dead rabbit, but after a long while he gave up waiting and walked back into the woods. Snow had a way of erasing everything, and the things it covered took on another shape that was unrecognizable.

Perhaps for the last night they would have in the cabin together, Liz and Jim slept next to each other. Both lost in their dreams; maybe moving in and out of them with this silent dance of love that seemed to elude them in the daylight. It was uncanny how comfortable they had become with each other while trying to survive in the frozen tundra. It was an unpredictable situation that could go either way. Jim moving closer and Liz pulling away. But on that rare occasion that she gave in, she felt a shift in her emotions and heart that could easily nail down the song that was forming between them. A love song. If she didn't pull away too many times.

Chapter 36

It wasn't the echoing sound of a chopper that awakened Liz out of a dead sleep. She sat up in bed and wiped her eyes, her pulse racing. She could have sworn she heard a knock on the door. She glanced over at Jim who was still sound asleep, and shrugged her shoulders. Maybe she'd been dreaming. She lay back down on her pillow and a heard a muffled knock again. She nudged Jim and he opened one eye.

"Jim! I just heard a knock on our door. Who in the world would be coming around here?"

He squinted and checked his watch. It was 9:15. "I have no idea. No one has been around the whole time we've been here. We haven't seen another human being. I better get up and see who's there."

"You're not going alone." She grabbed her shoes and slipped into them, putting on her jacket.

They both walked quickly into the living room and waited for another knock. It seemed forever and their hearts were pounding in their chests wanting to know who was outside the door. Suddenly a loud knock came and someone called out to them.

"Anyone here?" It was a man's voice. In fact, they could hear two male voices.

Jim walked over to the door and opened it up. He must have looked a mess because both men stepped back and the look on their faces was a look of amazement.

"Sorry to bother you sir, but we are looking for Elizabeth Stone and Jim Wilson."

Elizabeth shouted out loud. "Wait! I'm Elizabeth Stone. He's Jim! You must be with Search and Rescue!"

The two officers came in the door and Elizabeth hugged their necks. "I'm Officer Hilton, and this is Officer Jones. We're so glad to finally find you! Your family is going to be so glad that you are alive and well." Officer Hilton grabbed his radio and dialed their base to report the good news. Jim could hear a shout on the other end of the line.

They turned and shook Jim's hand. "Sir, are you okay? It's obvious your leg is injured."

"I'm fine. It's begun to heal and really, I'm fine. We're both in pretty good shape considering what we've been through. You have no idea how happy we are to see you guys! How did you find the cabin?"

Elizabeth pointed to the sofa and the men sat down while Liz and Jim sat on the floor and started the fire up again. The room was freezing.

"It was nothing short of a miracle that we saw your downed plane. We flew over it several times before spotting the wrecked fuselage in the white snow. We saw your supplies in the plane and the fire you'd built which had gone out. But that gave us the knowledge that at least one of you was alive. We searched the surrounding area and saw no sign of life so we started walking and that was when we saw a few rags tied to trees. So we knew we were going in the right direction. Had your fire been lit, we'd have seen the smoke from the air."

Liz looked at Jim and smiled. "The fire was blazing when we went to sleep. But it always burns out before dawn. We kept a fire going at the crash site for days but after we found this cabin, the trips back and forth were just too exhausting for us. You cannot imagine what we've had to do to survive out here. It's so cold that you just cannot be outside for any length of time. However, the walk to the crash site took us over two hours."

The two men were eager to hear how they had survived, but time was of the essence. They needed to get Jim and Liz back to the crash site so that they could get them off the mountain before the weather changed.

"I want to hear all about your story, but we need to get going. How about you two getting your things together, and we'll walk you back to the chopper so we can all get out of here. Otherwise we'll be spending the night on this mountain."

Liz got up and walked into the bedroom with Jim. They looked at each other and there was sadness in their eyes. Jim whispered in a low voice in her ear.

"I've loved every moment here with you, Liz. The ball is rolling now. Our lives are going come rushing back to us with lightning speed. We may feel like we are losing each other, but after our feet are on the ground again, we will find our way back to each other. I love you, Liz. This isn't a fly by night thing. I really want to see you again. Do you understand?"

Tears were rolling down her cheeks. She didn't understand why she didn't feel elated about the rescue. Suddenly it felt like they were leaving a home. She looked around the room and started packing her things, which didn't amount to much. She went into the kitchen and cleaned up the little they'd left out. She decided to leave a short note to the owner of the cabin. They at least deserved to know that two people had used this cabin as a refuge from the cold. It had played a large part in saving their lives. She got her backpack on her shoulder and picked up the rifle that was in the corner. The bow was in the living room and she grabbed it on her way towards the door. Jim had broken up the fire and pushed the logs to the back of the grate so that there was no chance of a fire in the cabin. He stood up with his backpack and crutches and walked to the door, looking back one more time before he closed it. Their eyes met briefly and without a word they both knew things were going to change quickly. The two officers walked ahead of them, making a path in the snow for them to follow.

"Jim, I know what you meant back there. I don't know why I feel so sad. Maybe it's normal. We've been together in a very serious situation and have gotten so close. That cabin felt like home. Boy, it's going to be quite an adjustment hitting real life so fast. Our world moved pretty slow here. I know we'll step right back in line when we get off the plane and go back to our own worlds. But I want you to know I love you, too. You have been so good to me here. I'll never forget that, no matter what happens."

Jim smiled at her as he reached out and brushed a strand of hair off her face. He would miss looking at her when he woke up each morning. He would miss hearing her laugh. And he would even miss her little fits of anger when she wanted her way. But he didn't miss those three words he'd been waiting to hear.

The walk back to the plane was a long cold one, and when they saw the familiar sight of the plane wreckage and the fire pit, they both looked at each other. Liz climbed into the cockpit and pulled the rest of her luggage out of the plane and handed it to Officer Hilton. Then she got Jim's things and pulled them out. She checked the plane for anything else that she needed to remove and remembered the transponder. Joe would want that back. The chopper was waiting and she knew it was time to go home. They all boarded and it took off. The sound of the radio and the voices talking to Officer Jones brought so much back to Liz. It felt good to be off the mountain and headed back to reality. But it was going to be a change for her; more emotional than she expected.

"Your parents have been notified, Liz. They know you both are alive. As soon as we arrive at Bozeman Hospital both of you will be admitted. Jim, you may have some surgery to deal with on that leg, and they may want to keep Liz there overnight. Standard procedure. I want you both to be prepared for the press to hit. They're going to want your story, so better talk with each other and get that story nailed down. Watch who you talk to and what you say. They tend to print things you didn't say, or things you insinuate. Just a warning."

Jim grimaced and looked at Liz. "Never thought about the papers. We've been in the news, I guess. Well, we have quite a story, don't we?"

She smiled, rubbing her eyes. She was tired suddenly. Worn completely out. "Yes, we do. But I don't know if I want it all over the papers. You know?"

"We're not obligated to tell them anything. I'm certain our hometown papers will want to talk to us. But we sure don't have to talk to the press in Bozeman."

Officer Hilton turned around and looked at Liz. "I don't think you understand that America is going to want to know if you were found alive or dead. It's been in the *Wall Street Journal*. You guys were on national news. This is serious stuff here and I just want you to be prepared for what you're going to be faced with. TV shows are going to be contacting you to do an interview. All the local news stations will be vying for your time. Who knows? There may be a movie in the wings about your amazing adventure."

Liz looked out the window of the chopper and shook her head. Her father could handle some of that mess. She had no desire to be on television, although it might not be a bad thing for her career. And for Jim's. The fact that he was a physician was a nice addition to the story. They'd survived pretty treacherous circumstances and the experiences were memorable. She got lost in her thoughts until the chopper landed on the Bozeman Hospital pad. They were greeted by hospital staff, and Jim gladly stepped into a wheelchair.

The next hour was hectic getting admitted into the hospital, but then Liz was able to call her parents and Jim phoned his office. The reaction of Jesse and Martha was overwhelming to Liz. She had a difficult time convincing them that she was perfectly fine. Maybe a little malnourished, but other than that, she felt pretty good. It was amazing to hear their voices and it made her eyes water. She was ready to go home.

"Lizzie? We're so glad you're okay. You have no idea how many nights we've sat up wondering how you were. If you were still alive.

How you were able to survive the weather. There are so many things to ask you. So many questions." Liz could hear her mother crying in the background.

"I know, Dad. It's good to hear your voices. We do have so much to talk about and I cannot wait to get home. It will be some time tomorrow. Jim has to remain here for surgery on his leg. But other than that, we both fared pretty well considering the crash landing I had to make. Tell Mother I'm fine. I know this has been hard on her. Probably worse on you guys than me. It's been tough, Dad. Really a challenge. But I think you would've been proud of me because I was able to pull from what I had learned from you as a child. I saw the purpose of it all. But I am more than ready to come home. I'll call you guys tomorrow and let you know my flight time."

"Liz, we're relieved. And thankful. A lot of prayers went up for you both. So Jim has a broken leg? I bet that was hard to deal with out there in the cold. Tell him we wish him the best. I'll call Joe and Leigh and let them know. Leigh has been about to lose her mind. She gave Joe hell for allowing you to go."

"I was afraid of that. It wasn't your fault, Dad. Or Joe's. No one knew the weather would change like it did. We'll talk all about it when I get home. I'm kind of tired, Dad. I love you. I'll call tomorrow."

She hung up the phone and watched Jim talking to his secretary. He was laughing and really into the conversation. Suddenly she felt shut out of his life. It was no longer just her and Jim. Their lives were coming at them and they had to jump in. He glanced her way and smiled. But the distance between them had begun and she knew she wasn't going to like it. She was wondering if he felt it at all.

They took her into an examination room and her questions remained unanswered until they both were admitted to their own rooms. Her mind was racing from thoughts of their time on the mountain to wondering if Tom would be waiting for her in Knoxville. She still had that to deal with. She tried hard not to think about the complicated mess her life was going to be for a while. First things first. She had to get home. And she had to tell Jim good-bye.

Chapter 37

The X-ray of Jim's leg showed that the bone was beginning to heal and no surgery was needed. This was good news and when Elizabeth walked into his room, he was grinning from ear to ear. She smiled at him and shook her head. She had taken a shower and put on the last clean pair of jeans in her suitcase and a clean sweater. Jim was still a mess and was sitting up in his bed with a removable cast on his leg.

"Have you seen a mirror lately? I looked at myself and nearly died."

Jim laughed and patted the side of the bed he was sitting on. "Man, do you look good! Come here. I need a hug."

She walked over to him and sat down, leaning over to kiss his cheek and give him a quick hug.

"I know you've been through a lot of tests. What were the results? Surgery tomorrow?"

"You won't believe it, but I'm going home tomorrow just like you. The bone is mending and apparently our brace worked. No surgery is needed, Liz. It was a very clean break. They are amazed at the shape we are in. Granted a little malnourished, but we really did well out there, lady. And by the way, you look beautiful!"

"I've heard the same praise from the doctors I've seen. I'm proud of us. We did handle ourselves well and in an odd way it was quite an adventure, even though we both were frightened at first and in so much pain." She poked his side and touched his hair. "I took advantage of the shower, clean towels and soap. It feels so good to be clean. I almost forgot what that felt like. I actually smell good."

"I kind of like you dirty." He pulled her close to him and hugged her again. "I was used to it being just to the two of us. There are way too many people around."

She looked at him and her eyes watered. "I know what you mean. It feels strange not having you near me. I know we are going to have to say good-bye tomorrow. And it's going to be hard on both of us. This has been quite an ordeal and we fought it together. That's a pretty neat thing to share, Jim."

"Wonder what time we'll be released tomorrow. I don't think I have any more tests. They want me to see my own doctor when I get home. Are you okay? Anything mentioned about your health?"

"Just a little dehydrated and I've lost some weight. But don't worry, I'll have no trouble gaining it back. You've thinned down, too."

"I've never been described as thin before, so I will milk that for all it's worth. Wonder if they would allow us to have our meals in my room tonight? Wouldn't that be nice? I don't know about you but I'm starving for real food."

"I wish I knew someone around here who could bring us some food from a restaurant. But I'll take hospital food over deer meat any day!"

"Have you seen any reporters? Maybe the word hasn't gotten out yet."

"Nobody. But we've been pretty tied up with tests and doctors all around us. I really hope we don't see them tonight. I want some quiet time to work through where we've just been, Jim. I didn't realize I would feel the way I do right now. I'm actually nervous about going home."

"I have some trepidation myself. Not about going to work per se, but about being so far away from you. All along I have said that I wouldn't let you go. And I'm very serious about that, Liz." He pulled her close and kissed her cheek. "I love you, lady. It's for real."

Liz wanted to wrap her arms around him but she felt confused inside. She knew she would be talking to Tom but at this moment that seemed so far away. Unreal. Jim was the real thing. He'd been her partner in this survival. She might not have made it on that mountain without him. His support.

"I'm feeling things towards you that I was trying hard not to feel. You know how difficult it is for me to open up inside. To let you fully in. Jim, we leave tomorrow for our homes and our jobs. Life is going to kick in and it will be so easy to just let this drift away. Is that what you think will happen?"

"Let's not try to foresee the future, Liz. I know how I feel about you, and it is going to take some work. I'm not looking forward to the distance between us physically. It will take effort to stay in touch and stay close like we are right now. But people do it. We're not the first. If love is there and it's real, then we will make it work. That's all I know to say."

"I know you're right. I've pushed men away for so long that maybe I don't have the trust in love like I should. You show me the way, Jim. I just know I'm dreading tomorrow not because I don't want to see my parents and get back to work. But because you're going the opposite direction than I am, and I know how far away that's going to feel to both of us."

"I bet you have a big reception at home waiting for you. Your parents are going to be so glad to see you and know that you're okay. Let's ask the nurses' station if our meals can be served here. I'm hungry and we both need to eat a good dinner."

They were sitting in two chairs beside each other facing the window that looked out upon the ugly roof of the hospital. They had trays pulled up in front of them and food enough for two people on each tray. The hospital was being nice to them, making sure they had everything they needed. It had gotten around that they were the two people trapped on Beartooth Mountain.

Steam was rising from the hot vegetables on Liz's plate. She leaned over and took in the smell of cooked squash and potatoes."My mouth is watering and I cannot wait to dig into this food. Hospital food is notoriously bad but I bet this tastes like a meal from a fine dining restaurant."

Jim laughed, but his mouth was already full of food. He grabbed his tea because the food was so hot, but it tasted good going down. "I feel like a king sitting here with you. What more could I ask for?"

"Sure beats sitting on the floor of that cabin trying to cook deer meat without burning it or the stick. It seems so far away from us now."

"It sure does. You know that's going to happen, Liz. I'm sure it's normal. After you experience a traumatic event and you get back to your real life, it's sometimes hard to remember exactly what happened. I'll have to call often to remind you of just how bad it was!"

Liz raised an eyebrow. "I can tell that I'm really going to have a tough time with you. Even far away you will be pestering me."

"I will do my very best to make you miss me."

They were interrupted by Jim's doctor, who introduced himself to Elizabeth.

"Mrs. Stone, I'm Dr. Rutherford. I've heard so much about you from Jim. You've been very brave, to say the least. I'm impressed."

Liz blushed and shook his hand. "Don't believe a word he says. He's been without good food for so long he doesn't know what he's saying, I'm sure. In fact, he didn't know what he was saying most of the time we were on that mountain."

Dr. Rutherford laughed. "I can see how well you two got along out there all alone. Well, you both are headed home tomorrow morning. I am releasing you, Jim, at 11:00, so make your fight plans accordingly. I know it will feel awful good to sleep in your own beds."

"You have no idea." Jim swallowed another bite of food.

"I'm curious, Liz. How did you come to know how to hunt and use a bow? I mean, looking at you, one wouldn't guess that you were strong enough to gut a deer and build a huge fire to cook dinner. Weren't you frightened out there alone?"

"The old adage that 'you do what you have to do to survive' is really a true statement. I was taught at an early age to shoot a gun and use a bow. I have Indian in my blood. But I never thought I would have to use the skills I was taught in my lifetime. I guess a little knowledge turned out to be a good thing in this case."

"I'm amazed at what you accomplished. I'm sure Dr. Wilson was thankful you had those skills. He was kind of crippled up with his broken leg."

"He managed to help me tremendously out there. We both learned how to survive that unbearable cold weather. There were times it wasn't much fun, but we were thankful to have each other. I am certain I would not have made it alone."

The doctor shook his head and turned to walk out the door. He turned back and looked at Jim and Liz sitting there eating quietly. "I'll have to add that you did a pretty darn good job splinting his leg. That had to hurt the first few days and I don't know how he took the pain. But all in all, you both seem to be in excellent health. You're an inspiration to us all."

Liz and Jim turned and smiled at each other."No one will ever know how much griping we did while we were out there. It was tough as hell going through it. But we did manage to make the best out of the situation and I'm proud of us for that." Jim said, calmly.

Liz smiled at him. "Let's finish our food before it gets cold. I'm tired and I know you need to sleep, too. Tomorrow will be a different kind of hard for us."

Jim pushed back his tray after a few minutes. "I can't eat another bite. I think my stomach has shrunk. But it was delicious. I want to make sure I thank the kitchen staff for being so good to us."

"I'm full, too. Why don't you take a long shower and I'll walk back to my room and rest until you call. Then I'll walk back to visit with you until we are ready to sleep. Sound good?"

"I know you need to call your parents again. Tell them I said 'hello.'"

She smiled and walked out the door. Jim took his removable brace off and sat on a chair in the shower and turned on the hot water. It felt like heaven for about fifteen minutes. He soaped himself and washed his hair twice, trying to get nearly two weeks of grime off of everything. He felt like a new man when he dried off and put on some clean clothes. His jeans were a little looser but he looked pretty good considering. He went over to the bed and sat down, putting his brace back on and leaning against the pillow. He closed his eyes and fell into a deep sleep, dreaming about the cabin.

When he opened his eyes the room was dark and he felt something beside him. He turned his head and there was Liz lying on her side on his bed, with her arm across his chest. He smiled and moved over and kissed her forehead. It was going to be tough saying good-bye to the most beautiful woman he'd ever met. And it looked like she was not going to let go too easily, either.

He closed his eyes and fell back asleep, thinking of how hard she'd tried to hold back her feelings. It looked like she'd lost the battle and they might just have a chance to have a relationship. He couldn't believe how strong she'd been, how hard she fought not to love him. He kept his hand on hers the whole night, not wanting to let her go. Ever. The nurses came and went without waking either of them. And for one more night they were allowed to remain in their own little world. But it was going to change.

Chapter 38

The light coming through the window was incredibly bright. Jim shaded his eyes and found himself staring at a nurse who was taking his blood pressure. He quickly looked to his right and the bed was empty. He glanced back at the nurse and saw a smile on her face.

"She left about an hour ago. Went back to her room and climbed into bed. How do you feel this morning? Excited about going home?"

Jim cleared his throat. He grabbed the straw stuck in his water glass and took a long swig. "Yeah, in a way. It's been quite an experience for us. Hard to believe it's over. Now things are happening at the speed of light, when for the eleven days we were walking in quicksand."

The nurse nodded and walked to the door. "I guess you can get your things together and eat some breakfast. You'll be checking out around 11:00, Dr. Wilson."

"Thank you. You've been very kind."

As soon as she was gone, he jumped out of bed and nearly fell; he'd completely forgotten about his leg. He grabbed the crutches that were leaning against his bed tray, hobbled to the door and aimed towards Liz's room. He was hoping to have breakfast with her. The nurses saw him and smiled as he passed them going towards Liz's door. It was open so he walked right in. He found her sitting in a chair looking out of the window. She turned her head when she saw him come in. Her eyes told him a million things at once.

"Good morning, Jim. How you feeling? Did you sleep well?"

"You know darn well how I slept. You were right beside me most of the night."

She managed a grin. "I was. Didn't know if you noticed or not. It just didn't feel right with you in that room and me here."

"I'm glad you came to my room. It was a nice surprise. Breakfast is about to be served. Thought I'd eat mine in here with you."

"We're having separation anxiety, aren't we?"

"I think you could say that."

"When will it go away?"

"I hope it doesn't."

"That could create some problems for us if it doesn't settle down to a manageable level."

"And what would that level be for you?"

"Not to think about you for hours at a time so I could get something else done. Not to wonder about your leg. Or if you ate. Or how you felt."

He laughed but he knew she was sort of serious. "I'm having the same problem you are. But the fact is that we both are going to hit the ground running when we get home. That is the kind of people we are. You know that and I know it. Right now, we are just having a problem saying good-bye. But the immediate pain of that will dissipate when we get home to our own lives. Then after we settle in, a new ache will take its place. That's the one that I want to see."

"What? You mean how much I will miss you?"

"Yeah. This stuff we're feeling now will pass. It's perfectly normal to feel this way after what we've been through. But when you are back at your job with the fervor that I know is natural for you, I will want to know how you feel then. And me, too."

"I guess that all remains to be seen. It's not like me to get so attached to someone that I was trying too hard not to like in the first place. You just kept on whittling away at my wall. And now look at the mess we're in!"

He grabbed her and pulled her up to him and looked in her dark eyes. "We need some time away from each other to see if this is real. I want to take you home with me and never let you go. But we need to see if this is the real thing, Liz."

Breakfast was coming in the door so Jim pulled up a chair and they both sat down and dug into a plate of hot steaming scrambled eggs, toast, bacon and juice. It tasted like a million dollars and they were quiet long enough to eat most of the eggs and toast.

Liz savored the flavors and licked her fingers after putting the remainder of the bacon down. "Was that not the best meal you've ever had? Gosh, that tasted good."

"It was at that. Even though my stomach is in shock, I want to eat this whole plate of food. I was pretty sick of deer meat and I know you were. It's going to be fun to enjoy food again."

"So you going to work as soon as you get home?"

Jim nodded. "Yeah. I'll head into the office just to see if my secretary has held the fort down. I will need to make an appointment with my doctor about this leg. I imagine there will be nothing done for a while. Then physical therapy for a few weeks."

"I'll go in. My poor secretary is going to freak out on me. And I have to see my parents and Leigh and Joe. What a conversation that's going to be! I almost dread it because there is no way I can explain what it was really like on that mountain. How cold it was. How tired and hungry we were."

"Do the best you can and then just let it go. They'll never know what we went through. It was hard. Probably the most difficult thing we will experience in our lifetime. But we pulled it off, and I am so happy we made it out alive."

"Yeah, it was a challenge, all right. There were times I thought I wasn't going to make it. And I was thinking at night that we might not be found until spring, because the weather had just settled in on that mountain. It snowed the whole frigging time."

Jim laughed and pushed back his tray. He stood up and moved her tray and pulled her up to him, balancing on one foot. He set his casted foot on the floor to help balance and held her close. She sank into him and took in a deep breath, remembering his smell. His arms around her. His hair. He was so strong.

"Look at me, Liz. You know I love you and I want this to work. But you have to figure out if that's what you want, also. I know you are going to deal with this thing with Tom, and if I'm honest, it makes me nervous. Very nervous. Yet it has to be done in order for you to really see how you feel about me."

Liz tiptoed and kissed his face. "I don't know what's ahead of us either, Jim. Like I told you before, I don't know Tom anymore. It was good to see him and we spent a few hours talking and catching up. But old feelings of hurt came back, too. A lot to sort through. He is a nice guy but I know I need to find out what my feelings are for him."

She stepped back and held his hands. "You have been so good to me, and I will be waiting to hear from you when you get settled in."

"Are you joking? I'll be calling you tonight when I get home. I know you'll probably be at your parents' but keep your phone on, will you?"

"I will. Don't worry. I made my plane reservations and a cab is going to pull up any minute in front of the hospital. My bags are packed. I kind of planned to leave before you, or we would never be able to say good-bye."

"So you're leaving now?"

"I am, Jim. It's the best way." She raised up and kissed his mouth and he pulled her close one more time. They stood there in each other's arms for a few minutes and then she moved away. He kissed her again and walked to the door and looked back.

"You're my girl, aren't you Liz?"

"I'm afraid I am, Jim. But we will find out for sure very soon. Be careful going home. We'll talk as soon as we can."

As Liz headed to the elevator, Jim walked slowly back to his room, for the first time noticing the ugly green walls of the hospital. His world had suddenly gotten smaller and he knew it was time to go. His flight was about thirty minutes later than hers so he packed his suitcase and brushed his teeth and said good-bye to the nurses. He called a cab and walked to the elevator, feeling the absence of the woman he loved. As he went down in the elevator he rubbed his face. He could smell her on his hands. He put them next to his face and took a deep breath in. It was faint but she was there. He was really going to miss her being around.

The cab came and he carefully climbed in, throwing his suitcase and crutches beside him on the backseat. The cab was old and shabby and the driver spoke broken English. He told the cabbie to take him to the airport and enjoyed the quiet hum of the road going by, lost in his thoughts of Liz. The weather was cold and there was a bitter wind blowing. He wrapped his jacket around him and zipped it up to his neck and braced against the wind as he walked slowly into the airport. It felt good to be going home, although he had no one he was going home to. But his work was waiting and he had missed it. It would be a few weeks before he could do surgery again. But he could see patients and get his brain back into the medical world.

He glanced up at the headers and saw the flight to Knoxville was boarding. The announcement was called out across the airport. He was so tempted to try to get on her plane and surprise her. It was hard for him to let her go. But he knew the way things needed to go. It was difficult to trust that he would ever see her again, and the odds were against them because of the distance apart. But stranger things had happened and he was betting against the odds that she would find she didn't want to live without him.

As he boarded his plane, his chest felt heavy. She was such a beautiful woman. So intelligent. He hadn't really gotten to the real Liz yet and he knew it. There was more inside of her that she didn't want him to see. One day he hoped that door would open and she would let him in. Until then, He would remember her like he last saw her; in his arms with her face pressed close to his. How did he ever get so lucky? The plane took off down the runway and near the very end it rose up into the sky. He closed his eyes and let his thoughts drift to her. *Today might be the last time I ever see her.*

Chapter 39

Jesse and Martha had been at the airport early, anxious to see Elizabeth's plane land. It had been pure hell for nearly two weeks and they wanted her home. It was a windy day and even though the sun was shining it was cold outside. The windows of the airport were fogged up from the warm air inside and Jesse kept wiping the window so he could see the runway. It was a pretty good size airport and hundreds of people were scurrying around. They'd eaten a little breakfast in the café at the front of the airport and Jesse sat sipping his coffee, checking his watch every ten minutes.

Martha was beside herself but tried not to show it. She knew she was going to fall apart when she saw Liz walk through the doors. The waiting area was full of people waiting for the plane to land and there was a musty smell from all the water that had been tracked in on people's shoes. It had rained for a week in Knoxville; fortunately it had not turned to snow. But it was messy all the same, and now that the sun was shining, the glare nearly put out their eyes when it reflected off the standing water.

Elizabeth saw them first. She came through the door with her small suitcase and saw her parents standing at the windows. Her father's shoulders were sagged from worry and her mother was wringing her hands. She dreaded the first conversation, but knew it had to take place. It seemed strange to be home and she'd only been gone eleven days. But it felt like an eternity. And then there was Jim. Her father turned and saw her and came running over to her. Martha was fast behind him.

"Liz! Oh, my God! Come here. It is so good to have you back home!"

"Hey, Dad! Good to see the both of you. I know you've been worried sick."

Martha wrapped her arms around Liz and hugged her tight. "You have no idea how much we've worried. There was nothing we could do, Liz. Do you know how frustrating that was?"

Liz brushed her hair out of her face and nodded. "Yes, I do. We were on the other end of this thing, Mom. We only had each other out there in that white tundra. It wouldn't quit snowing. The front just hung over us. It was a nightmare!"

Jesse grabbed the suitcase and pulled Liz along while she and her mother talked. There was too much to say and it was better to wait until they got home. Martha held on to Liz's arm like a pit bull and walked her to the car. After they were headed to the house, Jesse spoke up.

"I can't believe I have you back home. Child, this never should have happened. I've beaten myself up because I made the wrong decision. I can't wait to get home so we can sit down and talk about it. I want to hear all about it, Liz. It's all I've thought about."

Liz was sitting in the back seat and her mother wouldn't take her eyes off of her. "I know, Dad. It's been tough on all of us. But it's over now. I'm home safe and sound. Boy, it looks good here. There's no snow!"

"I bet you're sick of it, aren't you?"

"Yes, Mother, I am. In fact I don't care if I ever see snow again."

"Are you hungry, Liz? We can stop somewhere and get you something."

"I had a good breakfast. I'm okay for now. But a home cooked meal would be great for later, Mother. I am quite sick of eating deer meat. And an occasional rabbit."

They all laughed as Jesse pulled up in the driveway. They walked Liz into the house and put her suitcase beside the sofa. "I guess my car is at the airport. Unless you and Joe took it to my house."

She turned and looked at her father and he nodded. "You knew I would take care of that, Liz. It gave me something to do. It's sitting in our garage."

They all sat down in the living room with Liz in the middle of her parents. There was so much to tell them that she didn't know where to start. They were full of questions and worry and her father just couldn't wait for her to get it together. She knew he didn't realize what an adjustment it was to find herself sitting on a sofa at her parents' house. Her thoughts were whirling as she began the slow account of what had taken place after the crash landing.

"Dad, things happened so quickly in the air. I had to make instant decisions, not really knowing if I was making the best one or not. When I knew I was going down, I looked around me quickly and found what seemed like the best place to crash land. The lake I spotted looked like it was frozen over. But that was simply a guess."

"I cannot imagine the terror you felt, Liz. It was a life or death decision."

"We hit pretty hard but slid across the lake and ran up on the bank into a mass of trees. It took one wing off and shoved the front of the plane into the cockpit. Jim's legs were pinned. I thought it had cut them off completely. He did lose some blood from some cuts on his leg, but there was a clean break on his right shin. We found that out later."

Martha put her head in her hands. "Oh, God, Liz. You could have died."

"Now, Martha. She's made it out fine. Let's not get morbid now. Go on, Liz. Finish telling us about what happened."

Liz took a deep breath and leaned back against the sofa. Her mind pictured the damaged fuselage and the broken windows. "Dad, you don't know cold until you've felt it on a mountain in the dead of winter. Neither of us was prepared for that kind of cold. I had taken other clothing and so did Jim, but nothing warm enough to block out that dreadful cold."

"How did you manage, Liz? What did you do?"

"After I discovered his injuries, we decided we had to get his legs out from under the cockpit control panel. It was going to cut into his legs and they were going numb from the pressure of the metal. Finally, I found the lever on his seat and moved it back slowly. Then I pulled him out with his help. He could use his arms and that helped tremendously. It was sheer luck that we got him out and into the back seat. I immediately got some sticks and we taped them to his leg to give him some support. We were in shock, Dad, and moving slowly."

"I know you were, kid. You did good. So did you build a fire?"

"We slept first. We were exhausted and so cold. We bundled up in the back of the plane and huddled together. It was the warmth of our two bodies that kept us alive that first night. And we were ready for a fire the next morning."

Martha had remained quiet, listening to her daughter talk about surviving something she couldn't in her wildest dreams have imagined. She put her hand on Liz's leg and patted it, smiling.

"Thank God you made it home safe, Liz. Thank God."

Liz smiled and leaned over and kissed her mother's cheek. "God was the only thing we had out there, Mother. The only thing."

"Did you kill something to eat, Liz? I know you took your guns and bow."

"I know you want to hear all about that, Dad. But this hunt wasn't for fun. It was how we were going to live another day. I killed a deer and had to drag it back to the plane by myself. Jim was in too much pain to be of any help. But when I had to gut the deer and get the meat ready, he did manage to help me then. I tell you, Dad, that meat tasted like a million dollars that day. And we kept it inside the plane for a few days and ate from it.

We got tired of being cold at night, even with the fire going outside the plane. The snow just kept coming down and by morning it had nearly put the fire out. I had seen a cabin off in the distance when the plane was landing and hiked nearly two hours to find it. That was our saving grace, Dad. That cabin became our home."

Jesse got up and walked to the window and looked out. "I can't imagine my little girl lost on a mountain with a man she barely knows, hiking in the snow and hunting for food. It's barbaric, Lizzie. Nothing short of barbaric."

"Tell me about it. I felt like a pioneer. And Jim was such a trooper about his pain. We had some ibuprofen and doled it out one pill at a time. It did help with the inflammation and pain. But it meant that I had to do most of the work myself. And that was tough. It pulled something out of me that I didn't know was there."

"I bet it did, Liz. I bet it did."

She got up and stood next to him.

"I don't know what's going through your mind, but if you're worried one minute about Jim, I can settle your nerves right now. He was a perfect gentleman, Dad. He treated me like gold. And I grew to really like the guy, in spite of my reservations about men."

"I'm not worried about you. You could always take care of yourself. But if you had told me that he tried something with you, I would have killed him on the spot."

"Oh, don't be that way. He was good to me. And we both learned from each other. I'm not going to tell you all I had to go through because it would just make matters worse. You've already worried enough over me. The main thing is that we're home safe and basically unharmed from the whole disaster. I am pretty excited about going back to work and getting into a routine again. And if I don't eat another bite of deer meat for the rest of my life it will be just fine for me."

"Liz, I know you had to get discouraged when the snow wouldn't lift. It nearly drove your mother and I mad. How did you cope? Did you ever see anyone around? Another human being?"

"No. We were totally alone out there. Except for the wolves, that is. Sometime I'll share that story with you. But not now. Not today. I think we've shared enough right now and I'm hungry. Mother, can we start dinner? I can't wait to eat your cooking again."

Martha stood up and smiled. "Of course we can start dinner. I need something to do! Come on in the kitchen and give me a hand.

"Joe? It's Jesse. Our girl is home!"

"Thank heavens! When she get in?"

"Couple hours ago. She and Martha are cooking dinner now and then I think she's gonna want to go home. Been quite an adventure, huh, Joe?"

"I know one lady who is going to be so happy to know Liz is home."

"I bet. I know Leigh's been going crazy like the rest of us. I imagine Liz will want to see you both tomorrow night. She's going in to work tomorrow—there's lot of catching up to do with Walmart. And the papers are calling. News reporters for television. She's going to have her hands full until this becomes old news."

"I don't envy her that part. I talked to Jim on the phone. He sounds pretty good, actually. A little travel worn, but he sounded pretty strong."

"Travel worn. Hell, they're lucky to be alive, Joe. She looks good. Real good. I'm so proud of her."

"We all are, Jess. Please tell her we are dying to see her. Leigh will call her tomorrow."

"I'll tell her. She's going to want to see ya'll, too."

"Thanks for the call, Jess. Been waiting for it."

Jesse hung up the phone and looked at Liz and her mother in the kitchen. His heart swelled in his chest knowing she'd made it on her own. She'd done what a lot of men couldn't have done. He might include himself in that bunch if he was honest. She was a strong girl and the Indian in her came out when she needed it the most. He stared at her for a few minutes and then walked to the living room to turn on the news.

The first thing he saw was his daughter's face with Jim's, and then he heard the newsman saying that they were home alive. He laughed and turned the channel. She was going to have to do some interviews before they would leave her alone. The whole world was watching to see if they would survive. But no one was as proud of her as he was. His knees went weak for a moment thinking about what he would have done if she hadn't come back. But he pushed that thought aside as Martha yelled at him that dinner was ready.

"Sounds like things are going back to normal pretty fast around here," he said to the air.

After taking a huge bite of salmon patty, Jesse raised an eyebrow and looked at Liz.

"You know, Liz, your friend Tom contacted us while you were out there on that mountain. He came by and asked what we knew about the crash. I was surprised to see him. I thought he was out of your life for good."

"I'm pleased to know he looked you and Mom up. That was a brave thing to do."

"Brave? I thought it was bold. A bit brash."

"Well, you couldn't have known that he paid me a visit before I left and we had a wonderful heart-to-heart talk. We shared about all the years apart and why he walked out on me. It was good to get all that out."

Jesse wiped his face with a napkin and frowned. "Does that mean you're taking him back?"

"It means we are talking again. That's all for now."

"What about Jim? How do you feel about him?"

"Dad, it's confusing at the moment. I really do care about Jim. But I need to finish this thing with Tom one way or the other. Emotions are running in every direction."

Martha tried to shush Jesse but to no avail.

"If I were you I'd write him off. He did seem like a nice guy and I finally warmed up to him. I could tell there was some real concern there for you. But in the back of my mind, I was remembering how much he hurt you. It was hard for me, Liz. I wanted to punch him out at first."

"Well, I'm glad you refrained. Now you're going to have to let me figure all this out, Dad. You and Mom have been wonderful and I needed this meal with you badly. I've missed you and knew you were worried sick about me. But things are going to go back to normal pretty quickly and I'll be busy as all get out trying to catch up with all the Walmart stores. But in the middle of all of this, I'll be talking to Tom to see where that is going. We may not go anywhere. Granted, he was married and I didn't hear from him for a long time. But he still seemed like the same guy I fell in love with. I know time will tell, and I'm asking you to give me that time."

Jesse pushed away from the table and stood up. His daughter was just like him. Independent and stubborn. "You don't have to ask permission from me, Lizzie. It's your life. I just don't want you hurt anymore. You've been through enough."

He looked down at her with his glasses slipping down on his nose. "You're my only daughter and no man is going to break your heart if I have anything to do with it. They have to answer to me."

"Dad, I'm too old for that kind of talk. Now calm down. I'm heading home and I'll keep you and Mom posted."

Liz got up from the table and hugged her mother. "Thanks for the meal, Mother, and I'm so sorry to have worried you and Dad like that. It feels so good to be home. On solid ground again."

Martha smiled and hugged her again. "You go home and rest, honey. You've been through too much. And don't pay any attention to your father. He's all talk. Tom seemed like a nice man and I don't blame you for at least looking into that relationship. But don't let what you had with Jim slip away, either. A good relationship doesn't come along very often in your life."

Liz didn't ask what that meant. She grabbed her purse and walked out the door, closing it quietly behind her. She felt better than she'd felt since the crash. Safe and full of good food. But also excited about what was ahead. When she got into the car she glanced up at the front window and saw her father looking out. He smiled and lifted a finger to his mouth. He was a grizzly bear sometimes but she couldn't help but love him. She repeated the gesture back to him and pulled out of the driveway. A smile found its way onto her mouth as she anticipated the conversation with Tom, just as a text from Jim came across her cell phone.

"I'm remembering the silent dance that went on between us in that cabin. Hope it hasn't disappeared from your mind. Talk to you shortly."

Chapter 40

When Liz opened the door of her apartment her phone was ringing. She ran to catch it and answered out of breath.

"Liz? It's Jim! I'm already missing you."

She paused and took in the sound of his voice. He seemed so far away.

"Hey, Jim! So good to hear your voice. How are you? How is home? How is your leg?"

"I would say we both miss each other. I'm fine, a little sore, and glad to be home. How about you?"

"Same here. Had a good visit with Mom and Dad and ate some of her cooking. It was like heaven. But it does feel good to be back in my apartment. I just walked in the door."

"Well, sit down and talk to me a minute. I've wanted to call you all afternoon but knew you would be visiting with your parents. I know they're glad to have you home."

"Oh, yes. I think they would've liked for me to stay there overnight, but I needed to get back here and unpack. Tomorrow is a work day for me."

"Same here. Do you miss me much?"

"I do! I kind of got used to having you around all the time. Feels like something is missing."

"I think we're having separation anxiety. It'll pass, but I don't like the feeling, either. I'll plan a trip your way very soon. I don't want to wait too long or you'll forget me."

"No chance of that, Jim. So have you been hounded by the news reporters yet?"

"Boy, have I. And I've seen our faces on television several times. I know it'll blow over, but it's the hot story right now. Nice to be missed, I guess."

"You anxious to get back to your office?"

"I am, but it'll be a few weeks before I can do surgery. My leg is healing well but I need to be able to stand for a couple of hours so it's going to take some time before all that happens. You got tons of messages on your phone, I bet, Walmart being the main one."

"I'm sure my secretary will fill me in tomorrow. I'm going to take a long bath and go to bed early. It is so good to hear your voice. I'm really going to miss having you around, Jim."

"I love you, Liz. I wasn't going to say it, but hey, we're practically roommates now. I'll let you get your bath, but promise you'll think of me while you are lying there in the bubbles. I miss you, lady."

"Call me tomorrow. Let me know how you're doing. I miss you, too. Sleep well in your own bed, Jim. I can't wait to get into mine."

Lying in the bathtub surrounded by hot bubbly water, Liz let her thoughts go and just tried to relax. It felt so good to be home again. So safe. She swore she would never again complain about her life after nearly having it taken away from her.

Just as she was really starting to unwind the phone rang again. She reached for it and regretted it as soon as she said hello. "Mrs. Stone? This is Mary Aiden from ABC nightly news. Have you got a minute to talk?"

"Actually, I was getting ready for bed, Mary. I haven't been home long and am worn out." She couldn't hide the frustration in her voice.

"I'm sure you are, Mrs. Stone. But the world is waiting to hear your story. Can you give me about a twenty minute interview over the phone so that we have something to tell your public?

Elizabeth stood up and stepped out of the tub, shaking her head. Water and soap bubbles dripped on the floor and the bath mat she was standing on. She grabbed a towel and wrapped it around herself and walked into the bedroom with a scowl on her face. *So this was how it was going to be.*

"Hold on, Mary, I'll dry off so I can give you what you want. It looks like I'm not going to get any rest until I tell you my story."

She put the phone down and dried off, slipping into her soft robe and climbing up on her bed, which felt like heaven. An hour later she was done with the interview and so tired she wanted to cry. All of the things that had happened—the crash, the horrendous cold, the fear, the hunger, dealing with emotions about Jim, wondering about Tom—all of them came crashing down on her and she lay her head back on her pillow and closed her eyes. No one would ever really know what she and Jim had been through for those eleven days of hell. No matter how she explained it, no one would realize how very difficult it was. She let her mind go over all the moments with Jim—the funny times, the horror of the wolves, his loving words, and her inability to really let go with him.

Suddenly, she missed him so much. She knew he loved her and was such a good man. The desire to call him was overwhelming and she knew he would love to hear from her again. To hear how she was feeling. She had held back for so long after Tom backed out of their relationship, that the feelings ripped her heart apart. But sleep was fighting her and she knew she had to give in. Tomorrow was going to another emotional day when she got to work.

Soon her eyes closed and she slept long and hard. Dreams came and went, but her body needed the rest and was going to take it regardless of the pain and restlessness in her heart. Nothing disturbed her sleep, not even the lone text she got around 1:00 am from Tom. Her phone lit up and the green light remained flashing all night long.

Liz, I know it's late. But I'm dying here. Wanting to know you are okay. I finally contacted your parents again and they said you'd gone home to sleep. It hurts that you haven't called, although I know you just got home. I understand, but it still hurts. I miss you and want us to find our way back to each other. Please call me in the morning. I do have to work, but I'll drop everything if I can talk to you. Just to hear your voice. Sleep well, angel. I am so glad you are all right. Call me, please.

Chapter 41

The warm rays of the sun burst through the window and stretched across her bed. She woke with a start, covering her eyes from the brightness. She looked at the clock and threw the heavy covers back. It was 7:00. She needed to hurry and get in to work. Stephanie would be happy to see her and heaven only knew what Walmart was doing.

She was eager to get back into the swing of things, but at the same time, her body was still recovering from the ordeal. She grabbed her phone and saw the green light. A text must have come in. She opened her texts and saw the one from Tom. As she read it, her stomach went into a knot. He was checking on her. He wanted to see her again. She knew it was coming, but his words made it real. She was going to have to deal with the feelings she had for Tom and see what was left, if anything, of their relationship. Too much was happening at once. She washed her face, brushed her teeth, and dressed quickly. Work had to come first.

The drive in to work was refreshing and she felt more awake when she went through the double doors of her building and up the elevator to her office. Stephanie was sitting at her desk, just like nothing had happened. But when she saw Liz walking through the doors, she jumped up and started crying. They hugged each other and sat down on the sofa to catch up on everything. Liz hugged her and they both laughed with tears streaming down their faces.

"Do you know how worried I was about you, Liz? Oh, my gosh! I started a blog about you and people from all over the world have been reading it. The news about you and Jim spread fast. The crash was all over the papers and the news. We thought you guys were lost to the world. It took so long for the rescuers to find you. To even be able to look. Did you go absolutely mad out there?"

Liz laughed at her for being so chatty. "You are so adorable. And I thank you so much for worrying about me like that. It was a nightmare, Stephanie. An absolute nightmare. No way else to describe it. The plane crash itself was bad enough. But actually, we made it through that with just a few injuries. Jim's was the worst—a broken leg. But if you saw the plane, you would've expected us to be dead. The toughest thing to deal with was the bitter cold and hunger."

Stephanie pushed her back and looked at her. "You look tired. I know you need about two weeks to recover from all of this, but Walmart is probably going to want to talk to you. Michael French has called several times. He has been nothing short of wonderful about your accident."

"That's good to hear. I am anxious to talk to him, too."

"Tell me, Liz, how *did* you guys make it out there?"

Liz sighed and sat back on the sofa. "It's hard to find the words to tell you so that you can picture how it really was. Very, very cold. Freezing. Colder than you've ever been in your life and there was no way to get warm. We built a huge fire beside the plane. We kept that fire lit most of the time. We huddled together in the plane to sleep, but you can imagine how cold it was inside that plane. The only good thing was that it sheltered us from the wind. Otherwise we would have frozen to death."

Stephanie put her hand on Liz's leg. "Do you know how freaking worried we all were? Your parents were about to lose their mind over the stress of it all."

"I knew they were worried. But I had no way to communicate with the outside. We were totally alone on the side of that mountain. And you don't know quiet until you are stuck in a snowstorm out in the middle of nowhere with no way of communication. It really brings out the best and worst of you. Jim and I worked through so many emotions out there in that snow. We had to be uncharacteristically close and we barely knew each other. We were forced into a survival mode and each of us had our own weaknesses and strengths. I pulled from him and he pulled from me. It was crazy, Stephanie."

"I know it had to be the most difficult thing you've ever lived through."

"Yes. And it will be a while before I stop thinking about it. I learned a lot about myself, though. What I can endure and what I cannot. I will tell you that you can go farther than you think you can. You can do without much more than you realize. I had one bar of soap. That's it. One bar."

Stephanie laughed and stood up. I know you are anxious to get into your office. I will go post that you are home and alive and well and get you all of the phone calls and files that you need. It is so good to have you home."

Liz stood up and walked slowly into her office and closed the door. She sat down in her chair and smiled. It felt so good to be there. As she was sorting through the stacks of mail, the phone rang. It was Michael. Stephanie put him through to her office.

"Hello, Michael. I know you thought I dropped off the face of the earth."

"It is wonderful to hear your voice, Elizabeth. We all were very worried about you."

"I'm doing fine now, with my feet on home soil. But it was an ordeal of a lifetime. I'm certainly glad it's over. It feels good to be back to work."

"That's what I wanted to hear, Liz. You have done such a good job for us that it was well worth the wait for you to be found and if you need time to recover, I totally get that."

"Actually, it will be better for me to just jump back in to work. I am ready and anxious to move forward if that is okay with you, Michael."

"Sounds good. Let me know if you run up on any unforeseen issues. I'm only a phone call away. And Elizabeth, you have no idea how many people in Walmart were praying for your safe return home. I will pass on the good news."

She smiled and hung up the phone. Nice to work for such good people, she thought, as she tackled the mail again. She spent two hours sorting through files and messages, returning calls that were more urgent and delaying other ones for another day. Stephanie had done such a good job holding things together while she was gone that her job was easy to just slip back into. Stephanie brought lunch in and they both sat on the sofa and ate croissants and chicken salad.

"I know you are curious about Jim. I can tell you are dying for me to talk about him."

"I was trying to hide that. But yes, I am dying to know. What did you think of him?"

"I had no plans to fall in love or anything like that. It was going to be just a simple plane ride to Montana and back. I knew we would talk and it would be fun to get to know him. He was a nice man. A gentleman. But I wasn't ready for anything. I'm pretty much a loner, as you well know."

Stephanie raised an eyebrow. "Yes, I did notice that."

Liz smiled. "Out there in the dead quiet, we were forced to talk. We learned so much about each other. We had to share everything and unfortunately, much of the burden was placed on me as far as food and shelter. He hated that. He is really a man's man. But his leg kept him pretty helpless in the beginning, so I had to do everything. Can you picture me hunting for deer? Rabbit? I had to do it. I had to clean the deer and cook the meat. Jim got to where he could help keep the fire going, and cook. But hunting out there alone in the white snow was harrowing, Steph. You could get lost in a second."

"How did he treat you? What was he like?"

"He was a gentleman. Of course, on the plane we slept huddled together. But I spotted a cabin right before we crashed and after hiking nearly two hours I found it and we were able to make a shelter out of it. There was a fireplace there so I had to cut wood to burn. Jim helped drag limbs from the woods so that we could keep a fire going at all times. Sometimes I had to hike back to the crash site and rebuild that fire. We didn't know how long to keep that going, and eventually we had to quit. It was just too much effort."

Stephanie wiped her mouth and sat back, taking a long drink of iced tea. "You fall in love with him, Liz?"

"I think he did me. But I am still on the fence because of someone else."

"Someone else? Talk to me."

Liz laughed. "That's another story for another time. I better get back to work. You get enough to eat?"

"I'm not the one who's been eating deer meat and rabbit. I hope that food tasted good to you. You could do with a little more weight, you know. You're a little too thin, Liz."

"I will enjoy gaining those pounds back, believe me."

The phone rang and it was Jim. Liz ran into her office and shut the door, letting Stephanie know she would be a while.

"Hey, Jim! Where are you?"

"In my office. Look, I know you're busy, and so am I. So much catching up to do. But I had to tell you that I've missed you and I just had to hear your voice."

"I'm so glad you did. I was just catching Stephanie up on things. So your leg better?"

"It's sore from the doctor messing with it today, but I know it's going to heal just fine. My main concern is being able to do surgery again. But I am seeing patients today and it feels wonderful."

"You sound good, Jim."

"Thanks, so do you. How is Walmart taking your homecoming?"

"Michael French couldn't have been nicer to me. Walmart put everything on hold until I was home safe and sound. He was glad to hear I was back and ready to work, so I'll start tomorrow in one of the stores in Memphis, which means I have to fly again."

"How do you feel about that?"

"I'm fine. But can't help but think about what we went through. I'm eager to work, though. It feels so good to be back."

"Say, I'd better get back to my patients. I'm going to plan a trip to see you within the next three weeks. So don't think for a moment that you are done with me."

"I was thinking quite the opposite, Dr. Wilson! You have a great day and call me later if you like. I'll be home tonight after dinner. I am going to Leigh and Joe's house to eat dinner, and then home. It won't be a late night, I promise you."

"I know Leigh can't wait to see you. And Joe. He's been beating himself up for almost two weeks about approving the flight in the first place."

"You're ears will be burning, because I know you and I will be the main topic of conversation."

"I'll call you later so we can catch up. This all still seems so surreal. I love you and I'm missing you, lady."

"It's been a whirlwind here trying to fit back into my life. I miss you, too, and we'll talk more about things tonight, okay? I better run. Love you, too."

Chapter 42

Liz tried to be prepared for the dinner ahead and all of Leigh's emotions, but once she set foot inside the door, she realized she'd done nothing to prepare for Leigh. There were balloons everywhere and flowers. And a huge banner saying "Welcome Home, Elizabeth!" Food was covering the table and there were a few people there that she'd never seen before. Joe came up and hugged her, taking her coat and purse.

"My God, Liz. I was so worried about you! Never will I ever do that again! I was sick these last two weeks, worried that you might not make it off that mountain. Was it the plane, Liz? Or did a wind current get you? We weren't even sure where you guys were. Much less if you were alive or not."

Liz backed up from him and pushed her hair off her face. This was going to be quite a night. "Joe, it wasn't your fault. We all studied the weather and made the best call we could. Now, looking back, it seems so clear. But we didn't know the weather would turn like that. The plane handled perfectly and I'm so glad I was familiar with it because that crash landing wasn't easy. I'm here! I made it back in one piece. So let's celebrate."

Leigh spotted her from the kitchen and came running out with both arms out. "Oh darling, I have missed you so much and have been nearly ill with worry. Come. You must sit down and tell me the whole story. And I mean the whole thing."

Liz laughed and grabbed a chair. "Where did all this food come from? Have you been cooking all day?"

"Heavens, no. People have brought food in. I let some of my friends know that you'd made it back alive and they all wanted to help us celebrate. You've been on the news, girlfriend. Everyone knew you were out there freezing to death. You look thin. Have you lost a lot of weight?"

"I'm sure I have. We both did. Not much to eat up there except deer and rabbit meat."

Leigh shuddered and hugged her again. "You just don't know how glad I am to see you."

"It feels good to be home, I promise you that."

"Joe? Come on in here and let's sit down so she can talk to us about this whole nightmare."

Joe sauntered in and sat next to Liz, putting his arm around her. She felt them both staring at her so she swallowed some wonderful raspberry tea and started talking.

"The trip from here to Ottumwa was perfect. We were talking and just enjoying the sights. But when we neared Montana the wind changed and I almost got caught in a nose dive. I knew we were going down but I didn't want to crash, Joe. I pulled up the nose and kept us from descending too quickly, but had to land on a thick layer of ice on one of the lakes up there. We skidded and hit the bank hard, going pretty fast. It caused us to jump the bank and plow through some thick trees. We came to a grinding halt after tearing one of the wings off. The front of the plane was shoved into the cockpit and trapped Jim's legs underneath. The windshield was blown out and the windows on either side of the plane. I had packed some blankets that I had to use to cover the windows or we would have frozen to death."

She stopped for a moment to sip some tea and noticed the look on their faces.

"It was harrowing. And I wouldn't want to go through that again. Jim was such a hero, though. Very tough. The fact that he was a doctor really helped when we were removing his leg from underneath the bent metal of the cockpit. He instructed me the whole way, telling me to get some small limbs to splint his shin. He was in shock but still functioning as a doctor. Pretty impressive. You would've been very proud of him."

"Were you wounded at all, Liz? How did you escape without a broken bone?" Leigh was sitting on the edge of her seat shaking her head.

"Only God knows. I was aching everywhere and in shock. So was Jim. But the will to survive kicked in and I pulled from what I'd been taught as a young girl. There is so much to tell you that my head is spinning. Hard to know where to start."

Joe butted in. "After you got his leg splinted did you guys just stay in the plane and try to keep each other warm?"

"I climbed through the bent door on my side and started a huge fire not too far from the plane. I used fuel from the plane to start the fire. I helped Jim out of the plane so he could sit by the fire to get warm. The cold was worse than I expected. It went straight to our bones. We both were shivering and still in shock. But it felt so good to have that hot fire burning our faces. We had plenty of water in the plane and some food I'd brought. So we snacked on some protein bars and fruit and spent the night in the plane, huddled together to keep warm. In the morning, I was hurting so badly I thought I was going to die. And Jim was in some serious pain. We had ibuprofen with us and meted it out to get some relief."

"Why don't you serve your plate, Liz, while you keep talking. We have roast pork and vegetables on the table and fresh yeast rolls. And five desserts to pick from!"

"This is more food than I've seen in weeks. You have no idea how hard it is to eat deer meat and rabbit. Nothing else. I feel like I'm in the Garden of Eden sitting here at your table."

Joe looked at Leigh and frowned. Liz knew she looked thin to them but it wouldn't take long to gain it back if they kept stuffing her with good food.

"So how did you get along with Jim?" Leigh had a twinkle in her eye.

"How did I know that question was coming?"

"Come on, Liz. How did you two get along?"

"He was a perfect gentleman. And even though he was in such pain, he still helped me after I shot the deer, and he kept the fire going. We both decided that the fire had to stay lit no matter what."

"You were in pretty close quarters, Liz. You guys had to get pretty personal in that small plane. Or was it all about surviving?" Leigh was pushing her point.

"For the most part we talked about our lives, and also how we were going to get our next meal. Food and water were what we thought about for the first few days. We had no idea how long it would be before search and rescue would find us. The weather just wouldn't let up. It snowed every frigging day. It got depressing and we were about to lose hope of ever being found when finally the weather let up. When the sun came out one morning, it nearly blinded us."

"Did you stay in the plane the whole time?" Joe interrupted Leigh before she could say another word about Jim.

"We stayed there the first couple nights. But I'd seen a cabin in the woods northwest of our crash site so I took off one morning into the woods to find it. It was hard because not only was I sore, but it was so cold. We layered our clothing but the frigid air just went right through our clothes. I did find the cabin and checked it out. I had to hike back the same day and tell Jim about it. He was excited but we both were worried about his being able to walk that far on the rough crutches we'd made for him."

"Sounds like a nightmare, if you ask me." Joe frowned.

"It was a nightmare. And it kept on going. We both thought it would never end. You know we were out there in all that whiteness. It felt like we were pretty much cut off from the world. No one knew where we were and we never saw a living soul. It caused us to depend on each other and be very creative in what we could come up with to survive. I'd brought ammunition and guns and plenty of blankets and flashlights and extra batteries. But that first trek through the woods with Jim on those crutches going painfully slow seemed to take us forever.

We were still not over the crash and our predicament sort of had to sink in. Our bodies were incredibly sore and bruised. We had plenty of time to think, and sometimes that's not a good thing."

"So did you make it to the cabin?"

"Yeah, we did. Finally. I carried some of the deer meat with me that I'd gotten a couple of days before. We melted snow for water as often as we needed it. I had one bar of soap, Leigh. One bar. It had to last us for as long as we were there, which was an unknown at the time. And I never really got to wash my hair. So you know how difficult that would be for a woman. Nearly two weeks of not washing my hair. It's a wonder Jim would even look at me."

"Oh God, Liz. I just don't know how you stood it. I hate that you had to go through such a traumatic situation. I was about to lose my mind with worry."

"We were aware that the people we loved would be worrying themselves sick. And we wanted to get off that mountain. But the snow would not let up. You wouldn't believe how difficult it was to hunt in the snow and to wake up every morning and it looked the same as the day before. We really lost our sense of time and place. We did turn to each other and that was painful for me. You know how private I am."

Joe and Leigh both laughed. "I wish I'd been a fly."

"We had our moments, Leigh. Believe me. Jim really is a nice guy and we had so much time to sit and talk by the fire. The cabin was our safe haven and we learned to treasure it with all of its rustic charm. We wondered who the owner was and laughed at the fact that we had just taken over his cabin and made it our own. The fireplace was a lifesaver and we kept a fire going until we went to bed. It slowly burned down in the night and we woke to a freezing bedroom. It was just a log cabin, nothing to write home about. But believe me, we were so thankful to have found it. We got to sleep in a bed and sit on a sofa. With our bruised bodies it was a blessing."

They got up from the table and carried their plates to the kitchen. Joe went outside to take a call on his cell and Leigh pulled Liz into the living room where they could talk in private. Liz knew what was coming and she also knew there was nothing that she could do to stop it. So she just sat back on the soft sofa and closed her eyes and waited for the questions to come. And they did.

Leigh put her arm around Liz and squeezed her tight. “I missed you so much and am so relieved you are home. Do you know how much you mean to me?”

Liz opened one eye and smiled. It was nice to be loved. “Yes, I do. I thought of you a lot while I was out there freezing to death. I even laughed one time, knowing you would’ve had a fit if you could’ve seen me hunting in the snow.”

“You had to do things you never dreamed you would have to do. You’re a lot stronger than me, Liz. I promise you that.”

“It’s funny what we are capable of when put in a dangerous situation. Life or death. We somehow muster up the courage to keep ourselves going at all costs. Jim was really hurt and I had to step up to the plate or we both would have died.”

“I guess when you put it that way, killing a deer seems trite.”

“Exactly.”

Silence for a moment and then the questions came about Jim.

“So, in all that time out there did you guys not fall in love? You spent every waking moment together, Liz. Talk to me.”

Liz smiled again. “We did grow into a wonderful friendship. We learned so much about each other. Probably more than many married couples, because of the environment we were sharing. He does love me, Leigh. He really was so kind to me. So loving.”

“I told you, Liz. I told you how great he was. Now you know for yourself, even though not under the circumstances I wanted you to find out.”

“But I do have this little situation about Tom. I need to contact him, Leigh.”

“Tom? Tom? How could you still be thinking about Tom? Have you heard from Jim since you got back? What is he saying?”

"He wants to make plans to come for a short visit. He doesn't want to wait too long, but he does still have a cast on his leg. Not sure how long that will remain. And he has a practice to tend to. I have a job, you know?"

"I know all that. But you've found someone you could spend your life with—"

"Hold on, Leigh. Give me a chance to breathe. I do love him, I'll admit. But he knows all about Tom and understands that I need to talk to him. Hear him out. We were in love, Leigh. Come on. You know all about him."

"I know he walked out on you. He was a real jerk. You were madly in love and he couldn't stand up to the heat. He backed out, disappeared, and not one word for years."

"Don't you think I know that? It was hell waiting for years to figure out what happened. But when I saw him a few weeks ago, it all came back. All those old feelings."

"Humph. You both are two different people now. He doesn't even know you."

"Neither does Jim. I mean we got to know each other, but it was a forced situation. We would need to spend more time together in the real world. See how we feel about each other over time."

"And you're going to give this guy Tom a chance? What if you lose Jim in the process?"

"He wouldn't do that. He said he understood."

"He said that while sleep deprived and wounded. In shock. Freezing to death. Now that you both are home and back to your lives, I bet he is going to want to nail something down so that you don't slip away."

"You might as well accept the fact that I'm going to call Tom. In fact, as soon as I get home I'm going to call him. He was here, waiting for me until he just had to return to his practice. My parents talked to him. It's something that I feel I need to do and I want you to give me room. To let me run my own life, Leigh. I love you to death, but I swear, sometimes you can be a bit smothering."

Leigh laughed. Liz knew her skin was so thick she could hardly pierce it. "Oh, go ahead and call Tom. I just know that Jim is the one. I'm sorry. I'll back off for now, but mark my words. You'll end up with Jim, Elizabeth. It's meant to be."

Liz laughed and pushed away from the table. "I am stuffed and really need to get home. It's a work night for me, guys. Joe, I don't want to hear any more about how you made the wrong decision. I could have backed out at any time. But I didn't. So we made it through this disaster and now we go forward. I trust you and my father with my life. But of course, I didn't think I would have to mean that literally!"

Joe walked up and hugged her. "It's just great that you are home. I can breathe now. We all can. Leigh was beside herself. I thought I was going to have to put her in the hospital. The lack of communication nearly drove us all mad."

"We felt the same way on our end. Worse, maybe. And I'm sorry about the plane, Joe. I should have never gone on this flight. But it's over. You guys were wonderful tonight and I loved all the food and decorations. Thanks for such a warm welcome home. But now I need to rest and be ready for tomorrow. I have to fly to Memphis tomorrow. Another Walmart to check out."

Joe winced and looked down. "Please don't apologize. I feel stupid having sent you out on this trip without really paying attention to my gut. We all felt hesitant but none of us paid enough attention to the warning flags."

Leigh walked her to the door. "You're not afraid to get right back on a plane, Liz?"

"Actually, it's the best thing I can do. I don't want the fear of flying to take over my life. It was a rare event. Once in a lifetime thing. I'll be fine."

"Okay, okay. Give me a hug. I love you. Keep me posted on what is going on. I mean everything. I love you like a sister, Liz."

"I'm fully aware of how you love me. And I love you, too. Thanks again, Leigh. Will talk to you soon."

Once out the door, Liz breathed a sigh of relief. *It was as tough as I thought it would be. She really is pushing me towards Jim. I wish she wouldn't. I would like to make that huge decision on my own.*

She drove home in silence, with the radio off. Her mind was racing and all she could think about was returning Tom's call. But in her gut, if she was really honest, she had her doubts. She didn't verbalize them—saying them out loud would have been too scary. But inside, in that place she hardly ever listened to, there were real doubts forming about any chance of reuniting with Tom. Of spending her life with him. This next visit would tell her a lot. She would be watching herself and trying hard not to just let her fickle heart guide her decisions. This was too serious. The pain Tom had caused years ago had been sitting in her heart for years like poisoned bile. His handsome looks and strong personality could sway a woman to do things that might not be good for her. She had to stay strong and focused.

As she pulled into her driveway, she felt exhausted and was almost tempted to just climb into bed and go to sleep. But she didn't. She picked up the phone and punched in Tom's number as she walked through the door. He picked up on the third ring, and the time went backwards for the next hour as the stronghold of memories past dug their claws into her heart.

Chapter 43

"I really don't believe you're on the other end of this phone."

Liz smiled. He was a charmer to the bone. "It's good to be home, trust me."

"It seems like forever since I saw you. I was so worried, Lizzie. Talk to me. Tell me how you are."

Liz fixed a cup of coffee and walked into the living room. She sat down on the sofa, curling her legs around her. Her heart was racing and she had to pace herself so she wouldn't just cave in. "It's a long story, Tom. A long story. I really wasn't sure we would make it home, to tell you the truth. It was a long time to be stranded in the snow."

"Two weeks is a hell of a long time to be worried that someone might not make it out alive."

"I know. A lot of people were worried about us. But through our determination to live, we pulled through near impossible situations. You would've been proud of me, Tom. I am proud. We did a good job with what we had to work with."

"I don't want to exhaust you with telling me the details tonight. I realize you are tired and need to rest. But I want to see you. Tell me when that can be arranged. I came home because I had some cases that were pending, but I am more than willing to fly over and take you to dinner so we can talk."

"I want that to happen, Tom. But we have so much to discuss. This isn't going to be an easy thing that you are attempting. My life is complicated now and we really don't know each other."

"Don't say that, Liz. I know you. You haven't changed that much. Neither have I. Well, hopefully, I have matured. I hope you can see that."

"We both have grown, but it's been quite a few years. You've been married. I've had a career that I've spent years building. I'm not ready to just drop everything and run to you. I'm not even sure how I feel about you. I was very glad to see you two weeks ago. It was a wonderful visit. But to think about us having a life together now, after all this time, is mind boggling."

"I know it's a lot to swallow right now, Liz. It is a goal. Something to shoot for. I just want a chance, is all. A chance."

"You find out when you can fly over and we'll go to dinner. I'm all for that. I look forward to it. But I just want you to know that it's not an easy deal thinking of 'us' back again. I'm involved with Jim to some extent. He does know you exist. But there are so many emotions that have come back up since you popped back into my life. I know you understand all of this, but keep that in mind when you're thinking about developing a long-term relationship with me."

"I want a chance, Liz. To spend some time with you to see if anything is left worth salvaging. If not, I will back out of your life forever. I think it would be sad not to try."

"Call me and tell me when you can come. I care about you and look forward to spending more time with you. But just don't get your hopes up too much at the beginning. I was caught off guard before I left and was overwhelmed with seeing you. You have a way of charming someone just by walking into the room. I'd forgotten how strong your presence is. But now that I've had time to think and I am not just listening to my heart, I feel we have a ways to go before we could consider having a life together."

She heard Tom clear his throat and knew it was not what he wanted to hear.

"It makes me sad that we even have to have this conversation, Liz. I did it to us. I hate it and if I could erase the past I would. It was so obvious to me that I'd made the worst decision in my life by walking out on you. But there is no changing the past. You are so beautiful to me. I need you in my life. I want you in my life. Just give me a chance. Let me get to know you again, and I want you to know me."

"That sounds good, but we live far apart. It takes time to know someone. And we both have careers. I'm not sure if it isn't setting us up to fail again, but I'm willing for us to see each other and talk. Let's not look too far ahead, okay?"

"Okay. That's fair. I'll set something up for the weekend. I don't want to wait too long. I'll call you and tell you when I'm arriving; I so look forward to this, Lizzie. I can't wait to see you again."

His deep voice was full of emotion. It would be so easy just to fall in love with him all over again, but she had to use some common sense. And there was Jim. She had so much to sort through. How in the world would she be able to decide which man would be best for her life?

"I'll wait to hear from you. I'm glad we talked tonight, Tom. I hope I haven't sounded too distant to you. It's just that I've been through so much and my brain is fried. I'm not thinking very clearly and am not dealing well with my emotions. Please know I do appreciate how you hung around here waiting to hear from me. And my father told me you went by to see them. That meant a lot to me and it took some guts on your part, considering how angry they were at how you backed out of my life. And it gave them a chance to see you again. I am certain my father was reserved at first. But he did say you were a nice guy. I got kind of tickled at that, Tom."

"There are so many emotions to deal with that I know will make it harder. But I am up for the challenge, Liz. I love you that much."

"I guess I need to end this so I can get some sleep. It's been a full day for me and tomorrow I have to fly to Memphis. So let me know when you're coming. And I will let you know if plans develop on my end. Fair?"

"Perfect. See you soon. And it's so good to know you are safe."

Liz hung up the phone and sat there alone in the quiet, letting his words sink in. She wasn't sure any longer how she felt about Tom. He was so handsome and charming. He had a good practice. She could tell he was eager to bring the love back between them and carry it forward into marriage and having children. But she wasn't sure she could get over his walking out. So much time had passed. She wondered if she would feel differently if Jim wasn't in the picture. Were her feelings for him getting in the way?

She stood up and shivered. It was time for a hot bath and sleep. She walked to her bedroom and ran a tub full of hot water and undressed. Her mind was tired from worrying. She really needed to just let things go for tonight and relax. As she stepped into the water and sank down into the warmth, she had a flashback of Jim watching her in the cabin. His face moved in and out of her mind. His gentle ways. His voice. The small window that had opened up in her heart for Tom wasn't open very wide. For obvious reasons she was afraid to trust him.

This time it was the moon's light that shown through her window as she pulled the covers up to her neck. She looked at her phone once more before closing her eyes, and there was a short note from Jim.

Lizzie, with my eyes closed I am still in that cabin in the woods, surrounded by deep snow, with you lying by me. Not touching, I could hear you breathing in the night. And that sound wooed me to sleep in spite of the pain in my leg. I miss you. Jim.

His sweet words bathed her in the moonlight. And she fell asleep with the knowledge that his love felt good to her. It felt warm and stable. Even though Tom was handsome and dashing, smart and quick on his feet, it was Jim's evenness that kept her leaning towards him. But confusion never was a good home for decisions. So she tried to clear her mind and drift off to sleep, the smell of clean sheets and the feel of warm covers soothing her spirits.

Chapter 44

At 3:00 in the morning, with the sound of the hall clock ticking away, Tom lay in his bed with his eyes wide open. He had an extensive court case in the morning that he was completely prepared to handle. An open and shut case unless the defense attorney was in one of his "I love to hear myself talk" moods. He couldn't sleep because all he could think about was his conversation with Elizabeth. She seemed so far away. So cold compared to the night before she flew out. He knew it was a long shot to expect her to just jump back into a relationship with him. After all, he did walk out on her. For no good reason. But he still loved her. He always had. The issue was, would she even give him an Eskimo's chance in hell to get to know her again? Would she even really want to try?

He rolled over on his side and thought about her face. He knew every single inch of that face. Her eyes, her hair . . . the mole on the back of her neck. He'd never forgotten all the talks they'd had. How open she'd been and how excited she was that he was going to law school. He had beaten himself up for years for thinking he was missing out on something by jumping into marriage too soon. What was wrong with him? He had it made with her and he had been stupid. His immature decision to walk out had cost him the relationship of a lifetime. Now he wanted just one chance to win her back. Just one stinking chance. And after that phone call, the way she had hung up, the tone in her voice; well, it didn't feel like it was going to happen. And that doubt was churning in his mind over and over.

He spoke out loud to the empty room. "I need to get over there as soon as possible. Before that Jim guy gets his claws into her again. *Who is this guy, anyway?* Where did he come from? Like out of the blue she suddenly is in love with him. I need to see her now."

He got out of bed and went to the bathroom, glancing in the mirror as he went by. *You better not let her slip away again, you stupid idiot. This is going to be your last chance. So you better make it good.* He flushed the toilet and it echoed throughout the house. He walked into the kitchen and poured a small glass of milk and rubbed his tired eyes. He was worn out and really wanted to nail the case shut in Judge Simmons courtroom. The judge was a short, stout man with little man's disease. He had taken to disliking Tom for some reason, and that was going to be the only "if" in the whole case at 9:00. The question in Tom's mind was; would he allow him to state his case without being constantly interrupted by that bozo DA Jeff Crankle? What a name! No wonder he ran his mouth. With a name like that a person would have no other obstacle as large to overcome in his life. "Crankle." He chuckled and went back to bed. This time he dozed off, which was nothing short of a miracle, and didn't wake up until the alarm went off at 7:30.

Pushing the wide mahogany double doors open at his office, Tom walked straight up to Susan, his secretary and receptionist, who was tall, brunette, and had legs that never ended. "Good morning, Susan. Any calls?"

"None. But you know you have court at—"

"Yeah, I know. Judge Simmons. I'm not looking forward to it, as you well know. Will you check on a flight to Knoxville on Friday, returning on Sunday night? I want the last flight out on Sunday and the first one out on Friday."

Susan studied his face and nodded. "I'll do it immediately. It's going to cost you more because you've waited until the last minute."

"Doesn't matter. I got to make this trip. Don't have a choice. So let me know. I'll be in my office and then you won't see me again until after court is out."

Tom headed into his office and closed the door, sat down at his huge hand carved desk, and pulled out the papers in reference to gas tank explosions due to rear end collisions. A nasty case against the manufacturer, but this was the bed he slept in every day. Trying to defend the auto manufacturer against unfair lawsuits. At the same time, someone had died in the accident because of the explosion. It wasn't a fun job but it paid good money. He surmised that every lawyer in town might say that about their job. The judges had gotten ruthless and were picking favorites even though there was an unwritten law against that. It couldn't be proven, but it sure was seen in open court every day.

Three hours later, he was walking back into his office and Susan held out a piece of paper with his flight itinerary written down. He glanced at it and smiled.

"Thanks, Susan. What would I do without you?"

She was quiet but shook her head. It was obvious that she knew very well what he would do.

He sat down and picked up the phone. His hand was shaking as he dialed Elizabeth's number. Her phone rang several times before he remembered she had a job in Memphis. She didn't say how long she was going to be there so he left a long message telling her the flight and time of his arrival. When he hung up, he swiveled around in his chair and stared out of the huge window behind his desk. He was on the tenth floor of the John Milton building and he could see the magnificent skyline of Houston. But his mind wasn't on what he was looking at—his thoughts were of Elizabeth. He wanted to plan a special night for her that was conducive for some type of reconciliation between them. He was so good in court. Why was he so frozen when he got in front of her? Surely he could make her see.

Just as he was about to leave the office for the day, Susan put a call through to him. It was Liz. His heart started racing as he grabbed the receiver. His mouth felt like cotton.

"Hey, Liz! So glad you called me back."

"Hello, Tom. I got your message and your flight time. So you need me to pick you up at the airport?"

"No, I'll get a rental car. I've already gotten a hotel reservation and planned dinner for us on Friday night. Anything you would like to do?"

He could hear her sigh on the other end. "I really haven't thought about it. But I will. I'll give it some thought. Listen, I need to run, Tom. Just wanted you to know I did get your call. I look forward to seeing you again and having a nice dinner. It'll be fun."

"I cannot wait to see you, Elizabeth. Have a productive day."

She hung up and he felt that emptiness again. She wasn't giving him much to hold on to. But he was strong and determined to give it all he had. *It would've been nice if she'd just acted a little more enthusiastic about seeing me. This Jim guy must really have made an impression on her. Or maybe it was my leaving her cold that did it.*

Tom left the office and drove home, his mood going downhill fast. He had fought depression since his divorce and couldn't seem to pull his life together. His business was thriving and he had more work than he could handle, but his personal life was floating in a pretty deep ocean. He felt like he was in a rowboat with one oar. He climbed the steps two at a time to his house and walked in, dropping his keys in the dish near the front door. His house was immaculate. He had hired a decorator to furnish the house to his taste, so it was rich with dark woods and warm grays and cream. It was comfortable but had a masculine touch. He opened the French doors out to the pool area and sat down, breathing in the fresh air. It was cool outside but he needed that crisp air in his lungs. He lay back in the lounger and closed his eyes and fell into a deep sleep.

Two hours later he shook himself awake and got up and went in to the kitchen. He needed to get some things at the store for the next two days, so he made a short list and jumped into his car, pulling off too fast and throwing a few rocks at the end of the driveway as he sped off down the road. It had been a beautiful day but he was more than ready for spring, which was a long way off.

All the way to the store he thought about Liz. How he could make her happy. He wanted to make her life easier. They could travel, have children if she wanted. They didn't have to live in Houston, but he figured she could do her job anywhere. He knew he was just daydreaming. She wouldn't even give him a glimmer of hope just yet. But the night he saw her, the one night he got to hug her, he felt hope then. He felt like there was a slight chance. He was holding on to that hope with both hands. Strong, handsome and very athletic, Tom made an impression when he walked into a room. He commanded attention. He handled himself professionally in every situation. But in this one thing, this love he had for Elizabeth that was the size of the freaking moon, he was absolutely frozen. His words were hollow and he found himself fighting to find the words he wanted to say to her. She was no help because she was holding back. That was obvious. Yet, somewhere in there he just knew she did care about him. The anger and hurt had worked their way into her heart and covered her words with bitterness. He hoped beyond hope that he could smooth that out of her. He just wanted the chance.

The grocery store was packed and it seemed a little hectic. In fact, when he walked in, there seemed to be electricity in the air. Something wasn't right. He grabbed a cart, noticing the hair on his arm was standing up. He scanned the room as he headed over to the vegetables and fruits. People were talking and laughing and children were everywhere. He made his way to the clear plastic bags and grabbed a couple, stuffing tomatoes and apples into two of them. He grabbed some bananas and headed towards the milk and creamer, filled his cart quickly, and pushed past some poor lost husbands who were trying to find a phantom cereal that their wives had sent them to get, shaking his head and laughing as he made his way to a checkout counter.

As he pushed the cart near the end of the line, he noticed a young man yelling at a lady in front of him. At first it sounded like they knew each other, but after a few moments, the yelling got louder and the man pushed the woman. She began to scream at him and yelled for the manager. The young man reached into his pocket and pulled out a small pistol and pointed it at the woman.

The whole room filled up with noise; people were screaming and running out of the store. Tom was trying to decide how to help the woman when the guy pulled the trigger and shot her. She fell backwards and hit her head on the counter where her groceries were piled up, and blood started running out of her mouth. Tom ran around his cart and tried to grab her before she hit the floor and the young man turned on Tom and pointed the gun at him, yelling words that made no sense at all. Tom suddenly realized the guy, who seemed disoriented, was speaking in broken English.

Just as he was about to reach the woman, the young man yelled out a threat to Tom and Tom lunged forward, trying to grab the gun away from the man. The gun went off and Tom fell to the floor.

The whole room exploded and cops came running into the store. "Get down! Get down!" one of them yelled.

Tom lay on the floor with blood all over his white shirt, unconscious. As the cops apprehended the wild-eyed young man and took his gun away from him, an ambulance came and two ENTs loaded Tom on the gurney and rolled him in the back of the ambulance and took off towards Houston General. Another ambulance carried the dead woman to the hospital as the police were scrambling to find out information on her family so that they could call someone. Tom had no relatives in Houston. No one to call. So they checked his phone and called the last number he had dialed. It was Elizabeth Stone. A message was left on her cell phone to call the police department in Houston.

At Tom's house, the clock was ticking in the hallway. There was a suitcase open on a bed in the room next to his. Travel plans had been made. Tickets purchased. He was planning to go see the love of his life. If she would see him one more time.

Like a life stopped in mid sentence or a letter unopened, Tom lay in the ER of Houston General with life slipping away. And Elizabeth had no clue what was taking place. She was on a flight back from Memphis, her cell phone off.

Her mind was running in two directions at once. But there was a slight turn in her feelings about Tom. A wondering. The memories of what was had found their way back into her mind. And she was allowing herself to go over all the times he had told her he loved her. The ring he'd bought. The dress she'd almost bought. The smell of his cologne. . . .A tear came to her eyes and she wiped it off her cheek. It was going to be a long way back to Tom. If it even happened. But she had made up her mind to give him a chance. She had told Jim this had to happen because she had to find out once and for all if there was anything left for her with Tom. And he was begging for that chance.

As the plane landed and she was walking to get her bags, she turned on her cell and saw there was a message. She grabbed her bag off the baggage collector and walked towards her car, shoved the suitcase into the trunk, and unlocked the car door. Throwing her purse on the passenger seat, she sat down and hit voicemail. What she heard made her turn white. And a panic rose in her chest that made it nearly impossible for her to start her car and drive home. *What did the police in Houston want from her? Why were they calling?*

Chapter 45

Houston General was a busy hospital, one of the best in the whole state of Texas. Doctors were standing over Tom. X-rays had been taken, and had revealed a bullet lodged in his chest. His skin was pale and he was unconscious. There was internal bleeding and his life was slipping away. Surgery was imminent but the doctors weren't sure he would make it through such a delicate operation. But there was no choice. So they rolled him into the operating room and as the big doors closed and they began the long surgery to save his life, Elizabeth was dialing the police department in Houston, waiting to see what in the world was going on.

"Miss Stone? This is Captain Russell of the Houston Police Department. Do you know a Tom Thornton?"

Liz could hardly speak. Her heart was pounding in her chest and she couldn't breathe. "Yes! I do know Tom. Is something wrong? Is he in any trouble?"

"No, no. He isn't in any trouble. He's been in an accident. How do you know Tom, Miss Stone?"

"We dated for years. In fact he is supposed to come and visit me this week."

She heard a deep sigh on the other end of the line. "Well, Tom was in an accident today. At the grocery store. He's been shot, Miss Stone. It's very serious."

Elizabeth sucked in her breath and froze. "What do you mean? He's been shot? Who shot him? What has happened?"

"I know it's difficult for you to understand, Miss Stone. But he was involved in an altercation at Barnhill Grocery Store. A young man pulled out a pistol and shot the woman in front of Tom in the check-out line. Tom stepped in to help and the man pulled the trigger on him."

Liz was so shocked she couldn't speak. There was silence on the end of the line for a few minutes and then the policeman spoke up.

"Miss Stone. We have no way of contacting his parents. Do you have any information that would help us locate any of his family?"

"I'm not sure if his parents are still alive. And I don't know where they live now. I'm really not going to be of much help to you about tracking down any family members. I'm so sorry."

"Of course. Your number was the last number dialed on his phone so we thought we would try you and see if you could help us to locate any family members. He has no one here with him. And as I said, things look pretty serious."

Liz stumbled and then spoke up. "I'll be there as fast as I can. I'll get a flight as soon as possible. Is he in surgery now? How long will the surgery last?"

"I have no idea. But yes, he is in surgery as we speak."

"I'll call the airlines immediately and fly in to Houston tonight if there is still a flight available. If he makes it through surgery, please let him know that I am coming."

"We'll do what we can, Miss Stone. Thank you. I am sorry to have to bring you such grim news about your friend."

Elizabeth hung up the phone and stood still for a moment. Then she grabbed the phone, looked up the number of her favorite travel agent and asked about a flight out as soon as possible.

"Janie! You have a flight to Houston tonight? I'm in a big hurry. A friend of mine was involved in an accident and I need to get there as quickly as I can."

"Let me look it up, Elizabeth. I'm sorry to hear there's been a problem. I show a flight at 6:00 arriving in Houston at 8:20. Would that one would work for you?"

"Book me for the 6:00 flight. That's pushing me but this is an emergency. Thanks, Janie."

Elizabeth hurried to pack a bag and phone Stephanie. She sat down at her desk in the hallway and put her head in her hands and closed her eyes. Too much too soon. She'd just gotten home and back to work; her body was worn out from all the emotions of the crash and the arrival home. Now this. Now Tom was injured and she felt like she had to go to him. There wasn't a choice.

"Stephanie. I know this sounds crazy, but bear with me. Tom has been in an accident. My old boyfriend. He's in Houston General, and I'm flying out at 6:00 to be with him. I have no choice. Please handle things tomorrow. I will fly back as soon as I know he's out of the woods. Call me if anything comes up. And I do mean anything. I'll answer you as quickly as I can."

"I'll take care of things, Liz. But you are in no shape to be flying to Houston. I know you used to love him; but this is huge. You haven't really recovered from the crash. It's about time you took care of you."

"I hear what you are saying and I know you're right. But this is important. He has no one. Or so it seems. I'll be in touch, Steph. Thanks for taking care for me so well."

She hung up and dialed her father. He was a little more understanding than she thought he would be, but was still worried about her health and mental state. "Dad, I've got to go. I have no choice. Surely you understand."

"I get it, kid. But you haven't been home long enough to recover from the whole traumatic situation you just barely lived through. I know you care about Tom, but there's nothing you can do if you go."

"I can just be there for him. I feel I owe him that. He was coming here to see me in two days. He wanted to try and develop our relationship again. I told him it was a long shot but he was determined. Now I'm not even sure he'll live through this surgery. I have to go, Dad. Please tell Mom, and I'll keep in touch with you both as soon as I land."

"Okay. I know better than to try to talk you out of this trip. But know I'm not happy about it. I'll wait to hear from you, Lizzie. Don't make me wait too long. You know how I get."

"Boy, do I! Talk to you soon, Dad."

She threw her clothes together, trying to think about what she would need, and headed to the airport. She put her lipstick on in the car and ran a brush through her hair. She had no idea what she was walking into, but she felt pretty sure it wasn't going to be good. She felt weak and tired, and wanted to call Jim. But she decided to wait until she saw the extent of Tom's injuries. And how he made it through surgery. No need in upsetting Jim for no reason.

She arrived at the airport in just enough time to check her bags and jump on the plane. There wasn't a minute to spare. As she sat down in her seat she breathed a sigh of relief and laid her head back and closed her eyes. The flight was a little over two hours long, just enough time for her to take a short nap. As exhausted as she was, she couldn't seem to fall asleep, so she found herself staring out the small window, looking at the clouds below, wondering if Tom would live through the surgery. It was hard to comprehend that he'd been shot at a grocery store. Nothing made much sense. But the timing of this event was even worse. They were really going to talk about moving forward. It scared her to think about it because she really wanted to see Jim again. Confusion was taking over her heart and she was incapable of making a decision because she needed to see Tom.

Just as she was dozing off, the plane was approaching Houston. She sat up and wiped her eyes, weary from her busy morning and stressed out because of what she was walking into. She knew without even knowing the extent of his injuries that he might not make it through surgery. Her heart was racing as she walked out of the airport and grabbed the first taxi lined up near the exit doors.

"Houston General, please." She leaned back in the seat and let out a deep breath. There was just no way to be prepared for what she might face. As the taxi pulled up to the hospital, she jumped out, grabbing her small bag, walked into the main entrance, and headed up to the information booth. The small woman with wrinkles around her eyes behind the counter smiled at her and asked if she could help.

"Yes, you can. I am here to see Tom Thornton. I believe he is having surgery today. He is a good friend of mine."

"Yes, dear. Go up to the fifth floor and when you get off the elevator, turn to your left and walk down the hall to the waiting room. Let the nurses know that you are there to see Mr. Thornton."

"Thank you." Elizabeth turned and walked hurriedly to the elevators and punched number five. The heavy doors closed and she felt her stomach tighten. She wondered how long the surgery had lasted and if he had survived it. That thought was hard to swallow and she really didn't want to face it.

She turned left after leaving the elevator and walked into the large waiting room, picking a seat near an end table. She sat down and pulled a bottled water out of her purse and took a large sip of water. She texted Stephanie to let her know she had arrived safely and sent another text to her parents. When she checked her messages there was one from Jim. He was worried because he hadn't heard from her.

She closed her phone, hoping to postpone contact with Jim until she knew more about how Tom was doing. It was like juggling two lives and what she really needed to be doing was concentrating on her career. Walmart wasn't going to wait forever for her to get the job done. They had been wonderful about her accident, but it was time to really get to work again. She wouldn't be able to stay with Tom for long.

After resting for a moment, Liz went to look for the nurses' station. She approached a young nurse who was standing outside ICU. "Excuse me. I am here to see Tom Thornton. Is he still in recovery?"

"Mr. Thornton is in ICU already. He is in a very unstable condition. I'll try to get the doctor to come out and talk to you. No family has shown up for him, so he will be pleased to see that you are here."

"The police phoned me about the shooting. I got here as quickly as I could."

"I'm sure it was a shock to you. His injuries were serious. The doctor will tell you more. Wait here and I will see what I can do."

Liz sat back down and waited for a chance to speak with the surgeon who had operated on Tom. Her head was spinning with doubts about his injuries and the outcome of the whole thing. Her father had texted her back, angry that she was pushing herself again. She knew she wasn't fully recovered yet, but she had to make a split second decision and she had chosen to be there for Tom. She knew she wouldn't regret it. No matter what the outcome.

Soon a doctor came in, his face solemn as he looked around for Liz. She jumped up and walked over to him, eager to hear about Tom.

"Doctor, I'm Elizabeth Stone, and I want to know how Tom is. Did he make it through the surgery all right?"

"Let's sit down over here, Elizabeth. I'm sure you've come a long way to see your friend."

"Yes, I have. But I'm worried sick and need to know what's going on."

"The bullet when into his chest and hit a major artery. We have tried to stop the bleeding but he lost a lot of blood before we ever got to him. Internal bleeding is worse than an open wound. The blood has to go somewhere and it fills up your body cavity. He is not in good condition. His body is fighting to survive. I can't even give you an idea of what the percentage is of his chance of recovery. We're just hoping to see some sign of life. He lost too much blood, Elizabeth. I'm afraid it doesn't look good."

Elizabeth felt like she was sinking. She sat back in the chair and just stared at the ground. When she looked back up, the doctor was rushing out the door. She got up and walked towards the door marked ICU. A nurse was standing just inside.

"Is there any way possible for me to see Tom Thornton? I know he's in a coma, but please, I've come a long way. Can I at least tell him good-bye?"

The nurse saw the look on Elizabeth's face and nodded. "You cannot stay long. His condition is critical. We're not supposed to allow anyone to visit at this time, but I know you won't take advantage of this time with him. You have fifteen minutes. That is all I can allow you."

Elizabeth saw the stern look on the nurse's face, but she also saw a woman who understood the situation. She nodded and walked through the door.

She wasn't prepared for what she saw. Tom didn't look like himself. And there were tubes coming out of every place on his body. He was on a ventilator and that was the only sound in the room. She walked up to the bed and put her hand in his, and then reached over and pulled a chair up to the bed so that she could sit down. Her back and legs were tired from the stress of the day and she leaned over and laid her head on the bed. She looked up a few times to see him and tears were streaming down her face, falling onto the white crisp hospital sheets.

She whispered quietly to him, telling him goodbye.. "Tom, I know you can hear me. Somewhere in there you can hear me. I am here. I love you. I never thought it would end this way. I know you were trying to help that lady but you are so fragile right now. I thought we would have a chance to talk. To start over. But I guess it's not meant to be. I just wanted to tell you that I forgive you. That I love you. And that I will never forget our last visit. And all the beautiful times we shared years ago."

She stood up and squeezed his hand again. For a slight second, so soft that she wondered if she had imagined it, she felt a pressure on her hand. A slight pressure. Tears came running down her face as she stood there waiting to see if it would come again. The nurse poked her head through the door and whispered that it was time to leave. She nodded and turned to Tom one more time. She leaned over and kissed his head, moving his hair off his face. She had a feeling she would never see those beautiful brown eyes again, smiling at her.

She squeezed his hand once more and whispered "I love you" in his ear. Again, the slight pressure on her hand. It caught her breath and when she stood up to look at his face, there was not even a hint that he knew she was there. Only the ventilator breathing for him.

She let go of his hand and stepped away from the bed. It felt like she was cutting off part of her heart. For she had truly loved him once. He had been the love of her life. And now it was almost certainly over.

She didn't even remember walking out of the hospital. Her body was numb. Somehow she made it to a hotel, checked into a room, and climbed into bed. She cried for what had happened to Tom and because any chance for them to try again was gone. Her body was worn out, but her mind was beyond tired. She slept fitfully, waking off and on during the night only to realize the brutal reality that Tom wasn't going to ever come out of the coma.

Early, when the sun was still struggling to push through the clouds, she sat up in bed and yawned. She had to check on an early flight home and get some breakfast. There were several messages on her cell that she needed to answer. The world was going on no matter what condition her heart was in. This seemed like such an irony that Tom would die in a freak shooting in a grocery store right when they were going to try to work things out or at least to see if there was hope. *What were the odds of that happening?* Her chest felt heavy and it seemed like she was walking in quicksand. Too much to process after the crash.

She called Tom's floor and the charge nurse confirmed what she had suspected—he had passed away during the night. She was able to book an early flight, so she showered, ate, and headed to the airport. Her flight was at ten and she had just enough time to get there and go through security and board the plane. She felt like she was in a bad dream. But she'd been through nightmares before that somehow had ended up as her reality and she had lived through them. A tougher shell was forming around her already bruised heart. It would be a miracle if she ever let anyone in. And then there was Jim.

Chapter 46

Jim leaned his head back against the pillows that were propped up against the headboard. He was tired and his leg ached. Had to be the cold weather and standing on his feet too long. His leg was still healing and he wasn't approved to do surgery yet. It would be a while. But that wasn't what was really troubling him. It had been three weeks since he'd heard anything from Elizabeth. He had texted her and left messages on her home phone, but she had never responded. Maybe she needed some time to sort through things. And he was ready to give her all the time she needed. But a word, something—from her—would help.

He yawned and checked his watch. It was getting late. He wanted to pick up the phone to try again, but he couldn't take the rejection. The silence. He cut the television on to hear any news that he might have missed at 6:00. It didn't surprise him that there was nothing going on of interest. He turned out the light and pulled the covers up over his head. It was going to be a long night.

An hour into his sleep his phone went off. Just a small sound. But the house was dead quiet and he was a light sleeper. He grabbed his cell and checked to see if it was the hospital. He was surprised to see Elizabeth's number on the text. He sat up in bed and grabbed his glasses and eagerly read what she'd sent. He noted that it was after midnight. What in the world was she doing up at this hour?

Jim, I know you've been trying to reach me forever. And I wanted to give you a good reason why I haven't responded but just couldn't find the words. Something has happened and I am having a hard time dealing with it. But I might as well be honest with you so that we can bridge this gap that has come between us. You were aware that Tom and I were supposed to get together and see if anything was left after many years of not talking. I also know your feelings about all of that. Well, on the same day he was supposed to fly in to see me, he was shot in a grocery store near his home before he even got on the plane. I was called by the Houston police and ended up flying to Houston to be with Tom. He didn't survive the gunshot wound. So you understand why I have been quiet for a few weeks. Work has been horrendous and I have a way of crowding out my emotions and focusing on my work, as you well know. Please forgive me. I do need and want to see you. I just had to wait and let things settle down. I am not sure even now if I have dealt with his death, but I had to contact you. Let me hear from you as soon as possible. And surely, if you forgave me for something as huge as a plane crash, then you can forgive my not answering your phone calls and texts? Talk to you soon. Lizzy

His heart was pounding. He sat back and smiled, leaning against the headboard, noticing his hands were shaking. She certainly had a way of getting to him. He had been in such a knot over not hearing from her, and now all the frustration melted into the bedcovers and all he wanted to do was pick up the phone and call her. He was worried about her facing Tom's death alone. Well, he knew Leigh would be there for her. But he wanted to be the one she leaned on. He felt so protective of her. Was it too late to call? He hesitated and then sat back up and dialed her number. She answered at one ring.

"Hello? Jim?"

"Liz! Gosh, it's good to hear your voice! I just got your text. I was sound asleep and woke when it came through. Immediately I was concerned as to why you were up at this hour. I'm so sorry to hear about Tom."

"Oh, Jim, it was a horrible. What are the odds of being shot at a grocery store? Some crazy guy pulled the trigger on him as he was trying to help a woman the gunman was harassing. I still cannot believe he is gone."

Jim felt his blood pressure rise. *Why am I so jealous of her feelings for Tom?* "Liz, I know you are sick about this and I wish there was something I could do."

"Well there is a small thing you can do, Jim."

He smiled. "And what might that be?"

"I was hoping you could fly out for a visit this next week. Any chance of that happening with your busy schedule?"

"Oh, I think I can arrange it, Liz. When were you thinking?"

"That's up to you. I do have a few things this week that have to be done. So Thursday looks like the best time for me. How about you?"

"That would be perfect for me. Can you sleep tonight? I don't like the thought of you sitting up in bed feeling so sad."

"We have been through so much, Jim, that I am almost numb. Our time on that mountain feels like a fairytale now. And it hasn't been all that long that we were wondering if someone would ever find us."

"I feel like it's been a year since I've seen you. I really look forward to our visit, Lizzie. Please rest and we'll talk tomorrow. I know you have to be worn out."

"I am, Jim. Thanks for the call and I'm sorry that I woke you up."

"I wouldn't have it any other way, Liz. I've been dying to talk to you, as you well know. Worried sick about you."

"I'll call you tomorrow afternoon. Thanks again, Jim. Just hearing your voice has calmed me down quite a bit."

"Good night, Liz."

Jim lay there for forty-five minutes thinking about the conversation he'd just had with Liz. She sounded so weak and fragile. He was sad for her that Tom was gone, but maybe in that disaster there would come some clarification concerning her feelings for him. She was torn between the two of them and now she had time to recover and enjoy the time they would spend together. He smiled just remembering their time on the mountain. The cold had been almost unbearable. But somehow they had survived it and now it would be interesting to see if they could build a solid relationship from their time together.

He closed his eyes and drifted off to sleep. He had a full schedule of patients tomorrow but his mind would be on that phone call near the end of the day. He still loved her. He still got lost in her voice. But it was when he looked into her eyes that he nearly stopped breathing. She had no clue how beautiful she was, how he loved the stubborn part of her—and how he longed to never leave her side. *The big stoic doctor who wasn't going to get that involved with anyone, and now, look at me. I'm putty in her hands. It's ridiculous. But I love every moment of it.*

Six states away, tucked underneath her down comforter, Elizabeth lay with her eyes wide open. She couldn't turn her mind off. Her thoughts were racing between Tom and his untimely death and her feelings for Jim.

She had really put herself into her work for the last three weeks and was making great headway with all the Walmart stores. They were pleased with her findings and Stephanie was already taking calls from some other major corporations who needed her services. She was going to be as busy as she wanted to be, but inside there was something else going on. A need to share her life with someone. She was realizing that she was tired of living alone; a thought she had never before believed she would verbalize. After her breakup with Tom she suddenly had no interest in developing close relationships, and now she had reduced that once iron-clad decision to texting Jim in the middle of the night.

She turned over and tucked her nose underneath the covers and closed her eyes. Her skin looked pale against the dark night and her eyelashes were dark against the white pillow. She was tired of feeling sad and tired of worrying. She needed some love in her life and someone who was stable to surround her world. Sleep finally came and she dreamed of the plane crash and the cabin. The cold nights. The deer meat. And the growing feelings for Jim that remained inside of her until he was able to pull them out.

The alarm clock snapped her into reality. But when she opened her eyes it felt like she'd just fallen asleep. And it was going to be a long day.

Chapter 47

There was someone else that had been ignored for a few weeks and she wasn't happy about it at all. Leigh poured a cup of coffee and sat down on the sofa and dialed Elizabeth's office. She usually didn't call her at work, but she wasn't going to wait any longer. Just before Stephanie picked up the phone, Leigh hung up. She quickly decided to change clothes, put on her boots, and drive to Elizabeth's office to talk to her in person. She knew only too well that Elizabeth would dodge her calls, so she decided to beat her at her own game. There was no way she would not see her if she was in the office. Leigh decided to take that risk and drove quickly through nearly noon traffic to Liz's office. It was sunny and the warmth of the sun felt good coming through the car windshield, but it was still cold outside. Winter was slowly losing its grip on the weather but fighting it hard.

Getting off the elevator, Leigh looked around to find a restroom and ducked in the door to refresh her lipstick and get her speech down pat. She wanted to hear all about Liz's work, but mostly about Tom and Jim. It was about time that Liz decided who she was going to love. And Leigh had her own justifiable thoughts on that matter. She walked nonchalantly into Liz's office, pulling open the double doors, and immediately Stephanie was on her.

"Hello. Can I help you?"

"Hey, darling. You must be Stephanie! Elizabeth has told me all about you. She was thrilled that you could work for her. By the way, is she in?"

"Yes, she is. But she is very busy, Mrs. ?"

"Miller. Leigh Miller. I'm her best friend. She'll see me."

"I'll go talk to Liz and see if this is a good time for her."

Leigh smiled glibly at that remark and sat down on the sofa by a huge window looking down on the busy street below. It wasn't two seconds before Elizabeth came out of her office, smiling and walking towards her with her arms open.

"What a nice surprise! It's been too long."

"I'll say it has. Where in the world have you been the last couple of weeks? I thought you dropped off the face of the earth, Liz." Leigh waltzed passed Stephanie with a smirk on her face.

Liz sat down beside Leigh and laughed. "No, not really. But we do have a lot to catch up on. You want to grab some lunch and we can visit? I don't have long but I can spare an hour with you."

Liz glanced at Stephanie and Stephanie nodded her approval. "Go for it, Liz. It will do you good."

As Leigh walked out of the office, she glanced back at Stephanie. "Quite some gal you got here working for you. Like a pit bull. She wasn't going to let me walk into your office for anything."

"She's my right arm. And she has to be that way or I would be tied up talking to people that I really don't need to be wasting my time with. I am sure she realized that you were a good friend."

"Best friend, dear. Best friend. And I cannot wait to hear what you've been doing."

They hurriedly walked down to the local café on the corner and found a seat in the back corner in the small crowded room. It was warm and cozy and the aroma coming from the kitchen was heavenly. The waitress jumped on them as soon as they sat down, so they ordered their meals and Leigh didn't wait two seconds before she started asking questions.

"So. What's been going on in your world? Heard from Jim? Tom? You have to catch me up on your love life, lady."

Liz took a deep breath and glanced around her. She didn't relish talking about Tom's death, but there was no way out of it. Leigh would want the gory details.

"I have something very serious to talk to you about. All kidding aside, Leigh. Tom and I were supposed to see each other three weeks ago. He arranged for a flight to come for a long weekend. Before his flight left, he went to a local grocery and while in line to check out, there was a crazy man standing off to one side arguing with a woman in front of him. For some reason the man was very angry and pulled out a gun and aimed it at the woman. She was shot and was falling backwards, and as Tom leaned over to catch her, the gunman shot him, too. The woman died immediately and they rushed Tom to the ER."

Leigh's face registered her shock. "Whoa, girl. I can hardly keep up with you. You mean Tom got shot in the grocery store? What kind of nut would do such a thing?"

"Hold on and I'll finish. They caught the guy and I am sure he was arrested and charged. Not sure what he was so angry about. But I was contacted and flew to Houston to be with Tom. He was in a coma and they were sure he would never wake up. It was horrible. I could hardly bear to be in the room with him; he was hooked up to so many machines. Leigh, you have no idea how hard that was."

Leigh reached over and put her hand on Liz's. "Honey, why didn't you call me? I would have gone with you. You know I would."

"I know. But there wasn't time. It was all I could do to book the flight and get there before he died. I am not sure he even knew I was there, but I had to go, Leigh. I had to."

"Of course you did, honey. You did the right thing. But now what? How are you dealing with all these emotions? I know you're angry about his death."

"I was devastated at first, and numb. We were just going to see if we had anything, after all the years of separation. Not sure anything would have ever happened but it was worth finding out. But now that is all gone. He is gone. I will never know, Leigh."

"Damn, Liz. But you did have that chance to see him again and that is huge. Don't you agree? At least you did see him and talk things through. He died knowing you knew how he felt."

"I am thankful for that. But I went into a funk for three weeks and didn't answer any of Jim's texts or phone calls. It's a wonder he didn't just write me off. But that's not Jim. Of course he was there, in the middle of the night—calming me down. Understanding. I know there is a point to all of this sadness, but right now it is difficult to see it. From where I am standing, it seems my life is a complete mess."

"Oh, don't be so dramatic. I know you lost Tom. And for that I am very sad for you. But let's face it, Liz. Tom was gone a long time ago. The chances of your developing a long-term relationship with him again were slim and none. On the other hand, you have a very handsome, loving heart surgeon who loves you to death and is waiting to get the okay from you to move forward. Now that doesn't seem so bad, does it?"

Liz laughed and wiped her eyes. She could always count on Leigh for a little sarcasm. "From your rotten perspective, it is almost fate. I don't believe in fate, you know that. But I have a funny feeling you do."

"Of course. I think I already know where this is headed."

"Eat your lunch, girlfriend. We only have a few more minutes. I don't even know where things are going. But I do plan to see Jim next week and I think it will be good for us both. No expectations. Just time together."

"I'm amazed you had the wherewithal to set up a date with him after what you've been through." Leigh reached across the table and grabbed Liz's hand. "You need to let your life settle down a bit, Liz. But don't run off the people around you who are good for you and love you. I'm one of them. Don't put your head into your work and cut off all the people who believe in you. Jim being one of them. You may have nine lives, but I'd say your are pushing it to the limit. We don't get that many chances to have a good life and I don't want you to pass this one up just because you are heartbroken over an old love. It wasn't that long ago you wouldn't even speak his name. You hated him for what he did to you. Remember?"

Liz looked down and smiled. "Of course I do. I really didn't want to let Tom in that night he came by. But he charmed me all over again. That is Tom. Sort of like Bruce Willis coming to your door. But Jim is more like Jimmy Stewart. I know which one you would say is best for me. I already know what you are going to say."

Leigh laughed. "We know each other too well, Liz."

Liz stood up. "I've got to get back to work. Jim is coming next Thursday and I will let you know how it goes. Until then, I'll be working on my Walmart account. It's almost over and they've been wonderful. But I am ready to move on to the next company." She paused.

"And by the way, Stephanie is like my right arm. It didn't take her five minutes to size my office up and take over. She watches over me like a mother hen. I love it. So go easy on her. She is vital to my work."

"Damn your work, Liz. I'm working on getting you married so that you don't have to work so hard. You need a man around. Someone to lean on. You don't have to be so strong, you know."

Liz laughed and hugged Leigh. "Thanks for the chat and the hug. I'll call you next week after Jim leaves. I love you. Thanks for caring about me, and I'm sorry for avoiding you. I will work on not shutting everyone out when I get in a funk about my life. It's learned behavior. Not very conducive if I am the slightest bit interested in Jim!"

"No kidding. Thanks for taking an hour of your time to spend it with your best friend. I'll try to stay out of your hair for a few days. But don't push it! Now get in the car and I'll drive you back to work."

Leigh smiled and shook her head as she watched Liz walk into her office building. There was something vulnerable about Liz now. A character trait she had not seen before. Hopefully it would cause her to take note of this man in her life that truly loved her. Leigh could think of nothing worse than living alone the rest of her life without someone to love. She would die if Joe wasn't around. He was her rock. She'd always been a little jealous of Elizabeth because she was so beautiful. She could have had any man she wanted. But that was where the sadness slept. She wanted no one. Or so it seemed. Maybe beneath those long eyelashes and a mane like a horse was a heart that was just wounded. After Tom had walked out on her, she had let no one else in. The crash that could have killed her might have opened up that heart again.

Leigh drove home hoping that Jim would step up to the plate now before that door closed in Elizabeth's heart. Funny thing, the heart, she thought. It pumped blood into the body and gave us life. But it also could break over a lost love. It wasn't a coincidence that Jim was a cardio man. A heart mender. Just that thought alone made Leigh smile. There was hope in the wind. A crack in the armor. If the Berlin Wall could come down, then there was a chance, slight as it might appear, that Liz would fall in love again. And she wanted to be there to see it. A front row seat. For if truth be known, she'd lost a lot of sleep worrying over that girl.

When she walked in the door, Joe was waiting at the kitchen table, poring over the newspaper with a cup of coffee next to his plate of cookies. He looked up guiltily and smiled. "Hey, sweetheart. You have a good visit with Liz?"

Leigh came over and wrapped her arms around him and kissed the top of his head. "Yes, I did! And I want to make a wager; not that I'm a betting woman or anything. I am betting that Jim and Liz get together before the end of summer. I just have a feeling about this, Joe. She just told me that her past love, Tom, has died from a horrible accident. He had booked a flight to see her and rekindle their relationship."

Joe raised his eyebrows and laughed. "Leigh, if I've told you once, I've told you a million times, you've got to stop trying to fix Lizzie up. She'll come around in her own time."

"Well, let's hope it's before she turns gray and wrinkled. If she blows this thing with Jim because of what happened to Tom, I'm going to pull all of that lovely brown hair out of her head."

"Oh, that will fix everything."

"Joe! It's perfect. I know he's right for her,"

"And why do you say that, Sherlock?"

"Because he is a lot like you."

Joe rubbed his eyes and stared at her. Sometimes she could come out with something that made his knees weak. "Come here, honey. Sit in my lap. I know you love her. I know you want her happy. Let's just trust Liz to make the right decision. And do you really think Jim is like me?"

Leigh laughed and laid her head on his shoulder. Just for a moment she lost herself in his smell and faded cologne. "There's no one like you, Joe. No one. But I think he comes pretty damn close."

Chapter 48

There are times in our lives when we should grasp the power of the moment. The fact that this just might be a turning point, a fork in the road, so to speak. A monumental time when our decision will be critical to the rest of our lives. A second when, if we fail to see it, will pass like a rainbow after a light rain, when the sun peeps through the half-gray billowy clouds.

Elizabeth was about to have that kind of moment. She had prepared a wonderful steak dinner and had chosen an appropriate wine for the meal. Candles were lit. She was dressed to the nines and had left her hair down. Yet her mind could not stay in the present. She was fighting memories of Tom and the way he died. He had slipped out of her life twice, only this time it was permanent.

She was more than excited that Jim was coming. There was no doubt in her mind that she would be glad to see him. To hear his voice again. And he sounded like he was in a great hurry to see her. She knew he loved her. Or at least he did love her before. But she had moved away emotionally from him and he had felt it. She was sure of that.

She brushed a stray hair out of her eyes and turned off the oven. The rolls were ready. Everything was ready. Except her heart. It was tucked away in a dark room. A room that had been there since Tom had ducked out of their engagement. But this time, she wondered if she would be able to find the key to unlock that door. Or even if she wanted to open it again. She was depressed and full of sadness. Not a good atmosphere for what she was about to face.

The doorbell rang. *He's here.* Her breath stopped momentarily and she took a little sip of red wine. It burned her throat and she felt it hit her empty stomach. She wiped her hands on her apron and walked towards the door. Jim was on the other side and she would have to put on her best smile and hope against hope that he wouldn't see the tears running down her broken heart.

As she turned the knob, Jim pushed on the door and he accidentally knocked her back as he came through the door. She didn't have a chance to say a word. He had his arms around her before she could even say his name.

"Elizabeth! I was beginning to think I would never see you again!" He kissed her forehead, her cheeks, and her lips. He held her close and she could feel his heart beating fast.

She pushed away gently and smiled at him. His eyes were gray blue. She had forgotten how beautiful they were. And her words caught in her throat as she fought back all of the emotions she was feeling.

"Jim! It's so good to see you again. I've missed you, too! Please come in and let me take your coat."

Jim took his coat off and laid it on a chair close to the door. "Don't worry about my coat. I just want to sit and look at you. You look stunning—absolutely stunning." He glanced over towards the table and sniffed. "I smell something wonderful! You've prepared us a special meal together."

"I wanted us to be here tonight. It's the first time in a long time that we will really be able to talk and catch up with each other. A restaurant isn't the best place in the world for a good visit." She smiled her best smile.

He pulled her to him again and held her hands in his. "Do you have any idea how much I've wanted to see you? How much I've missed you?"

She looked down and nodded. "I've had the same feelings, Jim. But it's been a whirlwind around here with me catching up on my work and then this thing with Tom. I've not been myself lately. I really didn't want to talk to anyone. Can you understand that?"

"Of course I can. Am I moving too fast here, Lizzie?"

"Maybe a little. But I'm glad to see you. Please don't think I'm not. Come. Let's sit down and eat. The food is ready and then we can spend time talking. I know you've had a long day and I bet you're hungry."

"I'm hungry. But I am not paying any attention to my hunger, Liz. I'm so elated to be able to see you again. You look lovely. A little tired, but lovely at the same time. I've certainly seen you at your worst, haven't I now?" He chuckled and winked at her.

"You sure have! I was hoping that image of me had faded a bit in your mind."

"It is like yesterday, sometimes. These last few weeks have been hard on me, not hearing from you. But let's not talk about that now. I want to hear about your work and how you've been." He pulled out a chair for her and waited for her to be seated before taking his seat across the table.

"I'm good, Jim. Walmart has been unbelievably supportive and I really feel I've extrapolated enough information concerning their operation in each store to give them the answers they need. It's exciting to make the right improvements that will bring about the results they need both financially and internally with their employees. I love my job!"

Jim was smiling at her. "I am hearing the words you say, but all I am seeing is you."

Liz blushed. "This meal is quite a jump from what we ate in that cabin on the side of the mountain."

"Yes, it is. But I may have enjoyed those meals more because we were alone. No one knew where we were."

"Jim! You can't mean that. We went through hell for nearly two weeks! Nearly starved to death. And the cold was unbearable."

"I can still feel the cold. The pain I had in my leg. What you went through to feed us. But that is where I fell in love with you. So I have fond memories of that time."

She swallowed hard but didn't respond to his comment. "Tell me about you. How is your leg? When will you get to do surgery again?"

"Probably next week. But I won't take on too much at once. One surgery a day until I feel strong enough. Will continue rehab until my strength is up to par."

"You look strong. It appears your work agrees with you."

"So let's talk about your last few weeks, Liz. Tell me how you're dealing with Tom's death."

"I think I'm doing great with it and then I get hit with emotions that I thought were buried."

"That's normal, I'm sure. You guys were close at one time and he was trying to reenter your life. Not that I wanted that, you know."

"I know this was difficult for you, Jim. You've been the perfect gentleman but I've probably pushed that snowball into a boulder by now. I really didn't know what my future held. I just wanted to give him a chance so that I could either put it behind me or go forward. I knew the odds were slim. I really didn't expect much from our next visit."

Jim swallowed his last bite of steak and pushed away from the table. "You haven't had any time to think about us. I know you've been busy with your work and then this thing came up with Tom. I've been busy, too, Liz. But you have never left my mind. Can we move over to the couch to talk? I'll take our glasses of wine with us, if that is okay."

Liz stood up and carried the plates to the sink. She was shaky inside. Jim was in love with her, still. And she was reeling from the impact all this was having on him. It wasn't fair to keep him hanging. She could hear Leigh in her head saying not to mess this night up.

Both of them sat down on the sofa and sipped their wine quietly. The fire was mesmerizing and it brought back memories of the cabin. They both spoke at the same time, interrupting each other.

"Do you remember the—?" "Jim laughed as she talked over him.

"I was just remembering all the nights we sat on that creaky old sofa trying to stay warm by that fire."

"I do, too! And cooking the rabbit over the coals on a stick. We were in heaven having something to eat besides the deer meat. I don't think I could eat any deer meat now if my life depended on it!"

"I know. I would gag. But it kept us alive."

"Yes, it did. Thinking back, we went through a pretty harrowing time together. It's a miracle we lived through it. You did most of the saving, Liz. If you hadn't been so brave we would have starved to death."

"I hardly think you would have allowed that. Even though your leg was in trouble, I know you would have gone out there and shot something. Anything. You would not have allowed us to go hungry."

Jim paused. He reached over and brushed her hair away from her face. She looked up and smiled. It was a weary smile, but there nonetheless. He seemed grateful for anything. Any sign that she still felt something for him.

"It's getting late, Liz. I know it's been a long day for you and you're probably tired. I did get a hotel room, but I would like to stay. I—" He saw the look on her face and paused.

"No. I have no ulterior motive. I just don't want to leave you. Come here, Liz. Lean back against me like we did in the cabin. I know you have been through so much. Just let me hold you."

Liz leaned back and let herself get lost in the scent of his cologne and the strength of his arms. It did feel good to just let go and not think. He made her feel so soft and feminine. So at peace. He was such a good man. Tears were streaming down her face and suddenly she turned and put her face into his neck and cried. He held her close and they sat like that for what seemed like hours. Jim pulled her down next to him on the sofa and they remained silent for a while.

"It seems like too much, Jim. Everything that's happened in the last six months. I guess I'm not as strong as I thought I was. I'm so ready for things to settle down and get back to some semblance of normal. But I'm not sure how to do that."

He took her hand and stroked her face. His voice was low and deep. "Sweetheart, no one else but you could have held up to what you've been through. Both of us are weary emotionally and it is going to take some time. I just wish I wasn't so far away from your world. You need me now. And I cannot be here day to day."

"I didn't think I needed anyone, Jim. For so long it has been just me. But this time is different. I don't feel so strong anymore. I'm so glad you came. I needed to see you more than I realized."

He lifted her face and kissed her softly. She gave in to it for a moment and felt her heart racing. He had such strong lips and his arms felt good around her weary body. She closed her eyes and relaxed against him, feeling his warmth and wanting to let him in. He kept quiet and seemed to be listening to her breathing. She lay there quietly listening to the distant sound of the clock ticking in the hallway. Without her realizing it, she fell asleep in his arms, and woke up hours later with a crick in her neck. Jim was asleep so she quietly climbed off the sofa and went into her bedroom and turned down the covers and fell into them.

Her dreams were fitful and she awoke to the smell of bacon drifting into the bedroom. Just as she set up and stretched, looking at the rays of sun coming through her window above the bed, Jim waltzed into her room with a smile.

"Good morning, beautiful! I've made you some coffee, and breakfast is waiting."

She smiled. "My gosh, Jim. Aren't you an early riser!"

"Only when I have you in the other room. I slept pretty good on that sofa of yours."

"I got up and moved in here because I was getting a crick in my neck."

He winked and waved his hand. "Come on. The food is getting cold."

She went hurriedly into the bathroom to brush her hair and teeth and walked into the kitchen. The fragrance of rich coffee and eggs, bacon, and toast lingered in the air. "What a wonderful way to wake up. I could get used to this."

"So could I. So let's sit down and enjoy this food and you can tell me what your plans are for today. It's Saturday and before you open your mouth, I am vying for the whole day with you. I hope that's on your list."

A sleepy grin tiptoed across her face and she wiped the sleep from her eyes. "I really haven't thought about what we would do today. We could go shopping, to the park, or a good movie. Or we could just stay here for the whole day and I could bake us some fresh cookies and plan a good dinner for you tonight. I am on the go all week long, so it is nice not to have to be anywhere on the weekends."

"I feel the same way. And you make me feel very at home here, as you can see. Why don't we go out for a bit, maybe get lunch somewhere downtown at a small café, and then spend the rest of the afternoon here. I don't want you to feel like you have to entertain me. I am perfectly content just being here with you."

He was pushing buttons in her and she knew there was a point of no return where she would just let her heart open up and then he would be in for good. There would be no going back. She loved her privacy and being single; in control of her life. But Jim was different. She'd learned a lot about him on that mountain in the cold. There was nothing to hide anymore.

"That sounds wonderful. And this breakfast is fabulous. I feel so spoiled."

He grinned. "Why don't you take a long shower or bath and take your time getting ready. I'll clean up the kitchen and shower when you are through. Then we'll go downtown and walk around. If you see something you want to look at, we'll stop. Then we can have lunch somewhere; I'm sure you know that area of town. Surely there's a neat place to eat."

She laughed. "I know just the place. I think they even have music going on at lunch. That would be fun!"

She got up from the table and walked back into her bedroom. Jim followed her to the door but she pushed him back. "You stay out of here, buddy. I won't be long."

She stood on her tiptoes and kissed him softly. "And thanks for the lovely breakfast. That was unexpected. And I loved it. And by the way, there's a shower in the other bathroom. Help yourself!"

He whistled his way back to the kitchen and she could hear him washing the dishes as she started her bath. This was turning out to be a wonderful visit and she could feel herself relaxing, and allowing herself to enjoy Jim. It was hard not to love him. He was almost perfect. But she'd thought that of Tom and he bailed out at the most intimate moment in their relationship. Of course, Jim was older. And more mature. Sure of himself. *There was no way to be dead sure.*

She stepped into the pile of bubbles and blushed when she remembered his kiss. She shook her head, laughing at herself. She was acting like a teenager and that was going to stop. This was too serious for her to get swooned by a kiss. However, if she had to rate it, it would probably be a ten.

Chapter 49

The streets were crowded with people and there was a mist in the air. Possible rain in the afternoon. But nothing took away from this day with Elizabeth. Jim was walking on air beside her, holding her hand and listening to the words she was saying but really only seeing her face. She was beautiful to him and he knew as they walked together watching people and enjoying the hectic atmosphere of the crowd that she was the woman he wanted to spend the rest of his life with. She might not know, but he did. And he smiled from deep within, squeezing her hand tighter, and closing in the gap between them with his words. Slowly. For she was fragile even in her strength. He could see that now. She could stand alone, but they were stronger together. And that was what he wanted for their life.

"Isn't that a café there on the corner? Waterstreet Café? I'm getting hungry."

She threw her head back and laughed. "You're always hungry."

"Yes, I think I am. But I'm not ashamed of that. Especially when I can dine with you."

"You are a charmer. Leigh was right. Now let's see if we can get a table in there. It looks crowded."

They stepped inside and a waitress hurried them to the back left corner near a window. They could see the skyscrapers downtown towering like great giants casting shadows in the sun. Elizabeth sat across from him and the light coming through the window made her hair look almost golden.

"Are you nearly finished with Walmart?"

She looked into his eyes. He had more than her work on his mind but he was being cautious.

"We talked about this last night. Yes! It has been a challenging endeavor but I have loved every moment of it. I can't wait until I get my next company. You can't imagine the satisfaction I receive when I have moved from one store to the next discovering what the problems are that are eating up the profits of the corporation. It is hard sometimes to let the manager of a store know that he is the problem. But more often than not, that is the situation."

Jim raised an eyebrow. "Really? I would never have thought that would be the case."

"I know. I felt that way at first. But it has proven to be the norm instead of a rarity."

"I bet they love seeing you coming. Word spreads. They must know that you are going to find the problem."

"They do. I can feel it the moment I walk through the door. But it has to happen for the company to be healthy. They cannot hide behind their titles and starched shirts anymore."

They ordered their meal and ate in silence, watching the hundreds of people moving through the crowded streets outside. There were cars honking their horns, police sirens, people laughing, and the smell of food cooking. All blended into one as they watched all the people going by. Jim looked at her and for a moment he watched every single expression on her face. Once her eyes settled on his, and he allowed himself to gaze into them without saying a word. He was aching to hold her. To tell her he wanted her to live with him the rest of their lives. But he just couldn't get it out. It wasn't the right time. It might even run her away. He was so caught up in his thoughts that he didn't hear her question. She repeated it, and reached over and touched his hand.

"Jim! You were lost in thought. Talk to me about your practice. How is it going? I know you are so anxious to get back into surgery full time."

"I am. I do enjoy surgery, practically giving someone a second chance at life. What's not to love?"

She smiled softly. She did everything softly. But he wasn't fooled by this trait because he also was familiar with the wall of stone she'd built around her heart. Her life. And he had only begun to chip away at it.

"I have never dreamed of working in the medical field. I don't think I could stomach it. But I admire you for it. We are so desperately in need of good surgeons."

"I've worked alongside some of the best in the world. And yet I am driven to learn more. That is the one thing we can count on in this world. There is always more we need to learn. Everything keeps changing. New technology. New ideas. It is impossible to keep up with it. But we have to try or we will be useless in our field."

"This is changing the subject, but have you heard from Sheila again?"

Now it was his time to grin. "Thank heavens, no. Not a word. I am cautiously optimistic."

"That's a great way to put it. Caution being the key word." She looked at her watch. It was mid afternoon and they were still sitting in the café sipping on coffee. He could have sat there all day until sunset but he knew that would be too long for her.

"You ready to head home, lady? I could use a nap at the hotel and then we could enjoy a late dinner. How does that sound?"

"Perfect. I do have some paperwork to do and some errands to run. Are you sure that is okay with you?"

"As long as you promise to go out with me tonight. My flight is early Sunday morning. So tonight is our last time together until I return."

He thought he saw a frown starting in the middle of her brows. She looked down for a moment and then back towards him. "I have really enjoyed today. And last night. It has taken my mind off my sorrow. And it has reminded me of all the good things I saw in you while we were stranded on that dreadful mountain."

"We both have many things we saw about each other that might not have come out in a normal situation. I go over and over that time with you in my mind. Let's get back to the car and I'll drive you home."

They walked hand in hand back to the car and were quiet all the way to her house. Jim was already dreading leaving her. This time was so precious. He just couldn't let her slip away back into her private corporate world where everything was predictable and controlled. He had to see her again, somehow. He wanted her to see how much he loved her.

When he pulled up in her driveway he reached over and pulled her close to him and raised her face so he could see her eyes. He swallowed hard. "Liz, I'm not playing games here. We are way past that. We've broken bread together. Or rather rabbit. Deer. I am very serious about how I feel about you. This visit was long in coming and I am enjoying every second with you. Not trying to be pushy, but time is of the essence. So I am speaking my mind."

Liz did not turn away. He could see that it was difficult for her to hear what he was saying. But he was pleased that she didn't look away. Her voice was almost a whisper. But he heard what she said very clearly.

"I know this is a critical moment in our lives, in our relationship. And I don't want to miss it. It seems I have missed several of these moments in the past and I am tired of it. So I hear what you are saying and I'm taking in every single word. Just let me process it, Jim. I promise you I'm listening. I know we have something special and I don't want to draw back and destroy such a rare thing. I know you are good for me and I love the way I feel when you are near me. It has taken me a long time to say that, even to myself. I am sorry I feel so far away at times. I am working on that."

He kissed her lips and the side of her face. She had a light fragrance that was having its way with his mind. But he wanted to stay in the moment. It was so wonderful he didn't want to daydream it away.

"I know you have had a lot on you since we returned home. Both of us have been so busy finding our way back into our lives. I think it will take quite some time for us to recover from what we went through. But I love that it was with you, Liz. I love that it was with you."

He could tell that got to her. But he meant it. There was no game playing going on. She leaned into him and laid her head on his shoulder. He held her close and then pulled away and kissed her again.. This time he went slow. He could tell she was as lost as he was in that kiss. But he broke away and winked at her.

"You go. I am going to take a long nap. We need to save some things for tonight. Let's be casual for dinner. I don't care if we get a hamburger somewhere. But I do want to make the most of our time. We need to discuss anything that is on our mind. Any questions that need to be asked. This is real, Elizabeth. This is what life is all about."

"You are awfully deep for a man. I am amazed that you are not afraid to go there, like most men are. I do want to know all about you. Go rest and we'll get back together around 6:00. Is that good for you? Is that what you were thinking?"

"Perfect. See you then. You better get out of this car or I'll change my mind."

He watched her walk into her house and close the door. What he really wanted to do was to sit there for three hours until it was time to see her again. Or better yet, to go up those steps and knock on her door and never leave. Neither of which was an option. So he drove away with good thoughts about the last kiss and when he reached the hotel he unlocked his room and sat on the edge of the bed. Thoughts were running through his head like cars in the Indy 500. But the one thought that remained through the whole day was that this was his time. He had lived his life for this one moment. To be with Elizabeth. She was the one he had been searching for all his life. He also realized in this vulnerable moment, that no one could help him over this crevice into her heart. He had to do it alone. And that was a most unnerving thought in his head. He had broken rib cages and held a human heart in his hand. But to tear down the wall that Liz had built around herself was much more difficult. That was a pretty tough thing to fall asleep on. But his years in medical school had taught him to sleep standing up. So nap he did. He slept so soundly that he nearly overslept for one of the most important meals of his life.

Chapter 50

Liz had no more gotten into the house when the phone rang. It was Leigh. The ring even sounded like her.

"Hey, lady! I know you are probably busy but I need to know. How are things going with Jim?"

Liz rolled her eyes. The woman just wouldn't quit.

"How did you know he was in town?"

"News travels fast. Mary Bernstein, my hairdresser, saw you at the Waterstreet today at lunch. So I couldn't wait to call. Did I wait long enough?"

"I just walked in the door. How have you been?"

"Busy with Joe. I flew to Memphis with him last weekend and we stayed with some old friends. Went to the Rib Shack on the river. It was delicious."

"Sounds like fun. I haven't done that in years."

"So how is he?"

"Leigh, for heaven's sake! We've spent some time together and things are going well. I love having him around. I know you want to hear that. But you have to understand how much I've been through lately with Tom's death. That was a real shocker. He was on his way to see me."

Leigh interrupted quickly. "Jeez, Liz. You've got to let that guy go. It wasn't meant to be. It didn't work the first time and I know the deal; he came back and wanted to try again. But he is gone now and there isn't going to be another time. I hate to think that you are mourning someone who walked out on you years ago, when you have this guy who probably is madly in love with you right under your nose."

Liz felt her blood pressure rise. "You have no idea what I'm feeling, Leigh. And besides, Tom had changed. Even I could see that. I just wanted to see. I know you're right. It probably would not have worked out. But I was going to give it one more chance. I do like Jim. I may even love him. But I have to find out on my own if I am in love with him. There is a difference, you know."

"I know. I'm sorry. But sometimes I have to pull your leg out of the past. I feel like you just won't get over Tom. Even though he broke your heart, dang it. You shut everyone out when that happened. Even me. I liked to have never gotten back into your life after that happened. I didn't think you would ever get over it. And granted, it was a terrible thing that he walked out on you. I know you adored him. But stay in the moment, if you can. Just try, Liz."

Liz sat down on the edge of her bed and leaned back against the headboard. "Leigh, he is good to me. He is brilliant, funny, and really seems to care about my life. I am listening. I promise. So let me get some rest, and I'll talk to you tomorrow. We're going to have dinner tonight and then he will head home in the morning. Sometimes it seems too good to be true, you know? I'm having to pinch myself."

"Just enjoy it. And I didn't mean to be so hard on you. I just don't want you to miss this relationship because you are holding on to something that dissipated into thin air years ago."

"Thanks for the call. And I know you love me. Otherwise you wouldn't be so ugly."

Leigh laughed and Liz hung up the phone and snuggled down into her pillow. She dozed off for a couple of hours and woke up feeling a little groggy, checking the clock. It was 5:30 and she wanted to freshen up. Her paperwork would have to wait until later in the evening after Jim left. She washed her face and redid her makeup, putting her hair up in a bun. She had the beginnings of dark circles underneath her eyes; she was pushing too hard. She decided to change into a red sleeveless sweater and dark jeans with red lipstick. It made her eyes look better and she loved red. She hoped Jim would, too.

Just when she was changing her shoes, the doorbell rang. She ran down the stairs, taking two steps at a time, and opened the door. Her heart was racing. It was Jim, of course, standing there looking as handsome as ever. She didn't know how he did it, but he looked totally refreshed. She could smell his cologne and he was holding a huge bundle of flowers.

"Where in the world did you get those?"

He leaned over and kissed her. "That is for me to know. Aren't they lovely? You have a vase I can put them in for you?"

She walked into the kitchen and pointed to a higher cabinet. "It's up there. Can you reach it?"

He stretched his frame and grabbed the vase. Then he put water in it and arranged the flowers. "You want these on the table or what?"

She took the vase and set it on the island in the kitchen and smiled. "Are you hungry again?"

"Not quite. Let's sit and talk. You have any music you can put on?"

"I sure do. Have a seat and I'll get you a glass of wine."

"Sounds good. That nap felt good. How about you?"

"I barely got in the door and Leigh called. I don't think I need to tell you what she called about."

He laughed. "I know without even asking you what she said. She is a piece of work. She ought to have a job as a detective. Or work for the mob. I don't think you could put anything over on her."

Liz laughed and sat down on the sofa. "She's nosy and controlling. But she does love me. So I try to take that into consideration when she goes too far. She gets very frustrated with me. She thinks I am dragging my feet."

He laughed and kissed her hands. "I think you are coming along rather nicely, if you want to know the truth."

Liz raised her eyebrow and leaned back against a pillow. "Oh, really? Well, we'll see how the night goes, Mr. Romeo. What time is your flight tomorrow?"

"Already thinking about my leaving, are you?"

"No. I just wanted to know if we would have time to share breakfast."

Jim blushed. "I shouldn't have spoken so quickly. If I remember correctly, I leave at 10:30. So we do have time for an early breakfast, which probably suits you better, anyway."

"It does. I do have to work!"

Jim moved closer to her and pulled her up next to him. She had no resistance left in her. "Come here, sweet girl. I just want to hold you. It feels so good to have you next to me; so natural."

Liz felt herself melting in his arms. He smelled so good and she was tired of trying to resist him. Maybe this was right. Maybe it was time for her to allow someone in.

He lifted her face up to him and kissed her long and hard. She loved being close to him and let herself snuggle into his chest. They sat there for a short time just thinking, enjoying being next to each other.

The music was doing its job in setting the mood. She was beginning to feel romantic and that was unusual for her. Jim could sense it and kept kissing her. She finally stood up and smiled, pulling him up next to her. He grabbed her, not missing a beat, and leaned in to her, holding her close. Their feet moved like practiced dancers; the swaying was hypnotic, and her brown ponytail was swaying like a young girl at the prom. The melody and the dimness of the room were creating the perfect atmosphere for love. And they both were stepping right into it. The rhythm of their bodies moving to the beat and the intermixing of their fragrances was intoxicating and for a short time Liz gave in. Her step lightened and she knew Jim could feel the resistance leave her body. She had never met such a loving man. Yet he was strong. Nothing weak about him. She needed a strong man and maybe, just maybe, this was the one she needed.

Her thoughts ran back to when they were stranded on the mountain. The way he talked to her when they were lying in the bed at night in total darkness. He tried so hard to get to know her and she was constantly pulling away. How he hung on through that was a total mystery to her. But now, with him holding her and dancing to the music, it just felt right. But those words would not leave her lips tonight. Not this night.

She whispered in his ear. “Are you ready to eat? We need to have something before it gets too late.”

He pulled away from her and shook his head. “Food wasn’t on my mind just then. But you are right. I know we need to get something. I’ll run out and get us some burgers if you like.”

“Let’s go together. We need a break from this dark room!”

“I disagree, but I’ll be a good sport and let you have your way.”

She smiled and grabbed her purse. Her heart was beating fast and she would have given in if he had pushed her. But that wasn’t his way.

The drive to Bob’s Burgers was short and they spent the time talking about music they loved. Ordering quickly, they pulled up to the window to pay and then to the next window to wait for their meal.

“That was nice dancing with you. I could have done that all night.”

She looked down, blushing. “It was nice. I have to admit.”

“You are a wonderful dancer, you know that?”

“Not so bad yourself, Doc.”

“I haven’t danced in years but it all came back when I held you in my arms.”

She looked at him coyly. “That sounds like a line from a good movie.”

He grinned. “Touché. But I was being honest, lady.”

“It felt wonderful, Jim.”

He reached over and kissed her. The guy at the window whistled and they both turned and looked at him, laughing. He tipped his hat and handed them the white bag with their burgers and fries.

“Well, he got a peek, didn’t he?”

Liz was laughing and blushing at the same time. “I feel like a teenager right now. We got caught kissing in public.”

“I love it. Let’s get back to your house so that we can eat this food and I can kiss you again.”

“Jim! You are a mess tonight.”

“Yeah, but I’m your mess.”

Chapter 51

Food wrappers were all over the coffee table. Two drinks were sitting on the table on top of coasters. The music was playing softly. And she and Jim were sitting at the kitchen table looking at three photo albums of Liz when she was younger. Jim was enthralled with her and was enjoying the old photos of her as a young girl. He could tell she was uncomfortable but it helped him to understand where she came from. Her parents—her past.

"I love these photos with you standing next to your father near his plane. Was that when you decided you wanted to learn how to fly?"

"My first time up I knew I wanted to learn, but Mother was so protective of me. She refused to allow me to talk about it for a long time. But finally, she realized I wasn't going to give it up. Dad was on my side from the beginning."

"Do you think it was because he lost his son?"

"Maybe. We all were kind of destroyed when we lost Zach. But I jumped in and took that position with him without even thinking about it. I loved everything he did."

"Did your mom resent it?"

"She was harder to know. I never felt very close to her, although she was a good mother. She didn't have a temper and she sewed for me. Always made sure I had a lovely dress for a dance or the prom. She was just more introverted. Maybe I am more like her than I like to believe."

Jim cleared his throat. *So that was where she got this closing up thing. Her mother.* "Did she give you a hard time when you were dating?"

"No. That was Dad. He always threatened to beat them up if they did anything at all to hurt me."

"Typical father."

"Yes. It used to infuriate me. I was always independent. I knew I could take care of myself. And I always thought it was stupid for him to behave that way. All the boys were intimidated by him, but because I was so stubborn, he really had nothing to worry about. I wanted to play sports and dance. I was both. Feminine and athletic. Mother wanted me in ruffles. I wanted a more tailored look. We compromised in the end."

"Well, I love how you turned out. Now come with me back to the sofa. I need some time with you before I leave for the night."

Liz looked at her watch and was amazed that it was nearly 10:45. "I had no idea it was this late. It must have been our dancing that ate the time up."

He ignored her statement and lifted her face to his and kissed her. She seemed to give in to him and respond so he knew she was coming around to the idea of having this relationship. He wished he knew how she really felt inside. But all signs were that she did care. Really care.

"Liz, in the morning I head back home. Not sure when the next trip here will be. I hope not too long."

"Well, maybe I could be the one to fly out to Montana in a month or so."

Jim frowned. "I hate thinking of not seeing you for a whole month. That is just too long."

"I agree. But we do have jobs, you know. I will be busy setting up this other account. I am not sure but I think AT&T is the next one. Coca Cola has approached me, too. I have a full schedule for the year, Jim."

He scooted closer to her and held her close. He didn't want to let her go. But how in the world was he going to manage the next month without her?

"I miss you already, Lizzie. When I leave, you will be all I think about."

"I have to admit, I will miss you, too, Jim."

"Let's commit that we will try to see each other once a month. One way or the other. Do you think that is manageable?"

"Yes, I think it is. If we wait any longer, it will put a strain on us. I am aware that distance does not always make the heart grow fonder."

"No, I am not willing to take that kind of risk with you."

"What? Are you scared I'll find someone else?" She was being coy again. But he loved it.

"I am worried you'll have a line of men waiting at your door when I leave."

She rolled her eyes. "A line of men? How about none? I haven't allowed anyone close to me for years."

"Except Tom. You were willing to let him in again."

"I know that is hard for you to understand. And probably stupid of me. But that option isn't open now, is it?"

Jim shook his head. "No, it isn't."

They both stood up and she walked him to the door. He held her in his arms one more time and kissed her. "Are you sure you want me to leave? I could sleep on the couch. I'm like a dog. I can sleep anywhere."

She grinned but raised her eyebrow. He knew where this was going. "There is no way you would stay on the sofa. I already know better than that. Next thing I know you would be lying next to me just like in that cabin."

"But I behaved. Right? I was a gentleman."

"Yes, you were. But I had a rifle not too far away. And you knew I could use it."

He fell out laughing and kissed her again. "Okay. I'm leaving. But I want you to call me before you go to sleep. Is that good for you?"

This time she stood on her tiptoes and kissed his lips.

"I would love to call you before I go to sleep," he continued. "I would do that every night if you asked."

He kicked himself for not thinking of it sooner. “Tomorrow we have breakfast together. And then I’ll be on my way. I dread that good-bye, Liz.”

“Don’t think about it tonight. Or you won’t sleep. I have loved tonight and I will text you shortly because we both need to get a good night’s sleep.”

He kissed her good-bye and hugged her hard. She breathed in his cologne one more time. And he smelled her hair. Her sweet smell. And he nearly died letting go of her and walking out the door. But there it was. The sound of the door closing. And then he was on his own, driving back to the empty hotel room.

The room was dead quiet except for his alarm clock making a slight ticking noise. He was waiting for her call. He had taken a cold shower and jumped into bed to catch a late night news segment. It was nearing midnight. Memories of her and that light fragrance she wore were going through his head and he sat up, rubbing his face. He was a wreck. Was this love? If it was, it was going to kill him. He was remembering her hair and her sweet lips.

Then, bingo! The phone rang. He nearly knocked the phone off the nightstand answering it.

“Hey! What did you do? Write a novel while I was waiting?”

Laugher on the other end of the line. Giggling. “Did I take that long? I had to bathe and write some notes to myself so I would remember to tell Stephanie in the morning. I thought I hurried. What time is it?”

He was drumming his fingers on the bed. “Near midnight. I was about to dial your number. I know, I’m pitiful.”

“So are you tired? Will you be able to sleep? I have so many things going through my mind that I don’t know if I can turn it all off.”

“Join the club. But we need to, sweet girl. Morning will come soon enough.”

"I realize that. So I guess we need to say good night. I loved our time, Jim. Thank you for being so loving. So sweet to me."

He sighed. "You are making it worse for me. I loved our time, and I don't want it to end, Lizzie. Sleep well. I wish I were on your sofa so I could peek in on you."

"I sleep with a gun aimed at the living room."

"You're trying to be funny but it isn't working."

"See you in the morning, Jim. I know you are smiling."

"Good night, love. Call me when you wake. Better yet, I'll call you. I don't think I can take the waiting that early in the morning."

"Good night. I'll be up early."

Chapter 52

The room was dead quiet. No sound at all except maybe a light snore from her lips because she was on her back. Deep inside her head she heard a phone ringing. It slowly roused her enough to where she realized it was real. She sat up, groping for the phone. Her voice was husky and her eyes were still shut. "Hello."

"I knew you wouldn't be awake. Are you okay, Liz?"

She cleared her throat. How could he sound so chipper? "I'm up. I'm good. I was awake."

"Yeah, sure you were. Better get moving. I'm going to be there soon."

"What time is it, anyway?"

"7:00."

She jumped up and nearly fell off the bed. "I'm moving now. See you soon, Jim. I need to get going here or you will not get breakfast."

"That would not be a good idea, after the miserable night I had. I'll see you shortly. Don't go out of your way on the meal. Just cereal will be fine."

"Okay. See you soon."

She fell back on her pillow and yawned. *So he didn't sleep well. And I crashed.* She laughed out loud and got out of bed, turning the water on at the sink to wash her face and teeth. She flipped through her clothes trying to pull together an outfit she could wear to work and chose some flats to wear. Her hair was messy so she ran a brush through it and pulled it back. *That seems to be the code for the day now. A ponytail.*

Tripping down the stairs she hurried and opened some refrigerated sweet rolls and turned on the oven. Then she set the table and took two plates out and silverware. She poured orange juice and make some fresh coffee. The house was beginning to smell good. *He will love that,* she thought. She opened the egg carton and gently picked out four eggs and made scrambled eggs, toast, and cut up some strawberries. Her head was spinning when the doorbell rang. She was almost out of breath when she opened the door. But she wasn't prepared for what she saw.

"Morning, beautiful."

He was standing there in gray pants, a sport coat and loose tie, with a bottle of champagne in his hand and a small gift with a pink bow. Was she dreaming?

"Hey, Jim! Come on in. I have our breakfast all ready."

"It smells heavenly in here."

She watched as he took off his coat and draped it on the back of his chair. He walked over and kissed her on the mouth and opened the champagne. She took two glasses down from the cabinet over the sink and he poured them a small amount.

"I don't drink in the morning and I know you don't. But we will just take a sip of this and then eat our wonderful breakfast you have so lovingly prepared."

They took a sip and she poured hers into the orange juice and sat down. He did the same.

"You smell good this morning. Are you ready to head back home and get back to work?"

"You know the answer to that question. Don't even go there. I am going to drag this hour out as long as I can before we say good-bye again."

They slowly ate their breakfast, stopping only to gaze at each other and talk about their day. The sweet rolls were a hit and they both ate too much.

He scooted back his chair and looked at her. "I may regret this statement but I would love to do this every morning with you."

She grinned. "Not a bad way to wake up, is it?"

"Not at all. So you apparently slept better than I did. You were comatose when I called."

She could not hide her grin. "I was. I conked out after you left. Sorry, honey. But I was exhausted."

"So was I. But I could not get you off of my mind. I have thoroughly enjoyed this short trip and will go home and look at my calendar to plan your trip to see me."

"Just let me know. I will try to get my calendar together after I make my first appointment with AT&T. I won't know anything until that job is in process. But I know I will have weekends off so that won't be an issue."

"I may want you to stay a tad longer this time. But we'll see how it goes. I don't know how many surgeries I have lined up. Plenty of patients needing my expertise. I'm permitted to do a few here and there."

"I know you must be in demand, as long as you have been doing this."

"I keep busy. But so do you! We need to think this through, Lizzie. This long distance thing."

He glanced at his watch and stood up slowly.

"I hate this time. I absolutely do not want to leave. Can you tell?"

She kissed him and walked him to the door. He slipped into his jacket and held her close.

"Let me know when you are on the ground, will you?"

"I will. Let me know when you want to spend the rest of your life with me."

She tried to hide her response. But his last sentence flat took her breath away. She really didn't know how to respond.

"I'm sorry. It slipped out. I have to run, honey. Thank you for this lovely meal. I have enjoyed every bite. And I will be thinking of you until we speak again."

He kissed her again, and again. She finally pulled away and he turned and left. She had a hard time closing the door but when he pulled away from her house she shut the door and walked into the kitchen. His glass was there and she walked over to it and took a sip out of it. His lips had just been there. She knew this was getting serious and it didn't bother her. That was scary.

Stephanie was waiting at the door when she walked in. There were twenty phone calls and a COO from AT&T was sitting in her office.

"Elizabeth. Mr. Frank Jenison is waiting in your office. Are you okay? You look troubled."

Liz forced a smile and shook her head. "I'm fine. We'll catch up later. I didn't expect anyone this morning from AT&T."

"Apparently they are in a hurry to get started with you."

Liz raised her eyebrows and walked into her office and introduced herself. "Hello. I'm Elizabeth Stone. We spoke on the phone two weeks ago."

Frank stared at her and she got uncomfortable. "Good morning. I know this may not be protocol but I was hoping we could get started right away. Instead of a phone call I decided to just stop by in person so we could talk face to face. Get this thing underway faster. It's how I work."

"I see. Well, let me look at my calendar. I am about to wind things up with another company this week. I can start next Monday. Is that good for you?"

"I was hoping for midweek. This week. But I will take what I can get. Your reputation precedes you and we are anxious for you to look into some of our stores. Some serious problems are popping up and I've heard how you work."

"I will do what I can, Mr. Jenison. No promises. I think I have a good track record; I'm sure you've checked me out. We spoke of this on the phone during our last conversation."

"It's 'Frank.' And we had no hesitation in hiring you. The time frame is a bit off, that's all. We need you yesterday." He stood up. "I appreciate your time this morning, and I look forward to hearing from you towards the end of the week. If anything changes in your schedule, please let me know."

Liz shook his hand again and their eyes met. He was handsome but very businesslike. That was reassuring to her. She felt him checking her out, but at least he was subtle, if there was such a thing.

"I certainly will. Have a good day, Frank. I will be talking to you soon."

"Sooner better than later."

He turned and left her office and she sat down and blew out a sigh. What a way to start the morning. Her mind was totally not on work. Jim was leaving and it was all she could think about. She let her mind wander for a moment and then snapped out of it. Work was waiting and Stephanie wanted her attention.

"Stephanie, come on in and bring us some coffee. My day is going to disappear and I wanted to talk to you before the train starts rolling."

Two seconds later, Stephanie walked in, set the mugs down on Liz's desk, and plopped down in a chair across from her boss.

"I want to hear all about his visit. Was it wonderful? Did you have a good time? And most of all, are you head over heels in love with him?"

Liz laughed. The young never were tactful. They jumped right in. "Yes, yes, and I don't know yet. I think I'm falling in love with him. It feels like it. But it's been so long and I've fought it off for so long that I don't recognize the signs anymore."

"The look on your face says 'yes.' But I know it is still new to you. So when will you see him again? Did he say he loved you?"

"I have no idea when we will get together. Our schedules are ruthless. It is my turn to fly out to Montana so I will have to see how things go with AT&T. I can't take off my first couple of weeks with them. Although I would just be looking at a long weekend."

"Was he wonderful? Do you think he's handsome? And when am I going to get to meet him?"

"That will have to wait until he makes another trip here. I'll make time for that, I promise. And yes, he's handsome. Strong. So thoughtful. Almost too good to be true."

"I'm can't wait to lay eyes on him. Size him up. But he better not hurt you or he will have me to answer to. And your father, I'm sure."

"That reminds me, my parents have never met him. I've spoken about him, of course. We talked all about the crash and how we survived that ordeal. Dad will want to meet him. But I'm not a child, Steph. I could elope if I wanted to and they would have to get over it!"

"Oh brother, drama queen."

Liz laughed. "Okay, let's get to work. I'm going to visit the last Walmart store this morning and see if I can figure out the dynamics of that office. I will keep in touch. There shouldn't be anything else that would come up that is critical, at least until I get back. Text me if you need anything. I love that dress, by the way."

Stephanie twirled around and smiled. "Got it on sale. And I love red. Stay in touch. And it wouldn't hurt for you to take some photos next trip. Don't you think?"

"I hadn't thought of that. You are right. Would be nice to have a photo of him on my desk."

"That's what I'm talkin' about."

Chapter 53

One month into the job with AT&T and Elizabeth had figured out some of the issues. She was learning that the managers in the stores were unequipped to manage employees and left the offices unattended too much. Sales were dropping. Customer service was poor. People were switching over to other phone companies right and left. The cell phone business was highly competitive so AT&T had to be at the top of their game. There were some holes in communication at the corporate headquarters and the gaps started from the top down.

The top executives had been with AT&T for a long time and wouldn't handle her digging into their routines and files very well. She had dealt with attitudes like theirs many times. They squirm, wriggle out of, and find all kinds of ways to pass off the issues they have failed to handle—it's always the lower guys on the totem pole that are the problem. Not them. But Liz didn't answer to them and she could be tough as nails when she had to be. That was why she was hired by the COO. He knew she wouldn't back down to those bulldogs who sat in their cracked leather chairs smoking cigars, drinking a Scotch at their desks.

This one morning, when things were tight, her cell phone rang. It was her father.

"Hey, Dad! Everything okay? I'm kind of tied up right now."

"Just wondered if you could squeeze in your mother and me for lunch today. I know you need to eat at some point. And we just wanted to talk to you; catch up, as you say."

She looked at her watch. It was near noon. "I'll meet you at Martin's Bar and Grill on Jefferson Street. Maybe 12:30. Can you make that?"

"We'll be there, Lizzie. Will be good to see you."

She frowned as she hung up the phone. He never interrupted her day like this. Something was up. She finished her paperwork and packed her computer into its leather case and walked out the door. As she climbed into the car Jim texted her to see how she was doing and she shared the lunch date with him and her concern. Then she pulled out of the parking lot and drove over to the Grill. It was not overly crowded so she had no problem getting a booth.

She ordered an iced tea and sat looking at the people who were coming in the door. The place had a great atmosphere. Beautiful wood ceilings, dropped fans, a chandelier over the bar, and music playing. She got lost in her thoughts and didn't see her parents walking towards her. But when she looked up she noticed her mother was using a cane.

"Don't get up, Lizzie. We'll sit down here and get our meal ordered so we don't keep you too long."

"Mother, when did you start using a cane? What's bothering you?"

"Now Liz, just relax. Your mother and I have something to tell you."

"Are you sick? Why haven't you called me?"

Jesse reached over and touched her arm. "Take it easy, Liz. You've had more than your share to cope with lately. We didn't want to worry you."

Martha sighed and slowly spoke. "Liz. Sweetheart. I have wanted to talk to you but there just hasn't been the right time. I've been busy and so has your father. We've had doctor visits and you've been working so hard. But we can't wait any longer to tell you. I have been diagnosed with Alzheimer's disease. It's in the early stages but I didn't want to wait too long. We don't know how fast this thing will progress."

Liz was speechless. The last thing she expected to hear was that her mother was ill. She stood up and walked around the booth and wrapped her arms around her mother. "I am so sorry, Mother. I had no idea you were dealing with this. What is the prognosis? How long do you have before this really takes hold of your mind?"

"Sit down, Liz. Let's order and eat our lunch. She'll be fine. She will get the best of care; all the current meds are already being prescribed for her."

"It's just such a shock. I had no idea. Mother, how do you feel right now? What symptoms are you experiencing now?"

The waitress walked up and they ordered quickly.

"My short-term memory is going. I have a difficult time remembering where I put my keys or what day it is. It's frightening."

"I'm sure it is, Mother. I'm so upset that you have to deal with this horrible disease. I hate it!"

"Now Liz, she'll be okay. Don't get so upset. I hated having to tell you but you would have found out sooner or later. There are things you'll want to talk to your mother about. I didn't want to rob you of that opportunity."

Liz smiled and took her mother's hand. "I love you. We will get through this together. And no matter what happens with your mind, I will know you are in there, Mother. I won't forget you are in there somewhere."

Tears were streaming down Liz's face as they finished their lunch. It was time to head back to work, but she had so much she wanted to say to them.

"I'll come for a long visit on the weekend. This isn't the place for us to be crying. I'll call you, Dad. We'll have a good long visit. Just let her rest. Watch her closely. Oh, Mother! I love you so much."

They all hugged and Liz wiped her tears as she climbed into her car. Her mind was full of emotions and she didn't even get to talk to them about Jim. She wanted to talk to him so badly. If only he didn't live so far away . . .

She texted him to call her and headed back to the corporate offices of AT&T. He rang her phone just before she pulled in to a parking space.

"Honey, are you okay? Is everything okay?"

"Oh, Jim, something horrible has happened to Mother. She has been diagnosed with Alzheimer's. I just can't believe it."

There was a pause and then he spoke softly. "Sweetheart, I am so sorry you had to hear that. How is she doing now?"

"Well, she is having short-term memory loss. But the worst is yet to come. I dread it, Jim. Absolutely dread it."

"We'll take one day at a time, Lizzie. You know I am here. You can always lean on me."

"I wish you were here. You have no idea."

"When are you coming? Have you thought about a time when you can get away?"

"I have. I think two weeks from now I can spend a weekend with you. I am going to visit Mother this weekend and spend some time with her."

"You need to do that, of course. So I can expect you the following Friday? Can you take off that Monday, too?"

"I should be able to do that. I'll let you know. But pray for my mother, Jim. She is suffering and it is only going to get worse. My poor father has to watch this happen. I don't know how his heart will take it. He does love her."

"I'm sure he does. You just take all the time you need, Liz, to adjust to this news. I'll call you tonight and we'll talk more about it. I'll research some of the newer treatments and we can go over what she is already taking. How's that?"

"Sounds good. Thanks, Jim. You always make me feel better."

"Go have a good day. This account is important to you, Liz. Keep your mind focused on your work right now. It will help you cope with what your mother is going through."

"I'm sure you're right, Jim. Actually, you're right about more things than one, I'm afraid."

"What do you mean by that?"

"Nothing. Have a good day. And let me hear from you later."

"Okay, Lizzie. But you're not going to get away with making a statement like that and not explaining yourself. Later. You hear? Later."

Chapter 54

Spring was the perfect time to be visiting Montana. Even though it was still chilly there, the snow had ended and this would be the first time Liz would be able to see where Jim lived. He was so excited and called her every day checking to make sure nothing had changed her plans to come. She did love him. She could feel herself missing him and wishing he was closer. It was driving her crazy and she was angry at herself for not being tougher. This wasn't good for her career. Men seemed to mess up a woman's world. If you didn't have one you were always looking for one. When you found him it was all you could think about. There was no way to win, except to just cut yourself off from him altogether. And she'd lived that way for years and done just fine. Until Leigh opened her big mouth.

Her flight left at 8:45 so she was up early and at the airport, sitting in the waiting area by her gate until it was time to depart. The airport was full of people early in the morning and she kept busy just watching everyone. The man next to her was snoring and the woman on her right was reading a thick sleazy novel. It took all kinds. Suddenly she heard her flight called. She stood up and grabbed her carry-on bag and rushed to the gate. She got a window seat and settled in for the flight. She'd brought a book and something to eat just to help with her nerves. She liked it much better when she was in the pilot's seat.

Jim had texted her a few minutes ago to say he'd be waiting for her when she landed. She couldn't wait to see him, if she was honest with herself. It had been a stressful couple of weeks after learning about her mother's illness. This was a well needed break from work and worrying about her parents. They were really too young to have to face such serious problems.

A couple of hours went by and she woke to the sound of the flight attendant announcing they were about to land in Helena. Her flight was over. She was relieved but she found herself getting nervous about seeing Jim again. She was really looking forward to this time away from work, but mostly to being near him. It was getting addictive. And she was not used to that feeling.

When the plane landed, Helena's weather was bright and sunny with a cool breeze blowing. She walked down the jetway knowing she would see Jim any moment waiting for her. She was in the middle of people walking off the plane and as she turned a slight corner she saw him standing away from the crowd, watching for her. He was so handsome! She loved his hair and the smile that she saw on his face as their eyes met. Butterflies. That was what she felt as she saw him. High school butterflies.

"Hey, beautiful! Gosh it's good to see you!" He grabbed her off her feet and swung her around, kissing her hard.

"How are you? How was the flight?"

She could hardly catch her breath. "I'm doing great. It's so good to see you! My flight was uneventful. I actually dozed off reading my book."

"Oh, Elizabeth, it feels like months since I've seen you. Come on. Let's get in my car and I'll take you to my house. I have something exciting planned for us. You'll love it."

They walked to his car. It was a perfect kind of day. She looked around her and saw the mountains looming in the distance. It was paradise. *Much different place when you aren't stranded on the side of a snowy mountain.*

"So did you have to take the whole day off, Jim? I got an early flight without thinking about your having to take off from work. I hope that wasn't an issue."

Jim looked at her and shook his head. "I would take off an arm to see you. So don't worry about my work. It will be there another day. I've got plenty of surgeons who will stand in for me. I need this time with you. We need this time. Nothing is going to get in the way of this weekend."

"Good. I feel the same way. I felt a little guilty leaving Mother but this disease is going to be around for a long time so I knew it would not help at all for me to be home. I just hate it."

He grabbed her face and kissed her. "Liz, this is our time. We aren't going to talk about my son or your parents. What we are going to do is love each other. Spend time together—find out more about each other. I want to show you where I live. What I do."

"And I want to see all of that, Jim. I want to know all about your life."

They held hands in the car and he drove slowly, talking about all the things they passed. The buildings, the landscaping, and of course, the mountains. Unfortunately, she was only too familiar with mountains and he wanted to change her view of them altogether. As they turned into his driveway she was overwhelmed by the beauty of the grounds. The huge trees lining the driveway were breathtaking. And as they approached the house, she sat back in the seat and looked quietly at this place where Jim lived. It was not anything like what she had pictured. A huge two-story home with a grand porch and shutters and trees and full landscaping. She loved it at first sight. But the inside was even more beautiful. She was taken at how comfortable it was. Warm and inviting.

Jim took her bags to a room upstairs. It had its own door that opened up to a balcony that overlooked the back yard, which was beautifully landscaped and surrounded by tall trees. The flowers had not yet bloomed but she could imagine what it would look like in late spring.

"Let's get you situated. Do you need anything? Are you hungry?"

"It seems all we do is eat when we are together! Yes, I am a little hungry. What were you thinking?"

"I wanted to take you for a short drive around town and then we could stop and get a bite to eat. We will spend the afternoon at the house just relaxing. I have great plans for tomorrow but we'll talk about all that later. For now I just want to make sure you feel relaxed and welcome."

"This is a lovely home, Jim. I am impressed. You've done very well for yourself."

"You don't exactly live in a shack, Elizabeth."

"No, but it's nothing like this. But even though it is large, it still feels cozy. I love it."

"Let's get into the car and I'll drive you around town. It won't take long and I know the perfect little place to eat lunch. You'll love it."

The café was quaint and located on the side of the mountain. The view was breathtaking. The trees were getting new leaves and the color was like fresh spring green. It couldn't have been a nicer day. They ordered their meal and Jim held her hand.

"I have to keep looking at you and pinching myself. It's hard to realize you are here. I've wanted this for so long. Well, we haven't known each other that long, but it seems like I've known you all my life. I've certainly yearned for this type of relationship forever. I feel so relaxed around you. I can be myself and you still want to be around me!"

"I feel the same way and I wouldn't have it any other way, Jim. I've been alone for years and if I cannot find someone who I can be myself around, then what's the point?"

"It looks different here compared to Knoxville, but you do have mountains there. So not a total shock, is it?"

"Not at all. The mountains here are much larger and powerful. And the snow, of course. We know all about the snow!" She paused and looked at him closely. "You look so good to me. I have missed you."

He leaned over and kissed her. "That's good to hear. I was hoping you had. I was really having trouble waiting for a month to see you. I had tons of work to do. Patients to take care of. But I really wanted to take off and come see you again."

"The distance between us is a challenge. I didn't think at first that it would be such an issue. But I have to admit, this time, it was not a good feeling seeing you leave."

The food came and they ate, talking about the scenery, his work, and how much they had missed each other. Jim couldn't take his eyes off of her and it made her a little nervous. She kept wondering what he was thinking and what he had planned for them tomorrow. But she was so glad to be there that soon she forgot about the questions that were running through her mind, and she let herself slowly slip into his world.

After two hours of conversation they headed back to his house. She was ready to relax and sit with him on the leather sofa, sipping coffee and looking out the huge windows at the mountains. He was charming and she felt so vulnerable. *What was wrong with her? Was it love?*

He was sitting next to her talking but she wasn't listening. She was staring at him, wondering why he was attracted to her. He was a very good-looking doctor. He could have any woman. *Why her?* She came back to the conversation right when he was asking her a question.

"So, Liz, what do you think of that idea?"

"I'm sorry, babe. I lost my train of thought. What were you saying?"

Jim laughed but had a worried look on his face. "Am I boring you? I shouldn't have been talking about the pool and the changes in the house. I know you are probably tired and need to just sit here and relax."

"I'm sorry, Jim. I had something on my mind. I'll share it with you. I was just wondering, why me? What attracted you to me like this?"

"Well, for starters, I spent nearly two weeks with you out in the middle of nowhere. We survived the elements together. I got to know you and I liked what I saw. Is that a crime?"

"No. But you saw me at my absolute worst. Yes, we were surviving but I was shut down. How did you ever really get to know me? I wouldn't let you in."

"You aren't telling me anything I don't already know. Trust me. I felt the wall you had up. I kicked it a few times with my bare feet. But little by little you let me in. I tried to be patient. There was a little give and take going on. Don't you remember?"

"I do. But I just have all these questions. Sometimes I think I over-analyze things."

He took her hand and looked her in the eyes. "I have something wonderful planned for us tomorrow. And I don't want anything to mess it up. So we are going to drop this conversation and eat a light supper and go to bed early. We have a busy day tomorrow but I just know you are going to be so surprised. If the weather holds, and it looks like it is going to, we are going to have a déjà vu moment. Now, can you just relax and trust me, Liz?"

She smiled and leaned back on the sofa. "Yes, I can trust you. And I will. Now what do I need to do for supper? What do you have that we can fix?"

He tickled her and jumped up from the sofa. "It's my turn to fix you something. Just sit back and rest. Enjoy the view. I'll be back shortly with your meal."

He left her and walked into the kitchen. She could hear him banging around in the pans and laughed out loud. She looked out the window at the mountains and the white hazy clouds that were hanging in the air. It was lovely. She closed her eyes and without knowing it, drifted off for a short time. She was awakened by his gentle touch and soft low voice.

"Hey, girl. I've got your supper ready. Can you wake up and eat?"

She opened her eyes and he had two large wooden trays with plates filled with small spring rolls sliced in half and a small salad. Fresh fruit. It was perfect.

"How did I get so lucky? This is a lovely dinner for us, Jim."

He was blushing. "Thanks, Liz. I love cooking, actually. And since I am alone all the time, I have learned to use cookbooks and do variations of recipes to fit my mood."

"Well, I am dying to try these. Sorry I fell asleep."

"I wanted you to rest. And it means you feel at home here."

She looked at him and smiled. The words would not form on her lips but she did feel at home. She took a bite and rolled her eyes. "This is heaven, Jim. Eating this savory meal with you and looking out at these mountains. It's almost like heaven."

He smiled and winked at her and turned on some music. They finished their meal and after he cleaned up the kitchen he came out and asked her to dance. And there she was, tiptoeing to reach his shoulders, watching the stars come out over the mountains. *How could it get any better than this?*

Chapter 55

It was a night to remember. And as she lay in her bed with the moon shining through her window, she had a desire to talk to her best friend. She picked up her cell and dialed Leigh's number. It was late, but she doubted Leigh was asleep yet. A night owl.

"Leigh? It's me. Did I wake you?" She had to ask.

Leigh smiled. "You know better. What are you doing? Where are you?"

"I thought you would want to know! I'm at Jim's house in Helena. Beautiful place here, Leigh. You would die. Right now I am looking out my window at the moon coming through the trees. Mountains everywhere. It is breathtaking."

"I can only imagine. You sound like you're happy."

"I am. Tired, but happy. He has been so good to me; he fixed me dinner and we danced in front of this huge picture window. I actually let myself enjoy him, Leigh. It felt good. Strange, but good."

"It's all I ever wanted for you, girl. Just to enjoy life. With someone who cares about you."

"Tom cared."

"Not like this, Liz. He walked out when you were the closest. When you were about to marry."

"I know. I remember only too well. But I wasn't ready for Jim when you introduced me to him. I didn't want to get hurt again. It had been years since Tom and I broke up. But I just closed myself off. It was easier that way."

"How do you feel now, Liz? Still want to stay closed off?"

Liz rubbed her eyes. She was getting sleepy. "No, I have to say that I really do want to get closer to him. He is so good to me. It feels good to be around him now. Even in the cabin there were times I felt myself slipping. How could I not? He was such a gentleman then. But he was trying even then. I knew he was falling for me."

"Give me a break, Liz. Any man in his right mind would fall for you. And you guys were stuck on the side of a freakin' mountain."

"I know! Looking back it all seems like a dream. One of the worst times in my life. But it really brought us closer. I learned a lot about him on that mountain."

"So what is the plan tomorrow? You guys going shopping or what?"

"I really don't know. He says he has a surprise. Makes me nervous a little bit, but I know we will have fun no matter what it is." Liz yawned.

"I know you're tired. Go rest. We'll talk tomorrow some time. Just know I was only pushing you because I love you. Joe gets so mad at me for doing that—'matchmaking,' he calls it. But you are like a sister to me. I didn't want you living alone the rest of your life."

"I know. I know. I'm stubborn, Leigh. Very stubborn."

"I think I'm hearing that you love him. Am I right?"

"I've not said it out loud to him. But yes, I think I do love him."

"Lord, I never thought I'd hear those words out of your mouth."

"Well, keep it to yourself for a while. I have to live with it a while myself before I go shouting it from the roof tops!"

"Are you saying I have a big mouth?"

"I would never say that. But—"

"I get it. My lips are sealed. Have a great time and don't ruin this. Don't let yourself slip back into that old stubborn maid role that you've lived for so long. This is the real thing. Not many people get this, Liz."

Liz hung up the phone and slipped underneath the warm covers, pulling them up to her chin. With the light of the moon on her face she slowly drifted off to sleep, unaware of someone watching her sleep.

Jim was standing at the doorway doing his best not to wake her. She was the most beautiful thing he'd ever seen, and he wasn't going to let her get away this time. Not for anything. He'd waited too long. He'd known since the cabin on the side of the mountain that he loved her. He had to pinch himself to make sure he wasn't dreaming. She was here, now, sleeping in his guest room. So hard to believe. She had been so cold at times when they were trying to survive. Not even a peek into her heart. But now he saw the real Elizabeth. And he loved her even more.

He walked into the room and leaned over and kissed her forehead. She stirred but didn't wake. He stayed there for a moment listening to her breathe. He wanted to climb under the covers and hold her. Kiss her. He stepped away and walked out, his heart racing. She had no idea how much he loved her. How he had missed seeing her. But tomorrow she would know. He just hoped that she wouldn't run. It was going to be a surprise to her, a good one. But he just hoped she was ready. It was so hard to tell.

He sighed as he lay down in the next room. There was something so settling when you knew for dead sure that this was the woman you wanted to spend your life with. He had repaired many hearts in his life; he had even held them in his hands. But her heart had been like stone when he met her. It was only now that he was beginning to see a crack in that stone. He smiled as he fell asleep. The woman of his dreams was sleeping in the next room. Not a bad way to end a day.

Liz woke in the night and put on her robe and walked downstairs. She was cold and thirsty, so she poured some milk and walked into the living room and stood near the big picture window that looked out at the mountains. It was so quiet. Not a sound in the house. Clouds were resting lightly over the mountain and there was a mist falling on everything outside. She was thinking about the evening. How sweet he'd been. And she was wondering what the morning would bring.

She finished her milk and walked to the kitchen, nearly bumping into Jim. "Honey, are you okay? I heard you get up."

Liz grinned sheepishly. "I'm fine. I was just thirsty. It's too early for us to get up yet."

"I know. I just wanted to see what you were doing. We have a full day tomorrow. I guess we'd better get back in bed."

He walked her up the stairs and kissed her. She snuggled into his chest and for a moment thought about climbing into his large bed. But she turned and walked into her room, waving at him quietly. She got into bed and covered up, smiling. It was too good to be true. He'd heard her get up. That meant that he wasn't sleeping too well, either. The tension in the house had increased as the night progressed. It almost made her giddy. He really did love her. She fell into a fitful sleep, knowing that she would need the energy for whatever he had in mind for tomorrow. But right before she went to sleep she faced the fact that she was head over heels in love with him. He was a good man.

A tear fell on her pillow as she closed her eyes. It had been a long, long time since she'd let anyone in. In one way, she was scared to death and in another way ecstatic. All those nights in the cabin when they lay next to each other but not touching, she had pulled away inside. She'd deliberately held back any emotions that might have arisen, because she didn't want to deal with a relationship again. But now, if sort of felt like she was ready. And how in the world he had remained so patient with that struggle was beyond her. Most men would have given up. But he kept right on loving her. He was the opposite of Tom. And maybe that was a good thing. He was a heart mender. And in reality, he'd mended her heart without even knowing it.

Chapter 56

Jim woke early and got a shower, his heart racing at the thought of what was to take place that morning. He hurried to the kitchen and made some coffee, set out the mugs and plates. He started the bacon and sausage, and turned on the warming drawer. He poured juice, cut up some fruit and made eggs and toast. Her breakfast was waiting for her before she came down the stairs. He had arranged for a guide to pick them up at noon, so he had time to show her the rest of his land and relax before they started on their journey. He was never more certain about anything in his entire life as he was about making Elizabeth his wife. But he wasn't sure about her feelings on the matter. That was what he was going to find out today. And he felt like a schoolboy asking the prettiest girl in school to the prom. Only this was for life. Not just one dance.

He looked up and saw Elizabeth coming walking slowly through the kitchen door. "Morning, beautiful!"

Liz brushed her hair out of her face and smiled. "You're pretty lively this morning."

"Did you get any sleep at all?"

"Some. Just restless. You've got me on pins and needles about today. What in the world have you planned?"

"Have a seat. I have your breakfast in the warming drawer. I waited to eat until you came down so we can enjoy our meal together and talk about our day."

She pulled out her chair and eyed him. "This all looks wonderful and I'm starving."

"Well, it tastes better when someone else fixes it, right?"

"I guess that is true. Now what's up your sleeve?"

"Can you relax? I'm going to share some things with you, but first let's just enjoy this beautiful morning. I'm sorry you didn't sleep well, but neither did I. With you in the other room, that was pretty much all I could think about."

She raised her eyebrows. "You slept right next to me for two weeks and managed to contain yourself. In fact, I think I recall you snoring in the cabin."

He laughed and took a swallow of cold orange juice. "I did not! And besides, I had a broken leg that was killing me. Remember, we were halving the ibuprofen at the point. I had to be tough and just go with the pain."

"You hid it well."

"That's because you were being so brave out there in the cold, hunting down a deer."

She rubbed her eyes and picked up the warm coffee mug and held it in her hands, smelling the warm, mellow fragrance. "I haven't forgotten the fear I felt when I came face to face with those wolves. Scary thought. They were right on top of me. They could have eaten me alive."

"Don't remind me. But you did manage to scare them away. And I did come to your rescue, albeit a little late."

"I never was so glad to see someone in my life. But we survived all of that and it has brought us to this point in our lives. And you still haven't told me what we are doing today."

He looked at her grinning at him and he smiled and shook his head. "Not going to say just yet. It's difficult enough to keep a secret, but with you sitting here looking so coy and lovely, I really just want to kiss you."

"Not now. Not yet, anyway. I've got to wake up. I feel like I've been up all night. What time is it, anyway?"

"It's 9:30. I'm glad you slept in a little bit. But look at the sun out there. It's an amazing day. And I love having you here with me. Do you know that?"

She blushed and pushed a lone strand of hair out of her eyes. Her cheeks looked pink and her eyes very dark against the light pink robe she wore. The sash was tied loosely around her small waist. Her toes were painted red and her nails filed short. Her horse mane hair was her strongest asset, but her eyes could stop his heart.

He stared at her for a few minutes as she tackled eating her eggs and toast. The room smelled of fragrant coffee, eggs, sausage, and the perfume she'd worn yesterday. His mind was struggling to stay on topic. He wanted to hold her in his arms. He wanted to skip the trip up the mountain to that cabin and spend the rest of the day with her next to him. He would have given anything to know what she was feeling inside. But he didn't feel he could just come out and ask. *Last night she was so open. She laughed so easily and embraced me when we danced. When we looked into each other's eyes it seemed she fell into mine. I am petrified that she will turn me down. After losing Tom—it may be too soon.*

He brought himself back to the present and found her staring at him.

"Do you cook like this all of the time?"

"Not really. I don't eat a big breakfast during the week. I usually do a protein shake and add things to it. What about you?"

"No. I don't cook that much during the week. I've been so busy and I'm on the road a lot. My schedule has been hectic and looks like it's not going to let up anytime soon. That's what happens when you're building a business. Time is no longer your own."

"I'm all too familiar with that scenario as a doctor and surgeon."

"I'm sure you are. This tastes so good. You have spoiled me this whole trip." She pushed away from the table, sighing.

"I'm stuffed. I guess I need to go shower and dress. And that brings me back to the question; what in the world are we going to do today? What should I wear?"

"Dress casual. Jeans and hiking shoes. Or tennis shoes. Something comfortable. We are going on a short trip and some of the time we'll be hiking."

"Sounds dreadfully familiar."

"We're in Helena, you know. Not all that far from the mountains."

She stood up and brushed the crumbs out of her lap onto the table. "Shall I help you with the dishes?"

He walked over to her and pulled her to him. "You look heavenly this morning. I know you don't want to hear that, but I could swallow you whole. I'm so glad you decided to come on this trip to see me. It is so wonderful waking up to you. Doesn't it feel good to you, Liz?"

"It does. You've been so loving to me. So thoughtful. I'm overwhelmed with it all. And your house is magnificent. I'm very impressed, Doctor."

He kissed her again and smiled. "You go shower and get ready. We have a little while before we leave, so take your time. I've got a phone call to make while you're getting dressed."

She waltzed out of the room grinning and he hurried to his office to make a call to the pilot that was flying them to the crash site. He'd decided to leave earlier so they would have more time to spend at the cabin. He should have planned it that way originally. And he couldn't contain his excitement any longer. She was pressing him for answers about his plans, and he wasn't going to be able to hold back much longer.

The ride to the airport was slow. Traffic was building even though it wasn't noon yet. Church was about to let out and the traffic would be unbearable. Elizabeth seemed nervous so Jim tried to distract her with questions about her parents. It worked until they pulled into the airport. She turned and looked at Jim and he wasn't sure whether she was scared or mad.

"Um, where are we going, Jim?" She took her seat belt off and grabbed her purse.

"Take it easy, honey. I'm going to take you for a ride in this plane. Does it look familiar?"

"Slightly. Just like Joe's plane."

"Yes. And Fred here is a good friend of mine. Called him and asked for a favor. Now I want you to just sit back and relax. We're in the hands of a professional pilot. He does this for a living."

"I've flown quite a few times since the crash, but not with you. This really brings back memories for me."

They climbed into the plane and buckled up. She was staring out the window and there wasn't a smile on her face. For a moment Jim wondered if he'd done the wrong thing. But he was going with his gut feeling. She was going to be so surprised when they landed at the crash site and walked to the cabin. It would be so pretty to see when the snow was leaving.

"Come on, Lizzie. Just relax."

She turned her face to him and he saw a smile forming. "I'm fine. Just momentary anxiety. I can't wait to see what you're up to!"

"That's my girl. You're gonna love it. Trust me."

"You buy your own island or something?"

Jim laughed and put his arm around her. "Not without your input, my dear. Did you let anyone know you were making this trip to see me?"

"I phoned Leigh. She was so excited I was going. I can't wait to tell her what a good cook you are!"

"I really like Joe. He's a trooper being married to her. I know how pushy she can be, but somehow he deals with it. At first, I thought she wore the pants in the family. But I've seen him put his foot down, so I know he can hold his own with her."

"She's a handful, but she would also give you her last dime."

"Probably true. She's fun to be around and I always love it when I stay with them. Entertaining, to say the least."

"I'm worried about my mother, Jim. It breaks my heart that her memory is going. That disease is so creepy. It just shows up unannounced. She's handling it better than I would. But I know Dad is sad and worried sick."

"It's horrendous and we need to pray that the progression is slow. She is too young to be dealing with this, in my opinion. I'm checking with some doctors who deal with that, to see if there are any new drugs on the horizon that might help her."

"Thanks, honey. That means a lot.

Jim paused and took a deep breath. He looked over at Liz who was lost in her thoughts for a moment. They were moving through some clouds and he reached over and grabbed her hand and squeezed it. She turned her head and smiled at him. He winked at her and kissed her softly and whispered in her ear.

"Lizzie, you are beautiful sitting in this plane next to me. I can hardly believe you're here. I know in the scheme of things we haven't known each other all that long. But I have thought of you every single day since the crash. Do you know how lucky we are to have found each other? If it hadn't been for Leigh, our little loud-mouthed friend, we would probably have never met."

Liz rolled her eyes and touched his face. "You have a way with words, Jim! I am very happy that we found each other. My world has been turned upside down since the crash. Nothing is the same. I guess I've had a difficult time coping with some pretty big issues on top of recovering from our wonderful two-week vacation on the side of a mountain in the dead of winter. My mind is going in so many directions. But since I've been here, I've really been able to just focus on us. On your world here. And I feel so loved and so cared for. It's just not normal for me to let someone in that close."

He turned her face toward him and kissed her again. "Don't be afraid of me, Liz. I'm not going anywhere. I've pitched my tent. I'm here for the long haul."

She giggled. "Pitched my tent? I don't think I've heard that before."

"It's a male thing. But it simply means I'm dug in. I'm so in love with you that I've already moved in."

Liz laid her head back against the seat of the plane and closed her eyes. "Something just came to my mind that my grandmother told me when I had trouble sleeping one night. She was staying with me while mom and dad were on a short trip. I was scared and didn't want to go to sleep. She explained to me that when she married my grandfather, she found that they were made from the same cloth. I asked her what that meant, and she said that they were so much alike that their minds ran in the same direction most of the time. So often there was no point in a conversation because they both were thinking the same thing. Their hearts were similar. Like the threads in a cloth, they were woven the same. You could hardly tell where one began and the other ended. I always wanted that in a marriage. I suppose it is hard to find. But I am wondering, just thinking, mind you—if perhaps you and I might have that in common."

Jim was taken aback by what she'd just shared. She was being so real about her feelings. He brought her hand up to his mouth and kissed it and pressed it against his face. "I surely hope we find out that we are, Lizzie. Because I love the cloth you are made from."

Chapter 57

The plane landed with ease not too far from the crash site. It was a beautiful sunny day with hardly a cloud around. Elizabeth slid out of her seat and climbed out of the plane; Jim came around the other side and grabbed her hand to help her out. His face was beaming, but he noticed the pensive look on her face.

"Liz, I thought it might make this trip very special if we revisited the site of the crash. We brought food and water, and Fred has another stop to make, so he will return in about three hours to pick us up. "

"You weren't kidding when you said we were going hiking."

"No, I was dead serious." He leaned down and kissed her red lips. "No, don't go getting serious on me now. This is going to be fun. And we'll have a picnic when we reach the cabin. Don't you want to see that thing in the spring? With no snow? Aren't you the least bit curious now?"

She paused and laughed. "Actually, I've spent a long time trying to get over the crash. It hadn't occurred to me to return here and revisit the hell we lived through!"

"Oh, come on. I know it was tough on us. But this is where I found the real you. We got to know each other here."

She took his hand and pulled him forward. "Okay, let's get going; I guess I'm a little bit curious to see it again. It's no short hike to that cabin, if you remember."

"How well I remember. Let's go."

There was still snow at a higher elevation, but where they were walking it had thawed and the trees were full of new green leaves. The air smelled so fresh and even though the breeze was a little cool, they both had light jackets on and the sun kept them comfortably warm. Elizabeth was intrigued by the change of landscape. Nothing looked the same as when it all had been covered in several feet of snow. Nothing looked familiar. They hiked for an hour and sat down on a fallen tree to rest. They both were silent while they looked around the quiet mountainside. Liz had seen a torn piece of cloth that she had tied to a tree when she was walking blindly in the white snow. She got goose bumps remembering how frightened she had been, not knowing if she was going in the right direction to find the cabin or not. She had relied totally on her memory as the plane was coming down. It had all happened so quickly.

"This sort of looks familiar. But the color is throwing me off a little bit. Is it bothering you, too?"

"Yeah. But I cannot wait to see that cabin. I know it will look so different to us when we see it now. Things look so out in the open to me now. Before, everything was laden down with heavy snow. You ready to start hiking again?"

Liz smiled and stood up. He grabbed her hand and they hit the trail with new energy. Jim seemed excited about getting to the cabin. She had other emotions going through her head. The feeling of starvation ran through her spine. The fear of what was out there. And the responsibility of finding food that had been on her. "It feels good to be able to see the ground and see where we are going. I bet we have another hour or more to walk. It seemed like it took me about two and a half hours to get there."

"I bet it goes quicker since we are not walking through deep snow. That slowed everything down, Liz."

In an hour and a half they arrived at the cabin. It was shadowed by low-hanging tree limbs. There was a clearing around the front of the cabin, like someone had been there since they'd left. A funny feeling came over Liz as they approached the door. The cabin seemed so small.

"Oh, my gosh! It's so small. I guess we were so desperate that we didn't notice the size. It was home to us. A respite from the cold and wind."

"It does look totally different. I didn't tell you, but I tracked down the owner. He is here now, waiting for us! But he was on his way home, so he won't be here long. Just long enough for us to see him. I thought it would be fun to meet him and let him know what this cabin meant to us."

"Did he hear about our crash on the news?"

"He did. But nothing was mentioned about the location of the cabin. Later, when he revisited this cabin, he could tell that we'd been there. Or someone. We left it clean, but he could still tell someone else had been inside. He was so nice about it. Let's go in. His name is Charles Stanford."

Jim knocked on the door, and after a few moments it opened. A round-faced gentleman stood there with a pipe in his mouth and a hunting cap on his head. He was grinning from ear to ear. He spoke with a loud booming voice that made Elizabeth smile. "Come on in! I've been looking forward to meeting you two!"

Jim grabbed his hand and shook it vigorously. "It's great to meet you too, Charles. This is Elizabeth. She was the pilot I was telling you about."

Charles reached out and grabbed Liz's hand. "Well, young lady, looking at you, it's difficult to believe you're a pilot. You've had quite an adventure on this mountain. She can be rather frightening in the dead of winter. She has a mind of her own, that's for sure. I guess you found that out all to well."

Liz shook his hand and laughed. "Oh yes. We became all too familiar with the dangers on the mountain. I learned more than I ever wanted to know about surviving the cold. I hope I'm never that cold again."

Charles laughed and spoke gently to them. "Have a seat on this old sofa. I'm embarrassed that this place looks so bad. But it's just a hunting cabin for me and my boys. We come up here from time to time during hunting season. Us boys don't need much, you know. Just a bed to sleep in and some food."

"We found it quite accommodating, compared to sleeping sitting up in all that was left of the plane." Jim said, grabbing Liz's hand.

"Frankly, I've never been so glad in all my life to find this little cabin. I saw it when we were coming down but it happened so quickly and I was so focused on landing without completely tearing up the plane that I barely saw it out of the corner of my eye. We were lucky to find it hidden among the snow covered trees." Liz shook her head.

"I don't know how you managed. I really don't. Jim said you had a gun with you. Several, in fact. Were you trained to use them? I was pretty impressed at the story he told me about how you hunted for food."

"Well, it's not that impressive, Charles. My ancestors were Indians so I was brought up hearing about how they survived. It did come in handy, I tell you that. I never thought I'd use that piece of information in my lifetime, but the ability to hunt and find food is pretty critical when you are stranded somewhere."

"Yes it is! I'm amazed. Might have to pick your brain sometime. And I heard about the wolves. Those creatures can be downright terrifying if you are out at night. That's when they hunt. And their howls are bloodcurdling in the darkness. Thank heavens you made it through all of that. I'm very impressed with both of you, quite frankly."

"We worked well together and fought through all the tough moments, and there were plenty of those to work through. Daily. Hourly. My gosh, we had to worry about melting snow for drinking water—and staying warm. It was a challenge. We built many a fire in that fireplace. It always went out before dawn and that bedroom was freezing. We could have written our names in the air it was so cold." Jim laughed and looked at Liz.

"The main thing I missed besides real food was a bath. I don't know how we stood each other out here without a bath for so long." She couldn't help but laugh at the thought.

Charles stood up and shook their hands again. "Well, I am so glad I got to meet you. I hate to rush out but I have several stops to make before I head home and I don't want to be caught up here when it turns dark without my gun. I am so glad you came back up here to see the cabin. Just close the door when you leave. I don't worry about locking the door because there's nothing much in here anyone would want to steal."

They stood and told him good-bye and watched him leave. Jim sat back down next to Liz on the sofa and they stared at each other. "It feels so weird to be here, Jim. He was such a nice man. I'm so delighted to have met him after all this time. He really is a sweet man."

"Yeah, I liked him over the phone. Couldn't wait to shake his hand. This cabin helped save our lives. Even without food, we would have never made it without this kind of shelter from the cold."

Liz stood up and walked around the cabin. It was tiny, but it had felt larger when they were so desperate. She walked into the small kitchen and looked inside the cabinets. Charles had loaded the shelves with nonperishable canned goods. It was stocked again for the next hunter. She poked her head inside the bedroom and noticed Jim was sitting on the bed, bouncing up and down.

"Not so comfortable now. But it felt like heaven, then, Lizzie."

She sat down beside him and laughed. "It felt like a down mattress to me. I was so tired and cold I'd have slept on wood if I had to."

Jim got up and tried to turn on Pandora on his cell phone but there were no bars. Dead as a door nail. So he grabbed her hand and pulled her next to him and they slow danced to his humming. She grinned as he spun her around. He started singing and she was surprised at his strong voice. They laughed and laughed and finally she plopped down on the sofa, out of breath. He came and sat beside her, and they reminisced about making a fire and cooking the then-cherished rabbit meat on a stick. He reached in the pocket of his jacket and pulled out a box. She didn't see him at first, but when he laid it on his lap she turned white.

"Jim what is that? Oh, no! Why did you bring me up here?"

Jim looked at her face. It looked like she was petrified. Scared to death. "Now, Liz. Will you calm down? Of course I had a reason to bring you here. Well, two reasons. I wanted us to return here and see what it was like in the light of day. Without that dang snow. But I also had another reason. And you know as well as I do, with our busy schedules and the distance, that we don't have much time. Your visit is fast coming to an end. So it's pretty much now or never, agreed?"

Before she could answer him, and there was an answer on her lips, he opened the box and handed her a light blue small box. She set it on her lap, opened it and just stared at it. It was the most beautiful, most feminine ring she'd ever seen. She couldn't speak and he wasn't going to give her time to object. He got on his knee and put his hand underneath her chin and turned her face up to his.

"Elizabeth. I have loved you practically from the beginning. When I laid eyes on you, I was pretty much gone. But the dates we had, the plane flight and crash (she smiled weakly), and the nearly two weeks fighting for our lives, well, I fell head over heels in love with you and I couldn't say one word of this to you. You would have died right here on this sofa if I'd told you any of this."

He put his hand up to her lips, staving off her remarks that were about to burst out of her mouth. "I know exactly what you're going to say. But I want you to hear me out. Then I'll let you speak. I have known a long time that I wanted to marry you. I kept quiet about it until I thought you were ready. And then I realized that you probably won't ever be totally ready to marry anyone. Even me. So I am stepping out for both of us; yes, both of us, to get this thing going. I love you with all of my heart. I am totally wrapped up in you. And I want more than anything to marry you and spend the rest of my life with you. I know it's complicated with you there and me here. But we'll figure all that out. The main thing is for us to not let this slip through our fingers. We will regret it and I'm just not willing to let that happen. This comes along only once in a lifetime. Most people never feel what we feel."

He paused and swallowed hard. "So, Elizabeth Stone. Will you marry me?"

Tears were streaming down her face. She was so full of emotion that she didn't know what to say. She had no words for the first time in her life. Her fiery temper had left her and she was alone sitting there on the sofa, unable to defend herself. She did love him. She knew he was right about the once-in-a-lifetime thing. She looked at his eyes. They were full of tears and watering, and she knew he was about to cry. She leaned over and kissed him and pulled away. She was so afraid.

"Jim Wilson, you are so sneaky. Fixing me meals, waiting on me hand and foot. And now this! You are so bad." She looked at him and smiled. Her stomach was in her throat but she kept talking. "Of course I love you. I don't know why it's been so hard for me to say it. But it feels good to get it out! Yes, I do love you. I'm not sure how this will all work out with your work and mine, but I guess we can talk about that later." She looked down at the ring he was taking out of the box. Her chin was quivering and tears were running down her cheeks.

"Liz, take this ring." He put it on her finger. Her hand was shaking.

She looked at Jim and kissed his cheek."You're the most loving man I've ever known. You treat me like a princess, but you also respect my intelligence. It is a wise combination, Dr. Wilson. For you know how independent I am. I guess I've discovered in spite of my stubbornness that I really do need you in my life. It was a while before I would admit that to myself, but it is pretty clear now."

He looked at her and raised an eyebrow. "Is that a yes?"

"Yes, it's a yes. I will marry you! But how in the world will we figure all this out? And what were you thinking? I really just got back into my work. They would kill me if I pulled out now or said I needed off for a wedding and honeymoon!"

"Now, now. Just relax. We don't even have to set a date right now. Let's take a deep breath and just enjoy the moment. It feels so good to me to hear that you love me. I was so afraid you would turn me down!" He blew out a deep breath and leaned his head back on the sofa. " It hasn't been very easy to get close to you, you know. Especially with that mile-high wall you constructed years ago that had to come down one brick at a time."

"Was it all that difficult to get close to me? If I hadn't been so evasive it might have been easier on you. You were such a gentleman. As cold as we were I really tried to maintain my independence with you but you don't know how difficult that was seeing as how we needed each other to survive. I'm sorry I made it so hard for you. I know you were only trying to take care of me the best you could. It was pretty sweet watching you do it with that broken leg. I am at a loss of words, Jim. You have blown me away."

He kissed her long and hard and pulled her to her feet. "Lizzie, dance with me. Not just now, but for the rest of our lives. I've waited for you all my life. And now that I've found you, I don't want to let you go."

They danced slowly for a while and then Jim glanced at his watch. "We'd better get back to the pickup area. We have a long hike back so we better hurry. Don't want to make Fred wait too long for us. It will be getting dark up here on this mountain. And we both know what that's like."

She kissed him and they put on their jackets and started the hike back to the pickup site. Liz was tired when they reached the plane. Fred had not been waiting long so it the timing was perfect.

The ride home was quiet but Jim held her hand the whole way home. After they had thanked Fred and got back into the car, Jim realized they had not eaten the food he'd brought for a picnic. He had left it in the plane. So they pulled in to a small diner and ordered burgers and leaned back in their booth to relax. It had been a long day, but the warmth of the moment in that cabin had not worn off. They both were giddy and smiling.

Liz looked at her ring. "I just thought of something funny. Think of Leigh's face when she sees this ring. She is going to die!"

"Let's wait to tell her until you get back. I want you to myself for the next hour. What time does your plane leave?"

"I think it leaves at 8:00."

"We don't have much time and I wish I didn't have to let you go, Liz. Not now, not ever."

She glanced at him and smiled. She seemed to be really seeing him for the first time since they'd met. "One day before too long, I won't have to go home. I already will be home."

Chapter 58

Liz stood in the front of the mirror staring at her dress. Even with her critical eye, it was the most beautiful dress she'd ever seen. White lace all the way down, flowing back behind her in a trail. She felt pretty for once in her life. And she had no doubts about what she was doing.

Leigh walked in and found her fixing the last strands of dark shiny hair and touching up her lipstick. She walked right up to Liz and kissed her cheek. "Lady, this is one for the history books. The day Elizabeth Stone got married. I still have to pinch myself to believe it is true. We've been friends for what seems like an eternity, and the one thing I never thought would happen was that you would walk down the aisle in a church and say 'I do' a man standing there waiting for you. It blows me away that you have accepted this."

Liz turned and raised her eyebrow. "Well, do you want me to call this whole thing off? Because I'll do it; you know I'm perfectly capable of doing such a thing."

Leigh laughed. "Oh, no you don't. I worked my butt off getting you two together. It took a freaking plane crash and what seemed like forever on the side of a snow covered mountain to pull it off, but dang it, it worked! So you are not allowed to let all that effort go to waste now, girlfriend."

Liz laughed and hugged her friend. "I am so happy, Leigh! And I guess I need to thank you for introducing me to such a kind man. So loving. I never dreamed I would ever find someone like him, and he just walked right in to my life." She looked at Leigh, who was about to say something smart aleck. Liz beat her to it.

"Well, not exactly *walked* right in. You had him over to your house. And you invited me. Begged me to come. I do thank you for that. But it is still amazing how it all came about." She paused and grinned. "I certainly hope this doesn't encourage your matchmaking obsession."

Leigh couldn't talk quick enough. "Oh! You and Joe! You're both so skeptical! You just can't admit that it worked. That I know what I'm doing. He hates it when I try to match people up. But this time, he had to eat his words. Look at you! You are beaming! So happy. It is worth all the sarcasm just to know I was right this time about two people. Jim is wonderful and you won't regret this, Lizzie. This is a lifetime thing. I just know it."

Liz kissed her and shooed her out of the room. She needed some quiet time before walking down the aisle. This was her last chance to be alone. Single. And she wanted to just sit and relish it.

The church was full and the music was playing. Everyone was sitting there waiting for the bride to walk down the aisle. Jim was at the altar and had turned to face the door. Jesse Stone was standing with Liz just outside the door where no one could see them yet.

"Lizzie, this is a wonderful day for us. I'm so glad your mother was able to come today and really know what's going on. Her mind is going quickly. She's so happy for you. You look breathtaking, sweetheart, and I'm so proud of you. Jim is a great guy and I think you'll be happy. That is all we want for you, Liz. Happiness. Someone to love and someone to believe in you." He kissed her cheek and hugged her. Tears were in his eyes and hers.

"Thanks, Dad. I was so worried about Mother. She looks so frail. But at least she'll see her daughter get married. I know that makes her happy. There was a huge doubt in both your minds that I would ever take this leap. And I was pretty sure I wouldn't. Jim has turned all that around. Effortlessly. I think it was meant to be, Dad."

"It does my heart good to hear you say that. Now let's walk down the aisle, Lizzie. Everyone's waiting."

All the days we spend
trying to make it . . .
wanting to understand,
needing to know . . .
so many questions,
so much pain
and the loneliness . . .
is so loud . . .

But one day,
one fine day . . .
we meet someone
who is made from the same cloth;
who sets their tent
in our life . . .
and then it all
makes sense.
it all comes together . . .

The music love creates is an invisible dance
With two people
Woven from the same cloth
Into eternity.

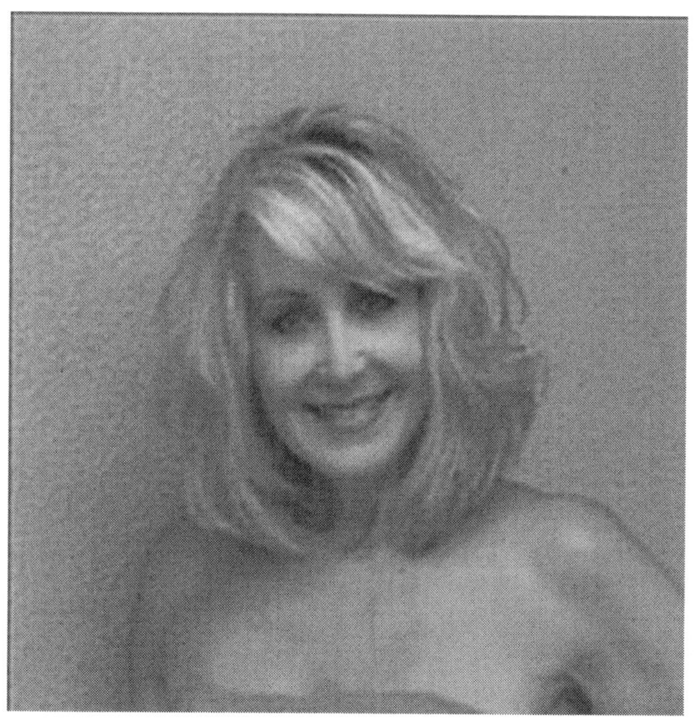

Nancy Veldman is an author, pianist and watercolor artist who lives in Destin, Florida with her husband Richard. She has written 100 songs on the piano and released ten CDs available on her Website and Amazon.com. She also has written six novels that are also available on Amazon.com, Kindle, and her Website. She received the Key to the city of Memphis for her humanitarian efforts and has set as her goal in life to help as many people as possible for the good. Nancy has owned Magnolia House, a boutique in Grand Boulevard in Sandestin, Florida, for twenty- two years. She spends her time working with the homeless, helping the poor, and talking to the many people who come through the doors of her gift shop.

Look for Nancy's music on iTunes, and soon on her own YouTube channel! You can read more about her on her Website, Magnoliahouse.com. She welcomes your comments.

Made in the USA
San Bernardino, CA
11 July 2016